PRAISE FOR TAHOE BLUE FIRE

"A GRIPPING NARRATIVE...A HERO WHO WALKS CONFIDENTLY IN THE FOOTSTEPS OF SAM SPADE, PHILIP MARLOWE, AND LEW ARCHER" - *Kirkus Reviews*

"A THRILLING MYSTERY THAT IS DIFFICULT TO PUT DOWN ...EDGE OF YOUR SEAT ACTION" - *Elizabeth, Silver's Reviews*

PRAISE FOR TAHOE GHOST BOAT

"THE OLD PULP SAVVY OF (ROSS) MACDONALD...REAL SURPRISE AT THE END" - *Kirkus Reviews*

"NAIL-BITING THRILLER...BOILING POT OF DRAMA" - *Gloria Sinibaldi, Tahoe Daily Tribune*

"A THRILL RIDE" - *Mary Beth Magee, Examiner.com*

"BORG'S WRITING IS THE STUFF OF A HOLLYWOOD ACTION BLOCKBUSTER" - *Taylor Flynn, Tahoe Mountain News*

"ACTION-PACKED IS PUTTING IT MILDLY. PREPARE FOR FIRE-WORKS" - *Sunny Solomon, Bookin' With Sunny*

"I LOVED EVERY ROLLER COASTER RIDE IN THIS THRILLER 5+ OUT OF 5" - *Harvee Lau, Book Dilettante*

PRAISE FOR TAHOE CHASE

"EXCITING, EXPLOSIVE, THOUGHTFUL, SOMETIMES FUNNY" - *Ann Ronald, Bookin' With Sunny*

"THE LANDSCAPE IS BEAUTIFULLY CRAFTED... PACE BUILDS NICELY AND DOESN'T LET UP" - *Kirkus Reviews*

"BE WARNED. IT MIGHT BE ADDICTING" - *Gloria Sinibaldi, Tahoe Daily Tribune*

"OWEN McKENNA HAS HIS HANDS FULL IN ANOTHER THRILL-ING ADVENTURE" - *Harvee Lau, Book Dilettante*

PRAISE FOR TAHOE TRAP

"AN OPEN-THROTTLE RIDE"
- *Wendy Schultz, Placerville Mountain Democrat*

"A CONSTANTLY SURPRISING SERIES OF EVENTS INVOLVING MURDER...and the final motivation of the killer comes as a major surprise. (I love when that happens.)" - *Yvette, In So Many Words*

"I LOVE TODD BORG'S BOOKS...There is the usual great twist ending in Tahoe Trap that I never would have guessed" - *JBronder Reviews*

"THE PLOTS ARE HIGH OCTANE AND THE ACTION IS FASTER THAN A CHEETAH ON SPEED" - *Cathy Cole, Kittling: Books*

"A FASCINATING STORY WITH FIRST CLASS WRITING and, of course, my favorite character, Spot, a Great Dane that steals most of the scenes." - *Mary Lignor, Feathered Quill Book Reviews*

"SUPER CLEVER... More twists in the plot toward the end of the book turn the mystery into an even more suspenseful thriller."
-*Harvee Lau, Book Dilettante*

"AN EXCITING MURDER MYSTERY... I watch for the ongoing developments of Jack Reacher, Joanna Brady, Dismas Hardy, Peter and Rina Decker, and Alex Cross to name a few. But these days I look forward most to the next installment of Owen McKenna."
- *China Gorman blog*

PRAISE FOR TAHOE HIJACK

"BEGINNING TO READ TAHOE HIJACK IS LIKE FLOOR-BOARDING A RACE CAR... RATING: A+"
- *Cathy Cole, Kittling Books*

"A THRILLING READ... any reader will find the pages of his thrillers impossible to stop turning"
- *Caleb Cage, The Nevada Review*

"THE BOOK CLIMAXES WITH A TWIST THE READER DOESN'T SEE COMING, WORTHY OF MICHAEL CONNELLY"
- *Heather Gould, Tahoe Mountain News*

"I HAD TO HOLD MY BREATH DURING THE LAST PART OF THIS FAST-PACED THRILLER"

- *Harvee Lau, Book Dilettante*

PRAISE FOR TAHOE HEAT

"IN TAHOE HEAT, BORG MASTERFULLY WRITES A SEQUENCE OF EVENTS SO INTENSE THAT IT BELONGS IN AN EARLY TOM CLANCY NOVEL"

- *Caleb Cage, Nevada Review*

"TAHOE HEAT IS A RIVETING THRILLER"

- *John Burroughs, Midwest Book Review*

"WILL KEEP READERS TURNING THE PAGES AS OWEN RACES TO CATCH A VICIOUS KILLER"

- *Barbara Bibel, Booklist*

"THE READER CAN'T HELP BUT ROOT FOR McKENNA AS THE BIG, GENEROUS, IRISH-BLOODED, STREET-WISE-YET-BOOK-SMART FORMER COP"

- *Taylor Flynn, Tahoe Mountain News*

PRAISE FOR TAHOE NIGHT

"BORG HAS WRITTEN ANOTHER WHITE-KNUCKLE THRILLER... A sure bet for mystery buffs waiting for the next Robert B. Parker and Lee Child novels"

- *Jo Ann Vicarel, Library Journal*

"AN ACTION-PACKED THRILLER WITH A NICE-GUY HERO, AN EVEN NICER DOG..."

- *Kirkus Reviews*

"A KILLER PLOT... EVERY ONE OF ITS 350 PAGES WANTS TO GET TURNED... *FAST*"

- *Taylor Flynn, Tahoe Mountain News*

"A FASCINATING STORY OF FORGERY, MURDER..."

- *Nancy Hayden, Tahoe Daily Tribune*

TAHOE
BLUE FIRE

by

Todd Borg

THRILLER PRESS

For Kit

ACKNOWLEDGMENTS

I owe huge thanks to my editors, Liz Johnston, Eric Berglund, Christel Hall, and my wife Kit. They put in hundreds of hours on this project, and I can't thank them enough.

The cover of Tahoe Blue Fire is especially intriguing. Because this novel has a story thread that connects modern day Tahoe to the Italian Renaissance, communicating that on the cover seemed an impossible task. Yet Portland, Oregon graphic artist Keith Carlson created a look I love, with a sense of mystery reaching back 500 years. The cover is magnificent.

I owe special thanks to Bob Hiland for teaching me something about poetry, no small task considering the depth and breadth of my ignorance. My head is now filled with the dance of prosody, rhythm and meter, free verse and rhyming verse, metaphor and theme, all kneaded into iambic beats.

As always, I couldn't have done this book without Kit's vision and support. She understands the picture of story as well as the pictures she paints. I'm a lucky guy.

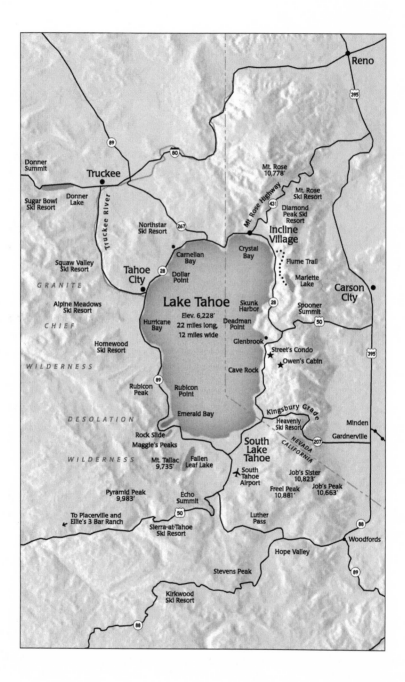

PROLOGUE

The big rotary snowblower was parked in the dark at the side of the road where the shoulder had been cleared of snow. The unusual snow removal machine was one of the huge ones, built on a double-engine chassis, designed for clearing highways.

The drive engine was idling quietly despite its size. The much larger blower engine was off. Because that engine made so much noise, the operator would fire it up at the last moment.

Three kills. Maybe four or five.

That's all it would take to get rich.

Three people who were in the way. People who deserved to die.

The money involved was the kind no one could ignore.

Not even a priest.

Not even a saint.

There was some footwork involved, some financial maneuvering, a disguise, a little bit of persuasion. If the killings weren't all done in the same way, there would be no consistent M.O. to track. If a victim or two couldn't even be found, better still.

The rotary driver knew from research that most murderers aren't that careful, yet many are never caught. Which made a careful killer almost impossible to find.

It had taken a week to prepare for the first kill.

Everything was in place. The victim had taken the bait.

It was midnight. A car drove by on the cross street up ahead. Its red tail lights were partially blocked by snow berms and trees, yet visible now and then. A block down, the car's tail lights went bright. The car turned into the large open field that had been filled with snow over the course of the winter, hundreds of dump truck loads carted off the highway that ran through South Lake Tahoe. When the field was filled by the beginning of March, they brought in a front-end loader and a rotary blower to clear some space. The loader broke up the worst chunks of ice. Then the rotary blew half the field's snow onto the other half, almost doubling the depth to 12 feet.

Now, the snow was starting to melt in the heat of spring sunshine, the third week of April. But it remained a thick layer of white ice, compressed like a glacier that never moved.

Two blocks down, a road grader was working the street, its blade scraping the asphalt, moving the snow into a large berm at the edge of the road. Other than the rotary driver, the grader driver, and the car driver, there was no one else anywhere close on the frozen spring night. Which meant that there was no reason for anyone other than the victim to turn into the parking lot. That alone almost guaranteed the victim's identity.

The car's tail lights pulsed with varying beats and intensities of red as the trees opened and then blocked the view. The lights went bright again as the car slowed. The car stopped, and the tail lights went out. The interior light went on and then off as the car's driver got out and shut the door.

It was hard to see through the trees in the dark, but it looked like the car's driver was walking over to the dead-end snow canal that had been cut out of the center of the snowfield. Now the car driver was silhouetted against the snowbanks. Even though it was night, it was easy to see him as he walked into the snow canal.

Proof that he was the correct person.

The rotary operator shifted into gear and gave the drive engine some fuel. The big 580-horsepower diesel rumbled as it revved. The engine was the size of the biggest engines on semitrucks. But it was nothing compared with what was to come.

The operator started forward, going easy on the accelerator. It wasn't that the vehicle's engine was quiet - it sounded like the huge truck it was - but there was no point in creating unnecessary noise. The rotary turned at the corner and began rolling down the street at a good pace.

The man who'd gotten out of the car might wonder at the coincidence of a rotary plow and a road grader coming near the meeting point. But their email exchange had noted that meeting during snow removal operations, which went on 24 hours a day, provided the cover of lots of noise and action, and allowed them total privacy.

Snow plows were a constant presence on the roads of Lake Tahoe in the winter and spring, especially near the snow storage lot. Even the specialized rotaries that were only used in the snowiest parts of the country were numerous in Tahoe. They weren't upgraded dump trucks with blower accessories bolted onto their front bumpers. These were single-purpose machines built like tall, square locomotives, big boxy monsters that prowled the highways at night. The rotaries had four-wheel steering and could crab sideways as necessary on icy roads. They chewed up the snow berms that had been pushed up by the road graders, and they shot the snow in giant 200-foot arcs out into the forest.

As the rotary approached the parking lot, the operator gradually accelerated, trying to find the balance between engine noise and speed, needing as much surprise as possible. Although the rotary wasn't currently blowing snow, the man waiting at the snow canal would probably assume that the rotary was going to blow some of the nearby berms.

The rotary driver turned into the closest corner of the parking lot, heading toward the most recent dump truck loads waiting to be blown onto the other half of the storage lot. The rotary was quite far from the man in the snow canal.

As the big machine got closer to the mounds of snow, its headlights briefly washed over the parked car. The man who'd gotten out of the car came into view for a short moment, illuminated by the light that bounced off the snow. He stood at the end of the dead-end passage as was agreed upon in their email communication.

Waiting.

No doubt excited at the promise he'd been given. Probably skeptical, too. He had, after all, failed at his job. But apparently, the email reassurance had worked. The promise of riches always enticed, even when the victim was scared.

Little did he know.

Now came the critical sequence.

As the rotary got close to the dump truck mounds, the operator started the giant blower engine. The huge diesel fired, then grew in volume to an amazing roar.

It was a rush for the driver, listening to the 1300-horsepower behemoth as the blower engine came up to full power. Combined with the big drive engine, the two power plants produced almost 2000 horsepower, and they roared like a rocket at liftoff.

Now that the rotary plow was fully alive, the driver flipped on the accessory lights.

Three thousand watts of floods and flashers lit up the night. The lights shined behind and to the sides of the rotary plow and still left six huge high beams to shine forward. The light level was in concert with the danger of the machine. The rotary plow seemed from a distance like a hostile alien invader. In reality, it was just a giant snow blower that could clear a path of heavy, compacted ice and snow eight feet wide. At the upper sides of the machine's auger housing were steel blades that pointed up at a forward angle, able to cut snow as deep as 12 feet. When clearing roads, the blades left smooth vertical walls as the cut snow fell down into the churning auger. Now those blades slid against the previously-cut snow walls.

The driver engaged the rotary clutch. There was a screech and a jerk as the auger came up to speed. The carbide-edged blades spun fast, flipping snow - and rocks and road trash and any other debris - into the impeller that rotated many times faster and shot the snow up into the directional chute and out into the air.

The rotary plow could move 11,000 tons of snow per hour. That was over 6000 pounds a second. It was the most powerful snow-blowing road machine on Earth.

When the rotary was close enough that the victim would not have time to run and escape out the entrance to the snow canal, the driver floored the accelerator, speeding up the rotary plow. The driver cranked the wheel toward the snow canal. The big rotary jerked to the side, the 50,000-pound machine nearly leaning over on two wheels. The lights came around as the machine pointed into the snow canal, aimed toward the man waiting at the end.

The victim reacted in an instant, telegraphing his understanding that he'd been set up. He darted left, then right, like a trapped bug who too late understands what his fate will be if he can't escape. The victim paused for a moment and held up his arm, trying to shield his eyes from the glare of the flood lights on the plow, which was now on an attack sprint. Perhaps he was trying to gauge if there was room for him to sneak past the side of the plow.

The man in the snow canal must have seen that the giant blower filled the snow canal side-to-side. He must have realized that there was no room to get past, for he turned away and ran to the snow wall at the end of the box-canyon. He tried to kick toe holds and punch his hands into the snow. But in the two days since the rotary had cut the canal, the snow had repeatedly thawed under the spring sun and then refrozen at night into a hard ice surface. It was now a solid wall of slippery ice.

The man was unable to get a grip. He backed up a few steps and then ran and leaped higher, attempting to hook his hands onto the top of the wall, which varied in height but at no point was less than ten feet high. The man couldn't reach the top, and he fell back to the icy pavement as the roaring monster charged forward, its sharp auger blades spinning at high speed.

ONE

"It would be too dangerous for me to come to your office," the woman on the phone said. She had told me her name was Scarlett Milo and that she'd wanted to meet and that she was in significant danger. She'd hesitated before saying her name, so I wondered if it was a pseudonym. She had yet to tell me any other info about what, where, when, why, and how.

So I picked one. "Why?" I asked.

"Someone is planning to kill me. And your office is in a public location. It would be too easy for him to lie in wait and pick me off. Or he could follow me home and burn down my house with me inside."

"Really?" I said.

"Do you doubt me?"

"It just sounds a bit melodramatic," I said.

She paused. "I thought you were a professional, an ex-cop who would care about innocent people."

The statement stung. While I considered it, I drank coffee that was cold enough to have lost its edge. Maybe I had lost my edge. I looked at Spot, my Harlequin Great Dane, who was sprawled in front of my desk. He looked so somnolent that I didn't know if he'd even raise up his 170 pounds for a steak. Maybe he'd lost his edge, too.

"Excuse me for being blunt, Ms. Milo, but if someone wants to kill you, he doesn't have to wait for you to meet me. He could come to your home now."

"He knows he has a target to kill, but he hasn't yet figured out where I live. But he knows that I'm onto him and that I will be cautious. He'll assume that I will seek help. So he would likely watch security people like you. Then he could figure out where I live and come and kill me."

"Now you've gone beyond melodramatic. Someone wants to

kill you but doesn't know who you are." I saw no point in adding that, from my perspective, calling me a security person was like calling a college professor a baby sitter. From her perspective, the nomenclature would make no difference. "I'm not the only so-called security person in Tahoe," I said.

"You're almost the only one. He's probably watching you as we speak. As for others like you, he could hire someone to watch them."

"Why don't you just tell me your concerns now? Over the phone."

"I could never trust the phone lines. I have something I need to tell you in person."

"How do you want to meet, then?" I said, wondering if I really wanted a paranoid client. But I couldn't afford not to have a client, paranoid or not. Besides, maybe she was just rattled by our recent earthquake, which had mostly shaken but not damaged area buildings. I'd met people who seem to lose their common sense when their house starts rocking.

"If you come to me, I can see you drive up the road below my house," she said. "I'll be able to tell if you're being followed. If not, I'll give you the directions."

"Why not just give me directions now?"

There was a pause before she spoke. "Because he might intercept you and force you to tell him where I live."

I took a deep breath. "He could do that after I meet you," I said.

"No. Because after I meet you, I'm going to go away. No one will be able to find me."

"How will you do that?"

Another pause. "I'm the only one who needs to know that."

Her statements were so over the top that my instincts told me to decline the job. Her fear was obvious and seemed genuine, but I suspected that it was fueled by an excessively-active imagination.

"If you doubt me," she said, "just humor me for the money. What's your standard retainer? Five thousand to start? Ten thousand? Tell you what. I'll give you my credit card number and you can run it before you come out. Now that I think of it, you will likely have some significant travel expenses before you're done with this situation. So run my card for twenty thousand. Then you can do your thing without having to worry about getting more money from me right away. When this is all over, you can refund whatever funds were in excess of your expenses."

Maybe I hadn't lost my edge.

I was about to tell her that it wouldn't be necessary until after we met, but I stopped myself. Why not let her pay to indulge her imagination? A substantial payment up front always separates the merely paranoid from the seriously worried.

"Twenty thousand?" I said just to check that I'd heard her correctly.

"That's what I said. I already called the credit card company and told them that a substantial charge would be coming through."

"Okay," I said. I expected her to balk and backpedal. Instead, she read off the card number and the security code and gave me the billing zip code.

"After you run the transaction, come up to Olympic Valley. You know where that is, of course?"

"Squaw Valley's official name," I said. "Where shall I go?"

She told me how far to drive up the valley toward the village, where to turn off, and where to pull over.

"If you call me from that point, I'll look down from my deck. Then, if I see that you aren't being followed, I will tell you how to get to my house. It is very important that you take this seriously, Mr. McKenna. So please engage in some obfuscation or whatever you call it when you want a tail to think you're just running errands, going to the grocery store, etc."

"Will do, Ms. Milo. I can obfuscate a bunch and still be there by three o'clock. Would that work for you?"

She hesitated. "I can tell by your tone that you're sarcastic and cocky and you think I'm just a fussy woman. But I assure you, I'm not being fussy."

"You've paid me, Ms. Milo. You can be sure that I give full service regardless of how I sound."

I let Spot into the back of the old Jeep with the new bullet-hole ventilation provided by the men who'd kidnapped Gertie O'Leary the month before. We drove clockwise around the lake so that I could cruise past Emerald Bay. The road and its steep switchbacks had finally opened after two months of near-constant avalanche closure. No matter how often I drive that route, I'm amazed at the spectacular vistas.

Spring was putting on a brag show. The sky was an intense light blue to complement the intense dark blue of the lake. Brilliant, snow-capped mountains were under full assault from hot, high-altitude sun, and they were shrugging off their winter snow cloaks. Five dozen streams and creeks rushed and danced and jived their way down to the big lake.

The Steller's jays had recently come up from lower elevations, and they squawked and strutted their color through the forest like showy, drag-queen bouncers, letting all the other songbirds know who was now in charge whenever the hawks and eagles and ospreys and falcons took a break from local raptor patrol.

The air was redolent of pine scents as the conifers readied their energies for the growing season that was still over a month away. Hardy sprouts of green grass poked up at the edge of the roadways, sustained by thermal-mass heat from the nearby asphalt even after the blazing sun went down and the temperatures were forced back down by hundreds of square miles of thick Sierra snowpack to the west.

I drove up the West Shore to Tahoe City and rolled over Fanny Bridge next to the dam that holds in the top six feet of the lake and stores it like a reservoir. Highway 89 turns west just north of the bridge. Before I followed it down the Truckee River Canyon to Squaw Valley, I stopped at a grocery store and bought two pastries. I was very vigilant as I did so, fulfilling, as with my usual attention to work responsibilities, my promise of discretion. Confident that no one was watching me, I paid for my purchase and went back out to the Jeep.

Just to reinforce my standards of diligence, I let Spot out and made a show of feeding him his breakfast treat while I ate mine, during which I surreptitiously studied my surroundings.

Everyone in view was focused on my dog, which meant that no one in view was focused on me. I'd seen it hundreds of times.

All people have a similar reaction to a 170-pound Harlequin Great Dane, regardless of whether or not he is ravishing a Danish. It's an open-mouthed stare that morphs into a grin and then to a raised arm and pointed hand and a shout to their companions to check out the giant, splotchy, black-and-white dog.

If anyone had an agenda that was about spying on me, they wouldn't fit the pattern and would thus stand out.

Obfuscation meets Holmesian deduction.

No one was following me.

I turned onto 89, driving next to the Truckee River on its way down to Truckee and then Reno before it dead-ended at Pyramid Lake out in the Great Basin desert, dumping its water there to eventually evaporate.

A few miles down the river valley, I went past the River Ranch Lodge and Restaurant and the road up to Alpine Meadows ski area. After another mile, the Olympic rings and the Olympic gas flame came into view, leftovers from the big snowfest back in 1960. I turned left and drove into Olympic Valley. The snow-capped peaks of Squaw Valley ski area came into view, a picture with a postcard quotient as high as they come. In the distance ahead, I saw the little dot of cable car carrying skiers from the base village up to High Camp atop the 2000-foot cliff.

My intersection approached up ahead. I turned off to the right and drove up to a curve that matched what Scarlett Milo described over the phone. I stopped and got out and dialed her number.

As it rang, I scanned the slope that rose above me. There were several nice homes visible in the forest and, no doubt, several that were hidden but nevertheless had views down to the valley floor, me included.

"Hello?"

"Hi, Ms. Milo, Owen McKenna here. I'm at the turn you described."

"Okay. Hold on." There was some background sound, a sliding door maybe. "Okay, I'm out on my deck," she said. "I can see you down there. You're standing near your car door and… Oh, what is that big black-and-white animal protruding from the rear window of your car? There's something pink, too."

"That's my dog. His name's Spot. The pink is his very large tongue."

"I see. Well, I don't see anyone else, and that was the purpose of this little exercise."

"The result of a prime obfuscation session," I said.

"Okay, come on up," she said. She proceeded to describe where and how I should turn and what to look for to know which house was hers, and then there was a snapping sound in the phone, followed by a deep crack that thudded in the air where I stood.

"Ms. Milo?" I said, sprinting for the Jeep. I jumped in, jammed the shifter into drive, and floored the gas. "Scarlett? Can you hear me?"

But there was nothing.

I raced up the slope, reciting what she'd said about left turns and right turns as I pushed the Jeep around the corners.

The house sat by itself on a section of curving road, out of sight from its neighbors. My tires scraped sand and grit as I stomped on the brakes. I jumped out, let Spot out, and ran for the woman's door.

"Scarlett Milo?!" I shouted as I tried the door. The doorknob was locked. There was also a deadbolt, and the door looked too heavy to easily kick in.

I ran around the side of the house. Spot anticipated my movements and ran ahead.

The house was on the lower side of the road, and the ground went down at a steep angle. I scrambled down a landscaped path to a broad stairs that climbed in a dogleg up to the deck. I took them two at a time while Spot took them three or four per leap.

Scarlett Milo was sprawled on her side at the far edge of the deck where she had probably stood to look down on me. Her throat was blown open, and blood gurgled out in large volume. I'd seen enough wounds to know this one was fatal. Because the blood was bright red and pulsed, I knew the bullet had hit her carotid artery.

By the shards of shattered vertebrae that mixed in with the messy, shredded wound, I knew her neck had largely been destroyed. There was no way to prevent further blood loss without strangling her.

Nevertheless, I knelt down and put my thumb across the main part of the blood flow. The blood gurgled out elsewhere. Just then, she made a kind of a coughing contraction. But there was no connecting windpipe to her mouth, so the exhalation just sprayed blood from her neck into the air and all over me and Spot, who stood a respectful several feet back.

I reached my phone out of my pocket with my other hand and set it on the deck to dial 911, a reasonable, if futile, move.

Her hand rose up, demonstrating that at least part of her spinal cord was still intact. She clutched at my shirt and pulled me down. Her mouth was moving. I realized that she was still conscious and wanted to say something. I bent down, my ear next to her mouth.

Because her windpipe was destroyed, she had no way to run air from her lungs through her vocal cords, if there were any vocal cords left. All she could do was make mouth movements.

Her hand shifted and reached for her pocket. In an astonishing feat of focus and control, she pulled out a pen and held it up.

I realized she wanted some paper. I let go of my phone and felt my pockets. There was a gas station receipt. I held it on the deck boards.

She scrawled some marks.

A voice came over my phone. "Nine-one-one emergency," a woman said. "Please state your name and location."

I reached for the phone.

Scarlett Milo tapped her pen on the deck boards.

I let go of the phone and looked at her. Except for the flowing blood and her moving arm, nothing else moved. She appeared paralyzed.

She tapped the pen again, the point making dots on the receipt paper.

I stared at it, trying to figure out the jerky writing.

"I'm sorry, but I can't tell what you've written," I said. "Can you try again?"

Scarlett once again raised her pen. Then her hand collapsed to the deck boards, and she was still.

TWO

I explained to the 911 dispatcher that the victim had died from a gunshot wound, and I told her who I was and where I was.

"Please keep the line open," she said. "I'll have officers en route immediately."

I looked at the scene, speaking as much to help me focus as to provide information to the dispatcher and anyone who would eventually listen to the recorded call.

"While I wait for your officers, I'll give you the details for your recording," I said into the phone. "A woman named Scarlett Milo was shot. I heard only one shot, and the wound appears to have been made by a single round. The entrance wound is at the back of the neck. It is a clean and symmetrical hole and I see no tattooing from gunpowder, so I'm guessing the shot was fired from a distance. Looking at the territory around the house, I'm guessing the shooter was some distance up the mountain.

"The exit wound shows substantial tissue shredding and what appear to be pieces of a broken vertebrae. It appears that the wound was caused by a high-powered round, which, despite likely deformation, exited the body and fell out of sight someplace below the house.

"The position of the body doesn't reveal which direction the shot came from. The victim may have twisted as she went down. But I see a faint spray pattern of blood on the back of the victim's collar. There is a much larger pattern of blood and other tissue on the deck, presumably from the exit wound at the front of her throat."

I turned and looked behind me to my right. "Behind me to the north is an opening in the trees on the mountain slope above. There is a grouping of large boulders. It's a south-facing slope, and the snow has mostly melted. I'm guessing the shot came from up among those boulders. Your approaching officers should know that there is access to that point from both Sandy Way and Squaw Summit Road. The shooter could still be up the slope, but I doubt it."

I thought of running up the slope with Spot to search for the shooter, but I was unarmed, and the dispatcher wanted me to stay on the line and report any critical information. And if I was up the slope when officers approached from multiple directions, I would be a distraction. They might even mistake me for the shooter.

Sirens sounded in the distance, a faint discordant warbling as some rose in pitch while others fell.

A minute later, the sirens swelled in volume as vehicles raced into the valley on Squaw Valley Road. Looking down from Scarlett Milo's deck, I could see two Placer County Sheriff's vehicles followed by a black-and-white CHP unit. One of the Placer County vehicles turned up the road I'd taken. The CHP vehicle turned off the main road, heading for a point east of the shooter's possible location. The other county vehicle drove past the road I'd taken. It went out of my sight before its sound indicated that it had turned onto another road to the west. They were trying to outflank the shooter, a smart move but one I didn't think would produce results. There were too many ways for the shooter to escape.

Two more vehicles with flashing lights came into the valley. One was another CHP vehicle, and the other looked similar to the Placer County vehicles but with different lettering. I guessed that it was a sheriff's vehicle from Truckee, which is in Nevada County, the next county to the north. Yet more sirens sounded in the far distance, a huge response for a rural mountain community, but a normal one for a place with vacation residences owned by celebrities, high-ranking government officials, business magnates, and foreign royalty.

One siren grew loud as it came up Milo's street and stopped at her house.

I disconnected from the 911 dispatcher and walked partway down the deck stairs so I was visible from the street. Placer County Sergeant Santiago ran over while his deputy stayed at the side of the SUV patrol unit, sidearm in his hand, crouching behind the vehicle, looking up at the mountain.

"McKenna," Santiago said.

"Sergeant."

Jack Santiago was the kind of man who most people would overlook. He seemed medium in every way, unremarkable in looks, height, size, demeanor, presence. Yet, when observed up close, one saw the intelligence in his eyes, the determination in the set of his jaw, and the strength in his shoulders. Santiago drew no attention to himself, but he won citations and respect. I'd rarely seen a more dedicated cop.

He looked around at the forest, taking in the lay of the land, the access points, the view corridors. Then he trotted up the stairs to the deck.

Santiago looked at Scarlett Milo's body for a long moment. He would be struck by the violence of the scene, but I knew he was also noticing everything about position and blood spray that I noticed and more. I was never good at taking an instant inventory of a crime scene. But Santiago would remember the victim's clothes and makeup and condition of her fingernails and skin and teeth, and from that he would already be building a picture of Scarlett's lifestyle and socioeconomic status on top of the obvious descriptors of height, weight, hair, and eye color.

I pointed to the slope above. "I think the shooter may have been up in those boulders."

Santiago looked up the mountain, then trotted down the deck stairs as he spoke into his radio. I couldn't make out the words, but the anger and frustration came through. Santiago stayed in the shadows next to the house as he continued to talk into his radio.

Down the street to the west, I saw a sheriff's vehicle come to a fast stop. Two deputies jumped out, looking up the mountain. Both had their guns out. One ran up the slope, then stopped as the other one played leapfrog. Each covered the other as they made their way up the slope.

"Any chance the shooter could have come down the mountain right here?" Santiago asked me. "Be near this house? In this house?"

"A chance, I suppose," I said. "But I doubt it. The front door is locked, and I've been up on the deck or down at the base of the deck stairs the entire time. No one could get to the deck door. Maybe there is an unlocked door around the other side of the house, but probably not. The woman was very concerned about her safety. I'd guess the shooter had an escape route planned. A mountain bike or skis or something. He could have run down to a vehicle on a nearby street and driven out of the valley as you came in. By now he could be on Interstate Eighty heading up over Donner Summit or driving down the canyon toward Reno. Or, he could have headed toward Tahoe City and melted into that community."

I glanced through the trees down to the pedestrian village at the base of the Squaw Valley ski area. "Otherwise, he's probably in the crowds down in the village, having changed clothes, maybe taken off a wig and wiped the perspiration from his brow. He could be sipping a beer at a cafe and listening to the sirens."

Santiago lifted his radio to his mouth.

"Forman, you and Johnson head up to that group of boulders and see what you can find. Rodriguez, you and Kylie take the streets. Start at the upper edge of the neighborhood and work your way down. Most of these houses are vacation homes, so there might not be anyone at home, but be persistent. Don't assume the houses are empty. Anyone answers, use the standard questions. Have they seen or heard anything unusual in the last two hours? Have any strange vehicles been cruising the neighborhood or parked on nearby streets in the previous week or two? Make them comfortable. Get them talking. Get their names and numbers. Leave them your phone number. If they want to know what happened, you can tell them that there was a shooting but no details are being released at the moment."

Santiago looked across at the deputy who'd ridden in his vehicle. "Fairbanks, stay put behind that boulder. Keep your eye on the slope and this street. Holler if you see anyone who isn't an officer."

Santiago walked back up onto the deck. I followed with Spot. Santiago looked again at Milo's body.

"Are you here as a friend?" he asked.

"No. Scarlett Milo called me at my office and hired me over the phone. She was afraid for her life. So I came up to Squaw Valley to meet her. She'd asked me to call her from that curve down below to get directions." I pointed to the place where I'd temporarily parked. "I heard the shot over the phone first. The crack came through the air about a half second later."

Santiago looked down toward where I'd parked to call Scarlett. "Sound travels a thousand feet per second. That intersection is about five hundred feet down. So your idea that the shooter was up in those rocks makes sense. The rifle crack would get to the woman's phone first, which you would immediately hear in your phone. Then the crack would get to you through the air a second later. Maybe less."

Santiago looked down at the body. "Looks like death was instantaneous."

"Not quite."

Santiago turned and looked at me.

"When I heard the shot, I raced up here. She was still alive when I got here. She couldn't speak because her neck was blown apart. But she wrote me a message." I handed him the receipt with her scrawled marks.

Santiago looked at it. "It kind of looks like 'Medic's BFF.' What's that mean?"

"I have no idea."

"You know the victim?" Santiago asked.

"No. She called me for help and said she was afraid someone was planning to kill her. She wouldn't tell me why over the phone. She wanted to meet, but she wouldn't tell me where she lived because she thought someone would get the information from me. She gave me her credit card number and told me to charge her twenty thousand dollars because she believed I would have a lot of expenses dealing with her mysterious problem."

Santiago raised his eyebrows. "That's a lot of bank. Did you run the card?"

"Yeah. I assumed it would be rejected, but it went through. She told me to drive to that place below her house and call her. So I did. When she answered, she walked out on her deck and told me that she could see me and that it looked like no one had followed me. So she told me her address and how to come here. I thought the whole thing was the elaborate melodrama of a paranoid woman. Obviously, I was wrong."

Santiago scanned the deck, looking at the blood spatter. He didn't comment on my understatement.

"How'd her blood get on you?" he asked.

"I put my thumb on her carotid artery to try and slow her bleeding, and she coughed," I said. "It sprayed out of the wound."

Santiago winced. "She have family?" he asked.

"I don't know."

"She live here full time?"

"I don't know."

"What was it that made her think someone wanted to kill her?"

"I don't know."

Santiago looked at me. "Do you know anything about her?"

I shook my head. "Just what I've already told you."

"I guess we've got a lot of work to do," he said.

I nodded.

THREE

As Incident Commander, Santiago directed all the law enforcement officers in the investigation.

He had them set up a roadblock at the entrance to Squaw Valley. No vehicles were allowed out without a check.

When I heard him say that, I had a disturbing thought. A shooter could put a rifle in a ski bag, loop the bag over his shoulders, ride one of the chairlifts up to the ridge at the southern boundary of Squaw Valley, and ski the backcountry down to Alpine Meadows Ski Resort, which is in the next valley to the south. From there he could leave by car and not have to worry about being stopped by any police. I told Santiago. He nodded.

Three more officers from Nevada County arrived, along with four more from the CHP. A half-hour later, a CHP helicopter appeared in the sky and flew overlapping circles above Scarlett Milo's neighborhood. Thirty minutes after that, an additional six Placer County deputies came up from the foothills.

The suspect search was spread out over a large territory, but the law enforcement response was huge. There were a dozen vehicles with flashing lights, multiple search parties, some officers combing through the neighborhood while others went up into higher elevations to search those areas that hadn't seen enough spring sun to melt off. Two of them were on cross-country skis. They angled up the slope on a shallow traverse. Three more had snowshoes, and they took a steeper route up.

Santiago remained at Scarlett Milo's house, directing the expanding crew with his radio and cellphone.

Two deputies came up onto the deck. One of them made a quick glance in my direction.

"No sign of anyone up in those rocks, sergeant," one of them said.

"You take pictures before you tracked it up?" Santiago said.

One of them held up a small camera. "Lots."

Santiago sent them down to canvas the streets below.

As Santiago continued to coordinate search efforts, I went over to Spot who was lying on the deck as far as he could get from Scarlett's body.

"You can give your statement later," Santiago said to me. "The medical examiner should be here soon. The evidence team is setting up a perimeter, and they'll start their search and bag and photo routine." Santiago looked up at the group of boulders I'd pointed to. "Good cover and not far, either. It wouldn't take an expert to make that shot."

I pointed. "If you move a bit to the left, you'll see another group of boulders higher up, maybe five hundred yards away."

"Hitting a target at that distance would take an expert," Santiago said.

I nodded. "Yeah, but a good hunter could do it. Military snipers often work from three times that distance. Even more."

Santiago looked out toward the valley below. "Let's say the shooter was thorough and there's no shell casing where the shot was fired. What do you think the chances are of us finding the round that hit the woman?"

"About zero. The only way for someone to hit her in that location on the deck would be from up the slope or from right on the deck. But I think she would have seen someone coming up onto her deck. She was wary. She would have said something while she was on the phone. The entrance wound doesn't show powder burns, so the shooter wasn't real close. Either way, the round went through her neck with explosive force. That argues for a high-powered shot, almost certainly a rifle. She was standing near the edge of the deck looking down on me." I pointed over the deck railing. "Even if the bullet was very deformed from hitting her bone, it would have probably fallen somewhere in those woods far below where I parked to call her. It might even have traveled far past me before it dropped to earth someplace out in the valley. It would take a miracle to find it."

"You think a search dog could find it?"

I looked over at Spot, whose prostrate form suggested depression. "My dog could maybe find a spent round if it was in a small area. But out there in the valley? No way. A professional dog would have a better chance, but it would still take a miracle." I waved my hand at the expanse of valley below us. "That round could be anyplace in two square miles."

Santiago glanced at Scarlett Milo's body, looked like he was about to say something, then hesitated. "Truth is, McKenna, I've never seen a gunshot wound like this. When you did that long stint in San Francisco, you probably saw some major stuff. It looks like her vertebrae shattered. You got an idea what caliber would do that to a person?"

"I'm no expert, but I don't think it would need to be anything really big. A thirty caliber could blow apart a woman's neck vertebra and barely slow down."

Santiago looked at Spot. "He looks weary."

"Human death does that to many dogs," I said. "Even if they don't know the victim."

"Why is that?" Santiago asked.

"It's a dog thing," I said, not eager to talk about it. I'd witnessed Spot's and other dogs' stress many times.

"Tell me about it," Santiago said.

"It's not a three-word answer."

"I'm just waiting for my men to report back after their searches."

So I told him. "Ever since we first began domesticating the gray wolf thirty thousand years ago, our efforts created what became the new species of Canis lupus familiaris. All of its sub-species, what we call dog breeds, evolved to be hard-wired to care more about people than even their own dog brothers and sisters. In exchange for guarding our camps from other tribes and large predators like bears and tigers and wolves, and helping us hunt, and keeping us warm on cold winter nights, we gave them what they needed. Food, protection, a place to sleep. To dogs, humans are gods. When the gods die, it's an emotional blow."

Santiago stared at me. "You sound like someone on public TV. One of those nature shows."

I walked over, bent down, and gave Spot a pet. "He's seen a fair amount of death. Always has the same reaction. His experience is not on the same level as what some of those military dogs or

earthquake dogs go through, but it's hard for him nonetheless."
Spot lay on the deck, his jaw propped between his front paws.

"Any chance you've got a shell cartridge?" I said. "Something
from a round that was discharged recently?"

Santiago frowned. Then he made a small nod. "You want to
send your hound on a search? You just made it sound futile."

"Trying to find the round is probably futile. But I was
thinking of a spent shell casing up near those boulders."

"Ah." Santiago nodded. "Like you said, maybe he'd be good
at searching a small area."

"Right. He's not a professional, but he's got the same sniffer
as other dogs. It's more a question of…" I paused.

"Whether he wants to," Santiago said.

"Yeah. Great Danes are lovers and loungers. They aren't as
eager to work as the other working breeds."

"I could fire my sidearm to get you a fresh shell casing,"
Santiago said. Then he turned and looked down from the deck at
his sheriff's patrol vehicle parked off to the side of Scarlett Milo's
house. "Wait. I picked up some large shell casings at the range
the other day and put them in the change compartment of my
patrol unit. I forgot about them until now. You think that would
work?"

"Depends on how recently they were fired. Let's try it."

We trotted down the stairs to his vehicle. He reached in and
pulled out three long shell casings.

"I was thinking they were two-seventy Winchester," he said,
a questioning tone in his voice.

"Looks like it," I said. "Or maybe two-sixty-four magnums."

Santiago smelled them. "I still smell the gunpowder, so maybe
these will work to scent your dog." He handed them to me. "The
way the dispatcher phrased it, it sounded like you heard just one
shot," Santiago said.

"Yeah."

"So there might not be a shell casing."

"Right," I said. "It may be that the shooter was using a bolt-
action rifle. Or if he used a semi-auto and the casing was ejected,
he could have picked it up."

"Worth having your dog look," Santiago said.

FOUR

I took Spot down to the street. I got my snowshoes out of the back of the Jeep and carried them as we headed up the south-facing slope. I didn't need them at the elevation of Scarlett's house, but I'd need them when we got up higher.

The soil was mostly grus, finely eroded granitic pebbles that slid underfoot as we walked up, making the climb a two-steps-up-one-step-back hike. Spot's claws are like studded snow tires, so grip was no problem for him. But he was lethargic with melancholy, and he lagged behind.

We climbed up through a forest that was heavy with scents of pine pitch from several species of conifer. We meandered between earthy aromas of impenetrable manzanita thickets and snow patches that lay four feet deep under the thick shade of fir trees. Snowmelt seeped and trickled and gathered into temporary creeks that gave the forest a backdrop of water sounds to go with the humidity of spring. The sun was dialed up to full wattage, and early-season songbirds flitted about, gossiping at high volume. The vibrant springtime renewal of life was on high speed as Spot and I hiked up to look for clues to Scarlett Milo's death.

When we got to the first group of boulders, I paused to look around. The air was cool, but the sun was hot. Spot immediately walked over to a patch of tree shade and lay down in the snow beneath it. He panted for a bit, blowing off heat, then calmed his breathing, put his jaw down on top of crossed paws, and appeared to sleep.

The boulders were grouped as if put there to create a shooting blind. There were multiple places a shooter could sit or squat or lie and get a sight line to Milo's deck. There was even a rock that would make a perfect rifle support.

Everywhere, the ground was marked with indistinct footprints, the most information that grus can deliver. Somebody, the shooter, or cops, or previous hikers, had tromped the ground since the snow retreated.

I lay down and sighted down through the rocks. About a third of Scarlett Milo's deck was in view, including her body with what looked like three more people nearby. Two wore uniforms. One - probably the medical examiner - was in plain clothes and was bent over the body.

"Okay, Your Largeness, time to perform your search magic."

Spot didn't move.

"I know, boy, life is hard, and people die. But you can help."

Maybe some really smart dog like an Australian shepherd would understand my words, but Spot slept on.

I could cajole and lift up on his collar, but you can't force a 170-pound dog to perform if he doesn't want to.

So I pulled out my emergency dog cookie, the kind that comes sealed in a smell-proof wrapper, has a pocket life of two years, and is warrantied to go through at least one laundry cycle without degradation.

I held it up and called Spot's name again. He ignored me. I walked over and held the dog treat in front of him. This time he opened his eyes, looked at the treat, and put his head back down.

This was worrisome. My dog was depressed. I needed to distract him, to get some joy into his heart. The best way to do that was to get some levity into my words and actions.

I tore at the little notch in the wrapper, but it would not open. I used my teeth. But the wrapper was some kind of spacesuit material, impervious to any alien weapon. I opened the blade of my pocket knife, put the dog cookie on a rock, and stabbed it through the heart.

Now the material tore easily. The cookie broke into multiple pieces.

Spot was finally interested.

I took the two largest intact cookie pieces and put them in my shirt pocket. Then I scraped up the rest of the crumbs and brought them over to Spot.

"A taste, Spot, a temptation of what's to come should you help me."

I held out my palm. He sniffed, unsure if he wanted the crumbs.

"Spot, this magnificent gourmet doggie cookie is like a Big Mac to a starving man." Spot's eyes drooped, unimpressed. "This is a Red Bull to a teenage boy. This is a ten-thousand-dollar, forty-year-old Macallan single malt to a Scotch connoisseur." That sold him. Spot licked the crumbs off my palm.

"Tasty, huh? C'mon, boy, let's do a little search and I'll give you another bite of heaven."

I lifted up on Spot's collar. He resisted, then gradually pushed out his front paws and walked them back until he was in a sitting position. I shifted my tug from up to forward, and he stood.

I pulled out the shell casings Santiago had given me and held them out to Spot.

"Smell these, Spot? Do you have the scent?" I held them near his nose, then reached out with my other hand, put it on his back, and gave him a vibrating shake. I wanted to make him understand that this was a special task, that I needed his attention.

"Smell these, Spot! Now find the scent!" I pulled the shell casings away from Spot and gave him a pat on his rear.

"Go find the scent, Spot!" I gave him another light smack.

He took a step forward and stopped.

"C'mon, Spot!" I pulled on his collar, trying to get him to at least make a pretend inspection of the area around the group of boulders. Spot took another step forward. He lifted his nose as if detecting some small scent on the breeze, turned to the side, and lay down in the dirt.

I squatted down and held out the shell casings once again, sticking them under Spot's nose. "Do you have the scent, Spot?!" I said, exuding enthusiasm, trying to tap into our past training efforts. Spot had to know that if he found the scent, he'd get more of the fabulous cookie treat.

But he didn't move.

Maybe his mood was not up to it. Maybe Scarlett Milo's death was too debilitating.

Then again, maybe there was no scent of spent shell casings anywhere nearby.

I turned and walked away from the boulders.

"C'mon, Spot. We've got more hiking to do."

I glanced back as I angled up the slope. Spot lifted his head and watched me go, then slowly got up and ambled after me.

I took a zigzag path up the slope, once again picking my way through the manzanita and around the snow patches. As we went higher, there was more snow coverage, and the snow patches were deeper. I found it harder to stay out of the snow and was forced to walk across the snow in places, stepping carefully to not punch through. The spring freeze-thaw cycles had hardened the surface. Every afternoon, the hot sun of late April had melted the snow's surface, and every evening and night, the high-altitude cold had refrozen it. The result was a firm snowpack with the top two inches turned by the sun into soft corn snow. Now and then, my foot broke through the crust, and I sank in past my ankles. I sat down in the snow and strapped on my snowshoes.

The microclimate of altitude change was noticeable after just a short hike. I hadn't gone up more than three or four hundred feet when the snow coverage became significantly deeper, despite the south-facing slope. Spot spread his toes to give more support, but he still broke through the crust. He began following me, stepping in my snowshoe tracks. I tried to make each step a hard marching stomp to compress the snow enough to help Spot.

The second, higher grouping of boulders was packed with snowshoe footprints and ski tracks from the cops who'd already searched the area. As before, I sighted through the boulders, checking the view down to Scarlett Milo's deck. Just as with the area closer to her house, this higher one was perfectly situated for a sniper. The only two differences were that this grouping was farther away, enough so that the shooter would have to be a relative expert. But the extra elevation and its snowpack would give a shooter the ability to ski away on a shallow traverse and travel a long distance very quickly.

I dialed Santiago on my cell phone.

"Sarge," I said when he answered. "I'm up at the second, higher, boulder grouping. It is snow-covered, and the area is trampled with footprints. I'm wondering if the cops who came up here found any footprints."

"Hold on, let me ask Forman." He clicked off, then came

back a minute later. "None," he said. "Forman said the entire area was untracked when they got there. They took pictures just in case, and then they walked freely over the snow to inspect around every boulder."

"Thanks," I said, and hung up.

"Okay, Spot, time for another search!" I radiated enthusiasm because, I hoped, that even depressed dogs might respond to enthusiasm.

Just as before, I pulled out the shell casings, had Spot sniff them, and gave him the command and the pat on his rear. Just as before he took one step forward, sniffed the air and stopped.

"Spot, find the scent!" I repeated, almost pleading.

Spot started to turn a circle in that manner that meant he was about to lie down, when he stopped. He lifted his nose, paused, nostrils flexing, then walked forward, slowly and deliberately. He angled a bit to the right, took several more steps and approached one of the big boulders.

I scrambled to be near as he homed in on the scent. He lowered his head and moved closer. I could see that whatever he smelled was likely in the small, dark crevice where the boulder rose from the snow and the snow had melted away from the rock.

I worried that Spot would paw at whatever he smelled and it would drop down into a gap to never be found. So when he reached out his paw, I was ready and grabbed his collar. I pulled him back.

"Good boy!" I said. I didn't want to lose the good behavior and reward connection, so I pulled one of the pieces of dog cookie out of my shirt pocket and gave it to him.

"Good boy!" I said again, petting him as he ate it without energy. Then I got down on my knees in the snow and knee-walked to the boulder, lowering my head to see into the little crevice.

In contrast to the brilliant sun on the snow, the area between snow and boulder was dark. I took off my sunglasses and lowered my head farther, putting my forehead against rock and my chin against snow. I peered down and to the left, down and to the right, hoping that a shiny brass shell casing would catch the light. Instead of a shell casing, I saw a dead mouse. I squinted, moving to get a better angle. Maybe it wasn't a mouse.

My thin gloves were in the cargo pocket of my jacket. I pulled them on and dug my hands into the snow, pulling back, digging a little trench to the mouse-like object. Gradually, I made a bigger opening, which allowed more light to shine in. The mouse morphed into a cigar butt.

It was a classic example of how dogs think. Ask them to look for a gunpowder smell and they will understand that gunpowder is the focus. But they will also understand that out in the woods, gunpowder is very foreign. So in the absence of gunpowder, they will alert on other foreign smells. Like a cigar butt where there should only be snow and boulders.

Careful not to bump the cigar butt deeper down into the crack, I plucked it out and held it up.

The butt was cold but had white ash on the perimeter, not yet spoiled by snowmelt moisture that would certainly wick into it in the next hour or two.

I held it out to Spot. "Is this the shell casing you were looking for?"

He sniffed it and made a single slow wag of his tail.

I got Santiago back on the phone.

"Your men who came up to the higher grouping of boulders. Any of them smoke cigars?"

"Cigars? Of course not. None of my men smoke."

"Are you sure? Can you check?"

"Why?" he asked.

"Because Spot found a fresh cigar butt. Someone left it here within the last couple of hours."

"You gotta be kidding me. Hold on."

Santiago came back a minute later. "No. No cigars among the Placer County men."

"Our shooter ain't so healthy," I said.

"Forman said there were no tracks in the snow," Santiago said. "He was adamant about that."

"Then our shooter was adamant about not leaving tracks."

"Except the cigar butt," Santiago said.

"Except the cigar butt."

FIVE

"How could someone not leave tracks on the snow?" Santiago said on the phone.

"C'mon up and I'll show you."

It took twenty-five minutes for Santiago and three other deputies to climb up the slope. Two of them didn't have snowshoes, which have ice claws on them to prevent slipping on ice and snow. So it was an arduous task to get up the mountain. As they approached, I could see them single file, carefully stepping in Spot's and my tracks to avoid sinking in deep. When they finally arrived, I held out my gloved hand, palm up, the cigar butt balancing. He looked at it.

"Your dog found that?"

"Yup," I said.

"After you scented him on the shell casings. I don't understand."

"Maybe there is no shell casing to be found. But he found something equally out of place in this landscape."

Santiago pulled out a Ziploc bag, turned it inside out with his hand inside, and picked the cigar butt off my palm and bagged it. He shook his head as if confused.

"It would be like if I said I dropped a quarter in the woods, and you looked around and could find no quarter. But if you saw something like, say, a ring, you would probably pick it up. Equally out of place."

"I guess it makes sense." Santiago looked around the setting. "A perfect sniper's nest," Santiago said. "From this distance, you'd have to be a pro with a rifle, but there is a great sight line to Milo's deck. So how did he escape? And how did he get here without leaving tracks?"

"If you walk on snowshoes, you leave tracks," I said, stating the obvious. "If you come in on skis, cross-country or downhill, you generally leave a track."

"The sun is pretty intense," Santiago said, "but any track would still show, right?"

"Yeah. But a skilled skier can come and go on spring corn snow without leaving a track," I said.

"I don't understand." Santiago was shaking his head. "You just talked about how a skier would leave a track."

I nodded. "Yes, if the skier skied forward in the traditional way. But you can side-slip down corn snow leaving only the faintest of marks. A skier going sideways on corn snow is like a smoothing machine. Like skimming sheetrock mud with a wide trowel. No tracks, no marks, except possibly a small line from the skier's tips and tails. And just a few minutes of hot sun would blend and obscure that."

The sergeant turned and looked around the sight. "You're implying that the shooter side-slipped into this space and took his shot. Then he'd have to side-slip out of here to leave without making tracks."

"Right." I walked to the upper side of the boulder grouping and pointed. "Somewhere up the mountain above this spot, probably a long way up, the shooter was skiing the normal way. He came to a stop, then started side-slipping down to this spot."

Spot lifted his head and looked at me.

"Not you, Spot," I said. "This spot. This place."

Santiago was frowning. "I'm not a pro on the boards, but I know that a good skier can control that kind of descent so that he gradually goes forward or backward as he slips."

"Right. I figure the shooter slid his way into this area through those boulders." I pointed above me. "He paused here, rested his rifle on this rock for support while he aimed and shot. Pleased with his shot, he tossed his cigar butt under that boulder. Who would ever find that, right? It probably didn't occur to him that someone would bring a dog up here. So he put his rifle back in his pack or sling or however he carried it, then side-slipped his way down through here. When he got far enough away that he thought it was safe, he probably skied away in the normal fashion. When he got to where the snow stopped, he would have taken off his skis and hiked down the slope. Or got into a car he'd previously placed."

Santiago thought about it, his eyes narrowed. "Even a long sniper rifle would slide right into a ski bag that he could carry in plain sight, wherever he wanted."

I nodded.

Santiago looked up the slope. "I don't like this at all."

SIX

When we got back down to Scarlett Milo's house, Santiago led me back up on the deck. Two officers were still there, collecting blood and tissue samples off the deck boards. The deck slider was open and two more officers were inside, one taking snapshot photos, the other using a camcorder.

"You said you haven't been inside her house, right?" Santiago said to me.

"Right."

"She gave you the impression on the phone that this was her house, and she said nothing to indicate that anyone else lived here or was visiting."

"Right," I said again.

"Dead people don't have many rights, and there is no obvious person to give us a consent to search. But she may have relatives or heirs, which means we need a warrant to play it safe."

I knew his point. "Because a search could lead to evidence that might implicate her killer, and we don't want that evidence to be inadmissible because we didn't get consent from whoever owns this house."

Santiago nodded. "I called for a warrant before I climbed up that slope. Hopefully, it won't be long before we get it."

"You've checked the place for other potential victims?" I asked.

"Yes. And photo documented the scene. To play it safe, we can't go through drawers until we get that warrant. But I'd like you to walk through the house and see if anything stands out based on what you spoke to Ms. Milo about."

"A look-see compatible with the plain view doctrine," I said.

"Right. We've already done that," Santiago said. "But something that looks benign to us might look like evidence to you."

"Got it," I said.

So I left Spot on the deck and walked through the house. Santiago accompanied me. Nothing of interest caught my eye.

Back on the deck, the medical examiner was speaking to two paramedics. They nodded, zipped the body into a black body bag, and carried it off.

Two deputies trotted up the deck stairs and handed an envelope to Santiago. He pulled out a sheet of paper and looked at it.

"Okay, we've got a warrant," he said. He looked it over. "It's thorough."

I took that to mean that they would be able to take her computer and look through her cellphone and anything else that might reveal a clue to her killer.

Santiago's men began a search of Milo's abode. I joined them, not participating but watching. Santiago called out to the youngest men in the group. "Jacob and Brian, I want you two on Milo's computer." He pointed to Scarlett's desk where her computer showed screensaver images of Sierra Nevada landscapes.

"You remember what they taught you in the computer forensics class," Santiago said.

"Yeah," Jacob said. "Document and photograph the make, model, serial number, and inventory number of the computer and any related media. Then we do a crash dump onto a virgin flash drive. That way we can save all the stuff in the Random Access Memory that would all be lost in a plug pull. After we've got that, we still pull the plug and we get to keep the hard drive as it was without any shutdown scrubbing."

"Okay," Santiago said. "Remember chain of custody. I want complete documentation at every step. Does our evidence kit have new flash drives still in the wrapper and the new crash dump utility?"

"Yes," Jacob said.

"Okay. Get to work."

One of them pulled a second chair up next to Milo's desk chair while the other got a fresh flash drive from their evidence kit and tore open the packaging. They sat down with a legal-sized pad of paper, moved Milo's computer mouse to turn off the screen saver, and started making notes as they proceeded to look into Milo's electronic life.

"On Milo's desk is an old-fashioned paper address book," I said to Santiago. "Okay if I look through it? I'll wear my gloves."

He nodded.

I pulled on my gloves, picked up the address book, and paged through it. It had obviously been in use for years. It had lots of names and phone numbers and pieces of Post-it notes with additional bits of info. There were entries in pen and pencil. There were cross-outs and eraser smudges. Here and there were scribbles that looked like gibberish, perhaps bits of passwords that only had meaning for Scarlett.

After my first perusal, I went through it again, forcing myself to look at each name to see if I recognized any of them. None seemed familiar. And there were no Milos listed. I looked to see if there were any notations that suggested that any of the entries were for people who might have been close to Scarlett, someone who could provide information about her. Nothing stood out, which wasn't surprising. People don't write sister-in-law or ex-husband next to names in their address books. They know who their family and friends are.

I put the address book down and walked over to Santiago.

"Nothing revealing in the book," I said. "Okay if I look in her file drawers? I won't change the order of any files or papers, but I'll take notes of anything interesting."

"Be my guest."

Still wearing the latex gloves, I found a blank piece of copy paper. I pulled a dining chair over to a filing cabinet that was part of the desk arrangement.

Milo's files were orderly, and the labels were clear.

First, I pulled out a folder labeled "Will."

In it were a bunch of papers with a lawyer's name at the top. They were filled with what looked to be the standard legalise that renders even the simplest statements inscrutable. But eventually, I figured out that Scarlett Milo had put her assets, which were substantial, into a kind of trust that would benefit several environmental organizations that focused on endangered species habitat preservation.

Several of her assets were mentioned. I scanned for information on another house that might reveal whether or not this house was a vacation home, but there was none. From her will, it appeared that if she had any relatives, they weren't close enough that she wanted to leave them anything.

I found a real estate file. In it was only the Squaw Valley house. The tax statement came to her name. If Scarlett had any kind of a life partner, they weren't part of the home ownership.

In her investment file, I found statements from several investment companies. In addition to cash and IRA accounts, she had stock funds, mostly conservative, large-cap companies. She'd been taking mandatory IRA distributions for several years, which put her age into her 70s.

To check, I found a file on her vehicles. In addition to the DMV information on an Audi and a Range Rover, I found a copy of her driver's license, which showed her age as 74.

There was enough money in her accounts to attract predators, but most of it was locked up in investment vehicles that would not make it easy to get immediate withdrawals. That took her out of the target range for the kind of scum that goes after older women.

But somebody wanted Scarlett Milo dead… Maybe it had nothing to do with money.

There were files for utility bills and charitable contributions and travel. I flipped through each and found nothing unusual. Scarlett was frugal with her heat and electricity, generous with her charity, and she traveled a lot. Her last trip appeared to have been to Florence, Italy, a place I hadn't visited. But I knew it was a popular tourist destination.

There was another file labeled Amazon and in it computer printouts that showed some kind of vendor account at Amazon. I looked over some of the pages. It appeared that Milo had written a series of books called "The Smart Single Woman's Guides." There were seventeen titles such as, The Smart Single Woman's Guide To Financial Power, The Smart Single Woman's Guide To Romance Without Commitment, and so forth. The books covered everything from traveling alone to coping with aging parents, from changing careers to legal strategies to finding a cultural passion, etc. I got out my phone, went to Amazon's website, and typed in Milo's name. Up came the book series. The books had lots of reviews and high ratings. The sales rankings showed that they were popular books, and they would produce a good income.

I wondered if they would produce any enemies.

I turned off the phone and took another walk around Milo's house, trying to see it anew, but I saw nothing notable.

I wandered over to her bookshelves. In the era of Kindle, her books were an impressive commitment to the long history and tradition of bound volumes of words on paper. The shelves took up one entire wall. The left side was fiction, mostly hardcover, classic 19th and early 20th century novels mixed in with more modern literary greats like Bellow, Updike, Barbara Kingsolver, and Toni Morrison.

The right side of the wall was nonfiction, biographies, histories, and even a few science books on the latest theories of modern physics. There was also a shelf devoted to Tahoe subjects, guidebooks for hiking and biking and cross-country skiing.

Most interesting to me was Milo's collection of art books, large volumes filled with color plates of the greatest art of the last 2000 years. She had more art books than I, and I had no doubt that she was much more knowledgeable than I was about the world of art. While I like to page through my books the way a five-year-old kid looks at picture books, admiring and pondering the art without much deeper understanding, something about Milo's collection made me think that she was much more academic in her approach. Perhaps she'd been a scholar.

The largest section of her art books focused on the Italian Renaissance, including monographs on Michelangelo, da Vinci, Botticelli, Raphael, etc. In addition to conventional art books with art reproductions, Milo also had several textbooks on the Italian Renaissance. I flipped through a couple of them. They were dense with information that didn't mean much to me beyond communicating the sense that the Renaissance was mostly about art and mostly about Northern Italy.

Below Milo's books were two shelves of vinyl records. I scanned the titles. Swing era music from the '40s and jazz from the '50s and '60s. The only music that spanned several decades was a large number of Frank Sinatra records.

There was nothing else especially notable about Milo's house. Her effects provided a picture of an educated, wealthy woman who'd done well writing guides for single women.

The last place I looked was the garage. It looked like any other garage, although perhaps neater than most. There was a cream-colored Audi and a black Range Rover, just as Scarlett's DMV file showed. Nothing was notable.

I went back out on the deck. Santiago was talking to one of his deputies. He turned to me.

"Find anything of interest?"

"A healthy investment portfolio, and an interesting collection of books, but nothing that seems like it might connect to her murder. I saw no indication of any family, and her will leaves everything to some environmental groups dedicated to preserving the habitats of endangered animals. How about you?"

He shook his head. "The only thing that stands out is we can't find her cell phone."

"I should've thought of that. She was talking to me when she was shot. It's got to be here someplace." I looked around at the deck, then over the railing.

Santiago gestured toward the house. "The portable phones are all in their cradles. So she must have been talking on her cell."

"Let's call her number," I said. "She gave it to me, and I called her when I got to the turn-off down below. Hold on, it should be in my phone."

I brought up the menu of my recent calls and redialed the most recent one.

I heard a distant ring.

"Below the deck," Santiago said.

Santiago's deputy ran down the steps as the ring came again. He leaned over, hands on his knees. It rang again. He moved over toward one of the pier foundations that held up the deck. Another ring.

"It sounds like it's coming from underground."

There were no more rings.

"The phone must have gone to voicemail," he said.

"I'll dial again," I said.

The faint ring came again. The deputy got down on his hands and knees. He turned his head like a dog trying to determine a sound location.

"Oh, wow, there's a little rodent hole. Her phone must've fallen down there. I'll try to dig it out."

He started clawing at the dirt. "How do rodents dig this stuff? It's mostly rocks." He kept digging. Santiago came down next to him. The phone kept ringing.

The deputy's hand was well below the surface, the dirt coming halfway up to his elbow. "You don't think a ground squirrel would attack me for tearing up his house, do you?"

"Never know," Santiago said. "But your big mitts are ugly enough, that rodent will probably be too scared. Be like Godzilla in his bedroom."

"Funny guy, sarge. You're a regular stand-up comedian. Oh, I felt something smooth." The phone stopped ringing. "Got it!" the deputy said. He carefully withdrew his hand. Delicately pinched between the tips of his index and middle fingers was a cell phone.

Santiago took it, pushed the button to turn it on.

"It's locked with a password," he said. "I bet it's got some clues to this woman's life. Maybe we can get a hacker to help us." He turned to me. "You got any other ideas about how to pursue this case?"

I shook my head. "Still in a bit of shock. I'll let you know if I think of anything. One more thing before I go," I said. "Do you mind if I make a copy of the note I gave you? The one Scarlett wrote on the back of the receipt? Scarlett has one of those all-in-one printer copiers on her desk."

"Sure." Santiago pulled it out of the notebook he carried. We made a copy, and he put the original back in his book.

I said goodbye, and Spot and I left.

SEVEN

The sun was nearly setting as I exited the valley out through Santiago's roadblock at the Squaw Valley entrance. I didn't know the officers posted there. It was faster just to let them search my Jeep than it would have been to have them call Santiago. I thanked them as they finished and let me through.

Out on the highway, I turned south toward Lake Tahoe. The mountain shadows were long, and I barely noticed a little puff of dust that seemed to pop up out of the hood on my Jeep. Then my right front tire blew, and the Jeep swerved toward the shoulder. I hadn't heard any sound over the road noise, but it all added up to gunshots, this time more than one.

I turned the wheel to get well off onto the right shoulder, then stomped on the brakes and slammed the shifter into park. I was out the driver's door in a moment. Spot was ready as I jerked open the rear door.

"C'mon, Spot!" I shouted as I sprinted around the rear of the Jeep. He followed and then passed me.

Because the right front tire had gone out, I figured the shooter was probably up on the mountains on the right side, the mountain ridge to the west that rose between Squaw Valley and Alpine Meadows Valley. I figured if Spot and I made it to a grouping of trees up against the slope, I'd be out of sight from whomever was above.

I pulled Spot into the trees.

But then I realized that the shooter could have gotten the front tire from down the highway in front of me, including the mountains on the east side of the highway.

So I shifted our position to block that view as well, and got out my phone.

The 911 dispatcher patched me through to Sergeant Santiago, and I explained what had happened.

The reaction was dramatic. He pulled a large portion of the officers out of Scarlett Milo's neighborhood, and they swarmed out onto the highway. They took up positions up and down the road, including the trees where Spot and I were hiding.

Multiple sheriff's vehicles raced up, sirens and lights blazing, officers jumped out, running, taking positions of cover, surrounding us. The CHP helicopter roared through the sky above. At first it seemed that such a rapid response would give them a good chance of spotting anyone up on any of the nearby ridges. But then I realized that the gathering dusk would give a shooter plenty of cover in just a few minutes. And if the shooter was on the steep ridge to the east, there were countless miles of trails one could follow and then emerge anywhere from Tahoe City to the Northstar ski area, or even as far away as Truckee to the north.

Santiago appeared, rushing toward the trees where Spot and I and other officers now stood. We went through a similar talk as we'd done at Scarlett's, discussing possible shooter locations and escape routes. Our conclusions were parallel to our previous conclusions. As darkness descended, we were unlikely at best to have any chance of finding the shooter.

I called my girlfriend Street Casey and explained that I was up at Squaw Valley dealing with a shooting, but I didn't give her details. She asked me to call when I got home.

An hour later, it was dark enough that Santiago felt it was reasonable to change my blown tire, although he wouldn't let me out of the tree cover.

"You're the target," he said. "No point in giving the shooter an easy shot. Maybe he's got a night scope or something."

"Maybe," I said.

When my tire was replaced, Santiago let me leave, and I cruised home through the darkness.

I went straight to my cabin. I wanted to shower off Scarlett Milo's blood, change my clothes, and clean up Spot as well.

Before I cleaned up, I called Street Casey again and asked if she had dinner plans.

"Yes, I was hoping you'd be done in time to join me, so I've been delaying. I'm chopping peppers for vegetarian stir fry. Want to come?"

"I'll grab some wine and show up when you say."

"I say come in about a half hour."

"Perfect."

I hung up. As I was about to get in the shower, the phone rang.

"McKenna," I said.

"Hola, amigo." It was my best friend, Douglas County Sergeant Diamond Martinez. "I'm calling because the shooting of the lady at Squaw Valley and the subsequent shooting at you has produced an amazing cacophony of buzz among local law enforcement. I'm in the area. Wanted to stop by and get the story straight from the source."

"I'm going to Street's for dinner in thirty minutes."

"Does she know about it?"

"The dinner, yes," I said. "The shooting, no."

"A report to an audience of two is more efficient than doing it twice," he said.

I thought about it.

"I will leave posthaste when you're done," he added. "Don't want to spoil a romantic dinner with a lady as lovely as the entomologist of local forensic fame."

"Meet me at her condo?"

"Gracias."

I hung up and dialed Street back. I told her that Diamond was stopping by for a quick visit. "Emphasis on the quick," I said.

Ever gracious, Street said that Diamond was always welcome at her abode, even when I was coming for a dinner-for-two.

I jumped in the shower, and Spot and I were back in the Jeep twenty minutes later.

From my cabin, Street's condo is 1000 vertical feet and two miles down a winding road. I have a key, but I never use it except for those times when Street makes a specific request for me to let myself in.

Spot began a slow wag the moment I let him out of the Jeep.

When I knocked on her brand new door, he stared at the new, reinforced steel panel and listened with the focus of a safecracker. Still wagging.

After thirty seconds, he lifted his head a bit and his tail sped up. He turned his head slowly as if watching something moving on the other side. His gaze tracked from right to left and eventually moved to the doorknob. A moment later, the knob turned and the door opened.

Street hugged him first and then raised up on tiptoes to kiss me. Spot pushed on past her, eager to consider any potential cooking smells and imagine what portion might be for him, vegetarian or not. The place was in fact filled with delicious food scents that I couldn't place. Accompanying the aromas was some classic Brubeck and Desmond.

"Just so you know, heavy front doors provide no privacy from dogs," I said.

"How is that?" Street said, turning around to glance at Spot, who was already in the kitchen, nose held high, nostrils flexing. "They can't see through a solid panel. Can they smell through closed doors?"

"Probably. But in this case, Spot could hear you. He knew exactly when you were about to open the door."

"But I'm wearing my slippers. They make no noise. And the music covers any other noise."

I shrugged as I came in and closed and locked the door behind me.

"Canine enigmas," Street said. "So many things work in ways that are unknowable. Like all the great arts. Poetry. Music. Painting. Dance. Dog perception."

I followed Street in and set the Wild Horse Pinot I'd brought on the counter. "Did you hear that, Spot? Street just called your detecting abilities a great art."

He wagged, then turned and looked back at Street's front door.

A moment later came a brief, two-tap knock.

I walked over. Even though I was armed with a 170-pound Great Dane, I bent down to look out the peephole. I didn't have a peephole at my cabin, but being at Street's, especially after the forced entry the month before, brought the responsibility of minimizing any potential threat to her.

I saw a fish-eye picture of a handsome man with skin the color of hand-oiled teak beneath black hair. Spot was next to me as I opened the door. Diamond gave him a knuckle rub on his scalp. Spot wagged.

"Sorry if I'm interrupting amore with business," he said.

Street came over and kissed Diamond on his cheek. "Vegetarian dinner isn't quite the same as amore," she said.

"If somebody like you cooked it for me, it would be."

Street smiled. "What's the business?"

Diamond gestured at me. "The tall gringo has the story."

Street frowned. "If we're going to be treated to a story, maybe you should get some wine out of this bottle, first." She handed me a corkscrew.

I pulled the cork as she got out three glasses. I poured an inch for Street and three inches for me. I raised the bottle to pour Diamond's and then paused and looked at him in his dress browns.

"Off duty twenty minutes ago," he said. "I'll change to my jean jacket in my patrol unit."

I poured three inches for him.

That would give Street an hour's worth of sipping and fifteen minutes each for Diamond and me.

So I told them about Scarlett Milo calling me and what had transpired. I finished with the shots at me, but explained, truthfully, that I wasn't in much danger because it is nearly impossible to hit an unseen driver behind a dark windshield on a moving vehicle. I kept it like upscale journalism, just the facts about person, place, and time, and I finished by telling them what Scarlett had written on the note. I did not include any editorializing or gratuitous details about the shooting. Street was very alarmed, but she had been involved in enough of my cases to know that things can get messy and disturbing, and she probably filled in the blanks with a realistic idea of what actually happened. Diamond had a better idea of the reality, aided by the reports he'd already heard.

"Gut sense?" Diamond said.

I shook my head. "It's obviously not a random event. Someone had targeted her, and she knew it in advance of the shooting. They probably targeted me simply because I'd been a witness of sorts to her shooting. Unfortunately, nothing she said and nothing we found other than the note she wrote gave us any indication of what caused someone to kill her. And the note is puzzling enough that it seems of no help."

Diamond said, "I heard that the note said, 'Medic's BFF.'"

"Right. Like a medic's Best Friend Forever. I made a copy." I pulled the folded copy out of my pocket. "Who knows what that means? But it gives us something to look into."

Diamond took the piece of paper and looked at it. Then he handed it to Street.

Street was frowning. "She wrote this before you got there? It doesn't make sense. Why would someone write an inscrutable note? Unless it was just a reminder to herself?"

"I guess I need to explain some uncomfortable details." I told them the sequence of events from when I called Scarlett from the street down below her house and how the shot came while we were talking over the phone. I explained how I'd found her on the deck, still alive but just barely.

Street looked sick. "She was shot in the neck, and she was bleeding to death, but she was able to write you a note? My God, that is both terrible and heroic. That gives those words great meaning. Medic's BFF."

"Yeah. Sorry to burden you with the image. It's not the stuff that makes for happy dreams." I put my arm around her shoulders and felt her shudder.

She said, "Imagine if people didn't mean harm to others. It seems like a fantasy to think of a world where no one would die at the hands of another person. What a different, wonderful world that would be."

We were silent for a moment.

Diamond's left foot made a barely perceptible tap on the floor, like a poker player's tell.

"What say you?" I said.

"People meaning well instead of harm would still cause other people to die," Diamond said. "It the unfortunate nature of life."

"Sure," Street said. "Accidents and such. But that's not the same, right?"

"Sometimes the difference between an accidental death and murder is a very fine line," he said. "The problem is trying to tell if a person meant well or not."

I drank wine. "Example?"

"Sure" Diamond said. "Thomas Aquinas addressed this in his Doctrine of Double Effect. You can intend one thing, but that can lead to another. It always gets down to intent. Exact same action, exact same result. But one way, he's a hero. The other way, he's a murderer. As an example, there's a standard philosophical conundrum that illustrates what Aquinas said. It's called the trolley problem," he said.

"I've heard of that," Street said.

Diamond nodded. "A runaway trolley is going to hit a group of five people and kill them. A person up the tracks sees an opportunity to pull a lever and send the trolley onto another track where there is only one person who will get killed. He pulls the lever. Instead of five people dying, only one person dies. The man saves a lot of lives."

"And some people will think he's a hero," I said. Then I realized where he was going with the scenario. "But it's possible that the person pulling the lever wants to kill the single person on the side track. Then he's a murderer."

"Right."

"Aquinas was a saint, right?" Street said.

I got the sense that she was eager to help direct the conversation away from Scarlett and her macabre murder.

"Yeah," Diamond said. "They knew Aquinas was a big deal back in the thirteenth century, and they made him a saint. He was an important theologian. But where he really kicked butt was as a philosopher."

Diamond picked up his wine glass and drained it. He set the glass down on the counter and turned to Street. "I'm sorry. In an effort to change the subject away from Scarlett Milo's murder, I went off a different direction that was no better. Please accept my apology."

Street started to protest, but Diamond smiled and said, "I should be going. Thanks for your time." He gave Spot a pet and then left.

Street and I looked at each other for a long, quiet moment.

Street spoke first. "I thought I'd grill the veggies on the perforated barbecue pan. Gives them great flavor. How about you light the charcoal while I pour more wine?"

I looked at her glass. It was down a half an inch. Either the wine was really good, or I'd stressed her talking about Scarlett Milo.

I picked up the box of wooden matches and headed out onto the deck. Spot pushed out before me. Like all dogs, he was always eager to figure out where the humans were going and then get in front of them and lead them.

I squirted lighter fluid on a pile of briquettes and lit them afire.

Street came out carrying our glasses. We stood at the railing, looking out toward the forest where here and there were filtered bits of lake view during the day, dense intimate forest at night. Spot stood to Street's side. He looked at her, then looked where she was looking.

When the coals were ready, Street brought out two bowls of vegetables, one onions and garlic cloves and the other peppers and carrots and broccoli and celery and bok choy. She sprayed olive oil into a pan that had hundreds of holes in it, then poured the onions into the pan and set it on the grill. The heat and smoke seeped through as she stirred, and within a minute, the aroma was grand.

After the onions began to cook, she added the other veggies, and stirred the mix continuously. Within a few minutes, she removed the pan, and I followed her inside.

I learned what the previous cooking smells were as she dished up a mixture of wild, black, and brown rice into broad-brimmed, cherry-red bowls and put the veggies on top. Maybe I could live without steak after all.

We sat across from each other at her small dining table, the lights down low, a single candle in the middle of the table, and her gas fireplace flickering off to the side. Tommy Flanagan had taken over the piano.

Street was wearing a dark red, silk shirt with three-quarter sleeves. It was open to the third button so that her simple silver necklace would show. She had on a matching silver bracelet, and she'd coated her nails with a clear coat that was glossy enough to reflect the candle light. I sensed the slightest touch of smoky gray eye shadow, which set off her hair that was no longer auburn but back to black and styled in a kind of wind-blown look. The combination might have been harsh in some lights, but with the low light of fire and candle, she looked beautiful, her cheekbones dramatic beneath soft skin.

Spot sat to the side of the table, opposite the fireplace, his ears and eyes like laser beams focused on Street's bowl, then my bowl, then back to Street's. Sitting on his haunches, his chin was significantly higher than the table, and his head gradually glided forward, closer, centimeter by centimeter.

"Spot," I said, snapping my fingers and making a downward pointed gesture that meant he should lie on the floor.

Spot looked at me. Instead of lying on the floor, he lowered his chin to the table and rested his head. With his head in one place, his eyes resumed their focus on our bowls of food. I thought of insisting that he lie down, then decided that his current position was okay as long as he wasn't drooling, something that would come instantaneously if we gave him any indication that he was about to get food.

When we were done eating, Street rewarded Spot for his gentlemanly behavior. His wagging tail nearly broke her sliding glass door as she brought a bowl of food out to the deck.

Later, we lingered with wine on the couch in front of her fireplace. Oscar Peterson was now doing his keyboard magic.

Street talked about Diamond's constant hunger for knowledge, from Thomas Aquinas's writings to how we judge the way people die.

I was noticing the way the firelight danced along the delicate lines of her neck and shoulders.

Street segued into Enlightenment philosophy and how

important it was to loosening the Catholic Church's constraining hold on society and teaching us tolerance for other religions.

I was studying Street's eyes and the little yellow flecks that made her nearly-black irises look mysterious.

Street talked about how philosophers taught us the importance of science and the value of democracy over monarchy.

I was thinking that the dramatic curve of her lips shortened my breath.

Street recounted how the most important points in our Declaration of Independence, the U.S. Constitution, and our Bill of Rights all had their origin in the writings of philosophers and how most of the great principles we hold dear today came from a few great thinkers.

I was looking at Street's face, all cheekbones and hollows in the flickering firelight, a non-standard beauty that was the equal of any.

As Street continued to talk, I thought it was nothing more than good luck that I knew people who looked outward more than inward, people who expanded my world instead of shrinking it, people who were primarily interested in the big questions rather than the minutia of their own lives.

I didn't have Street's intellectual firepower, but I was smart enough to treasure the wonder of her existence.

When it came time to go, we said goodnight with the candle still flickering and Gerry Mulligan performing his sax wizardry.

I was sorry to leave the woman of my dreams. But Street didn't invite me to stay, and she had said earlier that she needed to get up early. Although we had enjoyed many long evenings and sleepovers over the years, I understood her need to keep our lives from getting too intertwined, a need that arose from the very difficult childhood with parents who were evil.

I wondered if the powerful pullback that results from such abuse as a child prevents that person from fully enjoying a deep closeness in future adult relationships. I understood that close emotional connections and any degree of dependency brings with it the risk of revisiting unbearably painful memories should that closeness and dependency fall apart. Better to keep some emotional distance than risk shattering the balanced-yet-fragile psyche of an adult who grew out of the worst a child can experience.

But still I longed for her constant company.

Street and I hugged and kissed with Spot burrowing between us, and then Spot and I stepped out into the cold night. My eyes stung from the sadness of leaving Street as I walked to the Jeep.

When Spot and I were in the Jeep and driving back up the mountain, I said, "That girl back there is something special, isn't she? Like breathing some rarefied perfume. Like holding a one-of-a-kind flower in your open palms. I could spend my entire life with that girl. But instead, we just get visits, you and I. But I guess we need to get comfortable with that. Visits have to be enough, huh, boy?"

Spot stuck his head forward from the back seat and touched his nose to the side of my neck. He held his massive head next to my ear while I reached up and pet him.

"Visits have to be enough," I repeated as we headed up the dark mountain.

There was a folded piece of paper stuck into the crack of my cabin door. I pulled it out and brought it inside to look at it in the light. There was writing in blue ballpoint pen. All caps. The block letters were perfectly uniform, traced from some kind of template. It said, "WALK AWAY FROM THE MILO CASE OR YOU DIE."

Below the writing was a drawing printed upside down. I rotated the paper.

The image was printed from a computer. It was a five-point star. Within the star was a figure of a man. The man's head was positioned within the top point of the star. His outstretched arms were slightly raised to fit into the two star points to the left and right. His legs were spread to match the position of the lower two star points. At the perimeter was a circle that touched each of the star points, and at the center of the circle were crossed lines like the cross hairs in a rifle scope.

It was a disturbing drawing, and, despite the blinds on my windows, I turned off the lights and thought about it.

It appeared that whoever had shot at Scarlett and me knew where I lived. Maybe he'd simply followed me home.

I called Diamond and told him about it.

"It sounds like a seriously disturbed individual is after you," he said. "Is there anything about the warning that suggests who might have left it?"

"No. It's regular copy paper, an image probably printed off the internet, letters made with a template. No doubt it was handled with gloves."

"The star and man mean nothing to you?"

"No."

After a moment, Diamond said, "Want me to come over?"

"No. I can make a copy for you and give it to you in the morning."

"Stay low."

"Thanks," I said, and we hung up.

My little three-room log cabin was chilly, the wood stove having been cold all day. I got a fire going, and when the flames cast their flickering light through the glass door and it began to throw off warmth, it should have been cozy as always. But this evening stayed chilly in spirit even as the temperature rose. And when I turned off the lights to go to bed, the firelight seemed harsh instead of warm.

In the middle of the night, I couldn't sleep.

I got up and walked into the dark living room. Spot was asleep on his bed, warmed by the stove. I sat in the rocker in the dark, looking at the distant sparkle of lights around the lake one thousand feet below. If only my insomnia were simple loneliness. But I knew it was something deeper.

I went out the slider into the cold air that is a constant during Tahoe nights regardless of season. Spot jumped up and joined me, sticking his wet nose into my hand as he came through the slider next to me. Then he turned and trotted to the edge of the deck, thrusting his head over the railing, sniffing, listening. I followed and saw what had gotten his attention.

In the distance below were red flashing lights heading south down the East Shore highway toward the Cave Rock Tunnel.

There were two vehicles. Although they were a long way down, I could tell that one was a firetruck being followed by a rescue vehicle. They were no doubt coming from the Glenbrook Fire Station, going to assist on a fire somewhere south of Cave Rock. I watched until they went around the curve and disappeared into the Cave Rock Tunnel.

As I turned and went back into the warmth of the cabin, I thought of the heartbreak that accompanies fire.

Then I remembered what Scarlett Milo said. She had worried that someone might 'pick her off' or 'burn down her house with her inside.'

With my heart beating much too fast to sleep, I sat in the dark and drank a beer, staring into the red coals behind the wood stove glass. Spot sat next to me, lowered his head to my lap, and I rubbed his ears.

It was obvious that I'd screwed up in a major way. Scarlett was dead. I'd merely done as she asked, showed up at the turn below her house, there to be inspected from above by not just the client but the murderer as well. My complacent response to Scarlett's instructions wasn't enough. When a person calls to engage my help, it is up to me to gauge the situation and recognize threats that even the client doesn't see. I should have told Scarlett to stay inside, should have arranged for her to judge the situation in some other way. Whatever would have been the best way to respond eluded me still. But that only increased my sense of wrongdoing.

The situation was as breathtakingly simple as it was devastating. A client relied on me for help, and now that client was dead. There is no clearer definition of utter failure.

Like Diamond, Street was kind, at least to the extent of not judging me to my face. But how could either of them have not immediately thought that I'd made a tragic mistake, that as a detective for hire, it was my responsibility to know better, to figure out an approach to a client's problem that would keep the client alive?

Now I was up on the mountain alone with my judgment and my dog. And somewhere down below, other lives were likely being gutted as a fire burned.

EIGHT

I woke up with a pervasive discomfort. Tahoe is not the kind of place where snipers sit up on a mountainside and pick off people down below on their decks.

With no clues to go on, I called each of my main contacts at Tahoe's various law enforcement agencies and asked them if anyone in their jurisdiction had recently died, whether from a gunshot wound or any other suspicious or unusual circumstances. I started with Diamond even though I'd just spoken to him the previous evening.

"You get through the night okay?" he asked.

"Yeah."

"Good. First thing this morning, I checked for suspicious deaths in Douglas County and there haven't been any," he said. "But we did get a missing persons report. That is rare in our county. Also, the fire in Zephyr Heights last night appears to be arson. That's equally rare. Especially when there are people in the house."

"Don't tell me they died."

"No. Apparently, one of them was up with insomnia. His dog barked, alerting him to the fire. He woke up his sister and they both got out before the house was consumed."

I thought about how I too had been up, unable to sleep, as the Glenbrook Fire trucks raced south to help fight the fire.

"Any idea whose house it was?"

"No. They're currently at the neighbors. I'm on my way there now, so I'll know more soon."

"What about the missing persons report?" I said.

"A man named Malcolm Warner called from San Francisco. Said his twenty-seven-year-old son Sean went up to Tahoe for a last weekend of spring skiing. The dad said the boy always checks in every couple of days, but it had been several days since they'd heard from Sean. The dad is very worried."

"So it would have been about the weekend before last?"

"Sí."

"Why did the dad call your county?"

"Because Sean was staying in our territory," Diamond said, "a studio condo up near the Stagecoach chairlift at Heavenly."

"What was Sean's last communication to his parents?"

"He texted his mother that he was taking some unused vacation days and staying on in Tahoe for a bit. That text was five days ago, and neither the parents nor any friends have heard anything since."

"You turn up anything on the case?" I asked.

"Just one little thing. Sean's been working on his sheet. One for grand larceny. One for possession of a firearm without a permit. And two priors for burglary. Both were houses where he went in a window on an upper floor, giving him a rep as a second story man."

"He do time on any of these?" I asked.

I heard Diamond snort into the phone. "Father Malcolm has a lot of money. It's amazing what sufficient legal firepower can do. Sean did some probation, community service. Never spent a single night in the lockup."

"So our missing boy is another example of how the dregs of humanity get just as attracted to the excitement of Tahoe as the rest of us."

"Unfortunately, yes. We found the condo where Sean stayed. The manager said he never checked out. He just disappeared."

I was trying to think like a parent with a missing child. "The parents call the kid's workplace?"

"Yeah. The kid works at a tire store. He hasn't turned up there since he left for Tahoe. No one's heard anything."

"Maybe Sean met a girl up on the ski slopes."

Diamond paused. "I can remember a time when I might have gone AWOL had I met the right girl."

"Ha," I said. "You'd do that now."

"Have to be a really right girl."

"They're out there," I said.

"At least one, but you got her."

"I only got her three-quarters of the way. Any chance you found out what kind of car Sean drives?"

"A blue Toyota. His dad said it's dark blue. His words were, 'navy faded to dull dark blue.'"

"You check the Douglas County impound lot to see if it got towed in?"

"Yes I did, and no it didn't."

I thanked Diamond and asked him to let me know if he learned anything interesting about the Zephyr Heights fire.

I next called Santiago in Placer County. He said there'd been no other suspicious deaths either before or after Scarlett Milo's. He added that Milo's death was enough to satisfy any cop's appetite for crime solving for the next ten years.

I didn't have a current close contact at Washoe County, and Carson City County's claim at the lake consisted of a narrow slice of East Shore land that was mostly uninhabited. So neither was on my priority list.

I called Sergeant Bains of El Dorado County and asked him the same question. He said they'd had no recent unnatural deaths or missing persons report, but added that his records didn't include the city of South Lake Tahoe.

I dialed Commander Mallory of the SLTPD.

"Nope," he said in answer to my question. "We did have a woman go missing, but missing doesn't seem flashy enough for your shooter's style."

"Diamond just told me they had a missing person. Could he be referring to the same person?"

"A woman named Darla Ali?" Mallory said.

"No. Diamond's MP was a man named Sean Warner."

Mallory paused a bit, and I could hear him sucking the last drops of what surely was Coke in a can. "Darla's roommate reported her missing when she didn't come home from work."

"Descriptors?"

"Five-six," he continued, "blonde, blue, and, as her roommate Sanford Burroughs described her when he filed the missing persons report, twenty-four and fabulous."

"Boyfriend?" I said.

"No, he's not the fabulous-girls type. Real concerned, though.

He reported her missing two nights ago when she didn't come home from work, and he's called twice since then, wondering if we've learned anything."

"Have you?"

"Not much. I ran an errand with Officer Harlan first thing this morning. He and I were backtracking a suspect and we had some extra time. We were near Darla's place, so we stopped by. Darla and Burroughs share the top floor of a triplex. I'm sure Burroughs would be real pleased to have you stop by. Make him think the world cares about Darla."

"She have family?"

"According to Burroughs, yes, but Darla never told him much about them other than they were in Maine and she came to Tahoe to get as far from them as she could. Something about bad blood with the dad for bad things he did when Darla was younger, and bad blood with the mom for staying with the dad after she found out about the bad things. Burroughs said that Darla said she's never going to see or speak with her parents again."

"Lot of that going around," I said. "Job?"

"Waitress somewhere. I forget."

"Do you have the home address handy?"

"There's more to my job than playing secretary for you, McKenna. But hold on and I'll leave all these other robbers and killers and wife beaters and accident victims and ringing phones and unanswered emails and text messages while I look for you."

My phone went silent. I waited two minutes. Mallory and I get along pretty well, but that didn't mean he wouldn't attend to some business and fetch another Coke and maybe order some Chinese takeout before he came back.

The phone line clicked, and Mallory read off an address.

"What about her car?" I asked.

"No car."

"Anything else unusual happen in town recently?"

"Nope. Lemme know if you find anything."

"Will do. Hey, Mallory."

"What?" he said.

"You make a helluva secretary," I said.

He hung up.

NINE

I took Spot outside, wary of the forest. As an ex-cop, I knew to take all threats seriously. But all I could do was be careful. I walked Spot in the shadows, then let him into the Jeep, and we headed to the SLT impound lot.

As I slowed for the sharp curve entering the southbound tunnel of Cave Rock, I noticed a black pickup some distance back. Later, as I crossed the state line into California, I saw it again, although it may not have been the same vehicle. Black pickups are common in Tahoe. Just before I parked near the impound lot, there was yet another large black vehicle far back. But when I turned to take a careful look, it was gone. It was the kind of coincidence I didn't normally pay attention to. But after being shot at and getting the threatening note, I was more vigilant.

I got out of the Jeep as the impound lot attendant walked out of the office, stepping around puddles of melted snow. The spring sun came through the trees and hit the pavement here and there, making it steam. The man wore faded jeans and a faded jean jacket and his brown-gray hair was pulled back into a long, thin ponytail.

"Paperwork?" he said from the other side of a chain-link fence.

"No paperwork," I said.

He gave me that hardened look that all impound lot attendants get after two months on the job and they've learned that half the people showing up haven't paid their fine and they beg or lie or spin some story about having to get their car so they can drive their dying grandmother to the hospital.

"No vehicle release without paperwork," he said. He stood facing me, his thumbs tucked into the waistband of his jeans.

"I'm Detective Owen McKenna, here to look for a dark blue

Toyota belonging to a missing person name of Sean Warner. I don't want to take the car. I just want to see if you have it."

He squinted at me. Letting me in without paperwork was probably against the rules. "You try to lock yourself inside and start the engine, I'll cut the tires." He tapped a pocket on his jeans, the bulge of which suggested a large knife.

"I just want to look. There could be evidence in a murder case."

The man stopped squinting and frowned. "Sounds like BS, but okay, have a look."

He unlocked the gate and opened it. I stepped through. He locked it behind me.

"There's a dark blue Toyota at the far end of the fourth row." He pointed.

I walked toward it. The man followed me. Maybe to keep me from doing something devious. Maybe just to talk.

"People don't save for a rainy day," he said. "Somethin' happens, they get behind. Then surprise, the bank takes their ride. Or the cops, depending on. Me, I've got five hunnerd in the kitty. Well, almost five hunnerd. I could pay the fine. But no cop is gonna take my ride, 'cuz I figure if you got no cash for the meter, don't park. That's my motto for life. You gotta always have cash for the meter."

"Good motto," I said. "World would be a better place, we had more people thinking like you."

"Damn straight," he said.

The blue Toyota was unlocked, so I opened the door and leaned inside. There was a vague stink of old beer mixed with marijuana smoke. On the seat was a gray hoodie sweatshirt with dark stains around the edges of the hood and the cuffs. On the dash was a torn magazine with pictures of buxom, leather-clad women on motorcycles. Under the brake pedal was a single glove, dark enough to be almost invisible against the dirty carpet. The cup holder held an empty, dented Budweiser can. The steering wheel was thick with black grime. Hanging from the rear view mirror, looking out of place above the motorcycle mamas, was a string of purple rosary beads. Hanging from the rosary was a gold locket that held a picture of the Virgin Mary.

I opened the glove box and pulled out the vinyl car manual folder. Tucked in with the manual was the DMV registration. The car was in the name of Sean Warner, and the registration was two years overdue. I put it back and got out of the car.

"Any chance you have a key or a way to open the trunk?" I asked.

The man looked at me. He bent into the car and pulled the trunk release. The lid popped up. He grinned. One of his front teeth was missing.

I looked in the trunk. There was nothing revealing. I shut the lid.

"Can you do me a favor please and look up the paperwork on this car and tell me where it was towed from?"

The man thought about it. I could tell he was wondering if it was a trick question or if there was some aspect to the request that would bite him. He turned slowly and walked back to his office, which was a weather-beaten shack about ten feet square. I lifted the glove from under the brake pedal, stuffed it into my pocket, shut the car door, and followed the attendant.

The man pushed open the door of the office and, without even stepping over the door sill, reached in and lifted a clipboard off a hook on the wall.

He flipped through some sheets, stopped at one in the middle of the pile, frowned as he read.

"Snow dump," he said.

"Snow dump?" I repeated. "What's that mean?"

"Where the city dumps the snow from the main drag. You know, when the rotaries shoot the berm into dump trucks, the trucks haul it to the snow dump. Off Barbara Avenue. The Toyota was towed from there."

Then I remembered. "Does it say where at the snow dump that the Toyota was found?"

The man looked at the sheet, then shook his head.

"Thanks for your help."

"You think you can catch a murderer with what you seen?"

"Maybe," I said as I left.

Back in the Jeep, I took the glove from Sean Warner's Toyota out of my pocket and stuffed it under my seat. Spot would have already smelled it in the air and on me, so it wasn't an ideal scenting situation. But that didn't eliminate its potential usefulness.

My next stop was Darla Ali's triplex apartment. The address Mallory had given me was in a neighborhood by the "Y" intersection where Emerald Bay Road heads north out of South Lake Tahoe.

I parked nearby. Because it was the middle of the day, I figured that both Darla and her roommate Sanford might be out. I left Spot in the Jeep and walked over to the house.

It appeared that the main floor had been divided into two apartments. I went around the side to a flight of rickety outdoor stairs that climbed up the back of the house. I went up and knocked. The door opened. A large man in his late twenties stood there. He wore a muscle shirt and khakis. His black hair was greased straight back. He had a mustache and a Van Dyke beard, also black. The beard glistened with grease shine as well.

"Hi. My name's Owen McKenna. I'm looking for Sanford Burroughs."

"I'm Sanford."

"Commander Mallory of the SLTPD gave me your address. I'm an investigator looking into Darla Ali's disappearance. Mallory said she lived here."

"Yes. I'm so worried about her."

"Mind if we talk a bit?"

"Not at all." He glanced behind him at the apartment. It was a worried look that I'd seen many times.

"Don't worry," I said. "I don't care if you've got contraband lying around. I just want to ask a few questions about Darla."

"Okay, dude, I'm taking you at your word. C'mon in."

TEN

Sanford let me into a small apartment that was neat and clean but had the rich smell of pot in the air.

There was a small living/kitchen area. In the living section was a conversation area made up of four tall bar stools and an even taller, small, round table There was no bar in the place. If you wanted a back rest, you'd have to sit on the floor and lean against the wall. Sanford perched on one stool, his boot heel hooked over the cross bar. I took another.

"You have any idea about Darla's disappearance?" I asked.

"No. She went to work like normal. Four days ago. But she didn't come home. I couldn't sleep that night. I still haven't slept. The next morning, she still wasn't home. I was frantic. I called the restaurant, and they said she hadn't come in. I went to the police and told them she was missing. They had no clue as to where she went. I know something is terribly wrong. And now you're looking for her. Why? That's a bad sign, right?"

"I'm working on a case that probably doesn't connect to Darla. But it suggests that I look into any suspicious disappearances."

"Darla's dead, isn't she! That's why you're here, because you think she's dead. God, I can't stand to think of it!" Sanford hugged himself.

"Sanford, I'm only here because you filed a missing persons report."

"So I shouldn't jump to conclusions. That's what you're saying, right?"

"Right. Where does Darla work?"

"At the Elevation Seven Thousand Cafe on lower Kingsbury Grade. It's the new one."

I knew of the restaurant. It was across the highway and up a bit from my office. "Did you have any contact with her during the last day you saw her?"

"No. None at all. Except that morning. We talked over coffee and a banana, and then she went to work."

"What time did she leave?"

"She's been working the early shift. Normally, that means she leaves at five-forty to be on shift at six. But that day she left at five with me. She said she had to be there early. But when I called the cafe later, they said she didn't have to be there early. And anyway, she didn't show up."

"The Elevation Seven Thousand Cafe is quite new. Do you know where she worked before that?"

"Well, she was unemployed for awhile. And before that, she lived up on the North Shore and worked at the Cal Neva Hotel. She had to quit when they closed it for remodeling. So she moved down here because there are more jobs on the South Shore."

"Does Darla drive to work?"

He shook his head. "No, she doesn't have a car. It's at the top of her wish list, but she needs more money, first. She gets rides to work. Around town, too. Sometimes she takes the bus, although the schedule isn't real comprehensive. I give her rides, too, when I'm not at work." He pointed out the window. "I got a used Subaru Outback when I moved here. Best snow car there is. So Darla's happy to have me drive her." There was a silver Outback parked on the street next to a snow wall as tall as the car. On the roof of the car was a rack that held two pairs of skis.

"Where'd you move from?"

"Wow, you've got more questions about me than about Darla."

"Not really. In my business, I just automatically ask questions of whomever I'm around. The more complete a picture I can get of the world around Darla, the better I'll figure out where and how she fits in."

Sanford nodded, slowly, thinking. Maybe wondering if I had suspicions about him.

"I came from Vegas. That's where I learned to toss pizza dough. But the weather there is hell during the summer. Tahoe's perfect in the summer. I always wanted to try living here, so when I got passed over for a promotion, I thought that was my time to move."

"Where's work now?"

"I'm a prep cook for Pizza Pan International. They primarily do a lunch business. I do two half-shifts a day, making their pizza dough. You came here at the perfect time because I come home during the middle of the day and then go back to make more pizza crusts for the dinner crowd."

"Unusual schedule," I said.

"Yeah. Seven to eleven and three to seven. Most people would hate it, but it fits me perfectly. I can do errands during the middle of the day. Sometimes I ski a few runs, too."

"So you and Darla are both in food service."

"Yeah. That's how we met. The Chamber of Commerce put on a restaurant show a few months back to feature all the local eateries. The Pizza Pan booth was right next to the Elevation Seven Thousand booth. I was the pizza demo man, and she was the breakfast demo girl. We were both doing practically the same song and dance on either side of the convention booth drape. It was pretty funny. We had some good laughs, and we stayed in touch. She called me a few weeks later when her roommate moved out. I was looking for a better place, and I've been here ever since."

"Would she normally call you if she was going to be home late?"

"Yes, absolutely. We're best friends. She tells me everything. But she said nothing. She gave me no warning. She just never came home."

"What about her other friends?"

Sanford frowned. "Darla doesn't really have many friends. She mostly hangs with people from work."

"Do you mind if I look at her room?"

"No, of course not. You can look at anything. Just find her. Please." He pointed.

On both sides of the main room were bedrooms, each under a separate roof gable. I walked over and through a doorway and flipped on the light.

Darla's bedroom was about 10 by 12. The bed was made, and on the pillow sat a stuffed teddy bear propped up in a sitting position. On one wall was a dresser and a closet. On the dresser, leaning up against the wall, was a framed mirror that had broken. There were still some large cracked pieces of mirror in the frame.

"What happened to the mirror?" I called out to Sanford.

"It fell over in the earthquake." Sanford said from the other room. "Darla's still using it until she can get it replaced."

Draped over the top edge of the mirror was a rosary with a crucifix. It wasn't the same design as the one I'd found in Sean Warner's Toyota, but it struck me that I hadn't seen any rosary beads in years, and now I'd seen two in different places in the space of thirty minutes.

On the dresser were four pictures in stand-up picture frames. I recognized the images. One was a picture of Michelangelo's David, which looked magnificent even on a small card. The other three prints were of famous, old paintings. I picked up the frames and looked at the back. Darla - or somebody - had cut out the paintings' titles and painters' names and glued them to the back. One was Botticelli's Primavera. Another was Raphael's Madonna of the Goldfinch. The third painting was da Vinci's The Annunciation.

It seemed unusual to find such pictures in a young woman's apartment. I would have expected the typical 24-year-old woman in Tahoe to have pictures of her boyfriend or girlfriends or family, or a selfie of herself skiing or hanging out at the beach. Instead, this girl had four prints of artworks that were each created hundreds of years ago.

I stopped and took another look at the backs of the frames. The dates ranged from the 1400s to the 1500s. Maybe it meant nothing, but the artworks were all created by Italian artists during the Renaissance. I thought of Scarlet Milo and her Squaw Valley house with shelves of books about the Italian Renaissance. It was an unusual coincidence, as unlikely as the two rosaries. Although coincidences happen, as an investigator, my job was to assume there are no coincidences.

On the opposite wall was a window and below it a chair and small table that was being used as a desk. There was a spaghetti sauce jar full of pens and pencils and next to it a pad of lined paper with some kind of to-do list. Get new insoles. Return shoes to Amazon. Transfer $100 to checking account. Pay Sanford for the utility bills. Get shampoo, toothpaste, fresh veggies, whole grain pasta, almond milk, free range chicken, brown rice. Call Tammy for the fried rice/pineapple recipe.

Some of the items had been crossed off.

One item had been circled. It was an email address. TahoeBlueFire@gmail.com.

On the side of the desk was an old Apple laptop computer. I lifted the lid. The screen lit up. There was a box to enter a password.

"Hey, Sanford," I called out. "Do you know Darla's computer password?"

"No. She's quite private," he said.

"There's an email address written here. It says TahoeBlueFire at Gmail dot com. Is that her address?"

"No. Hers is something like Darla and then some numbers at Yahoo dot com."

"Does the Blue Fire address mean anything to you?"

"Sorry, no."

I shut the laptop.

I opened the closet. It was a small space that didn't hold many clothes. The only thing that stood out to me was that almost half of the clothes were purple.

I walked out of Darla's room. Sanford Burroughs was in the kitchen. He had a teakettle of water on the stovetop. It was popping and beginning to throw off tendrils of steam.

"Would you like some herbal tea? It's my own blend, very smooth," he said, his voice earnest.

"Sure."

He took the teakettle off the stove and poured it into a teapot. Then he lowered a tea strainer on a thin chain and shut the teapot lid. Behind him, lined up along the back of the kitchen counter were two long rows of empty beer bottles, every one a different brand of craft beer. On each bottle was a Post-it Note with penciled notes.

"It'll just be a few minutes on the tea," Sanford said. "Did you find anything?"

"Yeah. What was Darla's interest in Renaissance art?"

Sanford frowned. "Oh, you mean those little framed pictures on her dresser top. She got those a few weeks ago. I asked her what they were about, and she just said she found them in a shop in Carson City and liked them. Nothing more than that, I think. Why?"

"Has she spoken about the Renaissance?"

"No. I should've asked. I don't actually know what the Renaissance is. Something about art, right? But a fancier idea than just art. Artistic renewal?"

"Kind of," I said. "The Renaissance was a period of a couple of hundred years when there was an explosion of art production in Europe. Mostly Italy. Mostly the fourteen and fifteen hundreds." I knew it was a weak description that probably left out some of the most important aspects of the period.

I changed the subject. "Did Darla ever talk about leaving the area? Or traveling?"

Sanford shook his head. "You should know that Darla is just a down-home sweetheart. All she wants is to work her job, go skiing, say her prayers, and be good to her friends. She is a very good friend."

"Is there anything unusual about her? Anything you wouldn't expect?"

"No. Not at all. I mean, she has her dreams, of course. Everybody has their dreams, right?"

"What are Darla's?"

"Oh, the usual crazy stuff. Meet Mr. Perfect. Get rich. Live on an island in an exotic country."

"Does she ever act on those dreams?"

Sanford was shaking his head before I finished the question. "If you mean, does she look for Mr. Perfect on the internet or read books on living in another country, I don't think so. But she does have little flights of fancy about money."

"How do you know?"

"Oh, she'll do things like go online and look up treasure hunting. It's a kind of fantasy, I suppose."

"What kind of treasure?"

"Well, there's this author, Clive Cussler, who has some kind of operation where he looks for old sunken ships. I guess he's found a bunch of them. And some of them have had treasure. Like right out of the movies. So Darla, when she found out about that, she got kind of excited. She read up about it. Turns out that there have been hundreds of ships that have sunk over the centuries, and a lot of them have never been found. Some were known to have major money or gold or whatever on them. But the others, even without treasure, had some valuables. For example, I didn't know this, but Darla told me that all through history, most ships have had a safe on board so people could give their valuables to the captain and he'd lock them in the safe to protect them during the voyage. Well, Darla got to thinking about that. As she put it, that means that every sunken ship probably had serious valuables on it. So all you'd have to do is learn about ships that sank and then find them and go down and get the safe and bust it open, right? It wouldn't have to be ships that were carrying the king's gold. It could just be any ship."

"Sounds easy in principle," I said, "but the ocean is more than six miles deep in places. That would make finding a lot of sunken ships pretty tricky. And you'd only be able to search the ones that are close to the surface. Maybe a hundred feet or so. Much deeper than that, you would need specialized gear."

Sanford raised his eyebrows. "Yeah, I suppose you're right about that." He pulled two cups off of a little cup tree, poured tea, and handed one to me.

"Do you think that Darla suspected there might be a sunken ship in Tahoe?" I asked.

Sanford shook his head. "I doubt it. I mean, she never said anything to suggest it. Besides, Tahoe never really had any ships, right? I read about the Tahoe Steamer. That was pretty big. But they sank that one on purpose. So they must've taken any valuables off it first."

"Does Darla have any enemies?"

Sanford looked shocked. "No way. Everybody loves Darla."

"What about you? Are you and she close?"

"Yes! We're best buds."

"Have you been romantically involved?"

"Oh, no. I don't go for girls. But that makes it easier for us to be pals. Darla always tells me about her day."

"You said she likes to ski?"

"That was the main reason she moved to Tahoe. She's a great skier. I told her she should be a ski instructor."

I was thinking about the statistics that show the most common predator of a woman in peril - missing, abused, kidnapped, or murdered - is the woman's boyfriend or husband. "Did she ever mention the names of any guys she'd met?"

"No. She isn't a big dater."

"If I wanted to ask about her at the restaurant, who would I talk to?"

"I suppose her boss. He's the owner and also the main chef."

"Do you know his name?"

"Spooner. I remember because it's such an unusual name. Kind of cute, actually."

"Last name?"

Sanford shook his head. "She never mentioned it. Maybe he's one of those one-name types. It's called a mononym. Like Madonna or Sting or Prince. I wondered if I should get a mononym. Maybe then I could get some traction in the market."

"In the pizza business?"

"Oh, no. I have plans for a microbrewery some day. I could call it by my mononym. That would give it some buzz, don't you think?"

"Depends on the name, I suppose."

"I was thinking of Bold. Bold Brew. And I could just be known as Bold. When people are drinking my beer, they'd say things like, 'How 'bout a Bold?' It would be cool, right? And on the rear label, there could be a little origin story about Bold. Which would be me. What do you think? Origin stories are the latest marketing buzz. Everybody's got them."

"I don't know. I'm the last person to ask about marketing. Sanford, do you have a plastic trash bag I could have?"

"Sure." He opened a cupboard, pulled out a box that held a roll of white bags, and held it out.

"Perfect. May I also borrow Darla's pillowcase?"

Sanford frowned. "That's pretty kinky."

"I want it for her scent. To see if I can track her with a search dog."

"Oh, I get it. You mean like a bloodhound. And you would have the dog smell the pillowcase and then look for her."

"Yeah."

Sanford acted excited. "I've seen that on TV. God, I hope it works! But where would you go?"

"I might start from the cafe where she worked."

"Ah," he said.

I took the bag from him and turned it inside out so that my hand and arm were inside of it. I went into Darla's bedroom and gripped Darla's pillowcase through the plastic bag. I shook the pillow out of the pillowcase and then carefully rolled the bag back over the pillowcase so the pillowcase was inside the bag. Because I hadn't touched the pillowcase and had only touched what was now back on the outside of the bag, the pillowcase hadn't been contaminated by my scent.

The trash bag itself had a lemon scent. But I figured that would be less confusing to a dog than mixing human scents on the pillowcase.

"Do you have a picture of Darla?" I asked.

"On my phone, sure. A few. Let me look." He pulled his phone out of his pocket and scrolled through images. "Here's one that's good." He held out the phone for me to see.

"Yeah, that would help. Is there a way you can print it?"

Sanford thought about it. "I could email it to myself, open it on my computer, then print it."

"Great."

I waited while he did it, and he handed me the print in a few minutes.

Darla was a slender girl with short hair. There was something notable about her, but it wasn't her physical presence. It was something else I couldn't quite identify. Something about her attitude. Confidence? I didn't think so. Cockiness? No. Then I realized what it was. Ambition. The girl in the photo seemed imbued with a kind of hunger. I expected that she would go far.

"One more question," I said. "When Darla left for work on that last day you saw her, do you remember what she was wearing?"

"Of course. She had on her black velour pants, a lavender

blouse, and a purple dress jacket. She wore a necklace with an amethyst pendant and matching amethyst earrings. Her shoes were L.L.Bean hiking shoes, but of course in her bag were her white sneakers and apron that the restaurant has all the waitresses wear. She's a striking woman, Mr. McKenna. Straight men are always checking her out."

I thanked Sanford for the tea, gave him my card, and asked that he call if he thought of anything I should know.

ELEVEN

Back in the Jeep, Spot leaned forward from the back seat. He sniffed me all over and reached down to smell the lemon-scented trash bag.

I pushed it away. "Not now, Largeness. Just wait a few minutes and once again we'll see what your sniffer can do."

I kept watch for any black pickups as I drove over to the snow dump. I pulled over, parked and got out. It was a large open area in the sparse forest. After an entire season of snow removal, the area was covered in countless humps 8 or 10, or even 12 feet deep.

The city's snow removal crew fills the area with snow in a three-step process. First, the graders go down the wide, five-lane thoroughfare that runs the length of South Lake Tahoe. The graders make continuous passes during a storm, gradually pushing the snow into a huge berm that is 5 feet tall and 10 feet wide and takes up all of the center lane, which is normally reserved for turning vehicles. Next, a rotary blower goes along chewing up the snow and blowing it into a continuous line of slow-moving dump trucks that have matched their speed to the rotary. When each truck is full, it drives off and the next truck takes its place. The full dump trucks come to the snow dump lot and dump their load, gradually filling the forest with a monstrous, lumpy blanket of compressed snow.

Spot and I walked around part of the perimeter. Spot ran up onto the piles, then back off. It was a game. Up, then down. Up, then down. I envied his ability to find great joy in simply running around.

On the side of the snow dump was an unusual path cut into the piles of snow. It was like a narrow alley, cut by a rotary blower. The path had walls that were quite high, maybe 10 feet or more, and the cut went back about 30 yards into the field of piled snow and then stopped at an abrupt dead end. It was as if a blower driver had tried to chew a path through the snow dump and then gave up part way through.

"I need you to perform a miracle, boy," I said to Spot as I held Sean Warner's glove.

Spot ran around through the fresh snow, making circles around me. It was his favorite taunt. He knew I wanted him to do something, so he stayed close but kept up a high speed, thinking he'd frustrate me, which was true.

I waited while he burned off some energy. Then he slowed, picked up a pine cone that had recently fallen, and ran toward me. He did a quick stop ten feet from me and tossed the pine cone onto the icy pavement. It rolled to a point midway between us. It was a game he'd invented a year ago. Dare the slow human to try to grab the cone.

"Sorry, Spot," I said. I held up the glove and walked past him. He stayed behind, cranking his head around to watch me go, then turning back to study the pine cone. The sun caught his faux diamond ear stud and sparkled hot rays like those from a disco ball in a nightclub.

Eventually, Spot left the cone where it lay and climbed up onto the piles of snow to explore, no doubt appreciating that, unlike slogging through deep powder or walking gingerly on frozen crust and periodically breaking through, he could run on the compressed snow. The piled humps made it exciting, and he ran S-turns through them like a kid banking off the ramps and pipes of a skateboard park.

"Spot, c'mon," I tried again. "Let's get back to miracles." I pulled a dog biscuit out of the zippered cargo pocket where I keep them and held it up.

He ran over.

"You help me, you get a treat," I said. "That simple."

He stared at my hand. I put the treat back in my pocket. He stared at my pocket.

"Spot, I need you to find a scent. Do you smell this?" I pushed the glove up against his nose. "Do you have the scent?" I tried to put excitement in my voice. With one hand holding the glove, I took my other hand and put it on his back, giving him a vibrating shake to help engage his attention.

"Okay, boy. Find the scent!" I gave him a pat on his rear.

He ran off, circled around, and homed in on the pine cone. He scooped it up on the run and charged toward me. Spot skidded to a stop just in front of me and dropped the cone at my feet. He looked again at my pocket where I'd put the dog biscuit.

"No, Spot, I need your help. Please."

I went through the glove-scenting routine again, giving him the command and another light smack on his rear.

He took off again, this time at a lope instead of a run. He held his head high, which gave me hope that maybe he was paying some attention to whatever scents were in the air. On his second circular loop, he veered away from me and climbed up onto the snow piles. Like before, he weaved in and around the humps but at a much slower speed. I wondered if that would make any difference, pro or con. Spot slowed further, then stopped.

He turned around and retraced his steps for a bit, stopped again.

He pawed at the frozen, compressed snow, stuck his nose on the snow, sniffed, pawed again. Then he used both paws and did a little serious digging, right, left, right, left, shooting snow out between his rear legs. He went down about a foot, then stuck his snout into the little hole, grabbed something and pulled. The object he had was frozen in place. Spot pulled harder. I could see his shoulder muscles flexing. Then it came free.

Spot turned and trotted toward me. He was in no big hurry. But I knew he was thinking about the dog treat I had in my pocket. I got it out. When he got to me, he dropped a piece of fabric on the snow. I lavished him with praise and pets and gave him the treat. He chomped it once, and it disappeared. He looked back at my pocket.

I went back to the Jeep and got my large-sized bags out of the glove box. I opened one, reversed it, and picked up the fabric, sealing it inside. The fabric was shredded and frozen stiff. But it looked like it had been torn from a pair of blue jeans, and, according to Spot, its scent matched Sean's.

I felt discomfort in my gut. A man who parks his car and walks away for whatever reason doesn't tear off a portion of his clothes and bury it in the snow.

I praised Spot again and sent him on another search. This time, fueled by the actual taste of a doggie treat, he possibly felt more expansive. He went back up onto the piled snow but took a much wider arc and then zigzagged over a large area.

Once again, he found a promising place, did some more digging, and pulled a larger piece of fabric out of the compressed snow. He trotted back to me and dropped it at my feet. This time he had less enthusiasm.

I praised him and gave him another treat and reached down with dread to pick up a larger chunk of denim. It was folded over and bent and frozen stiff. I got it into another bag. Manipulating the fabric through the plastic, I untwisted it. I could feel something long and stiff inside, as if the fabric had been used to wrap a knife blade. But when I unwound the fabric, what felt like a knife was a gray, pointed object. On one side, it was stained a light brown. I realized I was holding a broken piece of bone.

TWELVE

I didn't want to believe what it meant, but the meaning was obvious. And while Spot got depressed when he found dead bodies, this was such a small portion that he didn't realize what he'd found. Not yet, anyway.

I called Mallory.

"I'm going to have to put you on the spam caller list," he said.

"Sorry for bothering you, but you'll want to see what my dog just found at the snow dump."

We talked for a half minute, and Mallory said he'd be over in a few minutes.

I hung up and waited for Mallory, my thoughts preoccupied with the enormity of what appeared to have happened.

A few minutes later, Mallory drove up in an unmarked, parking near my Jeep. He got out and came over. He held a can of Coke.

I reached out with the pieces of fabric and bone. With practiced precision, Mallory put the Coke between his forearm and his side so that he could use both hands. He held the bagged items and turned them over with both hands.

"Christ, McKenna, are you thinking what I'm thinking?"

"I hate it, but yeah."

"Could a rotary even do that? Chew through bone and such?"

"I don't know. Probably. The drivers couldn't make any progress if the shear pins broke every time a small branch got into the mix. Branches come down in storms. It wouldn't take much of a branch to be stronger than bones."

"But rotaries aren't like wood chippers, with sharp little blades," he said. "They're snowblowers. Sure, they're big as hell, but they're still snowblowers."

"I've read that simple little driveway snowblowers are responsible for more amputations than anything else," I said. "Extrapolate out to what a machine with one or two thousand horsepower can do, and it seems believable."

"Can your dog do another search?"

"He gets depressed when he finds dead bodies, but I don't think he's put this together, yet. We'll give it a try."

I went through the routine and sent Spot toward the piled snow. He climbed up on top and wandered without energy. What once was eagerness was now drudgery. Eventually, he went close to the deep cut the rotary had made in the center of the lot. Spot found a place that got his attention. He dug at the snow, sniffed some more, dug again. He made one more swipe with one paw then walked away and turned to look at the place from a distance. His ears were back and down. I recognized the meaning, the vivid mood change. He was somber. It made me feel guilty to have sent him on such a depressing mission.

"We'll need something to dig with," I said. I opened the back of the Jeep and pulled out my tire iron.

Mallory and I clambered up onto the snow piles and walked over toward Spot, slipping on the snow mounds.

Spot was standing listless, looking away from his find, hanging his head.

"Sorry, Largeness. I didn't see this coming." I rubbed his neck, but his ears were down and his eyes drooped.

Mallory took the tire iron from me and walked over to the place where Spot had pawed the snow. He stuck the iron in the snow and pried it back and forth. "Damn," he said as he looked down at the snow. He got on his phone and gave a long list of orders. I pet Spot some more, then left him to see what had Mallory so upset.

In a shallow depression in the snow was the major portion of a large hand, its three remaining fingers frozen into curved hooks, a gesture of high tension. I'd never considered that a partial hand, all by itself, could communicate terror. But as I looked at it, I felt chilled. My upper back and neck prickled with fear.

THIRTEEN

Whatever Mallory said into his phone created a big reaction. Within minutes, four black-and-whites appeared, sirens off but light bars flashing blue and red strobes. Two unmarked cars followed. I recognized one of the men who got out as the Chief. Mallory spoke to all of the cops. One of the sergeants gave some orders, and cops spread out over the snow piles. Two walked into the snow canal that had been cut by a rotary.

A road grader came up Sierra Blvd., making a loud roar and throwing out black diesel smoke. It pulled to a stop when the driver saw Mallory beckoning him. The driver got out and walked over to Mallory. They spoke. Mallory took him over to the snow canal in the center of the snow dump. They spoke and pointed and gestured. The grader driver shook his head and turned his palms toward the sky as if to say, 'I don't have any idea.'

I stayed back with Spot, petting him, reassuring him.

When confronted with a problem, dogs don't have our kind of linear thinking ability. They aren't as smart as chimps or gorillas or dolphins or elephants when it comes to problem solving. But they get a clear sense of the big picture. And their emotional intelligence with regard to what people want is far beyond that of any other animal. Dogs are the only animals that study a human's face. Dogs can tell what a human wants by the smallest of looks or actions. The most casual glance or concern on a person's face causes a dog to respond. If a dog sees the human look toward their leash or a treat, the dog jumps up in excitement. But if a dog sees grief or fear or sadness, the dog comes to nuzzle and give comfort or, if necessary, turn toward the door or window and growl. Dogs want nothing so much as to please people.

I'd given Spot the task of looking for a particular human scent. Which led him to a bone with the same scent. Bones and scents are both familiar experiences for dogs. But soon the discomfort set in as Spot realized that bones aren't supposed to have human scents. Add in the master's reaction - a quiet but obvious change in my manner and, no doubt, a huge, negative change in my own scent, the odors of horror and disgust - Spot realized that another human had died. Worse, he understood at some level that it was his discovery that brought the realization to his owner. He'd made the worst of discoveries, and it made him seriously depressed.

Over the next two hours, other city cops showed up as well as three CHP officers and a couple of El Dorado County deputies. One of the local cops had a K-9 unit, and, using Sean's glove for a scent source, the cop put his German Shepherd through multiple searches. The dog was a trained professional, much more focused than Spot, and he alerted over and over at multiple places. The dog and the officers dug out dozens of bits and pieces of body and clothing. Some were found in the snow piles, while others were found far out into the forest.

Mallory came over to me. He pet Spot as he spoke. In his other hand he held another Coke.

"Here's what we're thinking. You tell me if this seems wrong. The path cut down the center of the snow dump didn't go all the way through, as you noted. It looks like the killer cut it in advance as a trap. Somehow, he enticed the guy to walk into the cut in the snow. What he used for bait, I have no idea. Once the vic was in there, he came in with a rotary plow, the auger and impeller on high speed. The snow walls were too high for the vic to climb out, and he was trapped.

"Looking at the pattern of dispersal of human remains, it looks like he aimed the discharge chute a short distance directly in front of him. After he'd first chewed through the body, he continued forward and plowed through the remains again, re-processing the pieces so to speak, breaking them up into much smaller chunks. And on the second pass, it appears that the driver directed the discharge chute far out into the forest, oscillating it left and right as he drove. If you and your hound hadn't found this, it's entirely likely that when the snow melted over the course of the summer, nothing would have been noticed. The odd piece of fabric a hundred yards over there would have blown away. The odd pieces of bone or flesh a hundred yards the other way would have rotted and dried and been inconsequential. As for bigger pieces like the hand, coyotes would have carried them off. I'm guessing that when the killer was done with his evil deed, he probably blew a lot of fresh snow through the rotary, cleaning the equipment so to speak. Once the rotary was back at the yard, the rotary might not have shown any sign of what it had been used for. It would have been the perfect crime but for your hound dog."

Mallory rubbed Spot vigorously behind his ears. Spot seemed not to care. "Does that fit with your sense?" Mallory looked at me. I couldn't tell if he really wanted my opinion or if he was just trying to make me feel like a part of the process.

"Yeah, that seems a likely scenario," I said.

Mallory stared at Spot. Spot hung his head. Mallory's forehead was creased with deep wrinkles.

"My canine struggles with human death," I said. "This is a particularly brutal experience."

Mallory pointed over to the professional K-9. "The German Shepherd looks pretty bummed, too."

I turned to follow his point. The police dog was sitting in the snow next to its handler. The dog's tongue was out, panting. When you know the German Shepherd breed, you learn to see the difference between a vigorous pant to cool off and the stressed pant of anxiety. This was anxiety. The dog's ears were back. It hung its head. And its gaze went left and right as if searching for some sense of comfort.

"C'mon, Spot, let's go see if we can put on some cheer." I slipped my fingers under his collar and pulled him with me. When we got to the officer and his dog, I introduced Spot and myself. The man was in his late twenties, and he looked a bit gray with shock.

"I'm Christopher Benning, and this is Davis," he said, looking at his dog.

We shook hands.

"It's been a tough afternoon for Davis, huh, boy?" Christopher bent down and pet his dog. "Tough for your dog, too, I guess.

He's the one who found the first pieces, right? Sorry if that's the wrong word to use. I'm still pretty new at this stuff."

"No problem," I said.

"Someone said you were a cop in San Francisco."

I nodded. "After twenty years, I decided to come up here and try the private version."

"I started out as a rookie in Vacaville," Christopher said, "and then I heard about an opening on the SLTPD, so I transferred up to the lake. All I wanted was to ride. Snowboard in the winter, mountain bike in the summer. I love dogs, so I applied for K-nine training." Christopher looked down at his dog. "Davis is a natural. Smarter than I was in the third grade. He and I worked on his training for two years. He aced all the tests, and we were chosen to be a K-nine unit." Christopher looked around at the snow dump. He reached up and rubbed the back of his neck. "I knew being a cop would be tough at times. But I never imagined this."

I reached out and squeezed his shoulder.

"You focus on Davis, you'll get through these things fine."

"I guess. But this is nasty stuff. As long as you're here, would you mind holding Davis's leash for a minute. I need to check in with the sergeant."

I nodded and took the leash, and Christopher walked off.

Davis stood up, a bit startled at being left alone with me and Spot. I took the opportunity to introduce the dogs to each other.

Usually, dogs meeting each other is a happy affair, sniffing and appraising and taking in the doggie body language that helps them sort out their social structure. But as Spot came close to the German Shepherd, they regarded each other without much interest.

The shepherd was nervous, not because Spot was twice his size but because a man had died, and the shepherd had been tasked with finding many of the pieces.

When Christopher came back, Davis pulled toward him. He didn't wag, but he was obviously eager to go somewhere else.

A thought came to me. "Hey Christopher," I said. "I would like to do one more search on another item. My dog is clearly not the same caliber as yours. Would you mind sending Davis out again?"

"I suppose. He won't like it, but I guess that's part of his job. What kind of a search?"

"I've got another item, a pillowcase, from another missing person. I don't imagine that there will be anything to find, but what if?"

"I'll wait," Christopher said.

I went back to the Jeep and brought out the pillowcase in the plastic bag.

Christopher went through the routine with Davis, making certain the dog had a few good whiffs with the pillowcase over its nose. When Christopher gave the search command, Davis trotted off. There was no enthusiasm in the dog's movement, but his focus was obvious.

The dog went over to the edge of the snow dump. I saw no sign of scent recognition, but Davis was smart enough to go to the area that yielded the results on the first missing person. Davis went down the edge of the field of piled snow, then turned around and came back. Sometimes he held his nose near the ground. And sometimes he held his head high, air scenting. When he got to the corner of the snow piles, he turned and trotted down the side where the dead-end canal had been cut in the snow. The dog went past the opening of the snow canal without slowing. He retraced his steps and still found nothing.

Davis went another thirty yards into a new area. He stopped with a jerk so sudden, it was as if someone had an invisible leash on him and yanked it tight.

Davis lifted his nose into the air, turned a circle, then ran up onto the snow piles. He trotted along, up and down over the humps, then made another abrupt stop. He put his nose to the snow, then started digging.

Christopher started jogging toward Davis.

Davis went down a half foot, then lowered his nose into the hole and pulled out yet another piece of fabric. He turned and trotted off the snow dump, across the plowed area and out toward Christopher, who used an evidence bag to take the fabric. Christopher pet Davis vigorously. The two of them walked back to me.

Mallory was approaching from the side and got to me just as Christopher and Davis came near.

"Your dog doesn't have to keep searching," Mallory said to his officer. "We have enough evidence for now."

"Mr. McKenna asked me to do one more search using a different item."

"What item is that?"

I held up the pillowcase. "This is Darla Ali's pillowcase."

"The missing girl," Mallory said. He turned to Christopher. "Your dog found something?"

Christopher held up the bag. Inside was a large piece of fabric.

"That's purple," Mallory said. "Nothing like the denim or the other fabric pieces."

"Sanford Burroughs let me into Darla's room," I said. "I looked in her closet. About half of her clothes were purple. And Sanford said that she was wearing a purple jacket the last day he saw her."

"Christ," Mallory said. He crushed his empty Coke can into a wad so small, it was as if it were made of tissue. "The missing girl was butchered here, too? This isn't just a sick murder, this is a disaster."

FOURTEEN

Christopher sent Davis on several additional searches. The dog brought back multiple pieces of evidence that made it clear that Darla Ali had met the same fate as Sean Warner. The cops all stayed focused on the job even as a dark mood settled over everyone.

"You know how 'live finds' cheer up depressed dogs?" I said to Christopher after Mallory left.

He frowned. "One of the search-and-rescue trainers mentioned that, but it seemed a bit touchy-feely. We did lots of mock searches in training. But we all thought it was just about teaching dogs to perform search and rescue. Are you saying that it really helps their mood?" He looked down at his dog whose head was low.

"Yeah. Finding human bodies is the worst for dogs. Why don't you go hide and I'll send the dogs after your scent? When they find you, they'll be very glad to have found you alive and not dead. It'll make them feel better."

Christopher said, "Okay. Where do you think I should go?"

"Don't look around as I talk to you, or it will give it away to the dogs. What do you have that I can scent them on?"

"My cap or my jacket. We learned in search-dog training that caps and pillowcases are best. Anything that comes in contact with the head."

"Cap it is. There's a panel truck off to your left, down about a half a block. It's parked in front of a big snowbank. There's a slight breeze coming from that direction, so the truck is mostly upwind of where we are now. That would be a good place to hide. But let's not clue the dogs in advance that we're arranging something unusual. So be very casual and take off your cap." He did as I said. "Both dogs are watching you. Make a show of looking over toward Mallory on your right as you hand me your cap with your left hand."

Christopher did as I suggested. The dogs watched him turn and look toward Mallory. Christopher held out the cap with his left hand. Moving slowly, I took the cap and stuffed it into my pocket.

Scanning in the opposite direction from the panel truck, I looked toward the forest. "I'll take the dogs for a little walk into the forest behind those trees on the other side of the snow dump so they can't see you. That will put them a bit out of line from your scent trail. We don't want their search to be too easy. I'm guessing that your dog will be tempted to follow your walking path, bloodhound style. But he'll also be crossing your drifting scent plume. So he may abandon your trail and try to go directly to you once he's got your scent."

"Got it," Christopher said. "No doubt you saw how I send Davis on a search?"

"Yeah. Same approach I use with my dog. I'll walk away with the dogs. You go down that side street. Your dog will turn around to see where you're going. But after we're in the forest, you walk around the block, then get behind the snowbank on the other side of the truck. I'll count to one hundred. Then I'll scent the dogs on your cap and send them on a search."

"Got it," he said.

We both left on our missions. Davis came willingly on his leash, but he kept turning his head to watch Christopher recede down the block. He whined a bit, but I knew it would be worth it in the end. Spot was on my other side. Because of Spot's height, I don't need a leash. I just hold his collar.

I counted slowly as I walked. When we got to the forest and I knew the dogs couldn't see Christopher, I stopped. At the count of 100, I started talking, making my voice excited.

"Okay, boys! Do you want to do a search? Sure you do! Davis, are you ready? Spot, are you ready to search?" I put my hands on their chests and vibrated them. "Okay, time to smell Christopher's cap!" I put the cap on each of their noses. "Do you have the scent? Do you?" I unclipped Davis's leash and let go of Spot's collar. Then I dropped my hand in a pointing motion as I said, "Find the victim!"

I gave Spot a smack on his rear, his signal to search. But Davis was already sprinting away. He made little squeals as he ran back toward the place where we'd last stood with Christopher.

Spot ran fast, but a Dane is no match for a German Shepherd in acceleration. Danes can get up to high speed, but it takes time. Shepherds begin a run as if they were shot out of a bow.

As Davis came near to the place where we left Christopher, he did little leaps as he ran. He held his nose high, air-scenting. Spot was behind him. I couldn't tell if Spot was following a scent or if he instinctively knew that it made more sense to follow the trained professional dog.

Davis jerked to a stop, turned 90 degrees, nose high in the air, and turned again. Then shot off in a new direction, directly toward the panel truck down the block.

Spot followed.

My last glimpse of them was as they leaped over the snowbank.

I trotted after them and found Christopher romping with both of them. The dogs were both jumping with excitement.

"Wow, it really works!" Christopher said. "Look at them! Good boys!" He tried to pet them, but they were jumping around too much.

"Now we should both take our dogs home without letting them go back to the snow dump and those smells. They will leave this area with happy memories."

Christopher beamed at me. "Thank you so much. I never would have believed this if I hadn't seen it."

"Happy to help," I said.

FIFTEEN

I drove home thinking about the warning note that had been stuck in my door. I took Spot for a short walk on the trail that went north along the side of the mountain behind my cabin. Although the snow level on the mountain where my cabin sits had risen to about 6600 feet in the warm spring sun, the trail near my cabin begins at 7000 feet and quickly climbs up to 8000 feet. It was still heavy with snow. I didn't put on my snowshoes because I'd continuously tramped down the snow on the trail over the course of the winter. It supported my weight without my hiking shoes breaking through.

Ten minutes after we'd started, the sun, already low in the western sky, went behind a cloud. The sky immediately turned a cool blue gray.

Several times, Spot stopped and listened and sniffed the air. For what, I didn't know. He turned his head and looked up the mountain, but mostly it seemed that he was sampling the wind. I'd seen him do it many times before and in many different places. It always made me envious, and I marveled at the world of inputs available to dogs. I felt blind by comparison.

I followed Spot's looks toward the mountain above us, but all I saw was the undulating snow-covered slope, surprisingly dark under the heavy tree canopy. It was a condition that would provide perfect cover to any mountain lion or other predator that wanted to sneak up on their prey.

After we were back in the cabin, there was a double rap at the door. Spot was on his bed. He lifted his head but didn't bark. He wagged. Which meant friend.

I opened the door.

Diamond Martinez entered. Instead of his crisp, ironed, sheriff's uniform with the badge and patches, he was wearing a red flannel shirt, faded blue jeans, and cowboy boots. I'd never seen him in cowboy boots.

I pulled beers out of the fridge, opened them, and handed him one.

Diamond took it.

Spot was watching Diamond from his bed, and he thumped his tail on the floor. Diamond walked over and pet him.

Spot stopped the tail thumping and breathed big, deep breaths, which indicated that he was finally getting the affection he thought he deserved.

Diamond gave Spot a final aggressive rub, then stood up, walked over to the slider and pulled it open. I followed him out onto the deck. Spot jumped up and joined us. The sun was just moving behind another cloud. The lake immediately turned slate-gray.

I handed Diamond the warning note.

"The cross hairs make sense," he said. "Stop working the case or you'll be shot. But I don't get the star."

Diamond leaned back against the deck railing. He took another sip of beer, set the bottle on the railing, crossed one boot over another, and stuck his fingertips into his pockets.

"You're projecting an impressive Pancho Villa vibe," I said. "Cowboy boots and a casual south-of-the-border masculinity. You ever see Maria anymore? I bet she responds to that, huh?"

Diamond shook his head. "She's too focused on her improvements," he said.

"Improvements to what?"

"Me."

"Ah," I said. "Hard to tolerate the softening influence of a woman with a big personality. Be like lotion ruining your rough hands."

Diamond looked at me with cold, unflinching eyes.

"Like listening to opera," I said. I sensed Diamond trying to hold his tough look. "Going to art museums. Reading a novel that contains no horses or guns. Watching the ballet on PBS, right?"

Diamond said, "I've always noticed that tall, pale-faced gringos with beautiful girlfriends tend to indulge in an excess of judgment."

"Street would disagree in part. She thinks she's too thin and that her acne scars seriously mar the picture."

Diamond made a single head shake. "Common, negative self-delusion, something which many suffer and to which you seem immune. But lose the norte skin and ten inches of height, you might find yourself hanging onto what little defines you as a man. Mexican machismo is a gift of identity."

I tried to keep a straight face, but I couldn't help grinning. "You take a risk, don't you think, hitching your concept of masculinity to Mexican machismo?"

Diamond swigged beer. "As the novelist Carlos Fuentes said, 'I live through risk. Without risk there is no art. You should always be on the edge of a cliff about to fall down and break your neck.'"

"Like Pancho Villa," I said. "He tried to Robin-Hood Mexico away from the rich and give it to the poor and got assassinated for his efforts. Talk about risk."

Diamond turned his head and looked down at the lake. He gave no hint of his mood.

"Making any progress?" he asked.

"I found your missing person, Sean Warner. He was killed."

"I heard something of it on my radio. Where was it?"

I explained about finding his car at the South Lake Tahoe impound lot, using his glove for scent, and sending Spot on a search over at the snow dump where Warner's car had been found.

"You really believe that someone chewed him up with a highway snowblower."

"Looks like it. And they didn't stop at Sean." I explained about Darla Ali.

"Gives me a bad feeling," Diamond said. "That M.O. is a long way from Scarlett Milo's shooting."

I nodded. "The deaths could be unrelated. But Darla and Scarlett both had interest in the Italian Renaissance. Or at least art from the Renaissance. What're the odds of walking into a Tahoe abode and finding art from the Italian Renaissance?"

Diamond shrugged. "Not much. Now that you mention the Renaissance, the drawing on the warning note you got is kind of like the Vitruvian man."

"What's that?"

"You've seen it. Da Vinci's famous man in the circle. The one that's all about the proportions of the human body."

"Ah, right. So if that's what the note references, then it's another Renaissance connection."

Diamond nodded. "An inscrutable connection, but yeah."

"I found nothing to suggest that Sean Warner had any interest in the Renaissance, but he did have purple rosary beads in his car, and they are similar to rosary beads I found in Darla Ali's apartment. So we've got Darla and Sean with similar rosary beads and their bodies found in the same place. Then we've possibly got Darla and Scarlett connected by a common interest in the Renaissance. That possibly gives us a connection between three murders, but two M.O.s for the murders, shooting and death by snowblower. That's pretty weak, don't you think?"

"Tenuous linkage doesn't mean no linkage," Diamond said.

"You mentioned that the fire in Zephyr Heights was arson."

"Yup," Diamond said.

"When Scarlett called me on the phone, she referred to her potential murderer as picking her off or burning down her house."

Diamond's jaw muscles bulged. "So the question is, did she use the phrase as a figure of speech, or did she actually think someone might burn her house?"

"I don't know."

"We better take a closer look at last night's fire."

I said, "Have you learned anything more about it?"

"Not much. We have two victims who would have died but for some luck. You know the current Douglas County Fire Marshal, right?"

"Terry Drier," I said.

"Right. This morning, he figured out that someone threw a jar of petrol onto the front porch and tossed a match."

"A Molotov cocktail," I said.

"Not quite. Drier found a burnt wooden matchstick along with shards of broken glass on a part of the front porch that hadn't completely burned. It looks like the gas was tossed first.

Then it was lit. A Molotov cocktail has a fuse that you light before you throw it."

"I wonder why the arsonist didn't use the lit-fuse approach?"

"I asked Drier that question. He said that it was probably because Molotov cocktails often blow up when they're lit. They have a nasty habit of killing the person who uses them. I guess the right way to build a gas bomb you can lob is to use a fuse that's soaked in kerosene, which is less volatile than gas. But that's a hassle. Easier to just toss the gas, then light a match."

"Houses burn fast when you put gas on them," I said. "Whose house was it that burned?"

"Guy we all know. Although you maybe haven't met him. I get the sense he's somewhat reclusive."

"Who's that?"

"Adam Simms."

"You don't mean the famous nose tackle. Nine years on, what, three different teams?"

"All three hundred fifty-five pounds of him," Diamond said. "Football legends living among us. Practically in secret."

I thought back 25 years to Simms's glory days. "I remember the famous four quarterbacks who seemed to bring out his greatest power."

"Joe Montana, Dan Marino, Brett Favre, and John Elway," Diamond said. "Each was hit by Simms so hard that the press called them the Sacked-by-Simms Club."

"What happened to Simms's house?"

"Mostly gone."

"Simms got out of the house okay?"

Diamond nodded. "His sister, too. Felicite. Spelled with an E on the end. She's actually the owner of the house. She's had the place as a vacation home for years, and Simms has lived there for the last year or two. She lives in San Francisco, but she came to visit a few days ago. Their bedrooms were upstairs. The fire went into the front porch overhang and gutted the upstairs first. Odds are Simms and his sister would have died if he hadn't been up. But it turned out that he couldn't sleep, so he and his dog were downstairs in the kitchen when the fire started. They heard something hit the porch. The dog barked. Adam went to the front of the house and saw the flames. He yelled to his sister, then ran outside and turned on the hose. But the shut-off valve was off because it's winter. He went back in to check that his sister was awake. She was downstairs dialing nine-one-one. Then they ran outside and waited."

"The sister is normally in San Francisco?" I asked.

Diamond drank beer. "I understand that she isn't his sister by birth. They just refer to each other as brother and sister. Apparently, they were foster kids in a group home in New Orleans, and they've kept in touch over the years. They make a real odd-couple pair. She's a tiny little thing, probably weighs a fourth of what Simms weighs."

"You said her name is Felicite?" I asked.

"Felicite Genoveva. I couldn't understand what she said at first, so I asked. She said it's Creole, that her ancestors were free people of color who came to New Orleans from Saint-Domingue in the early eighteen hundreds."

"Where's Saint-Domingue?"

"What is now Haiti in the Caribbean. Around the time of the American Revolution, Saint-Domingue was a small French colony that produced half of all the sugar and coffee sold in Europe. All grown on slave plantations."

"And you know this because…"

Diamond shrugged. "Something I read somewhere."

"Sounds like Felicite's proud of her heritage, what with telling you that, but she grew up in a group home," I said.

"We hang onto whatever gives us a sense of self."

"Like machismo," I said, grinning.

Diamond made a single solemn nod.

"Does Adam have the same background?"

"No idea."

"They have any idea of why someone would torch their place?"

Diamond shook his head. "Logical answer would be someone who is targeting his celebrity. One of those deranged individuals who stalk and assault famous people simply because they're famous. But Simms might be targeted for more reasons than just rubbing up against his fame," Diamond said. "He infuriated a million sports fans over the years by hurting their heroes. Probably, some angry, sick fans might want to take him down as punishment."

"What about his sister?" I asked. "Could she be the target?"

"I floated that idea, and Adam scoffed. He said the usual things. That Felicite is sweet and kind, and everyone loves her. And Felicite admitted that she's basically invisible and unknown by anyone. She works at a tech company, but it's a low profile job. Only a few people in her company deal with her. Adam believes that he must be the target, and if Felicite is hurt, she's collateral damage. So he wants her to go back to San Francisco right away. She'll probably head back to The City as soon as she's done talking to us and the insurance company. If you want to talk to her, you should do it soon."

"Where are they staying tonight?"

"Their neighbor Ronald Baumgarter took them in. He's clearly awestruck by Simms. He's got a big house with lots of bedrooms, so it's logical that he offers space just because Simms and Genoveva are neighbors."

I said, "When you said that someone could be after Simms for payback because he specialized in sacking the most beloved quarterbacks in history, did Felicite have any comment?"

"Yeah. She said that Adam has been out of the league for two and a half decades and that he hasn't done any of the things that keep footballers in the limelight. He hasn't been a commentator, hasn't done anything controversial, hasn't bought into a team or joined any team's management. A lot of people have forgotten about him. Especially people under the age of, say, thirty, who were only five years old or younger when Simms ended his career. So the arson is very puzzling to her. She wondered if it was just a random event. Aside from the idea that someone tried to burn them up, I could tell that she was very upset about losing her house. She's trying to keep it in perspective. You don't want to focus on the loss of property when it may be that some demented fan is bent on killing your celebrity step-brother."

I asked, "Did either of them say anything that would indicate a possible connection to Scarlett Milo, Darla Ali, or Sean Warner?"

"No."

Diamond and I were quiet a moment.

"Is Adam employed?" I asked.

"No."

"Did he invest well?"

Diamond pinched his lips, making a sad face. "I didn't ask about it specifically. But from what I gather, he did like lots of sports stars. He lived the high life while the big money was coming in, and he didn't put much away. When the paychecks stopped, his life style burned through what little savings he had, and he's been struggling for the last decade or so. I got the feeling that without Felicite's generosity, he would be homeless. Felicite made it sound as if he had to move out of his East Bay place. So she let him stay at her Tahoe house."

"You get any sense that he's got enemies?"

"My only sense was that he seems as agreeable as a teddy bear and about as easy to get along with."

"Without a job, any idea what he does with his time?"

"He said he writes poetry."

"A noble calling," I said, "but hard to pay the bills."

Diamond nodded. "Even the most famous poets - the ones who win the Nobel Prize - most of them still have to teach to earn a living."

"It's a sweet, romantic thing for a fearsome tackle to write poetry," I said.

"Yeah, he's a smart guy," Diamond said. "But there is something off in him. He sort of goes blank now and then. Then he'll say the same thing twice as if he didn't remember that he'd already said it."

"I do that myself," I said.

The sun shifted and stabbed through the clouds. The twilight glow behind the West Shore peaks of Alpine Meadows went from a soft pink to a sudden brilliant orange.

Diamond leaned on the deck railing and held up his beer. "Here's to the world's greatest view."

I tipped up my beer to drink the last swallow and then raised it farther to get the last drops of the precious brew when the neck of the beer bottle exploded.

SIXTEEN

Chunks of glass blew into my eyes and face and down into my mouth. A loud crack snapped in the air a moment later. I wasn't sure, but it sounded like the sound came from up on the mountain above my cabin. I was too stunned with the blast of glass shards to react.

Diamond moved first. Before I even realized that I was unable to see well, he grabbed me and jerked me back from the deck railing. He put his arms around me and ran me backward over to the cabin wall like a linebacker driving me back. Diamond pulled open the slider, shoved me inside, and walked me over to the far corner of the living room where I sat on the floor on Spot's bed, clenching my eyes against the cutting grit of glass and spitting glass shards and slivers out of my mouth.

I couldn't see. I could feel Spot sniffing me. I listened as Diamond shut and locked the slider, trotted across my small cabin to lock the front door, then turned off the lights. I heard some other movement in the dark, the pull of a Velcro strip. It sounded like he'd pulled his weapon out of the concealed carry holster at the small of his back. He got on his phone and called in to report the shooting.

"You okay?" he said when he got off the phone. "Can you breathe?"

"I've got some glass issues, but yeah," I said. My words were slurred by a thousand prickly glass spears stuck into my tissues. My tongue and lips and gums all gripped and pulled and burned each other. "Feels like I've got diamond-grit sandpaper on the inside of my eyelids and sea urchins in my mouth," I mumbled.

"Don't move. We'll lie low in the dark until reinforcements come."

My eyeballs stung in a way I'd never experienced. The natural impulse to blink was excruciating, my lids stuck on my eyeballs by dozens of tiny razors gouging both eyes and lids.

"Probably lucky you tipped your beer bottle up another inch just as the shooter was pulling the trigger," Diamond said.

"No kidding," I said, only three syllables, but garbled almost to the point they were unintelligible. "Rather have this than have the bullet go through my neck or head."

"Probably hurts, glass in the eyes," Diamond said. "You want anything, let me know."

I mumbled, "I'm trying to keep my eyeballs staring straight ahead behind my clenched lids."

"They have those anaesthetic drops. You just need to hang in there until we get you to the hospital. Help will be here in a few minutes. We'll keep the lights off and hurry you out in the dark. That way, the shooter won't be able to get a clear shot at you. You think the shooter is on skis?"

I nodded, then realized that Diamond couldn't see me nod in the dark. "That would make sense," I mumbled.

There was a particular pain on my right eye, a red hot needle stabbing into my eyeball. I gripped the eyelashes of my right lid and tried to readjust the position. My eyes were streaming tears, but that didn't flush out the glass that was stuck in the flesh. "He no doubt had planned his escape," I said, torturing the words. "A sloping traverse across the mountain would take him down to the highway a long distance from here, and it could be done at considerable speed. As your men come up the highway from Stateline, one of the vehicles they drive by will likely be the shooter."

Diamond got on his phone and explained as much to someone.

When he hung up, he said, "Or the suspect could be driving north and heading over Spooner Summit," Diamond said. "Or he could also climb up and go over the east side of the mountains and drop down to Genoa or Jack's Valley."

I knew that Diamond was probably standing to the side of the living room window, peeking through the blinds out into the forest, trying to see anything in the darkening twilight, hyper aware of any potential sounds. He was talking just to help keep me focused on something other than the trauma of broken glass in my face.

"But going over the mountain would be very difficult," I said, words slurred, the glass in my tongue catching on the inside of my mouth. "This cabin sits at seventy-two hundred feet of elevation. Any decent shooting location with a view of my deck wouldn't be more than two or three hundred feet up behind the cabin. The ridgeline north and south of Genoa Peak mostly runs around nine thousand feet. To climb up and over would be a fifteen hundred-foot ascent followed by a four thousand-foot descent. That's a serious climb in what will quickly be total darkness, especially..." I gagged on something very sharp in my throat.

"Hey, you okay? Do I need to do anything? Maybe you shouldn't talk."

I tried to make an "Uh huh" noise without moving my tongue and throat.

"I'm guessing the shooter went down on this side," Diamond said. "There are many places off the highway where he could have left his car. The Logan Creek or Cave Rock neighborhoods, for example."

"You're probably right," I mumbled, concentrating on keeping my burning eyes still.

We continued to sit in the dark. Eventually, we heard a siren, then another, and then a third.

"Hang in there," Diamond said. "Ambulance will be here soon."

"I don't need an ambulance," I said. "Anyone can give me a ride to the hospital."

"I can't waste a deputy on that," Diamond said. "Besides, what if you need oxygen or something to keep you alive?"

"What I need is beer to numb the pain."

"Pretty sure the ambulance doesn't carry beer," Diamond said.

Five minutes later, Diamond led me out of the cabin. He held my arm as he guided me to the ambulance.

"Can you take Spot down to Street's?" I said.

"Sure. She at her condo or at her lab?"

"Condo. And go easy when you tell her what happened?"

"Will do."

They put me on the gurney and strapped me down, and we were at the hospital in South Lake Tahoe twenty-five minutes later.

Although I couldn't see, I could tell by his voice that Doc Lee was working the ER.

"Every time I'm here, you're working," I slurred, my eyes still shut. "You ever take time off?"

"No. I live at the hospital twenty-four-seven just to be sure that I'm here when you come in, which you do far too often. You need to give other people a chance to use our services. What I'm going to do is get some drops into your eyes. I'll lift your lids to do it. It will hurt, but not for long. Okay?"

"Okay."

"But when the pain goes away, try to hold your eyes still. Otherwise, the glass chips will chew up your eyes and eyelids."

He put in the drops, and the fire was intense. But then the pain went away fast. Doc Lee wore a very bright LED headlamp and magnifying glasses. He made a little murmur as he looked at my eyeballs.

"What's that mean?" I mumbled.

"What?"

"You made a murmur sound," I said.

"No, I didn't."

"Yeah, you did."

"I didn't."

"Okay," I said, "just tell me what you're thinking."

"I'm thinking that you had a really close call. Your eyes have so much glass in them, they look like those sparkly Christmas bulb ornaments for hanging on trees. What's good is that most of the sparkle is on the sclera. Very little is on your cornea. How'd you manage that?"

"I saw the bullet coming, and I looked away just as it hit my beer bottle."

"Wow. Fast reflexes. Let's take a look at your mouth."

I opened my mouth and the doctor looked around.

"Stay put. We need to get you an ophthalmologist and an ENT."

He went away. Fifteen minutes later, Doc Lee was back.

"Specialized help is on the way. In the meantime, let's see about getting some of the bigger chunks out. I'll just use my channel-lock pliers and wire cutters until the specialists get here."

I'd never heard Doc Lee make dry jokes. Maybe that meant I wasn't in serious danger. Or maybe it meant I only had moments before I expired.

He put the magnifying glasses back on and went over my face. I'd been so focused on the glass in my eyes and mouth, that I didn't realize I also had glass sticking into the rest of my face. Doc Lee found lots of little pieces in my cheeks and plucked them out with some kind of tweezer.

"You will have glass coming out of your cheeks and eyes and mouth for a long time," he said. "A good doctor knows his or her limits, I'm going to leave you for a bit. The other doctors will be here soon."

I lay there for an hour. Street showed up, raised her hand to her mouth in shock, but tried to be brave as she looked at me. I could see that she was shaken by my appearance. Her eyes teared up, and she bent down to hug me.

"Sorry, hon," I said in my garbled voice. "I know I look bad, but Doc Lee makes like it isn't that bad. Diamond stopped by?" I said. "Brought Spot?"

Street nodded. "He's in my VW. Diamond said you found a warning note suck in your door."

"Yeah. A strange figure in a star symbol of some kind." I pulled it out of my pocket and showed it to her. "Make any sense to you?"

"No. But it's very scary. Something about the drawing being upside down relative to the writing is creepy. Someone is serious about killing you."

"Kind of looks like it," I said.

"Unless you drop the case," she said.

I didn't respond.

"Which you won't do," she added.

"I don't think..." A woman wearing a white coat walked into the room, looked at me, and frowned. Street stepped back, giving her room.

"I'm Doctor Perez, ophthalmologist," the woman said. "I

understand you had a little accident involving broken glass in your eyes. I'll take a quick look." She wore mad scientist glasses with the various lens that could be swiveled back and forth. She also wore a headlamp. She flipped it on and looked at my eyes. Just like Doc Lee, she made a little hmm murmur.

"Bad?" I said.

"Not good. But I think your vision will be okay. This is going to take some time. We'll get the major pieces now and then you can come to my office for a more thorough appointment. Maybe tomorrow morning."

Street said, "I'll leave and get out of the way. Call for a ride when you're ready?"

"Will do. Thanks. Don't worry about me. I've survived worse."

Street made a little nod, wiped the back of her hand across wet cheeks, and left.

Dr. Perez went to work with a bunch of different tools. She used a substantial range of her mad scientist lenses. And she made a surprising number of grunts as she dug tiny glass shards out of my eyeballs and the inside of my eyelids.

Twenty minutes later, she said, "I've gotten the major pieces, but there is plenty of small detritus to remove another day."

"Boulders out by night, gravel out by day?" I said.

"Well, yes, I suppose you could put it that way."

My eyes still felt like sandpaper.

The doctor glanced at the clock on the wall, which said 10 p.m. "I have another appointment to get to," she said as she took off the mad scientist glasses. Maybe she wondered what I'd think of her schedule, but she was smart enough to know that she needn't answer my unasked questions.

"I would like you to come to my office tomorrow morning," she said, "and we'll have another look. In the meantime, you will be uncomfortable."

She left me with some pain meds and some eye drops and some kind of medicinal goo and specific instructions on what to do and what not to do. When she was done, I waited another half hour, and then the Ear, Nose, and Throat guy came, a doctor with an unpronounceable last name that began with the letter T.

"You can just call me Doctor T," he said.

He wore yet another version of Hollywood torture glasses as he examined my mouth and swabbed with an anesthetic and used long tweezers to mine for glass, finding it in my tongue and gums and at the back of my throat. He wrapped a cloth around my tongue so he could pull my tongue far out of my mouth while he dug around. It was not a joyful experience.

After another half hour, he said I'd live. "More glass will come out of your tissues here and there. You'll swallow some of them. But they are all very small. The likelihood is that they'll all travel through your system without a problem. Drink a lot of water and eat a lot of vegetables and beans, and you'll be fine."

"Great," I said.

"But call me immediately if you feel pain anywhere in your digestive system. If you can't reach me, go to the ER."

"Got it."

I called Street on her cell, and it turned out she was waiting in her car in the hospital parking lot. She came in and took me home. Spot was in the back seat. He stuck his head forward and sniffed with vigor, no doubt wondering about all the anesthetic smells.

I called Diamond en route.

"Any news?" I said when he answered.

"No. Too dark on the mountainside behind your cabin to see anything. We'll send two teams up there in the morning. Maybe they can do some ski track forensics. Meantime, even though the shooter is unlikely to try again from the same vantage point, you should try not to present yourself as an easy target."

"I was kinda thinking the same thing," I said.

SEVENTEEN

Diamond was outside my cabin when Street dropped me off. He told me that, if I insisted on staying at my cabin, he thought I'd be okay if I had Spot inside with me and I kept the doors and windows locked and blinds closed. But he stressed that it was my decision.

"You don't want me to take your advice, then die, then blame you," I said.

"Right," he said with a straight face.

I looked at Street. "Do you have a preference?"

"I'd rather you weren't at the place where you were shot at. But it also makes sense that the shooter would not come back here."

"Okay, I'll go on record as saying that I prefer to stay in my own cabin, and I accept the risks."

"Sounds good," he said.

I kissed Street, and they both drove away.

The next morning my eyes, my face, and the inside of my mouth were even more red and swollen than the night before. Every surface, inside and out, felt like 60-grit sandpaper. As I swallowed my morning coffee, it seemed that the liquid was filled with a fine abrasive.

When I stepped outside with Spot, I was a little wary. It had been less than 12 hours since someone had taken a shot at me. They could be anywhere on the mountain above me, waiting for a second chance. But I saw two Douglas County vehicles up the road and Diamond's men exploring the mountainside. I relaxed.

I let Spot into the Jeep and drove myself into town to see the ophthalmologist for my second appointment. Once again, she muttered and murmured and grunted from behind the monster glasses as if I weren't in the room. I wasn't a person so much as an interesting specimen.

"Large pieces of glass show up on radiography or ultrasonography," she said. "If we can find it, we can extract it. But I think I've gotten most of the bigger pieces."

"What about all the little shards?"

"They don't even show up on imaging. So we don't worry about them."

"You don't worry, but I do," I said.

"Mmm," she mumbled as she blinded me with her headlamp.

"What will happen to them?"

"Some will mostly stay where they are. Some will eventually come out and irritate you as they do so. Others will work themselves in deeper."

"Where they will poke me and hurt me inside," I said.

"Right."

"You weren't supposed to say 'right.' You were supposed to protest and convince me that my future was glass-free."

The doctor leaned back away from my face, swiveled several lenses away from her eyes and said, "Sorry. I thought you wanted the truth."

"I do," I said.

"The truth isn't pretty," she said. "But it isn't frightening, either. If you had embedded organic matter, then the likelihood of infection would be high. The problem with glass is simply that it irritates. But it is also inert, so if it doesn't bother you, it is often better to leave it in place. Removal causes more problems than it solves."

"But, is the glass that's inside going to make me eventually go blind?"

"No."

"Is the glass in my face and mouth going to screw up my health in a major way?"

"No."

"So it's basically all good news," I said.

"If your goal is to have vision and still be able to eat, yes."

"But," I said.

"But you won't be pain free. This will bother you for some

time."

"How long?"

She thought about it. A month, a year. Maybe several years."

"More good news." I thanked her and left.

Diamond had given me the addresses of Adam and Felicite's burnt house as well as where they were staying at Simms's neighbor, Ronald Baumgarter. I turned off the highway just south of Zephyr Cove, the home base of the M.S. Dixie sternwheeler. I climbed up and around on a twisting street and found the number on a house that perched just back from the street. Behind the house, the land dropped away. Highway 50 was somewhere out of sight down below. On both sides of the house were big Jeffrey pines, straight trunks two feet in diameter and rising up 40 feet before the trunks were interrupted by the lowest branches. Behind the trees was the blue backdrop of Tahoe, not unlike the view from my cabin although from a lower angle.

To the left of Baumgarter's house was the carcass of the house that had burned down two nights before. I left Spot in the Jeep and walked around its perimeter. The damage the fire caused was amazing. There was almost nothing recognizable left. I saw some blackened items I recognized, refrigerator, metal bed frame and bed springs, long metal strips that may have once been component layers inside of skis, a metal blade from a snow shovel.

Only a small portion of the house remained to suggest its former size and shape. The rear wall and one of the side walls were still standing although they were charred black. Part of the front porch remained. Everything else had been destroyed.

As the roof had burned, it collapsed into the house so that what was once a two-story structure was now a black pile of water-soaked rubble, eight feet high. I could tell that the house had contained a large room by the remnants of heavy timber-frame trusses. One had broken in two, the burnt, broken ends of the wood showing that it had been constructed of four-by-twelve lumber. And below the collapsed roof, the concrete foundation was cracked through, perhaps by the falling structure above and made worse by the temperature stress of cold fire-hose water dousing a searing hot base.

Tendrils of steam emerged from multiple locations. Outside of the burnt house was a perimeter of yellow crime scene tape secured to trees and several stakes driven down into the snow. I guessed the distance from the burned house to Baumgarter's as less than thirty feet. Baumgarter was lucky that his house hadn't caught on fire.

I pressed Baumgarter's doorbell. The door opened a short time later.

"Hello?" The man speaking was skinny, in his sixties, gray and balding, and wearing wire-rims that seemed held in place not by sitting on the slender bridge of his nose but by hanging from his giant, black eyebrows.

"Hello. My name's Owen McKenna. I'm an investigator looking into the fire at your neighbors' house."

The man nodded. "I'm Ronald Baumgarter. Terrible thing, a fire is. Terrible."

"I understand that Adam Simms is staying with you. May I speak with him, please?"

The man looked at me as if he were an art forgery expert studying a painting of questionable authenticity. Probably, he was trying to understand the strange, swollen, red glow of someone whose face and eyes had been augmented with glass shards.

"Yes, Adam Simms is staying here," he said. "It's like having royalty in my house. Come with me."

He led me through an entry and into a living room with a wall of windows to take in the western view. The windows had a sheer drape to reduce sun glare in the afternoon, but the filtered view of the West Shore mountains was still spectacular. To the side was the smoking wreckage of the burned house.

"Mr. Simms," he said, "you have a visitor." Baumgarter held out his arm like a waiter showing me to a table. "Adam, I have to leave for a couple of hours," he added. "Will you be okay? Is there anything you need?"

"No thanks," Simms said, his voice as deep as that of James Earl Jones.

"Then I'll leave you two to talk." Baumgarter nodded at me, then left.

Adam Simms was huge. I knew that from seeing him on TV

years ago. But in person, he was a black mountain, parked in an over-sized chair in the corner of the room, seemingly unmovable. I tried to visualize him running the 40 in 4.75 seconds as the records claimed. But it wasn't comprehensible that anyone of such size could get moving so fast.

He held a small sketchbook in his monstrous lap, a mechanical pencil poised above a page. It looked like a toothpick in a hand the size of a catcher's mitt. Simms's eyes turned up to me, white flashes in the dark face. In just a glance, he seemed soulful and lonely and confused. He glanced down at his sketchbook, then lay it open-faced over the broad arm of his chair like a saddle on a horse.

At the man's feet lay a yellow Lab, small enough and with a soft enough face shape that I thought it was a female. The dog jumped up and trotted over to me, tail wagging vigorously, friendly like all yellow Labs. I bent down and pet the dog while I talked to Adam Simms.

"My name's Owen McKenna," I said. "I'm investigating the fire that burned your house."

"Mr. McKenna," he said more to himself than to me. He added, "It was my sister's house."

He stood up in a single, fluid motion and took three large steps over to me. It wasn't a fast, spry movement, but he clearly wasn't suffering the mechanical problems so many of his contemporary football players had. That his knees still worked was a miracle considering his past job and the weight involved.

Looking at my chest, he reached out his hand to shake. "I'm Adam Simms."

We shook. Rarely do I feel small, but next to Adam, I felt delicate. At six-six, I was five inches taller than Adam. But Adam probably carried 360 pounds, which made him 145 more than me on a shorter frame. Imagining him coming toward me at full speed and hitting me with his singular, head-down tackle technique, was like imagining stepping in front of a charging bull. He was short compared to most pro football players, so he went under them, flipping them up and to the side as he desired.

"Good to meet you," I said. "I've long admired your skills on the field."

Adam glanced at my eyes, then went back to his chair, standing in front of it. I wasn't sure, but it didn't seem like my glass-infused eyes and skin put him off. It felt more like he was simply shy.

"Would it be okay to talk a bit?" I asked.

"Sure."

Adam's dog pushed her head into my hands as I pet her, then walked a circle around me and leaned against my leg. I pet her some more.

"That's Blondie," Adam said. "World's greatest dog. She was a rescue pup. She took to me like I was her long lost mama."

"Seems well adjusted," I said as I gave Blondie a neck rub.

"As long as she's with me," Adam said. "I've heard that she flips out when I'm away."

"You go away much?"

"No. But the problem is that I never know much in advance. She can always tell just before I go, and it makes her stress big-time."

Near Adam's chair was a kind of a sidebar desk opposite the window wall. I walked over to the desk chair, swiveling it to face Adam. As I sat, he lowered himself back down into the big chair.

Blondie sat down in front of me and lifted her paw as if to shake. I shook it. Then she circled around next to me, sat down again, and lifted her head up so that her jaw rested on my leg. I pet her, and her tail wiped the floor.

"Sorry, what did you say your name was?"

"Owen McKenna."

Blondie stood and trotted back to Adam. He patted his thigh, and she jumped up on his lap.

"Would it be okay if I took your photo?" he asked. "I have difficulty with recollection. My doctor says that photos are the best way to jog one's memory."

"Sure."

Adam made a little nod. He pulled out his phone, took my picture, then tapped on the phone. "McKenna," he said as he typed. It was impressive that he could hit the little buttons with his huge fingers. "Good name. McKenna. Sorry, but I'm slowly losing my brain. I forget names and other stuff. Most stuff, actually. They tell me to repeat names to myself. It maybe slows the effects of my growing… Why can't I say it. D something. Demen… The word that means total confusion."

"Dementia?"

"That's it," he said. "So I'm taking photos wherever I go. Then I look at them to see if I can remember taking them. Or remember the people in them. Mostly, I can't. The last two years, especially. And now it's getting worse fast."

"Is that from football?" I asked.

He nodded. "They have fancy words for it. TBI. Stands for Traumatic Brain Injury. It comes from banging your head. You bang your head enough times, you lose your brain. I never had a concussion. Not once. I just hit the guys with my head for nine years in the pros and four years of college ball before that. I thought the helmet gave me protection. Twenty-five years later, I'm learning it wasn't so much protection. Something about tau proteins running amok in my gray matter. I still have some good days. But eventually, it will all be gone."

"How soon is eventually?" Maybe the question was a bit forward, but it seemed that Adam led me there.

"Depends on if I have Early Onset Alzheimer's or if I have CTE. I forget what that means. With one, I'm supposed to last several years before I die. With the other, I have less time. They haven't decided which I have. Some doctors think I have both. If that's the case, I'll probably be dead in less than a year. Maybe a lot sooner than that."

EIGHTEEN

Adam's words were bracing. But he spoke with casual intonation. It was something he'd come to accept.

He glanced at me, then looked down as before.

"I'd like to ask you a few questions, if I may," I said.

He nodded.

"You were awake when the house fire started."

"Yeah."

"I believe it was around three in the morning?" I said.

Another nod.

"Where were you at the time?"

"In the kitchen." His voice was very soft.

"Why were you up?"

"I… I couldn't sleep."

"So you went downstairs to get something to eat or drink?"

He shook his head. Still didn't look at my face. After a long pause, he said. "I was working on an idea, and I got up to write it down."

"Would you be willing to tell me what your idea was?"

"I'm a poet. You probably wouldn't understand. It was a poet thing."

That was interesting. "I'm still curious," I said.

"If I tell you, you'll just roll your eyes. The big tackle fancies himself a poet." He picked up the sketchbook, glanced at the open pages, then closed it, holding the book with both hands as if it were precious and sacred.

"I won't roll my eyes. Terry Bradshaw is an actor and author. Rosie Grier from the Los Angeles Rams does needlepoint. That old Purple People Eater Alan Page is a Minnesota Supreme Court Justice. Chicago Bears linebacker Lance Briggs writes comic books. The Ravens kicker Justin Tucker is an opera singer. Poetry kinda fits right in."

"So you know about football players," Adam said.

"A bit."

Adam glanced right and left, shifting his weight in the chair. He rarely looked me in the eyes. "Okay. I was working on an issue of prosody," he said.

"What's that?"

He took a long breath. "Prosody is the flow of prose. The rhythms. Cadences. Beats. The meter. It's also about the sounds of consonants, vowels. Alliteration. Harmonies and dis... Dis..."

I tried to think of what word he might be searching for, but nothing appropriate came to mind.

"Discordant phrasing," he finally said. "I have the most trouble with D words. Anyway, the sensation you get from the cumulative flow of the words of poetry and prose is all affected by the prosody. Think of it as the music of words."

"That's what you were working on in the middle of the night?"

"Yeah. I call the importance of prosody Langston Hughes' law. My phrase. Hughes was a minimum daily required vitamin in the grade school where I grew up."

"He wrote Dreams, right?" I said.

Adam raised his eyebrows for a moment, surprised. "I've been holding onto my dreams from the beginning. And this poem I'm working on pays homage to Hughes' broken wing metaphor. Hughes was a master of prosody."

"And you were writing down an aspect of prosody," I said.

"One doesn't write an aspect of prosody. One writes something, anything, and then examines it for characteristics of good prosody or bad prosody. I'm working on a series of poems about wildness."

"Wildness," I repeated to make sure I heard him correctly. "Thus the broken wing metaphor," I said.

Simms continued, "Wildness is that aspect of the world that is being lost as humans put their stamp on every square foot of the planet. Thoreau said that 'in wildness is the preservation of the world.' And John Muir wrote about wildness as where we find hope for the world. There is almost no place where we haven't walked the ground at best, stomped and crushed the ground at worst. Almost all other species are under stress as a result of us and our lifestyle. Wildness is disappearing, and we can never get it back."

"It doesn't sound to me like you have any kind of brain injury," I said.

"It's like muscle memory. If I'm using the same circuits over and over, I remember. If not, my brain is on fast-evaporate."

"Have you written a lot of poems?"

He looked at the sketchbook in his hands. "I've filled ten or twelve of these."

I got a sick feeling. "I hope they didn't burn up in the fire."

Adam made a single nod. He held up the sketchbook. "This is all I have left."

"I'm so sorry."

We sat in silence for a long moment.

"Tell me what happened after you got up," I said. "Did you hear the crash of the firebomb on your front porch?"

"No. Blondie heard it."

At that, the yellow Lab lifted her head and looked at him. He pet her.

"And she barked," I said.

He nodded. "Yes. She ran to the front room and barked continuously. I followed and saw the flickering light from the flames coming through the drapes."

"What happened next?"

"When I saw the fire on the front porch, I knew the fire would go first into the overhang above the front porch. That's where my sister Felicite's bedroom was. So I shouted for her to wake up while I ran out to get the hose. But I couldn't find the hose faucet because it was buried in snow. I went back inside to check on my sister. She was dialing nine, one, one. Before the firemen could come, the house was de... de..."

"Destroyed?" I said.

"Yeah. The kitchen was at the back of the house. If Blondie hadn't heard the sound, the fire might have gotten into Felicite's room before I was aware that the house was burning."

I said, "Whoever tossed the bomb intended to burn the house down. The question is whether it was an act of arson or a specific attempt on your life or your sister's life."

Adam nodded slowly. "I've wondered that, too."

"Can you think of any reason why someone might want to cook you and your sister inside your house?"

"No. Except, wackos target celebrities, right? I'm not that much of a celebrity, but I still get nasty emails from people who said I was too hard on the quarterbacks. So I don't think Felicite was the target. And there is another reason why I could be a target."

I didn't expect that answer.

Adam could see that I was waiting for his explanation.

"I got a call from a woman," he said. "I only know her first name, which was…" He frowned. He pulled out his phone, tapped a few times, and said. "A woman named Scarlett. She said that she thought I was in danger. She said there were other people who were also in danger and she was going to call them, too. She said I should be extremely careful wherever I went, whatever I did. Then she hung up. I don't remember ever meeting this Scarlett. It was distressing. A stranger telling you that you and other strangers are in danger."

"Did Scarlett say anything to indicate how she knew you? Or knew about you?"

"No. Maybe she's a stalker."

"Have you talked to her at any other time?"

"Not that I remember. To my knowledge, we'd had no contact before. And I don't remember any time before the call when I might have met her. But I can't constantly make notes of everything that happens. And even when I think to myself that I should make a note about something, by the time I get out my phone, I often forget what it was."

"Any idea how Scarlett got your number?"

He shook his head.

I said, "There was a woman named Scarlett Milo who was shot and killed at Squaw Valley two days ago."

Adam jerked. Blondie lifted her head off his lap. He made a severe frown.

"It was the middle of the afternoon. That night, your house burned down."

"What do you know about her?" Adam asked.

"Very little. She believed she was in danger, and she called me. I was unable to prevent her murder. It's possible that she knew a young woman from South Lake Tahoe named Darla Ali. Darla Ali is also dead."

I watched Adam's face as I said the name. He looked shocked. "Never heard of her, either," he said. "What's going on?"

"Where were you at three in the afternoon two days ago?"

"Was that when Scarlett was shot?"

I nodded.

"You're wondering if I have an alibi."

"Do you?"

"No. I can't remember my days. Maybe Felicite would know. But I don't remember if she was around or not."

I continued, "You might have been dead, had you not been up when the arsonist lit the fire. Someone also tried to kill me yesterday evening. Presumably because I'm investigating the crimes."

"What happened? Did someone burn your house?"

"No." I explained what had happened and pointed to my red, swollen face.

Adam's alarm was palpable. "So Scarlett was right about everything she said."

"It would appear that way. Do you recall a person named Sean Warner?"

Adam shook his head. "Is that another person who's been killed?" He looked about to cry.

"Yes," I said. "Do you have any memory of recently meeting a young man or a young woman?"

"No." Adam looked sad and frustrated. "You said that Scarlett was shot. And you were shot at. How did the others die?"

"They were both run over by a rotary snow blower."

Adam's entire face seemed to fold into a mass of deep wrinkles.

"Were their deaths an accident?" He said it with a touch of hope in his voice, showing that universal belief that even though the result was the same, death by accident was somehow less bad than death by malice. It was what Diamond had said about

Thomas Aquinas. Intentions matter.

"No, their deaths look intentional," I said. "Let me change the subject," I said. "Do you know what the phrase medic's BFF means?"

Adam turned and stared at the wall. "I've heard of BFF. Or maybe I've seen it. I can't remember what it means."

"Some people use it as shorthand for Best Friend Forever. Does that ring a bell?"

Adam made a slow shake of his head. "I'm sorry, no. This is overwhelming. I'm getting very confused."

"I'm sorry, Adam."

"Me, too."

Adam's phone started playing the Jackson Browne song, Doctor My Eyes. "That's my timer." He picked it up and pressed a button. "It's a reminder for my doctor's appointment. I have to leave in five minutes."

"Where is your appointment?"

"It's in South Lake Tahoe. Near the hospital."

"Who's your doctor?"

He frowned again. "I don't remember. But I know the building and I know where the doctor's door is. Down the hall at the end. On the right. He does these tests on me. He says I'm helping the cause of science." Adam gently set Blondie on the floor, then stood up."

"Does Blondie come with you?"

"She goes everywhere with me. She's a service dog. I keep her bib in the truck. I put it on her when I go places so she can get into buildings."

"Ah," I said. He didn't volunteer what kind of service dog. Maybe he just meant it in a general sense. Or maybe his brain injury had given him a kind of Post Traumatic Stress Syndrome and Blondie helped him stay calm.

I stood up. "Thanks for talking to me."

He nodded. "Sure." He looked at his phone, tapped on it. "Mr. McKenna," he added.

"Right," I said.

I followed him out. From the front door of Baumgarter's house, Adam turned and walked over toward the burnt house.

To the side was a garage that was singed, the paint on the siding bubbled and peeled, but it hadn't burned. Adam lifted the garage door, walked inside and opened the door of a silver pickup. Blondie jumped inside, then Adam followed.

He started the engine, backed out of the garage, turned and drove away without seeming to notice me standing nearby. Maybe he'd already forgotten who I was. I watched Adam's truck recede around the curve.

I was about to lower the garage door when a black Audi drove up from the opposite direction that Adam had gone. The woman driver stared at me with concern. I stepped back to give her a wide space. She hesitated, then must have decided that I wasn't dangerous. She parked next to the garage. A tiny woman got out. She wore stylish clothes, brand new as if she'd been shopping. She had unusual black eyes that seemed part Asian and part African. Her skin was lighter than Diamond's. Her hair was cut very short and straight.

"Hi. I'm guessing that you are Felicite," I said.

NINETEEN

"Yes, I'm Felicite," she said. She stared at my swollen face and clutched her purse to her chest as if she thought I might be about to snatch it and run away.

"I'm Owen McKenna. I'm an investigator looking into your fire."

She frowned.

"You can call Sergeant Diamond Martinez for verification, if you'd like. I believe you spoke to him after your house burned down."

Felicite considered me for a moment.

"I've been talking to Adam," I said, hoping that would make her more comfortable. "He just left for his doctor's appointment. I'd like to ask you a few questions, please."

She looked around as if considering whether we should talk in the street. "Have you met my neighbor, Ronald Baumgarter? He owns the house where we're staying temporarily."

"Yes, we met. He took me in to see Adam, then left. After a bit, Adam's phone alarm rang, and he said he had to go to a doctor's appointment."

Felicite nodded. "We can go inside. I don't think Ron will mind."

I followed her back inside Baumgarter's house. Felicite didn't go to the living room where I'd spoken to Adam, but instead took me to a sun room on the mountain side of the house, opposite the side that faced her burned house. She probably preferred it to the living room because it didn't have a view of the rubble of her house.

The sun room projected out and had windows on three sides. There was a small couch on the back wall, and in one corner were two leather chairs arranged in front of a gas soapstone stove. Between the chairs was a small table and lamp. Day or night, it would be my favorite room if it were my house.

As with the living room's big windows, the sun room windows had sheer drapes that provided privacy from the outside but allowed views of the forest and the mountain from the inside. Felicite took one chair, I took another, and we both sat facing the stove and the mountain above.

"Adam told you about the fire," she said.

"Yeah. I'm wondering if you have any idea why someone would want to burn down your house."

"No. It was a mindless, senseless act. All I can think of is what Adam said. That it was either random arson or some disgruntled football fan who wants to punish him for tackling those quarterbacks all those years ago."

"Do you believe it?" I asked.

"I have no evidence to believe one thing or another. Adam's idea seems as good as any other idea."

"Can you think of any reason why you could be the target?"

Felicite looked at me with puzzlement. "You need to understand that I'm pretty much a nobody. I work as an accountant for Actuation Tronics, Inc., a tech company that no one's ever heard of."

"What do they do?"

" We make electronic actuators."

"What are those?"

"Actuators are devices that turn energy into physical movement. The incoming energy can be electric or wind or heat or wave motion or anything you can think of. They are used in a thousand kinds of industrial products. They come in every size from huge to microscopic. The kind of actuators that most people are familiar with are remote control door locks on cars."

"Ah," I said. "The world is full of people who earn a living doing something the rest of us have never thought about."

"That's my point. No one cares about what I do. Most people in the company don't even know me. I earn a decent income, but nothing that would get any attention. Not many people seem to like me much. But the flip side is that no one out there really dislikes me, either. At least, I hope not. I have no close friends, and no enemies, either. The only person who has ever really cared about me is Adam."

"Where do you live?"

"San Francisco."

"I used to be San Francisco PD. Where in The City are you?"

"In the Sunset district. The company I work for is in the SOMA district.

"South of Market," I said.

"Right. But even though SOMA is pretty close and I can take the bus, I mostly telecommute."

"Do you think that whoever lit your vacation house on fire knew you were up at the lake visiting?"

"Probably not. I just come up when I can to check on Adam. He has some memory issues, and I worry about him being alone. Adam still gets attention wherever he goes. But not me. So unless someone was spying on Adam, no one would know when I'm up at the lake."

"Does the term medic's BFF mean anything to you?"

"Well, I don't know about medic, but BFF is Best Friend Forever, right?"

"Yeah. Have you heard of BFF in any other context?"

Felicite shook her head.

"Do you know a woman named Scarlett Milo?" I asked.

"No, why?"

"What about Darla Ali?"

"No. Oh, wait, Adam said he got a phone call from a woman named Scarlett. The woman thought Adam was in danger."

"What about the name Sean Warner?"

She shook her head. "What's this about?"

"They are all people who've died recently."

"Here? In Tahoe?" Felicite's voice was shrill. She gripped her purse as if to crush it.

"Yes."

She breathed fast and hard. "Did they die in a fire?"

"No. But they were murdered."

"Oh, no." Felicite paled. "And someone tried to kill Adam and me. Are you thinking it could be the same person who killed them?"

"We don't yet know, but yes, it could be that there is just one perpetrator. Unusual clusters of murder are often related," I said. "So I'm looking for a possible connection between them."

"Did you ask Adam about the phone call from Scarlett?" Felicite asked.

"Yes, and he couldn't remember much. He had to consult his notes."

"I don't know what to think," Felicite said. She looked depressed. "Of course, Adam might have met those people and even spent time with them. But with his memory going, he might not remember their names." Felicite stood, still holding her purse close to her like it was a security blanket, and walked over to the sheer drapes. She pulled the cord and they parted. She gazed out at the mountains.

Felicite frowned and looked down at her purse. "Oh, my phone is vibrating." She pulled it out of her purse, slid her finger on the screen, tapped a few times. "My boss. She'll leave a message." She tapped again and was putting her phone back into her purse as the window in front of her broke. The tempered window made a loud crumpling sound as it fractured into thousands of diamonds, raining onto the floor.

"Move!" I shouted.

Felicite was frozen.

I rushed her as a rifle crack snapped in the air. It had been maybe a second or more since the glass broke. I wrapped my arms around Felicite from behind, lifted her up, spun her around, and ran with her into the center of the house. I set her down in the interior hallway.

"What's happening?" she said, her voice weak with terror. She stood with her back to the wall, raised her hands to her mouth and started shaking violently. Her knees buckled. I lowered her slowly to the floor.

"Sit still," I said as I got out my phone and dialed 911.

"Nine, one, one Emergency," a woman's voice said in my ear. "Please tell me your name and address."

"Owen McKenna. I'm in Zephyr Heights at Ronald Baumgarter's house. Hold for the address." I spoke to Felicite, "What's the address here?" She told me. I repeated it to the dispatcher. "The house is next door to the one that burned down two nights ago. Someone just shot out a window in Baumgarter's house. No one is hurt." As I looked back into the room where we'd been sitting, I realized that another window had also been shot. "Make that two windows. But I only heard one shot. From the lay of the land, I think the shooter must have been on the mountain to the east of the house, and the bullet went in one window and out another."

"Please stay on the line. I have officers en route."

It was a phrase that was getting very old.

"Call Diamond Martinez. He was the incident commander on the fire next door and the shooting at my cabin yesterday evening. He will want to know immediately."

"Will do," she said. "Please sit tight."

I handed my phone down to Felicite where she sat on the floor, her back to the wall. She looked at it like it was a grenade.

"Take it," I said. "The dispatcher may have questions for you. I'm going to make a quick check outside."

"No! You could get shot!" Her voice shook as she began to sob.

"The shooter is probably already gone. Even so, he was a long distance away, and his view through the trees is limited."

She took my phone. "You just said there was a shooting at your house?"

Felicite's pronunciation was so thick with fear that I could barely understand her words.

"Yeah. That's why I have bits of glass in my face." I didn't want to think that the shooter had followed me, that my presence had put Felicite at risk. But it seemed obvious. I unlocked the door and went out before she could protest. I ran to my Jeep.

Spot had his head out the window, ears up, no doubt curious at the rifle shot. He wagged as I approached.

"You okay, boy?" I grabbed his head, then opened the door.

I took his collar and ran with him back to the house. We rushed in the front door and back to where Felicite cowered on the floor.

She made a gasp as Spot and I approached.

"This is Spot," I said. "He's friendly. He will guard you." I pointed. "Spot, lie down."

He resisted and instead leaned toward Felicite to sniff her. I pushed down on his collar. He finally lay next to Felicite, reaching his head over to sniff her.

"Pet him," I said to Felicite.

She looked at me with wild eyes. She was breathing fast, her nerves on edge.

"I'm serious. Give him a pet so he knows you're friendly, too."

She slowly reached out and touched her hand to the top of his head." Her hand was tiny between his ears.

"Don't just touch. Give him a real pet."

She drew her hand over his head and down his neck. Spot began panting.

"Perfect. Now he's happy, and he'll stay with you." I reached for my phone. "Put your hand in his collar and hang onto it. I mean it. Hold his collar."

She did so.

"He likes that," I said, which was true. But more importantly, I could see that she was calming. All people under severe stress find a giant friendly dog to be a comfort. "Stay here with Spot," I said. "I'll be outside. You'll hear sirens coming. Don't worry. I'll talk to the cops. We'll keep the shooter away, and Spot will protect you."

I left them on the floor.

As I stepped outside, I heard the first siren.

While it was nearly impossible to see someone at a distance in the mountain forest, I watched for any sparkle or flash of metal catching sunlight or any movement as someone skied away from the shooting location. But there was no clear shooting location, just a broad mountainside of trees.

I saw nothing.

It was like Scarlett's shooting at Squaw and the shooting at my cabin. A distant sniper who has an escape plan is nearly impossible to catch. The only difference is that this time the sniper was less accurate than he was with Scarlett. Less, even, than he'd been with me the evening before. It had been impossible to see where the bullet struck because tempered glass is designed to shatter into harmless pieces. Perhaps the round came as close to one of us as it had with me the night before.

The houses in Zephyr Heights were at a lower elevation than my cabin. Here and there on the mountain were bare areas where the sun had gotten through and melted the snow pack. But the mountain still had lots of areas of snow. The shooter could ski down to any number of areas where he could have left a vehicle. He also could have trekked south toward the neighborhood above Round Hill. And if he was in good shape, he could do a gentle climb to the south, bypass Round Hill, and head for Upper Kingsbury. There was no way anyone could predict where he'd come out.

More sirens became audible. I walked out into the middle of the road where there was heavy tree cover between me and the shooter's probable location. As the first Douglas County patrol vehicle came into view, I stood in the middle of the street.

The vehicle came to a stop and a door opened. I heard someone say, "That's McKenna." Two deputies got out.

"I believe the shooter was somewhere on the mountain." I pointed. "Although he's probably long gone by now."

"A sniper like the other shootings, huh?"

"Yeah," I said. "I'm guessing the same guy who killed the woman at Squaw and took a shot at me from up behind my cabin yesterday. But of course I don't know that."

"Who's inside the house?"

"Felicite Genoveva, a step-sister of Adam Simms. He was here earlier, then left for a doctor's appointment." I pointed toward the burned rubble. "They're the ones whose house was torched two nights ago."

Another patrol vehicle raced up behind the first and stopped fast with the scrape of tires on grit. Diamond got out.

"Sergeant," I said.

"You okay?"

"Yeah." I restated what I'd told his deputies.

He looked around at the forest, then spoke to his men. "I'd like you two to go over to that ridge so that the shooter can't sneak up without being seen. When the other guys get here, I want you all to spread out and make a secure perimeter so we can get the woman out of here without more exposure."

The men nodded and headed into the trees.

I took Diamond back into Baumgarter's house. He nodded at Felicite who was still sitting on the floor with Spot. She nodded back, obviously recognizing him from his investigation of her fire. She was much calmer, one hand rubbing Spot's ears, a fingertip unconsciously touching his ear stud.

Diamond and I went into the sun room. The floor with its cover of glass pieces was like a theater stage made to look like a fantasy world of gemstones.

Diamond looked through both broken windows. "No way to get a clear sense of the shooter's location," he said.

"No."

He stepped back to the interior hall to talk to Felicite. "Do you know when Adam is supposed to be back?"

"He went to his doctor appointment. That usually takes an hour." She looked at her watch. "He will probably be back in about twenty minutes. Let me call him." She pulled her phone out of her purse and dialed.

I said to Diamond, "Any chance you still have access to the... What did your guys call it? The Douglas County Safe Deposit Box?"

Diamond nodded. "The house of our patron, the guy whose daughter I rescued from the carjacker methhead. He thinks I'm like a Marvel Comics superhero or something. Able to swoop in to save young damsels from the clutches of Dr. Doom."

"That was an amazing shot," I said.

"Hours at the range mixed with some serious luck makes for the kind of outcome we always hope for but rarely get. You're thinking that it's time to sit on Adam and Felicite."

"At least put them in the box. Give them some space to breathe."

"Makes sense," Diamond said. "They had the fire and now a shooting, all in less than 48 hours. So yeah. The house is still ours to use, webcams and all. Let me call the office. They keep a schedule of the house. The owner comes up about four times a year, and he likes to stay in his own house when he comes."

"Right," I said.

Diamond got on his phone as Felicite put hers in her purse.

"Adam says he's on his way and he'll be here in about ten minutes," she said.

"Good. Diamond's checking on something. Then we'll make a plan."

Diamond was talking. He stopped and waited. Then he said, "Thanks. No problem. I know the keypad code." He hung up and put his phone in his pocket.

"Adam's almost here," I said.

"We'll go outside and wait for him."

We went out, and Adam showed up a few minutes later. He let Blondie out of his truck. She was now wearing her Service Dog bib. She ran around.

We explained to him about the shooting and told him that it would be good for his sister's sake if he stayed calm.

He was very somber as he looked over at the blown-out sun room windows.

We went inside the front door. Blondie stopped fast and stared at Spot. Her tail was on high speed.

Spot looked at me.

"It's okay," I said.

He pushed himself up and walked over to Blondie.

"Dog's huge," Adam said. "Will he be friendly to Blondie?"

"Yeah. And she can tell."

Adam looked at Blondie who was quivering with excitement.

"I guess you're right," he said. "You know your dogs."

Spot and Blondie sniffed each other, both wagging. Blondie spun in a circle.

"She's never seen a dog that big," Adam said.

"Dogs don't care about size," I said.

Adam bent over, helped Felicite stand up, and gave her a hug, his body almost completely enclosing her.

Diamond said to them, "We're taking the two of you to a safe house. So you might want to grab a few things."

Adam said, "What's that mean, a safe house?"

"A place the sheriff's office is able to use, a place where no one can easily shoot at you or burn you down."

"Are we being detained or something?" Felicite asked.

"No. We just want you to be in a safe place so you can get a good night's sleep without worrying."

"How does it work?" Adam asked.

Diamond said, "Up above the top of Kingsbury Grade is a house that's owned by a Bay Area venture capitalist. We did a favor for him once, and he's been trying to help us out ever since. The house sits up high on a ridge, and it has a fence around it. There are other houses nearby. Two of them are owned by the same man, and he rents them real cheap to Douglas County Sheriff's deputies. There are lights on motion detectors. There are webcams inside and outside the house, along the fence, and at both roads and hiking trails on the nearby ridges. They send continuous video feeds to computers at the owner's company."

"So it's totally safe," Adam said.

Diamond shook his head. "No. No place is totally safe. But no one can come or go without being recorded. That is a powerful deterrent to anyone who might try to come close. The drive has a gate powered by a garage door transmitter, and there is a four-car garage. You can come and go relatively unseen. The house has reinforced windows and doors and is made of fireproof materials. There is also a sprinkler system. If you keep the blinds shut, no one will be able to easily target you."

"Are you saying we can take our cars there?" Felicite said.

"Yes. And you can come and go as you desire. Although your cars are the place where you are the most vulnerable."

"We both have window tint," Adam said.

"Good. That helps."

"What if I want to go back home?" Felicite said. "I've got work to do. And, frankly, I want out of here."

"Whatever you want is fine with us," Diamond said. "I just need to get your statement about the shooting."

Felicite frowned. "Could you take my statement at the house? Then I could go there with Adam, make sure everything's, you know, okay. Maybe I'll stay one night."

"Certainly," Diamond said.

"When would we go?" Adam said.

"As soon as you get your things."

"We have no things. Everything burned up. We have the clothes we're wearing. I have my poetry book. Ron Baumgarter gave us toothbrushes. Which makes me wonder, does this place have a washing machine?"

"Yeah," Diamond said.

Adam and Felicite went to get their few items.

"Where do you think the shooter was?" Diamond asked me.

I pointed out the window toward the mountain behind the neighborhood. "If you stand at the windows that were shot out, you can see a range of areas on the mountain from which someone could fire a single shot that would go through both windows. The shooter had lots of choices. Finding the place he used would be very difficult."

"How far away do you figure he was?"

"From the moment that the window broke, I'd guess it took about a second or a second and a half before I heard the crack of the rifle. So that's one thousand to fifteen hundred feet. If you cross-reference that distance with those areas from which one could shoot out both windows in the sun room with a single rifle shot, that narrows it down but still allows for a lot of territory."

"Lot of stuff a sniper has to think about to make that kind of shot," Diamond said.

"Yeah. And it gets exponentially more complicated as the distance increases. Military snipers take into account dozens of concerns. Gravity, wind, temperature gradients, the Coriolis effect of the spinning earth. But this shot doesn't involve that kind of distance."

"Sorry that I never think of you as Sherlock," Diamond said. "But you obviously deserve the moniker now and then."

"What do you think of me as?"

"A lucky gringo who has a brilliant girlfriend who isn't fixated on shopping and doesn't talk incessantly about children and future grandchildren."

"You're saying that your perception of me is basically about your perception of the woman I'm connected to and that I'm lucky for that connection."

Diamond shrugged. "Well, I perceive you as tall. That's not about Street."

"Not about anything I've earned, either. No credit to me."

"Still sound like Sherlock."

He turned and walked into the sun room, stepping gingerly on the diamonds of broken glass, then sighted through the windows, gauging where the shooter might have been.

Adam and Felicite appeared at the door. Adam held a paper bag with their few belongings in it.

Diamond got on his radio, said a few words, then clipped it back on his belt. We all hustled outside. Adam seemed worried. His grip on Blondie's leash was tight.

Diamond gave crime scene instructions to four deputies and left them behind.

Adam and Blondie got into his pickup, and Felicite got into her Audi. Felicite followed Diamond on one route, and Adam followed me on another. It wouldn't fool a team working with the shooter, but it would make it more difficult for a single individual to track us.

Diamond and I took circuitous routes that eventually led to the top of Kingsbury Grade, where we turned off on North Benjamin and snaked our way up into the high country.

Most of Tahoe's neighborhoods are down by the lake. This was one of Tahoe's highest neighborhoods, up above 7500 feet. Although the east part of Tahoe gets less snow than Tahoe's West Shore, the elevation of Kingsbury Grade makes up for it. The snow walls were six feet high.

I found the turnoff and made a series of turns to the house, which sat up on a ridge at about 8000 feet. Considering its spectacular location with views of Tahoe to the west and Carson Valley to the east, the house was modest, large but not ostentatious.

When I got to the gate, I pulled over. Diamond came up from the rear. He got out and punched the code into the keypad, and the gate opened. We all drove in through the entrance, and the gate closed behind us. There was a plowed parking area. Diamond got out and once again used the keypad at one of the garage doors. In a few moments, he brought two garage door openers out to Adam and Felicite and had them both pull into the garage.

Because Spot was a calming influence on Felicite and, probably, a stabilizing presence for Adam and Blondie, I let him out of the Jeep. We walked into the garage with Diamond.

Diamond hit the buttons to lower the garage doors, then we all walked through the door that led to an area off the kitchen.

Diamond took Adam and Felicite through the house, showed them which bedrooms they could use, pointed out the food pantry and the fridge and freezer, which were well stocked. He explained the controls for the lights and heat and showed them how to set the alarm.

Then we gathered in the kitchen.

"Any other questions?" Diamond said.

"Yes," Felicite said. She was obviously tense and worried, and her voice wavered.

"Ask anything you want."

"Do you think we're going to die?"

TWENTY

"No," Diamond said. "I think you'll be okay. But be cautious. No more open drapes."

Adam sat at the kitchen table. Spot was making a careful inspection of the cracks where the cupboards opened, searching out food smells. Blondie was exploring the adjacent living room.

Felicite leaned against the granite-topped center island. Her arms were crossed, her knuckles white as each hand gripped the opposite elbow.

"But do you think the rifleman will make an attempt on us up here at this house?"

Diamond looked at me as if he were handing off the ball.

I said, "It appears that his assaults have been well-planned. It takes time to scout locations and escape routes and set up for such a shot. He's obviously very motivated. I would consider your situation dangerous. But I agree with Diamond. He's not the kind of shooter who is going to attempt a home invasion. So I think you'll be okay."

Felicite said, "I ask because since the fire, I've come and gone in my car. I've been on display going into Ronald Baumgarter's house. Yet he hasn't taken a shot at me. But when he finally took his shot, he did it when Adam was gone. How do you explain that?"

"I can't for certain," I said. "But my best guess is that he was aiming for me, and I'm very sorry about that. He's already shot at me twice. However, because of the fire, we have to consider that you or Adam are also targets."

"You think this house is safe enough?" she asked.

Diamond answered. "The locks are strong, but the greatest security comes from the fact that anyone approaching knows that their vehicle and license plate and their face have all been broadcast to internet storage before they can even get close to the house."

"But someone could still break in."

"It would be difficult, but yes. The question is, who would want to. With a comprehensive alarm and two deputies living nearby, law enforcement is very close. Much easier to catch up with your victim elsewhere."

Felicite seemed skeptical. "What about a shooter from a distance like what just happened to us? There are places around here where a shooter could hide in the forest."

I said, "There are no great sightlines to the house from any close location. There are lots of distant locations from which someone could see the house. But shooting from long distance isn't as simple as aiming a gun."

"How do you mean? Hunters have those scopes."

"Yes. But they are still relatively close to their prey." I pointed toward the view out the window. "These distances are much greater. To be that good, snipers have to have highly specialized gear and training."

Blondie came trotting through the kitchen on her exploration. She stopped as if she'd hit a wall, then turned, ran over to Adam and jumped up against his leg. She moaned and cried, then jumped on him again. Then she spun around, frantic, and leaped up and hit his chest with her paws.

"Hurry," Felicite said to Adam. "Let's get you to a bedroom. Hurry!"

Diamond looked at me. I looked at Adam. He'd started to move, started to turn around as if looking for something, but in the unfamiliar surroundings, he was confused. His eyes began to looked glazed and unseeing. "I should get on the floor," he said.

"No," Felicite said. "We have time to get you to a bedroom." She turned to me. "Help me." She took one of Adam's arms. I took the other and, following her lead, walked him into the bedroom.

"Help me get him down onto the bed."

I had no idea what was happening, but clearly this was something she had experience with. We turned Adam around and backed him up to the bed. The backs of his knees hit, and he sat back. As we got him to lie down, he tensed up, his flesh becoming strong and rigid. I realized that he was having some kind of seizure.

Blondie jumped up onto the bed, crying, whimpering. Felicite shooed her off to the floor.

Diamond appeared in the doorway. He pulled out his phone.

"No, don't call nine-one-one," Felicite said, nearly shouting. "This is a routine seizure. Sort of. We follow the doctor's instructions."

I realized that Adam was completely motionless. "He's not breathing," I said. "His face is going gray."

"It's okay," Felicite said. "It's stressful to watch, but it only takes a minute or less for him to start breathing again."

Spot came into the room but stopped a respectful distance as if he understood that something serious was happening.

After a minute, Adam started breathing, then began having dramatic convulsions. His eyes rolled up, his hands made fists, his knees pulled up toward his chest, and he bucked and jerked. Froth formed at his mouth, and he made a kind of repetitive, growling cry.

Felicite kept her hand lightly on Adam's arm, and she jerked as he jerked.

Blondie jumped her front paws up onto the bed, whined, dropped back down to the floor, turned a circle, jumped her paws up again, whined more. She jumped up on the bed a second time. As she reached her nose toward Adam, his convulsing legs jerked and hit her in the nose with his knees. She cried, jumped off onto the floor, then ran back and forth making little yips and worried squeals. She turned more circles. The poor dog was desperate. She crouched down on the floor and cried. She moved her head back and forth on the floor, despondent. I'd never seen any animal so sad, so distraught.

"Can I do anything to help?" I asked.

"No," Felicite said. "We ride it out. He's unconscious. The seizure will stop in three minutes. It'll take him ten minutes to regain consciousness, then he'll be foggy-brained for a couple of hours after that. It's important that everything stay calm when he comes to. If medical personnel are around, that will freak him out. Much better for him to gradually come to the recognition that he's had another seizure."

Blondie was still crying. I tried to reach and give her a reassuring pet, but she pulled away. She resumed jumping against the bed, bouncing off, lying on the floor and thrashing. Spot came forward, but I held out my hand. "Spot, no," I said in a loud voice.

After a couple of stressful minutes, Adam's convulsions slowed and gradually eased to a stop. Felicite wiped the foam from his mouth. He seemed to go into a deep sleep.

"Help me roll him onto his side," Felicite said.

Diamond and I both stepped forward and mimicked her as she put her hands under the side of Adam's back. We lifted until he was on his side in the fetal position.

"This is his recovery position," she said. "It helps him breathe." She patted the bed. "Okay, Blondie."

Blondie jumped up on the bed and lay next to him, her brow wrinkled with worry. She cried and pawed at him and gradually calmed herself. Felicite lifted Adam's arm and draped it over Blondie. That helped calm her, although his arm was so heavy, I didn't know how long she could take the weight.

It is at times like these that I have a powerful perceptual shift about luck and fate and the chaotic randomness of life. Those of us who have so-called normal lives without undue stress and fear and worry and pain rarely know how fortunate we are. Then we see a man like Adam who's famous even if unemployed and who lives at his sister's house and struggles to manage, and we're tempted to think he should snap out of it. He's obviously intelligent, and he has no apparent disabilities. So we think, you're smart, go out and get a job, and make yourself a normal life.

Then we learn that the man has Traumatic Brain Injury and medical issues that can rip normalcy in two, and we realize that one of the main problems is in ourselves for failing to consider that not all other people have our good fortune of functioning bodies and brains, with emotional and psychological landscapes that are level and fertile and stable and predictable.

I stood there watching Adam helpless in the fury of some

kind of neural-electrical thunderstorm in his brain, and a bit of my expansive personality contracted hard, overwhelmed with sympathy, empathy, and the callousness of living each day of my life never considering that I had been given a thousand gifts that I had not earned. I hoped I had the sense to remember him the next time I judged someone whose shoes I hadn't hiked in and whose life I hadn't witnessed up close.

When the room was calm and Adam was asleep and Blondie was calmer, I said, "Blondie knew he was going to have a seizure, didn't she?"

"Yes." Felicite took her hand off Adam's arm and gently pet Blondie. "Adam needed something to help him track and give him purpose. So we went to find him a rescue dog. Blondie was a skinny puppy with a mess of fleas and mange, and she was scared of everyone in the world. She cowered at the back of the kennel and wouldn't come near me or the woman who was working in the shelter. But when Adam bent down and put his fingers through the cage, Blondie walked right up to him and she licked them. The shelter lady opened up the kennel and Blondie climbed right into Adam's arms. The lady was amazed. Astonished. But clearly, Blondie and Adam had finally found some kind of emotional safety in each other's presence. So we took Blondie to the vet and had her treated, and, in Adam's constant presence, Blondie came alive. And it was in Blondie's presence that Adam found better ways to cope with his problems."

"The seizures look very difficult," I said. "Do they have any idea what causes them?"

"The seizures are the result of his CTE. He probably mentioned that to you."

"He mentioned it, but he couldn't remember what CTE stands for."

"Chronic Traumatic Encephalopathy. It refers to the brain disease that comes from banging your head. He gets a full tonic-clonic seizure at irregular intervals, usually every two weeks or so. He's tried the various medications available, but none of them works with him. Yet, in the big picture, the seizures are the small part. The big part is he's losing his mind. Tons of football players are dealing with this. It's the dirty little secret about pro football, and it's the subject of that huge lawsuit. Right about the time that former football players start to be forgotten - twenty years after they retire - their brains go to hell. It doesn't happen to all players, or even most players, but the number is still large. First, they lose their short-term memory. Some of them start having seizures. After awhile, the disease progresses faster. They lose their long-term memory. After that, they lose it all, their sense of self awareness, their physical control of their body, their bladder and bowel function, their awareness of anyone they ever knew in their lives, everything that it means to be human."

Diamond said, "All because they hit their head too many times."

"Yes. It's a tragedy. And what happens to these older guys mostly goes unnoticed because it's all overshadowed by the fame and excitement focused on the current crop of younger players."

"These guys are our Roman Gladiators," Diamond said. "All through human history, people have thrilled to see the biggest, strongest men go to battle."

"Right," Felicite said. "And twenty or thirty years after they retire, they disappear into dark corners as their brains rot."

Adam moaned.

Blondie lifted her head off the bed and looked at him, her brow furrowed with worry.

"He'll start to wake up in another few minutes," Felicite said.

I looked at Blondie. "How does she sense a coming seizure?"

"We don't know. The characteristic is reported in something like ten percent of all cases where people who have seizures have a dog in the house. Dog people are working on concepts of how to formulate a standard procedure for training epilepsy therapy dogs. Obviously, the dogs smell a change in a person before they have a seizure. But we don't know what that smell is. If we could figure it out, then we could train any dog to be an epilepsy therapy dog."

Felicite ran her fingers over Blondie's face, caressing her ears and nose and cheeks.

"After the first couple of experiences, Blondie understood

that Adam's smell change, or whatever it was, predicted the coming seizure. So now she freaks out. In some ways it's stressful, but I wouldn't have it any other way because a little advance notice allows Adam to get down onto a bed or the floor so he won't fall and hurt himself. We got Blondie a Service Dog bib, so she's allowed to go wherever he goes. She even saved him once at the grocery store. He was in an area with shelving units that had sharp corners. When Blondie started her panic attack, Adam got down onto the floor before he passed out. For all we know, Blondie might have saved his life."

"What's his prognosis?" Diamond asked.

"You want it straight? He's dying. The epilepsy is a symptom of the CTE. It's a steady downward course. When it gets to his present state, the progression is inexorable and fast. It won't be long before he needs in-home care. Another few weeks, maybe. Shortly after that, he'll have to be put in an institution. And not long after that, we can expect that he won't even know who he is."

Like all adults of a certain age, I'd known several people who'd fought health battles and lost. I thought I was used to it. But this time seemed different. I didn't know if it was something about Adam's innocence, or Blondie's devotion, or maybe just a change in my own view of the world.

For a brief moment, I thought of Street and how I assumed she would always be present in my life, thus took her for granted in some measure. I realized that I shouldn't take her for granted, but I pushed the thought away. There are some kinds of darkness that are too hard to face.

"Is there anything that can be done?" I asked. "It's not about money, I hope."

"No, there's nothing that can be done. And it's always about money. The medical industrial complex needs to be paid. Adam didn't have insurance for years, the result of a pre-existing condition."

"What was his pre-existing condition?"

"Partly, blood pressure. Mostly, he weighs too much. The body mass charts don't make a distinction between fat and muscle. Then with the new insurance law, he got insurance where there is supposed to be a limit to his out-of-pocket costs. But what they don't tell you about are all the things that aren't covered. When he first seized, we went to the Emergency Room. Turns out the hospital wasn't part of the insurance plan, so no coverage. Then they brought in a consulting doctor, and that doctor wasn't covered, either. Surprise. Our only hope is that the lawsuit settlement will cover his expenses. They've even tried to come after me for Adam's medical costs because they think we're family. But I'm not related to him. I just refer to him as my step-brother because we grew up in the same group home."

Felicite reached over and stroked Adam's temple.

"I remember one of his poems," she said. "There was a line in it about how all you can do is keep fighting. And when the sunrise no longer warms your soul, you still go into battle, your sword held high, and you never stop fighting."

A phone rang in another room. Felicite said, "That's mine." She walked out of the bedroom, answered, came back to the doorway and looked in at Adam as she talked.

"How important is it?" She paused. "No, I couldn't get there in less than four hours. I'm in Tahoe with Adam." Pause. "Okay, I'll call as I'm approaching the Bay Bridge."

She hung up and looked at Diamond and me.

"It's never the crisis that she makes it out to be. But when my boss gets her blood pressure up, nothing will calm her until she knows that all the troops are rushing back to the fort."

"Good to be important to your company," Diamond said.

"I wish I weren't." Felicite looked down at Adam. "When he wakes, he will be groggy but placid for an hour or two. Eventually, he will realize that he had another seizure. At that point he sometimes gets stressed, but Blondie always calms him."

Diamond said, "Does he need someone to stay with him?"

"Normally, I would say no. But this is a new environment. It will confuse him. He probably won't remember where he is. I could write him a note explaining where he is. Is there any possibility that one of you could stay here until he wakes up? I can pay you for your time."

"I'll stay," I said, "and I've already been paid by my client. This is a related activity, so there's no problem with that. A quick question, please. With Adam's seizures, how is he still driving?"

"He's not supposed to be. I tried to talk to him about moving to an apartment where they have a bus for errands, but he wouldn't hear of it. He said that if Blondie ever alerts while he's driving, he'll pull over immediately and shift into park. He said he's even rehearsed it."

"He's taking quite a risk," I said.

"I know. But what else can I do? Turn him in?"

"Let's hope that Blondie is good enough that nothing bad ever happens."

TWENTY-ONE

Felicite and Diamond left. Adam woke up and, as Felicite predicted, was confused. He looked around at the room. Blondie was excited. She licked his face and pawed at him. She made his adjustment to strange surroundings much easier.

Adam didn't remember my name, but as I spoke to him, it seemed he started to remember me. He continued to lie in bed for half an hour as we talked, then he sat up.

"I had a seizure," he said.

"Right."

"You saw it?" He looked very uncomfortable.

"Yes. It wasn't anything to be embarrassed about. I felt bad that you had to go through it."

Adam pet Blondie as he seemed to stare at the wall.

In soft words, he said, "If I were religious, I'd think this is how God is punishing me."

"What makes you think you should be punished?"

"I've done bad things."

"Like what?" I said.

"Just... stuff."

"Lots of people have done bad things in their lives," I said. "Doesn't mean they should always be punished. Sometimes just their understanding that it was bad is enough to bring a bit of justice to the world."

Adam didn't respond.

After a bit, I said, "If you want to talk about it, I'm a good, non judgemental ear." I felt bad as soon as I said it because I realized that it wasn't necessarily true. If Adam confessed to a minor crime, I might ignore it. But if he confessed to a bad crime like murder, I would turn him in.

But Adam went silent and said no more.

Eventually, he became less morose and more like the Adam

I'd met before his seizure.

I re-explained about the safe house and showed him around the place once again and reminded him that he could come and go as he liked. He was quiet, but it seemed that he understood.

I found a pizza in the freezer and made a meal. I knew Adam could easily eat the whole thing, so I had just a single piece to be sociable as I explained that Felicite was called back to the Bay Area by her boss, and that I had to leave. When it seemed that he was cognizant of his situation, I gave him my card with my numbers, and Spot and I left.

When I got down Kingsbury Grade, I called the SLT police and got put through to Mallory.

"Commander," I said when he answered, "I'm hoping for some kind of an intro to the city plow drivers."

"We've already grilled them," he said. "But maybe you can learn something new. Hold on." He put me on hold. "Here's the number," he said when he came back. He gave it to me, and I wrote it down. "Brann Crosen is the guy who more or less organizes the city's drivers," Mallory said. "You probably recognize that name."

"Sorry, but no."

"After Brann Crosen was hired by the city, there was suddenly national press coverage about him with regard to a lawsuit against his former employer in SoCal, a construction company. Turns out Crosen had quit the company after just two days on the job. He claimed he'd been the victim of harassment aimed at new employees."

"Like a fraternity hazing?"

"Yeah. So his lawyer brought a civil suit, charging the construction company with intentional infliction of emotional distress, all of which supposedly happened the first two days on the job."

"From the press coverage that resulted, I assume that Crosen won the lawsuit."

"And got an award of a hundred big ones."

"Nice pay for two days' work," I said.

"No kidding." Mallory's anger was obvious. "Anyway, be

aware of who you're calling on. That guy would sell his mother to a pet food manufacturer if he got a good price."

"Thanks," I said.

"Oh, one more thing," Mallory said.

"What's that?"

"There was mention in the initial press coverage that Crosen had changed his name. I don't recall if they followed that up or if anyone knew what name he grew up with. But you might want to know if you end up looking into his background."

"Got it." I dialed the number Mallory had given me.

"Brann Crosen," a voice said.

"My name's Owen McKenna. I'm an investigator working with the SLTPD. I need to speak to someone about your highway snowblowers."

"The rotaries? What about them? We have seven street maintenance crew. We have five equipment maintenance crew. We have a code enforcement officer. We have seasonal employees. We have graders, plows, dump trucks, rotaries. If you have a problem with a ticket or a towed vehicle, your best plan is to keep your vehicle off city streets. That simple. Keep the street clean, we don't get mean. Do the right thing, we won't ding your bling."

He was a fast talker, and he wasn't going to make it easy to butt in. So I made it harsh.

"Got it," I said. "I'm calling about the man and woman one of your machines chewed up and spit out at the snow dump."

He went silent for a bit. "That's just an urban legend."

"It happens to be a true story."

"I've got nothing to say."

I continued, "It'll be less talked about if you talk to me. I'm easy when you help. You want to obstruct, I'll have Commander Mallory call the mayor and the city manager and tell them how helpful Brann Crosen is to justice in this town."

Another pause. "What can I help you with?"

"I want to know about rotary security."

"We don't have any rotary security. We use them as needed and park them in the city yard when we're done. Not like somebody is going to steal a fifty-thousand-pound snowblower with the city logo painted on it."

"If one of your employees didn't borrow it for a little moonlighting, then I'd like to get your input on that. Tell me where to meet you in fifteen minutes."

More silence on the phone.

"Or Mallory can set up an appointment at the PD. Maybe they assemble a Grand Jury and grill you for a few weeks."

"I'm at the yard on Industrial Avenue," he said. He told me about the fence gate that looked locked with a padlock but really wasn't.

"See you in a few," I said.

I parked on the street, told Spot to be good, removed the unlocked padlock from its hasp, pushed through a rusted gate, and walked into the yard. There was a pole building open at the sides where there would normally be walls. I could hear Frank Sinatra singing "Nice Work If You Can Get It."

The place was a boneyard of large, rusted snow removal equipment, old hydraulic hoses and pumps, snow blades with broken mounts, bent impeller wheels, a transmission up on concrete blocks, an engine hoist, and a sand and salt spreader that was designed to be bolted onto the rear of a dump truck. Just to the side of the roofed area were two dump trucks that were next to a six-wheel grader that was missing a wheel, which was next to a rotary plow. The rotary was the size of a small train locomotive. Its huge corroded auger looked dangerous even with the machine turned off.

Frank's song was coming from a boombox over in one corner of the yard where a slim guy in his mid-thirties was working on a large, old differential and axle. He saw me and walked over.

"May I to help you?" He had a touch of Mexican accent.

"I'm looking for Brann Crosen."

"Oh. I am Emilio. Señor Crosen is to work in the small of the offices." He gestured.

"Thanks," I said.

Emilio walked back to his work and his boombox.

A man came out of a metal-clad building at the corner of the yard.

"Help you?" he said.

"Owen McKenna. We talked on the phone."

He wasn't a huge guy, but he obviously worked out with the aid of steroids. He stood about 5-8, and was broad enough at the chest that I guessed he could slap three forty-fives on each end of the bar and press three sets of six reps each. He looked at me the way a lion looks at a giraffe, a predator gauging his superiority over a larger but older and less capable animal. He knew I would be no threat if he had the rest of the gym-rats pride around him. But running solo made him wary. He didn't speak. Up close, I saw that he used a small touch of eyeliner on his eyes. Maybe there was some eyebrow shaping as well. He was clean shaven except for a little U-shaped line of hair that went from the corners of his mouth down and around the bottom of his chin. The effect didn't seem especially flattering, but what did I know. Maybe it was part of the body-builder thing. Maybe it drove body-builder groupies wild.

I pointed at the rotary. "How many of these blowers do you have?"

"Total? Or how many that work?"

"Working."

"Three. And one of the working three has a permanent case of the flu. Drive engine works great, but the blower engine gets emotional each time we use it. Lately, it's been running sixty forty against cooperation." He pointed out toward Emilio. "That's why we've got the Hispanic guy. He can make any engine run."

"Where are they now?"

He pointed to the one in front of me. "This is the one that doesn't work. It has more problems than we can fix. But buying new is out of the question." He patted the machine on the side of its intake housing. "These babies are spendy as a yacht."

Crosen turned and pointed to the far corner of the yard. "That one over there works, but it's waiting on another set of shear pins, and we ran out. The distributor sent pins for a hardware store blower. What were they thinking. The one with the flu is sidelined over on Emerald Bay Road. Fred's got the third working rotary up on Keller as we speak. Nice days like this give us a chance to catch up and clear out berms. Late April can still bring on serious dumps, so we don't let up until June."

"Do you know which rotary was used on the two victims?"

"We never noticed any rotary out of place. Everything's been business as usual for the last many weeks. I won't agree that one of our rotaries was the culprit. And anyway, the cops sent two guys around here to take samples or swabs or whatever you call it off the machines. Looking for DNA, I guess. I never heard that they found anything."

"The act of blowing snow kind of continuously cleans the machines out, doesn't it?"

He shrugged. "Probably."

"Do you ever clean them in any other way?"

"Sometimes when we accidentally scoop up mud and other debris, we hose them out."

"So a machine could chew up a person and not show it after, right?"

"I s'pose."

"Are there any rotaries around the south end of Tahoe that don't belong to the city?"

"Most don't. Douglas County hires private snow removal for their roads over on the Nevada side. Seems to me their contractor usually has one or two working the Nevada side all season. But the main rotary inventory belongs to Caltrans. They've got thirty-six of them for District Three, which includes Echo Summit and Donner Summit. Of those, quite a few rotate through the SLT sub shop."

"Do you know all of your drivers personally?"

"The city drivers, of course. Caltrans drivers, no, although I've met some."

"Have any of the city drivers ever been in trouble? Drug problems? Money problems?"

"Look, a guy who spends his nights crawling snow berms in a machine that kills your hearing and shakes your brain 'til your fillings fall out, isn't your typical soccer-coaching, church-going guy who takes his mother-in-law out to breakfast once a week. Even so, we've got drivers with families. A couple of them even go to church."

I could still hear Emilio's boombox. Frank was now singing "New York, New York."

"What about Caltrans drivers?" I asked.

"Like I said, I've met some. But there's a lot of guys. A woman, too, according to what I've heard. Although I can't imagine what kind of woman would want to drive one of these beasts. Yeah, the power's a rush, but the work sucks. You're constantly staring through a fogged-over windshield that's scratched and dulled, and you usually work during storms when you can barely see where you're going, and you mostly work at night when traffic and pedestrians are minimal, and you have to concentrate every second to make sure you don't hit someone walking their dog or some kid who's got earbuds cranked up so loud that they couldn't hear a ship's foghorn ten feet away. The stress from all that is crushing." Crosen paused. "Anyway, you could check with the Caltrans dorm here on the South Shore. They've got eighteen beds. A bunch of guys room and board there during snow removal season."

"Where is that dorm?"

"At the Caltrans maintenance station out in Meyers. They've got eight rotaries based out of that location, plus plow trucks, graders, sanders, loaders. Kind of like us only a lot bigger."

"In your opinion, if someone wanted to borrow a rotary for a short mission, how would they do it? Would they need to steal a key to the yard and sneak in at night or what?"

Crosen was shaking his head before I finished the sentence.

"It doesn't work like that. The world of snow removal doesn't have security like the TSA at airports. Sure, we try to keep track of our operations. But we send our drivers out night and day. They have a territory and a general plan of attack. But they need to adjust their route according to conditions. If they come upon a pile-up, they don't just sit there waiting for two hours until the wreckers clear it. There's too much work to do. So they change their plan and keep working. If they get stuck and their cell phone battery is dead from when they were lying in slush trying to fix a broken tire chain, or their machine is down from scooping up a manhole cover, they leave the rotary in the street and walk for help. Maybe they remember to lock the driver's door. Or maybe they're driving the one without door locks. There's no GPS tracking on these old rotaries. The city can't afford to know everything about every rotary at every hour. But the idea of someone taking one? That'd be like stealing a rhinoceros. Who'd want to? Whatever you wanted a rhino for, there'd have to be a lot easier way."

"Nevertheless, if someone saw an opportunity to borrow a rotary, use it as a murder weapon, and then put it back where he found it, it's possible that no one would even know. Someone could have even taken it out of this yard, for example. Right?"

Crosen was shaking his head. "You're suggesting something that is technically possible. But practically, I don't buy it. You'd have to have a lot of stars lined up to get away with it." Crosen's voice had risen, his agitation pronounced.

I was thinking about the timeline for the rotary murders. The previous day, Sanford Burroughs had told me that Darla had gone to work four days before and didn't return. I said to Crosen, "Can you look at your schedule for the period of three to five days ago and see if there were any rotaries near the snow dump?"

"Probably," he said. He turned and walked to a little metal shed that was tucked under a corner of the big open-sided pole building. I followed. We went inside. He pulled a homemade schedule pad off his desk and flipped back two pages. "Yeah, we had a rotary near the snow dump on each of those days. We also had a grader doing cleanup on the streets near the snow dump."

"What's cleanup?"

"After a storm, we attempt to clear all streets within twenty-four hours. If no other storms are on track for a follow-up dump, we go out and scrape the streets a second time to pick up ice and snow that's loosened in the sun, and we move the berms over another notch to widen the streets. When the streets are cleaned and the snow is bermed as high as the graders can push it, then we send out the rotaries. Only after the rotaries go through is our city back to the way we want it."

"Could one of your rotaries have been left unattended near the snow dump?"

"Sure, although that would be unusual."

"How hard is it to drive a rotary?"

"I know what you're really wondering," Crosen said. "Could your average Joe hop up into the cab on one of these things and drive it away? The answer is that it wouldn't be easy. Someone who has heavy equipment experience could figure out how to start the engines and shift. But learning how to drive and steer and run the blower and control two engines is a specialty skill. You would either need experience, or you'd have to have someone explain it in great detail."

"Could one research it? Study it online or something?"

"I suppose it's possible, but it seems unlikely. Here, take a look for yourself."

He walked me over to the parked rotary. "Go ahead, climb up the ladder and look inside. The door's open."

So I did. The only thing I recognized was the steering wheel. There were knobs and levers and sliders and switches and dials and gauges and odometer-styled readouts.

One item looked especially foreign.

I called down to Crosen. "What's this lever?" I pointed and leaned sideways so he could see.

"That's your rear steering joystick. You use it to set your crab angle. Four-wheel steering."

Despite the cockpit's complexity, it looked primitive. The machine was obviously very old. The glass on two separate dials was broken, fogged by a wavy bead of silicone glue. One switch was held in place with duct tape, another with yellow filament tape crispy with age. The metal dash had torn as if from flexing deep within the interior of the machine. The vinyl seat was cracked with exposed foam shedding yellow powder like dander.

I backed out of the door and climbed back down.

Crosen was gone. I looked around and saw him going back into the office in the metal building.

Over on Emilio's boombox, Frank had switched to "What Kind Of Fool Am I?"

I walked over and stuck my head in the door. "One more question, please. You ever hear of a woman named Scarlett Milo?"

"No," Crosen said, not paying much attention. He was bent over the desk, looking at a yellow slip of paper, like what you get on a triplicate form where the top copy is white, the next is yellow, and the last is pink. He was frowning.

"Find something?" I said.

"Rotary number four, the one Fred's got up on Keller."

"Yeah?"

He held up the yellow sheet. "This is a repair order. I remembered that this took place during the time you were talking about. When your urban legend victims supposedly died."

"What about it?"

"Rotary number four was sidelined over by the snow dump."

"What happened to it?"

Brann Crosen looked down at the yellow sheet. "One of the gauges showed no oil. Our driver assumed that there'd been a leak, and he worried that without oil, he'd burn out either the drive engine or the blower engine. On this order, it doesn't say which oil gauge was affected. But either engine would cost a fortune to replace if it was destroyed by running without oil. So he left the rotary on the side of the road."

"What happened?"

"It turns out that it hadn't sprung a leak. The sensor was down. The engines were okay."

"Which means," I said, "that someone could have borrowed the rotary, then put it back in the same place, and possibly no one knew what had happened. Passersby or local residents wouldn't have paid attention. The only people who would know the rotary was being borrowed were just your drivers, none of which were in the area."

Crosen didn't speak. He stared at the yellow sheet.

"Is there some other related info on that paper?" I asked.

After a time, he nodded. "Yeah. The notes by the repairman say that the wire to the sensor was severed."

"Meaning cut on purpose."

Crosen looked at me. "Yeah," he said.

TWENTY-TWO

When I was back in my Jeep and about to drive away from the city's yard, I got a call.

"Owen McKenna."

"This is Sanford Burroughs calling. Darla Ali's roommate." The man's voice wavered with what sounded like nervousness.

"I remember."

"When we talked yesterday, you asked me to call if I thought of anything else that might help you find Darla."

"Are you at home? I'm close to you. I can stop by in five minutes."

"Okay. See you soon."

As I drove to the house Sanford shared with Darla, I thought about whether I should give him the news that we believed we'd found evidence of her murder. I decided it wasn't appropriate to tell him until we knew for certain. I was willing to pass on the bad news, but only after Commander Mallory made it official.

I parked in the street and walked around to the stairway.

Sanford must have heard me on the stairs. He opened the door as I got to the top. I walked in. Sanford shut the door behind me, walked past me toward the barstool conversation area, about-faced, came back toward me, stopped. He didn't sit. He shifted his weight from one foot to another.

He said, "I remembered overhearing something Darla said when she was talking on the phone. It was a few days or so before she went missing. At the time, it seemed a little unusual but no big deal. I thought she was talking to her boss. But this morning, I realized it might be something entirely different, something that might connect to her going missing. I've been freaking out about this, trying to examine it like, you know, the way a detective would think about it. So I called you."

"What did she say on the phone?"

"Well, I don't remember her exact words. But it was something like, 'I don't want a fee, I want a percentage. I've worked hard at this. I deserve it.' Then, she said something like, 'If you don't agree to that, I might change our agreement. I don't care what you say. My contribution is worth it.' At the time I heard it, I just thought it was a conversation about work. Like she was, in effect, asking for a raise. But I was in my own world, plotting my takeover of the microbrew world in South Lake Tahoe. But when you stop to think about it, what waitress gets paid on a percentage basis? When I realized that this morning, it seemed obvious that she wasn't talking to her boss at all."

"Do you think this could have something to do with her going missing?"

Sanford hesitated. "I don't know. It's just that it seemed like she was disagreeing with the person on the phone, right? She wanted a percentage of whatever, and the other person just wanted to pay her a fee. So what if the disagreement was a bigger deal? Then maybe that other person did something that caused Darla to run away or get in trouble?"

"You look like you've got more to say," I said.

"Well, I told you before about how Darla liked to read about sunken treasure. About how she had fantasies of getting rich?"

"Yeah?"

"As soon as I thought about it, it seemed like what she said on the phone could have been about finding a treasure. I mean, doesn't it seem that way to you? The whole percentage thing?"

"Maybe."

"If she and this other person had found a treasure, and if they fought over how they would share the proceeds, then maybe it escalated into something big. Maybe Darla got hurt. Does that make sense?"

"I don't know, Sanford."

"I learned from Darla that sunken treasure is real. They find it all the time."

"I'll keep that in mind," I said. "I'm glad you called me."

"Do you think that could help you find her?" There was a lightness to Sanford's tone that suggested hope. But something about him seemed disingenuous. Maybe he was purposefully sounding hopeful. If so, that would suggest that he was trying to convince me that he didn't know she was already dead.

"Every bit of information is helpful," I said.

I thanked him and left.

TWENTY-THREE

After I left Sanford, Diamond called. "Wondering what happened with Adam Simms," he said.

"Simms woke up after his seizure, adjusted to his new surroundings with the help of Blondie, ate pizza with me, and told me that maybe God was punishing him for doing bad things."

"What bad things?"

"He wouldn't say."

"Are you concerned?" Diamond asked.

"Yeah. In the meantime, I just learned how the killer of Darla Ali and Sean Warner got the rotary plow he used on them. I should tell you about it."

"You want to meet?" Diamond asked.

"Yeah, let me check in with Street and Mallory. I'll call you back.

I started with Commander Mallory. He couldn't meet, so I told him that Brann Crosen found out that one of their rotaries had been sidelined near the snow dump around the time of the murders of Darla Ali and Sean Warner.

"Crosen say why? Mallory asked.

"Someone cut the wires to the oil gauge. Made it look like the machine couldn't be driven when, in fact, it could."

"Very interesting. Good work."

We talked some more, then hung up. I called Street, and she said that she was at a meeting on the West Shore, so we agreed to meet at the Beacon at Camp Rich on the South Shore, one of the few restaurants in Tahoe directly on the beach and a place that was central to our current locations. I called Diamond back, and he said he'd join us.

We three sat out on the deck and shared an order of calamari. Despite the cool air flowing off the lake, the spring sun of late April was still warm as it lowered toward the West Shore mountains. With the sun's rays on our faces and the beach free of snow, we could imagine the coming summer, something hard to do when up in the deep snow of higher elevations.

I brought Street and Diamond up to date on what I'd learned about Adam Simms and the rotary plows.

"So Adam Simms is a poet," Diamond said. "You get a chance to read any of his stuff?"

I shook my head. "No. But Felicite sort of quoted some lines from one of his poems. I can't remember them, but it seemed like real poetry. Not that I would know. It didn't rhyme."

Street smiled. "Nothing wrong with free verse. But it's harder to write because one has to make word music without the crutch of a rhyme structure."

I sipped beer. "Artists always need to make something new."

"Ain't new," Diamond said. "King James Bible was free verse. And when the Whitman dude wrote Leaves Of Grass, he supposedly used Biblical cadences."

"Shows what I know," I said. "What's the point of rhyme, then?"

"That's just one kind of structure," Street said. "Rhyme, meter, and other sound patterns."

"Simms talked about that," I said. "He called it prosody, the way prose sounds. It's more than just the meaning of the words. I guess you can get all that without rhyme."

"Rhyme's coming back, anyway," Diamond said. "Garrison Keillor's latest book of poems has a whole lotta rhyme."

Street took the tiniest bite of calamari and followed it with an even tinier taste of beer. Not that I minded because I usually got to eat and drink what she didn't finish.

"I tried to get Adam to talk a bit about his poetry, but I don't think he lets anyone read it."

Diamond said, "What did you think of his story about Scarlett calling him to warn him?"

"I can't make sense of it."

"The killer will try again, right?" Street's forehead was creased with worry. "He was probably shooting at you, not Felicite."

"I imagine so. Thanks to Diamond and his patron, Adam

and his dog are currently in the safe house on upper Kingsbury. And Felicite is presumably safe down in San Francisco. If I'm careful, I'll be safe, too."

"You've found a correlation between the two women victims," Diamond said. "Both had interest in the Italian Renaissance. What's next?"

"I don't know."

Street spoke. "Any chance you asked Mr. Simms about the note Scarlett wrote you?"

"Yup. No luck. He'd never heard of a medic's BFF. Neither had Felicite."

"Can I see your copy of the note again?" Diamond said.

I pulled it out.

"Medic's BFF," he said as he read it. "What're these blackish smudges?"

"There was blood on the original."

I saw Street wince.

Diamond handed the note to Street.

She looked at it, then carefully smoothed it out on the table as if pressing it might reveal its secrets.

I looked up and saw Diamond staring at Street and the note, which was upside down from his perspective.

I looked back at the note. Something about it gave me a new thought.

"Let me see that again," I said, reaching out my hand.

Street handed it to me.

I turned it around. "Her handwriting is a hybrid of sorts, printed letters with little embellishments," I said. "But this apostrophe..." I pointed at the apostrophe in the word 'medic's.' "This is just a copy, but even so, when I look close, the apostrophe doesn't seem to have even a hint of a curve at the top."

Street said, "Lots of people just make a short, vertical mark for an apostrophe."

"Right." I pointed to the note. "But look at the little entry curve as she wrote the letter M. And the exit curve on the D. The style of the other letters would suggest a curved apostrophe like a small, cursive, numeral nine."

Diamond was staring at the note. "What's your point?"

"I'm wondering if Scarlett wasn't making an apostrophe at all, but some other letter that she didn't finish. A letter that begins with a short downstroke."

"She'd had her neck shattered by gunshot," Diamond said. "Makes sense her handwriting wouldn't be very polished."

"Of course. But the rest of the letters are completely formed, even if shaky."

"If not an apostrophe, what unfinished letter might she have intended to write?" Street asked.

"Considering the context," I said, "the little mark may not have been an apostrophe at all but a truncated I."

"You're thinking that she may have meant to write Medicis." Diamond pronounced the last syllable like 'cheese.'

"Exactly," I said.

Street said, "The premier family of the Italian Renaissance!"

"Right," I said. "Even a humble ex-Homicide Inspector knows of them. Scarlett Milo had lots of books on the Italian Renaissance, including some books on the Medicis."

Diamond reached out for the note. I handed it to him. He stared at it. "Now that you've pointed it out, I can't see this note as Medic's BFF, I can only see Medicis BFF."

"You've probably read about them, too, right?" I said.

"Everybody has," Diamond said in an astonishing over-estimation of general awareness. "They were art patrons, bankers, and city leaders in Florence," Diamond said. "They ruled the city for over a hundred years. And four of the Medicis were elected Pope. Without them, Italian history would be radically different. The Renaissance as we know it might not have even existed."

"That's a grand statement," I said, fully aware that Diamond, more than anyone I knew, had the knowledge to make such grand statements with confidence. "I'm curious about that. The Renaissance was basically an explosion of art, right? How could a single family be so critical to that development?"

"Because the Medicis more or less invented secular art patronage," Diamond said. "Prior to them, art was mostly done for the church or had other religious purposes. Artists were selected and paid by the church to produce art that glorified God, and, before Christianity, multiple gods. That was the main purpose of art. The idea that someone might enjoy art for a non-religious reason was rare. Along came the Medicis, who were the richest family in Europe. They asked artists to make sculptures and paintings that often had little to do with religion. They were narcissistic and wanted portraits of themselves, of course. But they also wanted other beautiful, non-religious art for their walls and gardens and places of business. This concept of leaving religion out of art was on par with the tenth century Chinese invention of making paintings without people in them, thus inventing landscape painting."

Diamond finished his beer, then made another pronouncement. "The Medicis were as important to art as the greatest artists they promoted, Michaelangelo and da Vinci, for example. For without the Medicis, those artists and many others would never have been discovered or hired to make their art in the first place."

"If what you are suggesting is true," Street said, "that Scarlett was really writing the word Medicis, does that suggest any meaning for BFF?"

"Got me," Diamond said. He looked at Street.

"If the Medicis had a best friend forever, who might that be?" Street asked.

"Ain't that brushed up on my Medici knowledge," Diamond said. "Botticelli, maybe. Did a bunch of portraits of the Medici dudes."

Street pulled out her phone and tapped at it. We waited. "When I Google Medicis BFF without any apostrophe," she said, "I get nothing specific that would pertain to this note."

"Not surprised," Diamond said. "BFF is current-day idiom. Even if the family did have a best friend, it's likely no one has written about that using the BFF acronym."

"It can't be that hard to find a Medici Renaissance expert who might know," I said. "I could go to UNR and ask. You think they have a Medici Studies department?"

Both Street and Diamond grinned.

"Maybe Renaissance Studies," Diamond said.

"Wait." Street was frowning, looking inward. "When I was in grad school at Berkeley, I knew a woman who was pursuing her doctorate in Classics. She worked as a teaching assistant in Greek and Latin literature classes. Her name was Olga Decker."

We waited as Street worked her phone. By the speed of her finger motions, it was obvious that her tech skill set was closer to that of a kid than a slow adult.

Diamond commented. "Woman's good with her thumbs."

"Sure, but can she work an Underwood?" I said.

"Your specialty," he said. "But the same stimulus that causes someone else to dial up their thermostat causes you to reach for a wood-splitting maul. Not sure you're living in the appropriate century."

"Definitely not."

Street was still doing the thumb dance. Her rhythms were more like jazz than classical, I thought. It occurred to me that I'd never noticed if her other rhythms fit that mold. I started thinking about the activities where her rhythms were most pronounced.

"Okay," Street said, interrupting my thoughts. "Olga Decker is currently on sabbatical but is spending it in the Berkeley area. She's trying to reserve all of her Sabbatical days for writing, but she says you can always call and leave her a message."

"Wait, are you saying you and she have just texted back and forth?"

Street gave me the grin that made me think of a certain king-sized bed in a Hawaiian condo with a large lanai out the slider and crashing waves beyond that. "There's a lot you could learn from me," she said.

"No argument there."

I found a pen and was going to write Olga Decker's contact information on a paper napkin when Street said she'd already emailed it to me. So I thanked her and kissed her and stood up.

I put money down for the bill, and we left.

TWENTY-FOUR

We'd come in separate vehicles, so I said goodbye to both of them and joined Spot in the Jeep. My vehicle had been parked in the shade as twilight descended, so I let it warm up as I dialed Olga Decker's number. She'd just been available to text Street, so it might be my best chance to get her on a phone call.

She answered fast. "Street Casey texted me your name, so I white-listed Owen McKenna in my contacts folder. Otherwise, your call would have gone directly to the phone call composting heap, there to rot in company with telemarketing pitches."

Whatever I expected a Classics scholar to say, it wasn't that.

I gave Olga a brief explanation of my current job investigating a murder that may have a connection to the Medicis of Italian Renaissance days.

"Quite the extravagant proposition," she said. "Entertaining, at least, if not realistic."

"Could you spare a few minutes sometime in the next few days?"

"Well, I'm on writing sequester. Can't you talk right now? I can spare a couple of minutes."

"Yes, of course. Here's my situation. I need to solve a puzzle, and I very much hope you can help. Two women and a man were murdered. As one of the victims was shot and lay dying, she wrote two words on a note. 'Medicis BFF.' That woman and one of the other victims were enthusiastic about the Italian Renaissance. Before they were killed, I believe they were excited about something connected to the Renaissance. I'm trying to figure out what Medicis BFF refers to."

I could hear Olga Decker breathing. "Some of my students use BFF as an acronym for best friend forever."

"Right."

"Which has nothing to do with usage in the era of the Medicis. So if this is really about the Medicis, the woman who wrote the note was probably referring to something other than best friend forever."

"And whatever that thing is," I said, "it's possible it was motive for the murders."

"I can't help you," she said. "I could teach a four-credit course on the Medici family, but this is meaningless to me."

"Can you point me toward someone who might be of help?"

"I can point you to lots of people, but I have no belief that you would find anyone who knows more than I."

"I'd like to ask anyone I can find," I said.

"Okay, here's a remote possibility. Two years ago, I had an exchange student named Antonella Porto from Florence, the epicenter of the Medici family dynasty and the most important town of the Italian Renaissance. This student often referred to a legendary professor she had at the University of Florence, a man who, like some of Berkeley's finest scholars and me, believes it is good to reach down and teach intro classes to freshmen and sophomores. It's remedial work, believe me, but it is eye-opening to see where young college students are in their nascent brain development."

"Does this professor specialize in the Renaissance?"

"More than that. Antonella said that, in Italy, he is considered the foremost Medici scholar in the world. Of course, whether that is true or not, I don't know. As with most careers, the reputations of professors are made more on the basis of their charisma than on their knowledge."

"Did your exchange student mention his name?"

"Oh, you wouldn't believe. It was as if she belonged to a cult, and this man was the leader they worshiped. She mentioned him constantly. I've never heard such fawning adoration. His name is Drago. Professore Giovanni Drago. The name stuck with me because of its Italian meaning of Dragon. Believe me when I say that I was glad to have Antonella go back to Italy just so that I would never have to hear her say his name again."

"Any idea how I would contact this Professor Drago?"

"You mean phone number and email? No. Antonella Porto made him sound like royalty. You're not going to get royalty on the phone, are you. Now maybe if you speak Italian, you could make some international phone calls. But to hear Ms. Porto tell it, you would probably have to visit. And when you get off the plane, just ask for Professor Drago. Surely, everyone in all of Italy knows this celebrity."

"You don't like this guy very much, do you?"

"I've seen professors with that kind of popularity in this country. They are all self-aggrandizing jerks who care more about the attentions of the cute students, male or female, than they do about the quality of their writing, their lectures, or their research."

"If there isn't an easy way to contact Drago, what about contacting Antonella Porto?"

"Well, I certainly don't carry her number around in my head. I suppose you could go to the university and ask the other students coming and going. Or you could Google her. That probably works as well for Italian girls as for American girls. They're all addicted to their Facebook presentations. But I've gone overtime. I have to go."

"Thanks for your help," I said as she hung up.

TWENTY-FIVE

The next morning, I got busy on the phone and on the computer, trying every way I could think of to contact Professor Drago in Italy. But I could find no number or email. Neither could I find anyone who would confess to knowing him and be willing to take him a message. Nor could I find contact info for his student Antonella Porto.

Frustrated, I headed over to Street's bug lab. Her VW beetle was parked in front. She answered my knock, opening the door with one hand and holding a jar of white rice in the other. Spot pushed in past her, exploring the thousand scents of bugs, which, I knew from experience, are not like the scents of flowers.

"Lunch?" I said, looking at her jar of rice. "Oh, I guess not. The rice is moving."

"Maggots," she said, "endlessly offering themselves for science. And by the way, maggots have much more protein than rice. Many people around the world eat them. It's considered a delicacy in some cultures."

"Not my culture." I stepped past her, giving wide berth to her jar.

"Don't be scared," she said. "It's not like they're going to bite you."

"So you say. You were wrong once before."

"Really? When was I wrong?"

"When you said I'd like Brussels sprouts better than cheeseburgers."

"That was clearly a joke," she said. "Hyperbole in pursuit of levity, which I hoped would lead to a playful, open-minded desire to try new foods."

"Yes," I said. "I did try Brussels sprouts. And I might even like them if they were grilled and covered with melted cheese and lots of barbecue sauce."

"Which is made of high fructose corn syrup. The whole point of Brussels sprouts is that they're healthy."

"As are maggots, so says you. Doesn't mean I'll eat them."

"Stuck in your ways," Street said.

"That's good, because I'm stuck on you, too."

Street set down her jar and hugged me. "Thanks."

Spot saw us and immediately came over and thrust his nose between us, wedging us apart.

"Spot, can't you see I'm trying to hug my sweetheart?"

He wagged.

Street let go of me and bent a bit so she could hug Spot.

"He wants in on the love," she said.

"He wants you to hug him instead of me. And it's working."

"Yeah, he's effective at this amore business. Everybody loves him."

Spot was still wagging.

"Speaking of amore," I said, "wanna take a trip with me to the amore capital of the world?"

Street let go of Spot and straightened up. "Are you going to Italia?"

"Your charming friend Olga said that the foremost Medici expert in the world is Professore Giovanni Drago, and he lives and works in Florence. I believe Scarlett Milo would want me to spend her funds investigating the Medicis up close. I also think she'd recognize that I would need an assistant on my travels."

"Will I be assisting with amore as well?"

"Part of your duties, sì."

"When would we leave?" Street asked.

I looked around at the shelves of jars of bugs in Street's laboratory. "As soon as you can tear yourself away from your beloved companions."

"How long would we be gone?"

"Don't know. Just a few days. Adam is in the safehouse. I worry about leaving him for very long. But his stepsister Felicite says he has seizures roughly every two weeks, so he's probably okay for a bit."

"Have you appointed yourself protector of an athlete who - what did you say - is the size of a piano and can sprint like a race car?"

"Kinda," I said. "He needs it when someone is trying to burn him and shoot at him."

"I thought the shooter was aiming for his sister or you."

"Yeah, but I also consider Adam a shooting target by association."

"Well," Street said, thinking. "It would take me some time to tie up loose ends, catch up on email, and get this place ready before I could travel overseas." She looked around at her lab.

"So when do you think you could leave?"

"Probably not until tomorrow."

"That long?" I said. She was amazing. "Okay, I'll put off leaving until then."

TWENTY-SIX

After Street's agreement to join me, I once again looked up Antonella Porto, Olga Decker's exchange student.

I found no contact information, but there were several Facebook pages and other websites with information on multiple Antonellas. One seemed especially promising as it mentioned her fascination with the Medicis of Florence. The same page also referred to her job at a Florentine restaurant called Trattoria da Tacito. I was able to find a phone number for the restaurant. But when I dialed, I got no answer. I'd have to pursue it when we got to Florence.

I called my bank and had them overnight in some Euros, and I reserved a pair of roundtrip tickets online. Diamond's schedule for the next week was too heavy down in Carson Valley for him to babysit His Largeness up at my cabin, but he agreed to take Spot in at his abode.

The next morning, Street and Spot and I made the trip up and over Kingsbury Grade and down to Minden in Carson Valley. When Diamond opened his front door, Spot raced around Diamond's yard to show his excitement, no doubt enjoying the feeling of grass instead of high altitude ice and snow between his toes. Spot didn't even notice when we said goodbye and drove off, his standard reaction when faced with the prospect of hanging out with Diamond, the man who'd introduced him to danishes.

To get to Europe, Street and I first had to fly the opposite direction from Reno to Los Angeles on a small jet, rickety with age. The plane shook as if it were shivering from the cold at 35,000 feet, and the metallic banging from within its walls was so loud that the only possible source of noise was a hundred loose bolts bouncing around the plane's ribs. At LAX, we waited for three hours, then walked onto a newer 747 stretch that was bigger than many ships. The plane spent an inordinate amount of time getting its lumbering bulk up to speed before it gradually lifted off and climbed up over the Pacific. The pilot put the beast into a big banking turn and held it until we were cruising northeast, the shortest route to Europe from L.A., going nearly over the North Pole. We flew into nighttime as we crossed the northern Rockies, cruised starlit skies across Hudson Bay and on to Greenland, then saw dawn as we came back southeast toward Ireland and Great Britain. After eleven hours and nine time zones in the air, we dropped down into Frankfurt and changed back onto another rattle-shake oldster for the third leg of our trip to Florence.

Soon after we crossed the glaciers that scoured the north slopes of the Swiss, French, and Italian Alps, we dropped down over the long, twisting waters of Lake Como and then out across the verdant fields of Northern Italy. There were sixteen shades of green in the patchwork of vineyards and forest and hay fields and vegetable farms. Stone farmhouses and barns dotted the landscape. As we descended closer to the ground, we saw sheep and pigs and horses. On the top of every tall hill were castles and churches in fortress towns. Rarely did we see any building that didn't look hundreds of years old. Eventually, the rural land began to disappear under a profusion of structures. In the distance we could see the dome of the big famous church that was the center of Florence, the most significant of Northern Italy's medieval city state towns.

Our first indication that Florence has one of the world's shortest runways came when the captain publicly announced his concern about local rain showers and muttered that if the runway was wet he needed to know in advance so he could detour to Bologna. Apparently, the landing strip had dried enough, and he put the plane down in a quick-stop maneuver that was so hard and abrupt that it was like landing on an aircraft carrier and being caught by the cable that jerks you to a stop just before you pitch off the deck into the high seas. Our pilot knew his stuff, and our plane stopped rolling with an easy 15 or 20 feet to spare before the end of the runway.

Florence has no taxiway, so the plane about-faced and rolled halfway back down the runway before it turned off and parked on a lot not much bigger than the tarmac at a modern American gas station. We walked down the gangway stairs into spring Tuscan sunshine that was noticeably softer than Tahoe's high-altitude scorch torch. Although Florence is farther north than Tahoe, it sits at much lower elevation, so there was no snow. Unlike the dry air of the Sierra, the Tuscan air was humid, and on the moist breeze were luscious floral scents over the verdant smells of the vineyards in the surrounding countryside.

The bus driver must have been a dodge'em-car champion. He threaded the big coach through medieval streets that had been generously built so that two people could walk abreast. I stared as he raced past ancient stone walls and signs and bicycles with margins of two inches. When the bus stopped at the Florence train station, 21 hours after we left Tahoe, we were happy to get off and begin transporting ourselves in that oldest, slowest, and most healthful way, the movement of walking a relief after the sarcophagus-sized space of mass transit seats.

We'd walked for only ten minutes when we came to the church that is shown in every depiction of Florence and was featured in an article in the airline magazine. It was huge and decorated with hundreds of impressive sculptures that nestled in little nooks on the outer walls. I'd learned from the article that the church, like much of Florence, was built during the Renaissance, which made it about 600 years old, the approximation of date necessary because those slow-poke Renaissance construction workers took over one hundred years to haul and carve and hand cut and stack all that stone. The church was bathed in golden light giving it a pink glow against the cerulean blue of the sky as the afternoon moved toward dusk.

"The duomo is something," Street said.

"Duomo?"

"The Italian word for church."

"Oh, right. I saw that in the magazine," I said.

"Look at the crowds. And this is the off season." Street gestured toward the masses holding up their phones to take pictures.

"Yeah. Old sells," I said. "I thought our Spanish missions in California were old at two hundred forty years, but I guess that age wouldn't impress these tourists."

"I'm pretty sure most people think gigantic stone temples are more impressive than little wood and mud-brick missions."

"Ah," I said.

We turned down a side street. There was a nice doorway in a plain stone building, and on the wall was a little sign that said Residenza.

"You think this is a hotel?" Street asked.

"We could ask inside."

I pulled open a huge wooden door with a brass doorknob in its center, and we walked into a small marble entry. A dark, narrow passage went back, and a well-lit stairway with an ornate cast iron railing rose up to the side.

"Your choice," I said.

"Up," Street said.

We took the stairs. A second floor hallway led past several doors to a small room with a desk.

"Buon giorno," a woman said.

"Parla inglese, per favore?" Street said.

"Sì," the woman said and then spoke rapid-fire Italian.

Street said a few Italian words mixed with English words. I heard "hotel" and "rooms" and the other woman spoke more fast Italian and they nodded and gestured and eventually Street turned to me and said, "Do you want this on your credit card?"

"It's an expense that Scarlett Milo is covering postmortem, so yes," I said as I pulled out my card, and the two women made the transaction. When they were done, the woman gave Street an actual metal key that inserts into a lock, and Street said "Grazie mille" twice.

Street turned to me. "We're on the second floor." She walked back down the hallway and headed up the next flight of stairs.

"You said we were on the second floor. We already came up one flight."

"Right. This is Italia. The second floor is the third floor."

"Then where is the third floor?"

"On the fourth floor," she said.

We hiked up the stairs. "How did you know how to say all those Italian words?" I asked.

"When you were watching the movie on the plane, I was reading the phrase book."

"Always the perfect student," I said.

Our room was large and spare and beautiful, and had a polished oak floor, a fifteen-foot ceiling, crown moulding, heavy velvet drapes, and a partial view of the duomo out the tall narrow windows. "Ain't like no Holiday Inn," I said.

"Ain't indeed," Street said. "How lovely."

We showered and headed out to wander the city and find dinner and libation in the form of pizza and Chianti.

The next morning, I got out the sheet on which I'd printed a Google map of the address for Trattoria da Tacito.

"Tell me again about this restaurant?" Street said.

"It was on a Facebook page that mentioned Antonella Porto, the exchange student I learned about from Olga Decker in Berkeley. Apparently, Trattoria da Tacito is where Antonella works."

Street nodded and went into the bathroom.

I noticed that I'd printed the map at a large scale, so there were no street names anywhere near the little Google teardrop marker. The only thing to go on was the irregular pattern of streets and blocks that were all different shapes and sizes. I spread out the big store-bought map of Florence to compare with the Google map.

After a minute, Street came out of the bathroom, saw me staring at the map, and said, "Need help?"

I looked up. She was slipping a turquoise hairclip into her hair. It matched the turquoise of the lacy camisole that snugged around her torso and hung from string-sized shoulder straps. It also matched the turquoise underpants that were a design exercise in how to construct clothing using the least amount of fabric.

"If you don't put on more clothes," I said, "you're the one who will need help restraining me. But if you do put on more clothes, then no one will know how color-coordinated your underthings are."

"You will know."

"That's the problem," I said. "How am I gonna focus on detecting?"

Street pulled on a thin, loose, drapey black sweater and tight black, elastic pants. She slipped her bare feet into pointy black shoes not much more substantial than ballet slippers. Last, she put on a silver necklace from which hung a tiny turquoise pendant.

"Better?" she said.

"Yes and no. Come help me with this map, but stand a little behind me so I can concentrate."

She came near. She emanated the tiniest aroma of freesias.

I pointed to the maps. "No street names came through on the small map I printed. So I thought I could find the street shapes on the big map and tell where to go. But it's like a jigsaw puzzle."

"Those shapes are right here." Street pointed.

"How did you find that so quick?"

"I have a Ph.D. in Entomology."

"Learning about bugs teaches you map reading?"

"Yes, actually," she said. "The patterns of Italian streets are like the tunnels and galleries that bark beetles carve under tree bark. Confusing, senseless, and utterly captivating. Anyway, half the streets on the big map don't have names, either."

"More frustration than captivation," I said.

"You need to get in touch with your inner Italian romantic," Street said. "Come on. We'll find the restaurant by exploring." She hung her passport pouch around her neck, slipped it under her sweater, picked up her little turquoise clutch, and moved to the door.

TWENTY-SEVEN

We walked down the block toward the duomo.
At the corner, I opened up my map and compared it to the church and the adjacent roads. "The church is tall. So if we get lost, we can always come back to it, right? It will be our center, like a homing beacon."

"And keep us safe," Street said.

"You're making fun of me."

"No, but you do sound a little like a priest," she said.

"Maybe I'm in the wrong line of work," I said.

"Maybe. But if you were a priest, you wouldn't have the opportunity to appreciate how the color of my lingerie coordinates."

"There's a deal breaker."

"Not all priests obey the rules about celibacy," Street said.

"I'd have to be discreet," I said, "and only admire you in public from afar. Then we'd arrange to meet in the secret catacombs for…" I paused.

"Closer admiration?" Street said.

"I was thinking of different words, but yeah."

We walked down a block. I checked the map. Turned and pointed. Walked down another block where I checked the map again.

"You're advertising your tourist status to the whole world," Street said.

"I am a tourist."

We continued the process and worked our way into a labyrinth of Florentine passageways south of the big church. We went down streets that dead-ended, streets that doubled back in a U shape, streets that were only seven feet wide. At every corner we looked for street names. At most, there were none. Occasionally, there was a stone plaque on a building with a street name carved in it, probably from 600 years ago. Twice we followed a street and saw yet another stone plaque on the same street but with a different name.

"I think this one might be it," I said, pointing to the map. "See the way it turns at a slight angle to the left here, and then it makes a hard right?"

"Right," Street said, "which means we've walked most of a big circle. Good to get exercise. Here's number sixty-three."

We were looking for number 39. I checked the map.

We walked down the next block. Most doorways had no number. Street pointed to a navy blue door about halfway down the next block. "There it is."

There was a small sign above the door that said Trattoria da Tacito.

We went in.

There was a man behind a counter. He spread his arms wide and made a little bow. "Buon giorno," he said.

""Buon giorno," Street repeated. "We're looking for Antonella Porto. Is she here?"

"Sì." He grinned and pointed back toward the kitchen. "I am Sylvio, and I will be your host with a smile, and I have this nice table here, no? Antonella would love to be your waitress." He grinned some more, came around the counter and ushered us to the table. He pulled out a chair for Street. "Antonella is the best in Florence. Our food is the best in Florence. And you will smile when you are eating!"

The man walked back toward the kitchen, called out, and returned with a young woman who had short black hair over white skin and a scattering of freckles behind round, wire-rimmed spectacles. She looked more like the Irish than the olive-skinned Italians. "Please meet Antonella," Sylvio said.

"Hi," Antonella said, nodding and smiling.

He talked to her in Italian and, with just a little input from Street, it was decided that we would have the house specialty, some kind of pasta and grilled vegetables. Sylvio waited at the table while Antonella wrote down our order.

"Can you recommend a good wine?" I asked Sylvio after Antonella went back to the kitchen.

Sylvio opened a wine menu and pointed at the selections. "Of course, there is the Chianti Classico that our region is famous for. But if you want a wine to really make you smile, you might try the Brunello from just to the south of here."

Street saw the Brunello on the menu and raised her eyebrows.

Sylvio was standing sideways to Street. He winked at me with the eye that Street couldn't see. "Is very good for amore," he said.

"Brunello it is," I said.

Sylvio grinned as he left.

"Sixty-eight euros," Street said. "Twice the Chianti Classico. Is amore that important?" Her mouth hinted at a Mona Lisa smile.

"There's nothing more important."

Sylvio came back with the Brunello and made a show of having me taste it and then pouring it into two large wine glasses. His performance was over-the-top, but he exuded charm, and I could see that when tourists went home to Iowa, they would remember their meal at Trattoria da Tacito better than they would remember the duomo.

Street and I chatted while we waited. The Brunello was excellent. The wait stretched out to twenty minutes. Sylvio returned two different times to refill my wine glass and add two drops to Street's.

I leaned to the side to better see the kitchen, wondering if they'd had to go pick the vegetables, and harvest and grind the wheat to make the pasta.

"Italians don't rush," Street said. "They take it easy. Slow meals. Two or three hours off in the middle of the workday. It's like low blood pressure is the national goal."

"What about the twenty-five percent of tourists who expire waiting for food," I said.

Street grinned like Sylvio. "That still leaves odds of three out of four that you'll make it."

Antonella brought our first course, which was delicious red and green peppers, zucchini, and eggplant.

After we'd eaten, Antonella brought us a second course of

pasta in a cheese sauce. She asked in perfect American English if our meals were okay. She gave us a gap-toothed smile as she spoke.

I answered. "The food is great, thank you. We actually came here on the recommendation of someone you know."

She raised her eyebrows.

"I understand that you were once an exchange student at UC Berkeley. I spoke to one of your professors, Olga Decker, when I was doing a little research on the Medici family. Ms. Decker told me about you and said that we should look you up if we came to Florence."

"Oh, how nice to meet you."

Street and I introduced ourselves.

"How is Professor Decker?" As Antonella said it, her tone was so harsh she might have asked after Street's maggots.

"Very well," I said. "She also told me that you know a Medici scholar named Giovanni Drago."

"Oh, just barely. In my second year at the University of Florence, I took two classes from Professor Drago. My focus was viticulture, but the university thinks that even grape growers should know the history of Florence. Any class on the history of Florence is naturally focused on art history. And a big part of Florentine art history is the history of the Medici family. As we learn here, the Medicis rocked Florence."

"Can you tell me how to locate Professor Drago?"

"I suppose you could ask at the university. It's not far from here. The duomo is that way." She pointed toward the side wall of the trattoria. "And the university is just three blocks north of the duomo. It's at the Piazza San Marco."

"Do you know where the faculty offices are? Or is there another office where we should ask about him?"

"There is a reception desk. They will help you. Professor Drago is a full-time professore, so he…" she stopped, thinking. "Wait. Once per session, he brings his class to his house where he has several notable sculptures and paintings and quite the art library. He owns a small Giotto fresco that came from a church that collapsed. And he showed us his copy of da Vinci's Codex Leicester. That's the one that the Microsoft guy, Bill Gates, owns. It's the most expensive book in the world. It's not like the professor's copy is so special. After all, you can see all seventy-two pages online. But the professore wants his students to see what an art-focused life is like. So he brings all his students to his house to hang out among his art treasures for an afternoon. Anyway, I probably still have the address in my phone. Can you wait?"

"Of course."

Antonella went back toward the kitchen. She returned with her phone, scrolling and tapping on the screen. "Here it is." She angled the phone toward me. "Do you want me to text you?"

"Let me give you my number," Street said. "Owen is still learning how to work his phone." Street stated her number.

Antonella typed it in and tapped the phone. "There. I don't know how fast a text gets to an American number when the phone is over here in Italy, but…"

Street's phone chimed. She picked it up and looked at the screen. "Got it," she said.

"Between that address and the university, you should be able to find him."

"Thanks so much," I said.

When we were done eating, I left Antonella a good tip and thanked Sylvio for a great meal.

"Grazie mille," he said, smiling, spreading his arms wide, then taking a bow.

As we walked away, I said, "Charming guy."

Street said, "That's the essence of the Italian personality."

"Where do you think we should try finding Drago? The university?"

Street looked at the time. "It's already the middle of the afternoon. I'm guessing that most professors would be heading home soon if they haven't already."

"His home first, then."

Two blocks down, we saw a cab and waved, but it didn't stop. Another block, another cab, which also ignored my wave.

"I think I remember reading that you don't flag down taxis in Italy," Street said. "You have to go to a taxi stand."

"How do we find that?"

"I have no idea," she said.

"Didn't you once get a ride with that Uber app on your phone? Could we use that?"

"I did it back in San Francisco where Uber started," Street said. "But I don't know about Italy. There was some big transit strike in Europe because the taxi drivers don't like Uber. I heard it practically shut down France."

"Wait, you're saying that because some tech guy in San Francisco came up with a ride app, the result was that transit was crippled in a country on the other side of the ocean?"

"Yeah."

"Write an app, change the world, get rich," I said. "I wonder if I could've been a techy."

"Were you the smartest kid in your college?" Street asked.

"I had to get extra credits just to graduate from preschool."

"There's your answer."

So we walked about a mile before we found a taxi stand. There were four other groups in line. After ten minutes, we were in a cab. Street showed the driver her phone with Professore Drago's address.

"Please take us there," Street said.

The man nodded, spoke back, sped off.

Taxis in Florence are a dance with danger. We jerked around corners, dashed in front of fast-moving buses, screeched the brakes on many occasions, some of which even involved stopping. We went over a bridge that crossed the Arno River. In the distance down the river was the Ponte Vecchio Bridge, covered with multiple stories of shops suspended above the water. As the turns multiplied and the streets flashed by, it felt like we were in a maze.

Eventually, the driver pulled over and pointed at the doors across the street. None of them had numbers that I could see.

I pointed out the window. "Where?"

The man turned toward the back seat and pointed at Street's phone, which she was still holding.

"Dove è il numero di casa?" Street said.

The man pointed again at several doorways across the street and spoke many Italian words.

"La porta blu?" Street said.

"Rossa, rossa."

"The red door," I said, slowly catching on.

"Sì."

"Grazie," Street said as she opened the car door.

When we were out of the cab, Street pointed to a huge building a block or two over. "That's the Pitti Palace," she said.

"What's that?"

"Today, it's basically a giant museum. Back in the Renaissance, it was one of the Medici residences."

"That giant place was one of their houses," I said.

"Right."

"Yikes," I said.

Street turned around to the place we'd come to see and the rossa doorway the cab driver had pointed at.

The building was like many others in Florence. It was made of stone and was unembellished except for a shiny magenta-glazed, wall-mounted pot that held red geraniums the same color as the red door. We walked over to the door.

As I was about to knock, the door opened and a man walked out. He was tall and thin and dressed neatly but in drab colors. I guessed him at about seventy.

"Professor Drago?" I said.

He stopped on the sidewalk and looked at me. The expression on his face was the one that movie stars save for paparazzi.

"We'd like to ask you a question about the Medicis," I said, thinking that there was a decent chance a professor would speak English. "Could you please spare a minute?"

"No. I'm busy," he said in perfect BBC English. He shook his head and walked away.

"Could we talk to you later this evening?"

He spoke over his shoulder as he walked away from us. "If you want to know about the Medicis, go to the library."

"Please, I'm only asking for a minute."

Without turning back toward us, he lifted a hand and made an abrupt wave as if to flick off a troublesome insect.

"Well, that didn't go too smoothly," Street said.

"Let's wait a bit, then follow him," I said in a quiet voice.

Street looked at me. "What's the point? What if he's going on a long walk?"

When he got down toward the end of the block, I started walking after him, but I lagged, allowing the distance between us to increase.

"There was something furtive in the way he looked around when he came out of the doorway," I said.

Street turned away from me and looked at the man as we walked. She frowned. "Furtive," she said. "I didn't sense that. Is that a detective thing? Can you read people at a more nuanced level than ordinary mortals?"

"Maybe if I'm sensing fear or anxiety or bad intentions."

"Like predator or prey," Street said. "The emotions connected to the criminal world."

"Yeah."

"So you want to follow him? Because of a single look?"

"That, and I'm put off that he wouldn't talk to us."

"It's about a bruised ego."

"A little. I've learned to go on instinct. When I want information from someone, and that someone acts in a certain way, I've learned to watch and see what I can learn."

"Because you might get some leverage," Street said.

"Maybe."

Up ahead, the man went around a corner, out of our sight. I picked up our pace. We came around the corner. The professore was down the block.

"Which of those predator/prey emotions did that man have?"

"I'm not sure. Anxiety mixed with anticipation."

"That's quite the subtle observation."

I shrugged.

Drago went down several more blocks, heading toward the center of Florence. At one intersection, we could see the duomo in the far distance. The man turned another corner and went into a small shop. There were some angled bins in front of the shop that were filled with oranges and apples and melons. We stopped a half block away on the other side of the street. We stood so that a van was between us and the shop. We could still see the shop entry, but we were largely obscured by the van.

A couple came out of the shop. They each carried a bag. A baguette protruded from one. A camera hung around the neck of the man, and the woman held up her phone to take a picture of the fruit display in front of the shop. Tourists. A man went into the shop, followed by another tourist couple. A young woman walked up. She looked unusual in that, despite the warm sunny day, she wore what looked like a light frock over her clothes, and she carried a pair of spike heels, her fingers hooked through the little straps. She glanced up at the windows in the stone wall above the shop, then went inside. The second tourist couple came out. They carried a bag of chips, and the man carried two large bottles of beer. Another man came out of the shop, carrying nothing.

Street said, "It sure is easy to tell the tourists from the locals."

"Yeah," I said. "The tourists come out with groceries, and the locals don't."

As I said it, two young women came out. They each wore a lightweight coat, open at the front, revealing black cocktail dresses. They both had on high heels, and they carried nothing.

"Maybe they live in apartments behind the shop or up above," Street said. "The shop owner could be the landlord."

"I don't think those girls live there," I said. "I think that's where they work."

Two men passed each other in the doorway, one going in and one going out. No groceries.

Street looked at me. "You think the men without groceries are buying something else there? In apartments above the shop?"

"More money in that than selling groceries or simply renting apartments."

Street grinned. "There's your leverage if you need it."

"Yup," I said.

TWENTY-EIGHT

Professor Drago came out fifteen minutes later. His shirt was tucked in a little more neatly than before.

"It's only been fifteen minutes," I said. "Not much time for amore. Just a job to get done."

"Aren't you the romantic," Street said. "You know, some men and their prostitutes fall in love and get married and live happily ever after." She pointed at another young woman who was approaching the shop. This one carried a bag that was just big enough for, perhaps, stiletto heels. Her coat was buttoned up, but the lacy hem of her red dress was visible. "Like that girl," Street said. "She's probably got a girl-next-door personality that would make a great wife."

"Pretty rare," I said. "But if she looks like you in turquoise underthings, amore and a marriage proposal will come fast."

"What if her john found out that she studies bugs for a living?" Street said.

I put my arm around Street. "That would be the delightful bonus that would make her irresistibly exciting. Just so long as she doesn't let her john look inside her laboratory fridge."

We followed Drago back the way we'd come. I was about to approach him at his door, but he was too quick. He stepped in through the doorway and shut the door before I could get there.

Street and I trotted up to the door and knocked.

I expected him to open the door immediately, but he didn't. We waited.

I knocked again.

We waited some more.

The door finally opened. A woman in her sixties looked out. She was short and wide and had jet-black hair with inch-long, chalk-white roots. She wore a frumpy black dress like something a hotel maid might wear. But she was quite beautiful.

"Buon giorno," Street said. "Parli inglese, per favore?"

"A little," the woman said.

"Grazie," Street said. "We're looking for Professore Giovanni Drago, please."

"I am his wife," the woman said. "What do you want with him?"

I spoke. "I'd like to speak with him, please."

"What about?"

"My name is Owen McKenna, and this is Street Casey. We've come here from Lake Tahoe." As I said it, I realized that many people around the world don't know that name. "California," I corrected. "Two people have referred us. One is his former student."

"And what is his name?"

"Her name," I said. "Antonella Porto."

"I do not know this name. Professore do not know this name."

"I understand. I still hope you'll help us. Our question is about the Medici family. Antonella told us that Professor Drago was the man to talk to."

I heard the sound of a car coming to a stop behind me. A door opened and closed. A woman in her mid-thirties trotted up in an obvious hurry. We stepped aside as she said some fast words in Italian, two of which were 'Ciao mama.' The older woman opened the door farther to let the younger woman in. They kissed cheeks. The mother looked at me again.

"The professor will want to talk to us about the Medicis," I said. I tried to make it sound like I was referring to something significant.

She shook her head. "Professore is busy man. Important things. No time for question."

"This is very important," I said. I raised my voice loud enough that Drago could probably hear me from inside. "Please let the professor decide if he wants to talk to us. He will, trust me."

At that, the professor appeared behind his wife. He said something, and she moved away. He looked at us with distaste.

"I already told you that I'm busy. You are persistent to the point of displeasure. Please go away."

"This won't take long. I'm an investigator from the United States. I'm pursuing a murderer who, I believe, is motivated by something that connects to the Medicis. Special information, perhaps. We don't really know."

The man's face took on a cold look. "I'm sorry, but I don't have time for this kind of nonsense." He began to shut the door.

I put my foot in the opening.

"I would like you to make time, please," I said. "This murderer has killed three times, and we have reason to think that he is planning more murders. Your help could save a life or two."

"So you say. I've heard ridiculous things about the Medicis before. Each time it turned out to be a false story perpetrated by treasure hunters who think they can track down a missing work of art with my help. I simply don't believe you."

"Give me ten minutes to convince you," I said.

"Sorry." He tried to shut the door again. "Please move your foot or I will call the police."

"There are lives at stake. If you don't help me, I will consider ways to pressure you."

"I have a strong constitution. I don't succumb to pressure."

"What about your recent walk to the little food shop? Do you want that kept private?"

The man's face colored, and he looked very sad. It made me feel terrible for bringing it up. I had to remind myself that it was in service of stopping a killer.

The professor spoke in a soft voice. "Please allow a man a vice or two if they don't harm anyone."

"Would your wife agree that there's no harm?"

"My wife knows."

"Your daughter, then." I hated to say it.

Drago narrowed his eyes. "You would do something as cruel as telling her?"

I knew that I wouldn't, but he didn't know that. I said, "It would make me have contempt for myself, but I'm trying to catch a murderer. If you have information that can prevent more people from dying, then it would be worth it."

Drago stared at me, hate and disgust in his eyes, as he thought about it.

"You are vile."

"If you talk to me, I think that you will find that my overall intentions are good. In the big picture, I mean no harm. And I am not a treasure hunter. But if I have to hurt one stubborn person to save the life of another innocent person, I'll do it."

The professor's jaw moved back and forth as he took a deep breath through his mouth. "I don't have much time." He spoke directly to Street as if I weren't there.

"Thank you," I said. "It shouldn't take long."

He turned and walked inside. We followed him into what seemed like the center of the apartment, a small, elegant, circular atrium with a spiral staircase that rose at the room's perimeter. Natural light came from a ring of windows three floors above. At the atrium's center was a white marble fountain with a sculpture of a nude woman, languorous in her pose as she bathed in burbling water.

With the base of the staircase at noon on the atrium's layout, the room had three arched doorways at three, six, and nine o'clock. The man walked past the fountain and through the doorway at three o'clock.

As we followed him, Street said, "You speak impeccable English. You must have spent time…"

"I went to Oxford," Drago interrupted. "Took my doctorate in Renaissance Studies. I came back home to spend the next forty-five years helping the Italian government understand just what an astonishing collection of art they possess. Even most Renaissance scholars and aficionados don't comprehend the depth and breadth of artistic innovation produced here in the fifteenth and sixteenth centuries."

The room we entered had a sitting area and what looked like an old harpsichord in the corner. The top had a classic design made of inlaid wood around the perimeter. There were two windows, very tall and narrow. They looked out at the Pitti Palace in the distance.

"Have a seat," he said, still talking to Street as if I weren't in the room. He gestured toward a formal grouping of chairs with straight wooden backs designed to be uncomfortable. Drago sat in a chair next to a small table with a glass and a pitcher that was dewy with condensation. He poured some water into a glass and took a drink. He did not offer us water. My threat had made him give us some time but nothing more. Drago checked his watch, a large gold chronograph with three small, separate faces. The big watch dwarfed his bony, arthritic wrist. When we were all seated he said, "Tell me about this murder."

TWENTY-NINE

"There were three murders. One was a woman named Scarlett Milo who believed she was targeted for death. She asked me to investigate. She was shot and killed as I was meeting her. The second woman was Darla Ali. I never met her, but we linked her to the first."

"Both women," Drago said, his voice low. "But it doesn't sound like it was any kind of sex crime."

I shook my head. "No. The third murder was a young man named Sean Warner."

"You must have developed some possible reasons for why these people were killed," he said.

"Yes, but on the basis of flimsy speculation. The two murdered women were both focused on the Italian Renaissance and the art it produced. In San Francisco, California, this would not be unusual. But in Lake Tahoe, this is highly unusual. Although it would be hard to explain just how unusual to a person who lives and breathes the Renaissance every day."

Drago looked out one of the windows. He sighed.

As I described the situation, it sounded ridiculous to me, and I wondered if I was so desperate to find justice for Scarlet Milo that I'd flown a quarter of the way around the world on a silly whim.

"As Scarlett Milo lay dying, she scrawled a note to me. The writing was hard to read, so we're not sure what it says. But it originally looked to me like it said 'Medic's BFF.'"

"What does BFF mean?"

"I don't know about acronyms here in Italy, but in the States, BFF is often an abbreviation for Best Friend Forever. It's used primarily by younger women to refer to close friends, especially when they are texting each other. I did some research on what a medic's best friend forever might be and came up with nothing of substance."

"And you think this has something to do with the Medicis of the Renaissance," Drago said. "Why?"

"Scarlett Milo had many books on the Italian Renaissance. And in Darla's apartment, there were four pictures of artworks done by Italian Renaissance artists, Raphael, Michelangelo, Botticelli, and da Vinci. It's obviously not much of a connection. But Tahoe is not a place where people focus on Renaissance art. That two of them ended up murdered makes the Renaissance connection more possible if still unlikely. So when I looked again at the note the dying woman wrote, I thought that instead of 'Medic's BFF,' perhaps the woman meant to write Medicis BFF. Of course, if she did mean to write Medicis, then we had the question of why a dying woman would refer to a powerful family from five hundred years ago and six thousand miles from Tahoe."

Drago moved his hand through the air as if waving away cigarette smoke. "Conspiracy theories abound everywhere. It is people like you and these women who died who keep such crazy ideas alive."

His dismissive manner irritated me. "It is because of the women who died that I'm tracking it down," I said. "Whether it is something real or just a crazy idea is what I intend to find out." I took a deep breath as I looked at Drago. It would do me no good to show anger.

"I made a photocopy of the note the dying woman wrote," I said. "Humor me, please. Maybe looking at it will give you an idea." I pulled it out and handed it to Professor Drago.

He took it. The look on his face was scornful as if, without even looking, he knew the note was inane or even gibberish. Drago pulled eyeglasses out of his shirt pocket and slipped them on. He held the note out in front of him and moved it forward and back to get it into focus. He squinted at the note, then lowered it to his lap. "There is nothing here to go on. Despite your speculation, this Best Friend Forever concept is meaningless in the context of a multi-generational family like the Medicis. I couldn't even begin..." Drago stopped talking and frowned. He lifted up the note and looked at it again. In two or three seconds, his face reddened.

I waited a moment. "What are you thinking?"

Drago swallowed. "It's..." He stopped.

"From your reaction to the note, it appears that it does mean something to you," I said. I looked at Professor Drago and waited. "Please tell us what you make of it," I said. "If it is merely a conspiracy, as you referred to it, I'm eager to hear the details."

After a moment, Drago spoke. "Yes, it means something to me, although it's nearly impossible to believe it is anything but a silly rumor that is hundreds of years old. It's not a widespread rumor, so to have the rumor surface in America is startling."

Drago took a sip of water, swallowed, set the glass down. He rubbed his nose, pulled his glasses off and put them back into his shirt pocket, then spoke.

"The long history of the Medici family - a family that controlled much of the business of Florence and actually ruled the city and the Catholic Church for many years - included several tantalizing stories that have never been substantiated. Scholars believe that they persist simply because they make good stories." Drago gestured with Milo's note. "This one - let's call it the BFF rumor - is just like the other rumors. It has never been corroborated with any evidence. I personally looked into this rumor a couple of decades ago, and I believe it is complete nonsense." He paused, staring at the note.

We waited.

"For you to understand this rumor," Drago said, "I have to explain about one particular member of the Medici family, a young man who was on the periphery of the power center, a young man named Tommaso de' Medici."

Professor Drago drank more water, then took a deep breath before he began talking.

"In fifteen nineteen, Lorenzo Two de' Medici and his wife Madeline De La Tour gave birth to Catherine de' Medici. Catherine, you may remember from your history, was married off to Henry the Second in fifteen thirty-three. Henry, of course, became King of France in fifteen forty-seven, making Catherine Queen of France. After Henry died in fifteen fifty-nine, each of Catherine's three sons ended up serving as king.

"During the time of Catherine's youth, there was talk that Catherine de' Medici had a fraternal twin brother who was named Tommaso de' Medici. If the rumors are true, Tommaso was given up to be raised by a distant cousin."

"Why would they give up one baby out of a pair of twins?" I asked.

"We don't know for sure. We do know that Tommaso had dark skin and full lips and looked of African descent, so his father was likely different than that of his half-sister Catherine."

"Catherine did not look like Tommaso?"

"No."

"I thought you said they were twins," I said.

"Yes. Fraternal twins who were sired by separate men."

Street must have sensed my confusion. "It's called superfecundation," she said. "It's a situation that is not uncommon and results in fraternal twins by different fathers."

I thought about it. "So Catherine's mother Madeline must have had sex with two men in a short period of time. Each fertilized one of her eggs, and the two eggs developed in the womb together as twins."

Drago nodded.

"And," I continued, "Catherine's father was white and Tommaso's father was black."

Another nod. Drago said, "I should point out that in Renaissance Europe, blacks occupied every social strata. Yes, there was discrimination. Some blacks were slaves, and certainly many blacks were treated very badly. But other blacks were merchants and professionals and artists. One, Benedict of Palermo, was made a saint. Saint Benedict is now the patron saint of African-Americans. So the Medicis were accustomed to dealing with blacks as friends and associates and, apparently, as lovers."

"No surprise there," Street said. "We've had American presidents with black mistresses."

Drago made a faint smile. "For many of us Europeans, our favorite American president is Thomas Jefferson. That he kept slaves and defended their enslavement was certainly reprehensible. That he had children by one of his slaves, Sally Hemmings, does not detract much from his reputation but instead suggests he had a more expansive view of humanity than other men of his time. In some ways, he clearly thought that blacks were second class people. Yet he obviously felt they were worthy of his love, and he believed that Hemmings was acceptable and worthy as the mother of his children."

"Why do you think that Tommaso was given up to another family?" I asked.

"We'll never know. But the perspective of a Medici back then was probably similar to what a husband might think today. Which makes the likeliest explanation that Lorenzo couldn't tolerate raising a son who was the child of his wife's lover. The fact that her lover was black probably mattered less than the fact that another man had fathered Tommaso."

"What happened to the mother Madeline? Did she stay in touch with her son Tommaso?"

"No. She died fifteen days after Catherine and Tommaso were born, on the twenty-eighth of April, fifteen nineteen, just six days before her husband Lorenzo died. The cause of death is thought to be the plague or syphilis. Catherine was raised by relatives much the way Tommaso was."

Drago picked up his glass of water and drained it. A drop of water fell from his lips to his jacket. He pulled out a handkerchief and dabbed at the spot.

I said, "What does Tommaso have to do with the BFF rumor?"

"For that I have to tell you the story of the most famous gemstone in the world. Have you heard of the Hope Diamond?" Drago asked.

I looked at Street.

"A huge blue diamond, right?" she said. "Isn't it in the Smithsonian?"

"Yes. The gem that eventually became the Hope Diamond was acquired by a French gem merchant named Jean-Baptiste Tavernier from the Kollur Mine in southeast India around sixteen fifty. In the beginning, it was a huge gem, one hundred fifteen carats, and it was known as the Tavernier Blue. Jean-Baptiste Tavernier sold it and many others to King Louis the Fourteenth in sixteen sixty-nine. It began to be called the French Blue. The price was the equivalent of about five million euros today, which, compared to modern diamond prices, was a huge bargain. Louis the Fourteenth had the diamond cut to a much prettier shape that really sparkled. This process shed about half its weight so that it was only about sixty-five carats. Of course, that was still very large. It then became known as the Blue Diamond of the Crown of France. But some still call it the French Blue."

Drago put his fist to his mouth and cleared his throat. "Skip ahead one hundred twenty years to seventeen ninety-two. The French Blue was still part of the French Crown Jewels. King Louis the Sixteenth was under siege from his own people at the beginning of the French Revolution. He and his wife Marie Antoinette were convicted of treason, and they were beheaded. During the turmoil, thieves stole all the crown jewels. Many were later recovered, but not the French Blue Diamond, which disappeared, never to be seen again. Or so people thought."

Drago paused to breathe. Just to tell the story made him winded and upset.

"Twenty years later, just as the statute of limitations on the theft of the crown jewels ran out, came reports of an amazing blue diamond in London. This stone was forty-five carats, smaller than the French Blue because it had been recut to disguise its source. However, in recent times, new scientific measurements combined with detailed historical descriptions have proven that this new diamond was actually the French Blue.

"The history of this supposedly new diamond was hard to trace. Some people think that England's King George the Fourth had acquired it for his collection, but no one reported actually seeing it. When King George died, it turned up in the hands of a rich London banker named Thomas Hope. From there, the various owners of what became known as the Hope Diamond have been numerous but documented. It went from London to New York to Turkey to Paris to Washington D.C. where a dramatic socialite named Evalyn McLean liked to hold big parties during which she put the necklace with the Hope Diamond over the head of Mike, her Great Dane, and he trotted around with the diamond swinging from his neck."

Street looked at me, grinning.

"What?" I said.

"That would be a nice complement to Spot's ear stud, don't you think?"

I smiled.

"What is that?" Drago asked.

"Sorry. Nothing," I said. "How did it get to the Smithsonian collection?"

"After Evalyn McLean died, her children inherited it, and they later sold it to a diamond merchant named Harry Winston. Winston exhibited it for many years, and then donated it to the Smithsonian." Drago looked off through the window, his eyes vacant as if visualizing the diamond. "Sometimes wealthy people do a very nice thing and give their art and gems to museums to be enjoyed by everyone."

"Interesting story," I said. "How does it connect to our question?"

Drago turned away from the window, back toward us. "What I've just explained about the Hope Diamond is all true, verified by countless experts and historians. The history of the Hope Diamond is extensive and, except for the twenty-year gap from Louis the Sixteenth to Thomas Hope, largely comprehensive. The point of telling you that history is to show that the documentation of ownership, what we call provenance, is critical to a gemstone's value, just as provenance is critical to a painting's value.

"The story I'm about to tell you now is all rumor. Not one part of it has been verified. There is no documentation at all. It is in the contrast between these stories that we find the difference between truth and fiction."

"Understood," I said.

Drago continued, "As I said, the Hope Diamond originally came from the Kollur Mine in southeast India. While the gem that became the Hope Diamond was mined around sixteen fifty, a similar gem had supposedly been found about a hundred years earlier. It was a little smaller and not quite as perfect. Nevertheless, it was huge and had a blue color very much like the Hope Diamond."

Drago shifted in his chair. "You remember our Tommaso de' Medici. Tommaso was a very awkward child, especially around girls. And he was unable to shake that as he grew to an adult. More than his illegitimacy or his dark skin, it was because of his awkwardness that he was kept at the periphery of Medici power. Not being in the inner circle, he was excluded from all major decisions. Even so, his adoptive father was prominent in the family and a very successful businessman. So Tommaso did have access to certain discretionary funds to use as he pleased."

Drago took several breaths as if he'd been swimming and just come up for air. "According to the rumor, Tommaso de' Medici received a proposition by courier back in fifteen fifty-three. He was thirty-four years old. Tommaso de' Medici was understandably eager to make a name for himself and show the rest of his family that they'd underestimated him. Perhaps Tommaso was the Medici contact by chance. More likely, the sender of the message knew that Tommaso chafed at not being granted family power equivalent to his cousins, and the sender thought that Tommaso would be more likely to grant the sender an audience for his proposal."

Drago again glanced out the window. It appeared that he was looking at the Pitti Palace.

"The courier came from Constantinople, which had just fallen to the Muslim Conquest and had become the capital of the new Ottoman Empire. This courier, who may have been a thief or may have been legitimate, is said to have brought a letter that described the death of a Persian businessman. After this businessman's death, his fortune was reportedly stolen and scattered, and his widow was left with almost nothing from her former life. She wanted to sell the diamond her husband had given her for their marriage. The diamond had never been seen by anyone at the time because it was so valuable that her husband had insisted it be hidden away from the moment he gave it to her."

I was getting impatient. "This is about the BFF rumor?"

After a long pause, Drago said, "The letters BFF refer to this diamond, the diamond that had supposedly come from the Kollur Mine one hundred years before it produced the Hope Diamond. This diamond was reputed to sparkle unlike any other diamond ever found.

"When Tommaso received the courier's letter, he was intrigued and realized that this might be his opportunity to prove to the rest of the Medicis that he was worthy. Tommaso turned out to be a skillful negotiator, and he arranged to purchase the Persian widow's diamond for a good price.

"After Tommaso received it, he gathered all of his family at the Pitti Palace in the presence of Florence's most celebrated diamond experts and revealed the diamond. The experts inspected it at great length, and all agreed that it was the most impressive diamond they had ever seen. Tommaso named it Fuoco Blu di Firenze."

Street figured it out first. "The Blue Fire of Florence," she said.

"Scarlett Milo's BFF," I said.

THIRTY

Drago nodded. "As you can see, the story is enticing. It is precisely because of this that the story endures despite no evidence whatsoever."

Drago paused as if gathering his words.

"According to the rumor, the acquisition of what at that time was the most impressive diamond ever seen gained Tommaso the credibility that he desired among the family. And Tommaso was apparently so impressed by Fuoco Blu di Firenze's singular quality, that, like the Persian businessman, he hid it away so that it could never be stolen by a thief or even his Medici cousins."

"What happened to it?" I asked.

Drago shook his head. "That's the point. No one knows. The creative storyteller who dreamed up this diamond neglected to fabricate any supporting details or records. Nevertheless, it became part of the oral history of the Medicis. And now the legend has been passed down for five hundred years."

"If we were to operate on the notion that the story is true, where might we learn more about it?"

Professore Giovanni Drago stood up, turned away from us, and walked over to the window. He looked out at the Pitti Palace as if he were gazing back into history. After a minute, he turned, came back to his chair, and sat.

"I hate to continue with this. I don't want to think that you or anyone else could attach my name to such nonsense."

"But…" I said, waiting for Drago to continue his thought.

"There is a man named Bruno Valenti, originally of La Cosa Nostra."

"The Sicilian Mafia," I said.

"Yes. A few decades ago, he was convicted on murder and racketeering charges and sent to prison for life. After many years, he was let out under the laws of libertà condizionata, the Italian version of what you call parole. Now he is an old man and living in a town in southern Tuscany. I've heard rumors that he's in very bad health."

"You think he had something to do with the Blue Fire of Florence?"

"No. But if there were such a thing as the Blue Fire of Florence, and if someone were to have obtained it through theft or purchase or fraud, my guess is that Valenti would know about it. His specialty was acquiring hard-to-acquire things. Paintings. Rare automobiles. Ancient illuminated manuscripts. Stashes of gold, silver, and platinum. Historical artifacts. Jewels."

"Do you know how I might approach him?" I asked.

Drago shrugged. "I suppose you could simply knock on his door and ask him. He is in his dotage. I don't imagine that there is any kind of a moat to ford."

I appreciated Drago's small sarcasm. It made him seem a little less like a stuffed shirt.

"Having said that," Drago continued, "even if the Blue Fire of Florence existed and Valenti knew about it, I can't imagine that he would be forthcoming to you."

"Do you have any idea of his address?"

"No. But I can make a call to someone I know in the prosecutor's office."

"Thank you. I'd appreciate that."

Drago stood. "Wait here, please."

He left. We waited. We didn't talk. I think both Street and I felt that getting all of this information had been a tenuous procedure at best. Talking might distract Drago if he could hear us from wherever he went.

Drago returned ten minutes later and handed me a slip of paper. On it were letters and numbers written in cursive. Most I recognized, some I didn't. Italians use the same alphabet as other western countries, but they form certain letters differently.

I got out a pen. "Let me double check what you've written." I rewrote what he'd written. He explained where I was confused.

"This town you've written," I said. I sounded it out syllable by syllable. "Roccatederighi."

"Yes, that is close to how we say it," Drago said.

"You said it is in southern Tuscany."

"Correct. I'll show you on a map." He left again, then returned shortly with a map of northern Italy. He opened it and pointed. "Here is where we are in Florence. An hour south of here is Siena. An hour south of Siena is a turnoff to Roccastrada." He traced with his finger. "From there, you follow these little mountain roads up to Sassofortino, then continue on to Roccatederighi. I've been there, but it was long ago. I don't remember the streets. Perhaps you can get the map details from your Google company."

"Thank you, professor. I very much appreciate your help. I'm sorry for the time it took out of your day. And I'm very sorry that I felt I had no choice but to pressure you."

He made a small nod. "I'm sure you will discover that the Blue Fire of Florence is one of the great fictions to come out of the Renaissance." Drago spoke as if he was done with us.

"There is one more thing I'd like to ask you," I said.

Drago looked frustrated and impatient.

I pulled out the warning note that had been stuck in my cabin door and handed it to him.

"Does this image mean anything to you? It looks a bit like da Vinci's Vitruvian Man drawing with a star and circle drawn around it."

Drago looked at the piece of paper. "This has nothing to do with da Vinci. This is Agrippa's pentagram."

"What does that mean?"

"Heinrich Cornelius Agrippa was a Renaissance magician from Germany. He wrote three important books about occult philosophy. This pentagram was in one of the books. It is a symbol of magic. The signs at the points of the star are astrological symbols." He lifted his head from the paper and looked at me. "I assume you know about the Reformation."

"Not much, no."

"The protestant Reformation, which, literally, was an attempt to reform the Catholic Church, began during the Renaissance. The church fought back. The resulting turmoil brought a renewed focus on people who didn't worship exactly as the Church wanted. Specifically, the Church fixated on witchcraft and on those people, especially women, who practiced ancient traditions of magic. The Church felt that many kinds of magic had Satanic inspiration. Agrippa noted that this was one of the main symbols of magic."

"Is there a reason the drawing is upside down in relation to the writing?"

"Yes. A pentagram that points up refers to white, or good, magic. An inverted pentagram refers to evil magic, otherwise known as Black Magic."

"What does this mean for me?"

"It suggests that you are being targeted by someone who believes in evil Satanic ritual, someone who practices modern-day witchcraft."

I stood, and Street joined me.

"One more thing I should tell you," Drago said.

We turned back.

"This man, Bruno Valenti. He is old. Maybe eighty, maybe eighty-five. And he is also ill. He will seem feeble. But don't let that lull you into thinking you don't need to be careful. Bruno Valenti is a sociopath, a very dangerous man. As bad as they come. He has no empathy. He cannot understand anything from another person's point of view."

"Got it," I said. "I've known many people like that. No empathy means they'll kill you without concern beyond whether they might get caught."

"Exactly," Drago said.

"Thanks for the warning," I said.

We left.

The next morning, we asked the woman at the residenza desk if there was a train that ran to Roccatederighi.

"I've never heard of this town."

I glanced at Street. She raised her eyebrows. She pulled out her phone and showed the woman where it was on the map.

"Oh, there. There are so many places I haven't been. But I have been to this nearby town, Roccastrada, and I can tell you that the train does not go there. So it won't go to Roccatederighi. There are many towns... how do you say, of no account. In the middle of the country. You would have to rent a car."

"Is there a car rental at the train station?"

"Sì."

We said our grazies and walked to the train station.

A rental agent put us into a tiny Fiat 500, which was cute. But it felt like something a forest fairy would ride to a hobbit meeting among the mushrooms. My legs straddled the steering wheel, and every time I let up the clutch, my left knee nearly hit my chest. But the car had gopower, and we could keep up with the big BMWs as we took the freeway south out of Florence.

On our map, the drive to Roccatederighi looked straightforward, a stretch of big freeway to Siena and then a smaller divided highway south until our turnoff. From there we would take a smaller road with many more turns, which itself was followed by an even narrower paved path that snaked through the country.

Because the speedometer was in kilometers per hour, I kept being startled when I glanced at the dash and saw that we were going 120 or 130. Even adjusting the kilometers to miles, we were still moving at speeds that would get us a ticket in the States.

"This little car goes fast, huh?" Street said as we raced toward Siena. The city had just appeared on a distant hill, a picture postcard with patchwork fields in the foreground and a rock-fortress with bell towers in the background.

"Yeah." I patted the dash. "This baby may have worked up a sweat, but there's still more oats in her tank."

"Is that guy speak or something?"

"Standard gearhead lingo."

"You being a gearhead and all," she said.

I didn't turn to look at her, but I knew her eyes were rolling. I said, "Whenever I get the chance, I pop the hood of my Jeep and leave it up so people can admire the motor."

"I thought motors were electric and cars that run on gas have engines."

"Motors, engines, whatever," I said. "Anyway, it's the guy stuff in me that appreciates the way you look in your turquoise confetti. You wouldn't want to forego that, would you?"

"If it means that you keep the hood of your Jeep closed, yes. I would die of embarrassment if you left it open when I'm around. The guys who do that are the ones who walk into the Seven Eleven without a shirt on, buy a six-pack, and then pop a can open and guzzle it before they get out the door."

"You've never been with me when I do that?"

Street smacked me on the shoulder. "We're in Italy, the essence of high-style, refined living. You should squelch your primitive impulses and..." she trailed off.

"And start listening to opera?"

"Yeah, that would be a good place to start."

"My buddies will think I'm no longer a real man if they hear Puccini on my stereo."

"Better than having them discover that you don't know what an engine is."

We flew through the outskirts of Siena and continued south. Forty minutes later, we found our exit, a road that headed west across the valley and began to climb in twisty switchbacks up to Roccastrada. The countryside was beautiful, like the northern California counties of Marin and Sonoma and Napa.

Once we were outside of Roccastrada, the smaller road seemed designed to be a car-sickness testing track. Curves on top of the curves and hills on the hills and narrow passages that narrowed even more so that two motor scooters would have to touch handle bars to pass. There were stretches with drop-offs that would make a mountain donkey pause.

Street kept one hand gripped on the door handle and the other one up on the dash for support or, perhaps, crash resistance.

Street rolled down her window as we crawled through the medieval towns that graced every hilltop with a castle and a church and an accompanying cluster of buildings that served as homes, shops, and schools atop vertical fortress walls.

The single masterstroke of Italy's formation in the 19th century - when someone had the idea that maybe all these city states could stop warring and get along - was for the new government to recognize that these towns, with all of their art and history, were the essence of what made Italy great. So the government made it mostly illegal to change them in any way. They created, in essence, the architecture police, the cultural police, the color police, the construction police, and the art police. The result was both a strangling bureaucracy and one of the most popular tourist destinations in the world, one that attracts millions of tourists who want to see what the Middle Ages looked like. Modern buildings in Tuscany are as rare as yurts and teepees in Midtown Manhattan.

We climbed up to Sassofortino, a group of stone buildings on very steep slopes. From there, we wound our way around to Roccatederighi, the town where, according to Professore Drago, the former mobster Bruno Valenti lived. He was now out on parole, living in solitude in an obscure hamlet that was a thousand years old and was almost hidden among hundreds of more spectacular tourist spots sprinkled throughout Tuscany.

As we approached Roccatederighi, there were amazing views of the fertile valley below. Stone buildings hugged the sides of the mountain. They each had a view that would give you thrills or vertigo. At times, the buildings were directly on the edge of the narrow road. If an approaching vehicle came at the wrong time and you veered an inch too far to the right, you'd rip off the side of your car on a stone wall.

Street had pulled up another map on her phone, and she gave me directions as I drove.

"When you come to the center of town, the road will make almost a U-turn to the right, at which point you turn left."

Which I did.

"Drive the equivalent of a couple of blocks, and when you come to a small square with no exit, park."

Which I did.

From the left turn in the middle of town, the streets were made of stone, no doubt laid down a thousand years ago. They were rough to drive on, but they didn't require annual pothole repair. We got out of the Fiat onto a small stone plaza. Street pointed to a narrow, cobbled road, walled in by medieval buildings. The path climbed steep, erratic turns.

Although the stone walkway may have been the main drag a thousand years ago, it wasn't big enough for any vehicle wider than a motor scooter. I raised my arms to my sides and was able to touch both walls with my palms flat on the stone. Two people could walk side by side only if they were coordinated on the uneven stones.

We went up the steep passage. Here and there were smaller side passages. Some went up at steep angles, and some went down at steeper angles. Many of the sloped passages were made of steps, but the steps were uneven and of varying heights. I caught myself thinking critically about the construction. Then I imagined myself as a stone laborer a thousand years ago. I could hear the monk in charge telling me, "Take your stone sledge hammer and chisel and cut this steep slope of granite into steps." From that perspective, the steps were perfection.

We walked up a passage that was spanned by an arched stone stairway bridge. The bridge looked like a good path that would have a view over the walls of the city to the valley below. So we hiked around a lopsided, five-cornered block to access the arched bridge only to find it wasn't there. We knew we'd been fooled by the multiple turns, but we couldn't solve the puzzle. We tried to retreat and retrace our steps but found ourselves on yet a different street. Another time, a path curved up and around to join a higher passage only to become a dark tunnel going under a building. The passages were a three-dimensional maze with a fun but ominous tone. Dr. Seuss meets M.C. Escher.

Everywhere were pots of brilliant red geraniums celebrating spring in Tuscany. Most of the flowers flanked entrances, some with painted doors in green or red enamel and others made of weathered planks held together by hand-pounded bands of iron. They looked their age at a thousand years or so. Some of the doors had rounded tops. The windows were made of small panes of wavy, antique glass, and their frames and sills were free-form in shape, some straight, most a bit curved to fit the shapes of the stones that formed the walls. Frequently, the streets and passages went under rooms of buildings that stuck out from the main structure, additions added on in the only space that was left to expand, above the street. Those added rooms were often built only five and a half feet above the street. I wondered if the people intended to build passages that required people to duck. Then I noticed that some of the buildings were so short that the height inside the interior spaces couldn't be more than five and a half feet tall. It was a dramatic indication that our species has grown a foot in the last millennium, a probable result of humans developing agricultural techniques that finally produced, for a sizable portion of the population, as much food as people wanted.

We climbed to the top of the village where an ancient church overlooked the town and the distant green pastures far below.

Street said, "According to my map, Valenti's place should be close, but I don't see any numbers at the various doorways."

"An ex-mobster would have money, right?" I said. I pointed to a bare, clean wall of dark, forest green stucco. "There's no number," I said, "but it fits the location, and the style seems befitting of an ex-mobster, don't you think?"

"I've never seen a mobster's house," Street said.

I looked at the expanse of wall. Inset into the green stucco was a large, lemon-yellow door. The paint was shiny enamel. On either side of the door were three windows in vertical rows. The windows were each made of multiple small panes, and the separating wood moulding pieces were also painted lemon yellow. The window panes were all wavy glass, whether actual antique or fake antique. Above the upper corners of the door frame were two wall sconces made of more wavy glass. On either side of the door sat two ceramic pots glazed in high-gloss yellow. In the pots were more red geraniums.

I walked over to the door. There was an elaborate brass knocker depicting a monk on his knees praying. I swung it three times. After a minute, the door opened.

A young man stood there, dressed in black jeans, black silk shirt, and black silk jacket. His thick arms hung slightly out from his sides, and his feet were apart in a typical, young man's tough-guy posture. Although handsome, he was built like a backhoe with long limbs on a thick body that appeared asymmetrical, as if he'd once been severely injured and then put back together crooked. The left side of his jacket bulged at the armpit, partly because of his asymmetry and partly because of his large sidearm.

He said nothing.

"My name's Owen McKenna, here to see Bruno Valenti."

The man looked at me, his face unchanged. A garbage can would radiate more warmth.

He made a nod and shut the door.

We waited.

Two minutes later, the door reopened, and the young man was back. "Mr. Valenti doesn't know you." His English was good.

I tried to think of what might get us through the door. "Please tell him we have information about the Fuoco blu di Firenze."

Another nod. He shut the door.

Two minutes later, he opened the door again and said, "Come in." He gestured for us to go past him.

We walked into a hallway with a polished marble floor.

"Straight ahead," the man said.

As we walked forward, there was a smell not unlike that in a hospital, a peculiar mix of antiseptic and something ozone from electric machinery.

"Turn left."

The hallway was wide enough for three abreast, but the young man stayed behind us, a good strategy in case we got out of hand and he needed to shoot us in the back.

We turned and walked into a beautiful room with large windows and white walls that reflected the sunlight and made the room very bright. The polished oak floor was stained a golden tone and gave the room warmth. The windows must have been in the outer wall of not just the Valenti house but of the original fortress walls as well, because there was nothing outside but a spectacular view of the valley below.

To one side of the room, facing the windows at an oblique angle, was one of those couches designed for reclining, like the one where Olympia reclined in Manet's famous painting. In place of a nubile seductress was an old man. He was as rotund as he was prostrate. His head was huge and bald, and his neck had fat rolls that went all the way around, a real-life version of the Michelin Tire Man. Clear, thin plastic tubes draped over his ears and dispensed oxygen beneath his nose. His wheezing was evident from a distance.

He looked permanently set in place as if he'd never move if he didn't have to use the bathroom.

"Mr. Valenti, I'm Owen McKenna and this is my companion Street Casey. We've come from California to talk to you about the Blue Fire of Florence."

THIRTY-ONE

"Maybe I heard it wrong," he said in English with a touch of Bronx accent. His voice was soft and wheezing and breathy. He inhaled several times, then added, "My assistant said you came here to tell me of the Fuoco blu di Firenze. What is the information?"

I was trying to think of a plausible story. "Someone is committing murders back in the States, and we think he's motivated by the diamond. So we're tracking its movement from Florence during the Renaissance."

"This is information? You are not telling me anything."

"The implication being that the diamond does in fact exist. We hope to find out where it's gone in the last several hundred years."

Valenti made a snort.

As we'd driven to the town, I'd thought I might have to challenge his tough-guy reputation to provoke him. But Valenti began to speak, his wheezing the kind that made everyone else feel like they weren't getting enough air.

"I was put in prison," he said. "Inflated charges. The government is corrupt. The prosecutors are weasels. They dart out to attack when they think they have opportunity. The rest of time, they are in the hiding. They conspire to make me the blame for the corrupt action of the politicians. Now I am out of prison. I will not go back, even if it means I play their game. I know nothing about the Fuoco blu di Firenze. But if I did, they would take that and create a new false charge and put me back in the cell. There I would die. But I will die here. With my view. With my wine. No more prison. Ever. You tell me something interesting, I will listen. But if you have nothing to say, leave me for my peace."

"When you suggest that you wouldn't speak of the Blue Fire

of Florence because of what might happen, you imply that you do in fact know something about the diamond."

"You are a big irritation. Like the last person who asked me about the diamond. I know nothing!"

"Who was the last guy to ask you about it?"

"She. I do not know who was she. She annoy just like you." Valenti squinted at me. His eyes reminded me of corroded metal.

I wondered if his statement referred to Scarlett Milo. "If I talk about the diamond and mention your name," I said, "the prosecutors will start thinking about what else there is to learn from you. Maybe they call your parole officers. Maybe they say you've violated the conditions…" I let the statement hang. After a moment, I said, "But I have no interest in talking to anybody else if you answer my questions."

"The libertà condizionata are the scum. They blame to me the crimes of others." Even though Valenti could barely breathe, his voice was like a razor, his eyes suddenly sparking like fire. "And you would make them think it more? Get out!"

The young man stepped forward and grabbed my elbow.

I thought of stomping his foot and spinning around. There was a decent chance I could disarm him. There was also a chance I could get killed. And Street was in the room.

I turned slowly, and we walked out.

When we were out on the stone path and the door was shut behind us, Street said, "That was scary."

"Yeah." We walked down the sloped street, away from Bruno Valenti's home, away from the ancient church that capped the top of the small mountain. In the distance behind us, I heard a motor scooter start up. But there was no revving of engine, no typical sound of acceleration.

"Hurry," I said to Street. "Down the street, just past that intersection, there's a passage on the left. Let's go in there."

We ran and turned in. It was a dark tunnel under an ancient building. A steep, stone stairway went up, then turned. We went up the steps and around the corner. The stairway emerged into a small open patio area. It was too narrow for sunlight to come down to the stones, but the sky above was blue.

"What are you thinking?" Street said, worry in her voice.

"The motor scooter. It could be Bruno's man. It didn't race away, but stayed idling. Like he was supposed to follow us. Like he was coasting behind us, waiting for an opportunity."

"Opportunity for what?" Street's voice had a tremolo to it. "You think he wants to hurt us?"

"Maybe. Follow me." I ran across the patio into another short tunnel and stairway that went up to the street above. I took the steps two at a time. The steps came out at what seemed like a rooftop. But at the far side, there was a doorway arch that opened onto another, higher pathway. The paths were all part of a latticework of passageways that went back and forth across a steep slope. I waited as Street joined me. We stood silent. In the distance was the motor scooter sound, this time from below us. It shifted, then got louder as the engine revved. Climbing.

I took Street's hand and led her up the stone pathway to a turn where we stopped in a dark corner. We were sheltered from most angles. On the upper side above us were tall stone walls. On the other side was the valley below. As we listened for sounds, we could see the dot of a farmer and his tractor, crawling across a distant field.

The motor scooter engine had gone silent.

Street must have noticed. She put her cupped hand behind her ear to aid her listening. She shook her head.

Maybe there was nothing to worry about. But in the next moment, I heard a scooter. Then it went silent. That didn't make it a pursuit. It was obvious that old man Valenti didn't like me. But that didn't mean he intended to have me harassed.

I whispered to Street. "Let's walk down this passage. I think it will intersect with one of the streets that go down toward where we parked. Just to be safe, let's stay against the wall and..."

A chip of rock exploded from the wall and hit my cheek accompanied by the snap of small-arms gunfire.

THIRTY-TWO

I grabbed Street, spun her around, and we ran back the way we came.

Another shot went wide. A third shot blasted more rock chips from the wall next to us. The gunfire was loud, but the edges of the sound were muffled. The gunman had a silencer.

There was a corner up ahead. I sprinted faster, dragging Street. I went around the corner, jerking on Street's arm. It probably hurt, but she didn't complain.

We ran down the passageway. The scooter engine revved. It grew louder as if the scooter were climbing up an invisible parallel passage toward us. Then the engine sound fell off. He must have made a sudden turn away from us.

I thought about the man as we ran. When we were inside Valenti's house, he'd grabbed my elbow with his left hand, which suggested he was a lefty. That meant he could shoot at us while he kept his right hand on the throttle. The streets of Roccatederighi were confusing to us. But he would know where we had parked, and he would be able to search all the streets to find us.

We ran and came to a sheltered spot, walls rising high on both sides. We stopped, panting hard, waiting to hear if the scooter sound changed. The sound dropped off. But after a few seconds, it grew slowly. The sound bounced off the stone walls. I couldn't tell which direction it came from, so I didn't know which way to move. The engine pitch rose as the scooter came faster. Street's hand gripped mine hard. I tensed, preparing to run, but I didn't know if the man on the scooter would come out in some other part of the Roccatederighi maze. Maybe it was best to stay right where we were, relatively hidden, out of view from anywhere but the narrow path down below us or the narrow path up above us.

As I started to think that the man was on the other side of the building to our side, the scooter popped into view in the passageway below us. He raced up toward us at high speed, his gun raised. I spun Street around, and we sprinted back up the narrow road.

There was a muffled gunshot, then another, then another. He had a high-capacity magazine, and his silencer would ensure that few people would hear his rain of bullets. Of those who did, the reputation of his Mob boss would keep anyone from reporting it or even answering questions about it.

We ran up the stone road and saw another opening to the side. We ran into the passage and found it was another stairway that went up through a narrow passage and then popped out into open air.

The scooter appeared below us. The shooter saw us up at the top of the stairs and raised his gun.

I pulled Street out onto an open area as the man fired from below. Bullets thudded into the rock next to us. The shooter revved his scooter, driving it up the stairway, its wheels easily gripping the shallow, granite steps.

We sprinted out onto the plaza of the ancient church, perched at the top of the small mountain near Valenti's house. I pulled Street with me as I jumped up two feet onto a stone-paved square. We ran across the square toward the far side where there was a short rock wall. Beyond the wall, the mountain dropped away down a steep slope.

The motor scooter revved behind us. Another spit of muffled gunfire came at us. I pulled Street to the left and then to the right as we ran, a serpentine motion to make us harder targets to hit.

There was more gunfire.

"Try to get over the wall and climb down the slope," I shouted to Street. "I'll see if I can stop him."

Street shouted at me, "Those sculptures in front of the church. You could use them!"

As Street ran for the wall, clambered over it, and lowered herself down the other side, I veered toward the front of the church and its two sculptures, one made of stone, one bronze. The bronze one might be hollow and lighter. It was about five feet tall, a man in robes, probably a saint. As I ran up to it, I circled around, grabbing it under its elbows, lifting, pulling, jerking.

It must have weighed 250 pounds. I dragged its feet off of its pedestal and moved in a rotating motion, lifting the sculpture with centrifugal force. I leaned back against its weight and spun around, keeping its feet in the air. I did one full rotation, then began another, the bronze saint's feet rising. In my peripheral vision, I saw the young man on his motor scooter. Somehow, he'd jumped the scooter up the two-foot rise onto the church plaza. He came straight for me, his gun raised. As I rotated around, I saw the dark eye of his gun barrel flash. I let go of the bronze saint. It clattered onto the stone surface. The saint's hand caught in a crack in the stones and flipped the sculpture over into the path of the scooter.

The scooter driver tried to slow, tried to evade. But he hit the saint on its chest, the thickest part. The scooter stopped fast, and the man went over the handlebars. He almost cleared the plaza without touching, but his head struck a glancing blow on the stone wall as he flew over it, and he flipped over as he went off the drop off just two feet from where Street had gone out of sight.

I ran to the wall and looked down. Street was crouched down beneath the wall, gripping a bush and digging her feet into crumbling dirt to keep from sliding down the mountain. Below her, the scooter driver was rolling, limp like a rag doll. He came to a stop against a boulder.

I reached down to Street's hand and helped her up and over the wall.

"We're safe now," I said, hugging her hard.

She trembled in my grip, but she didn't speak.

"I'm going to climb down to the driver. Are you okay waiting here? I don't think anyone else is out prowling and looking for us. But if you step around the back side of the church and flatten yourself against the far wall, no one will be able to see you."

Street nodded, still silent, the trauma of the chase obvious on her face.

She ran toward the church. I climbed over the stone wall.

The slope the young man had tumbled down was steep. I used both hands as I climbed down, grabbing onto bushes and protruding rock and tufts of grass. The man was about 30 yards below the wall, face down in the dirt, wrapped halfway around the boulder. As I got close, I saw that he was still alive. One foot was moving, turning back and forth. Both of his hands were visible. I looked for his gun, but I didn't see it. It could be far below us. Or it could be under his body.

I put my fingers through the back of the man's belt and lifted. He didn't resist. I got him turned over, face to the sky, still held in place by the boulder. One of his eyes was shut, the tissue around it already blue and swelling. The other eye was partway open, unfocused. There was no gun where he'd been lying.

I went through his pockets and took his keys.

The man was quite banged up, scraped and bleeding on his hands and forehead. There was a significant laceration on his left elbow. But it didn't look like his injuries were lethal.

I slapped his face. "Wake up."

His lips tried to form a word, but it sounded like gibberish.

It was possible that he had a serious concussion. It was possible that he had bleeding on the brain and would die in minutes, but I doubted it. From his movements, I guessed that he would be crawling back up the slope within an hour.

I scrambled back up to the church plaza and found Street at the back side of the church.

"Okay?" I said.

"I've been kidnapped twice in connection with your cases, but I've never been shot at."

"I'm so sorry about that." I hugged her again. She was shaking.

"Is the shooter…"

"He's alive, but he's unconscious and banged up. He lost his gun. I think he'll come around in an hour or two. We have some time."

Street made a small nod as we walked.

"You've been shot at multiple times," she said. "I don't know how you handle the stress."

"I just remind myself that the vast majority of all shots miss. Not that it's much comfort." I put my arm around her shoulder and got her walking. Movement is always good for psychological trauma.

"Actually, that is a kind of comfort," Street said. "Next time,

I'll tell myself that."

"Let's hope there's never a next time."

"Where to now? Do we call the police and a doctor for the shooter?"

"I'd first like to revisit Bruno Valenti, if you think you're up to that."

"But he's the one who no doubt ordered us killed."

"Right. And he's expecting his assistant to come back and report." I pulled out the young man's keys and showed Street. "Valenti won't know it's me until I walk into his room."

Street looked alarmed.

"If you like, we can go back to the car, drive away, and I can come back alone, later."

"No. I should come. I have to face these things."

"It could be dangerous."

"Yes. But I think that Valenti's houseman was the only other person there. And Valenti doesn't seem dangerous by himself."

THIRTY-THREE

Instead of trying Bruno Valenti's front door, we walked around to the side where I guessed the young man had emerged with the scooter.

There was an ancient stone overhang, large enough to be a carport if the streets allowed something as wide as a car to pass. Instead of a car, there was a stylish three-wheeled scooter. The front seat was like that on a motorcycle, with similar handlebars and controls. Behind it and above the two rear wheels was a larger seat with a back rest. The trike was no more than four feet wide, narrow enough for Valenti's assistant to give him rides up and down the steep streets of the medieval town. To the side of the trike was enough space to park a motor scooter. There was a door at the back of the stone carport. I didn't see a video camera or a motion light, but that didn't mean we weren't watched.

Moving quietly, I tried the doorknob. It was locked.

I didn't want to risk making noise by trying different keys in the lock. So I studied the key opening and then found the key that matched. I held the doorknob to help muffle the sound as I slid the key in, click by click. The key turned, and the door opened.

I motioned Street to follow. We walked softly into a kitchen, went through it to a dining room with large windows that showed the grand valley views. To the side was a hallway that looked like the one we'd been in earlier when we'd come in the front door. The next room would be the one with Valenti.

I put my hand palm out and pointed at the floor, letting Street know that I wanted her to stay here out of the danger range in case Valenti had a gun. Moving silently, I peeked around the corner. Valenti was still on his reclining couch, his hands folded across his chest, his head back, snoozing. I took silent steps until I was standing next to him, close enough to grab him if he reached for a hidden weapon.

I spoke loudly enough to wake him up. "You need a more reliable assassin, Bruno."

Valenti awoke with a jerk. His eyes were wide. "You…" His hands seemed to clench in fear.

"Yeah, your boy is a screwup. And you're an idiot for sending untrained help on a mission over his head. Maybe now we'll have a more productive talk, huh?"

"I don't know to what you are talking." Bruno stopped looking at me. His gaze went up toward the ceiling, his look was intense, the fear now mixed with confusion. His body tensed as if he were doing crunches. He started to vibrate. His right hand went to his left arm, squeezing it as if he had a sudden pain. His left hand reached down to the couch, feeling where the fabric of his bedclothes met the cushion. I tensed, ready to grab his arm if he brought out a weapon.

He pulled out a small vial. With practiced precision, he flipped open the top with his thumb, raised the vial, and popped a pill into his mouth. He shut his eyes and mouth. His lips and jaw moved as if he was getting the pill under his tongue.

"You want me to get help?" I said.

"No." Valenti managed to say, his voice soft.

Valenti breathed hard and fast. Street came into the room and looked at me.

"We'll wait a bit," I said to her.

Gradually, Valenti's breathing slowed. He stopped shaking. Valenti opened his eyes and spoke.

"I will not go back to prison. This is the end. Fifth heart attack. The doctor said if I had another, that would be it. I want to die here. Not in a hospital. In my home." He clenched again, his eyes shut tight, his upper body rising slightly. Slowly, he relaxed.

"Tell me about the Blue Fire of Florence," I said. "Otherwise, we call the police."

"No policia!" He said in a raspy whisper.

"Then talk."

He breathed hard several more times. His face was a peculiar gray. He closed his eyes as if calming himself, then spoke. His voice was airy and softer still.

"This is my end. I can tell. So now I will tell a story. What difference will it make?" Valenti's knuckles bulged as his fists tightened. He breathed shallow, fast breaths.

We waited.

"Back in early nineteen sixties," he began, "when I was in my thirties, I was in prime of life and making a name for myself in the business. I got unusual PO. I think it was nineteen sixty-one."

"What's a PO?" I asked.

"Purchase Order. A buy request. We had other names for them. If the PO was big, we called it - let me think of the English - a yacht builder. The way it worked, if someone would pay highest dollar for something, we were willing to get it for them. The buyer did not know that we were inventive to how we acquire these items. The buyer thought we were dealers."

"What kind of dealers?" I asked.

"It depend on what buyer wanted. If buyer wanted valuable painting, we were art dealers. If buyer wanted a piece of military, we were weapon merchants. The more hard the item was to get, the more the buyer needed specialty dealer like us. And the more expensive the item, the more resource we invest to find it." He stopped to breathe, over and over. He'd been speaking slowly. Maybe I could help him speed up.

"So if someone wanted the Blue Fire of Florence and was willing to pay big bucks for it," I said, "you were willing to pose as gem merchants to the buyer. So you made inquiries regarding its whereabouts, and then you went and stole the diamond."

Bruno Valenti's face was turning from pale gray to a duller gray. He took several more labored breaths. "Sì."

"How did you find and steal it?"

"My capo knew a guy who knew a guy who worked with Florentine mosaics. This is art of creating pictures with the colored Venetian glass and the gemstones. This man sold individual gems as well. He told that the Fuoco blu di Firenze was to be in the safe of a Florentine family who had the connections back to the Medicis of the Renaissance."

"So you and your men burglarized the family's house, then

broke into the safe and found the Blue Fire of Florence."

"It is very hard to break secure lock box. So we had the truck and the hydraulic hoist and took the safe. We cut it open at our warehouse. There were lots of jewels." Valenti sounded proud. "They were very amazing."

"And the gems included the Blue Fire."

He nodded.

"How did you know? How could you verify that it was the actual diamond? Did you have a jewel expert with you?"

"There was huge blue diamond in lock box. We knew the Blue Fire of Florence is red glowing diamond."

"What does that mean?"

"It's very rare. It happens only with certain blue diamonds. Just to be sure, we got special light from jeweler. He called it the ultraviolet color. We took the diamond to the darkest corner of the warehouse and shined the light. When we turned the light off, the Blue Fire of Florence glow like red fire. Very dramatic. That proved it was the real gem. The diamond's huge size was more proof. Of course, in the Medici time, there was nothing like these special lights. But the sun also has the violet color. If someone holds the diamond in sunlight and then brings it into dark room where you are waiting with your eyes already in the darkness, you will see it glow bright red. But the special light makes it easier to see."

"What happened to the diamond?"

"The buyer was in the States. He used a middle seller. A woman named Natalina Garaventa. Natalina got a message to us that she would pay two million dollars cash for the Blue Fire of Florence. That was a lot of money. But the diamond was most amazing. So two million was very good price.

"We made some questions about Natalina Garaventa. We learned she represent a rich buyer in the States. She lived in Hoboken, New Jersey. But she was originally from Italy. She spoke native Italian, and she had a sister in Genoa, Italy. "

Valenti shut his eyes and breathed many shallow lungfuls. I heard phlegm rattling in his bronchial tubes.

"So you sold Natalina the diamond."

"Sì. We brought it to Natalina's sister's house. Full service.

She had jeweler to confirm the authenticity. He brought one of the special lights and shined it on the diamond to see it glow red. He told Natalina - who went by the name Dolly - that it was real, and she paid us cash. Hundred dollar bills. Twenty thousand of them."

"Any idea where the diamond might be now?"

"No."

"Any idea who Dolly was buying it for?"

"Sì," Valenti said. He breathed some more, his lungs sounding worse. "Dolly had married a man who was also from Italy. A man named Antonino Martino Sinatra. Their son was born in Hoboken. He was the singer Frank Sinatra. He was the real purchaser." Valenti appeared distracted by pain.

Street leaned toward me and whispered, "There's your connection between Tahoe and the Italian Renaissance. Do you want to ask him about the Cal Neva Hotel?"

I nodded. I said to Valenti, "Back in the time you speak of, the early sixties, Sinatra owned the Cal Neva, a hotel at Lake Tahoe where we're from," I said. "He was reputed to have been involved with the Mafia, and the state of Nevada took away his gaming license as a result."

Valenti's head moved just a bit. Maybe it was another nod.

"Were you connected to that in some way?" I asked. "Beyond just selling his mother the diamond that you stole? Or, after you knew who the purchaser was, did you or your relatives get involved with Sinatra then?"

Valenti looked at me. Then his hands and abdomen clenched in another crunch-type move. He sucked in air as if fighting pain. Then his muscles loosened. He relaxed. The air came out of his lungs in a long, slow, rattling breath as if he were sighing.

It was his last sigh. He went still.

THIRTY-FOUR

I wanted to walk away. We'd gotten the information we came for. Bruno Valenti had died, and the injured young man was unlikely to talk considering he was the one trying to kill us.

But the ex-cop in me needed to play by the rules. Most of the rules, anyway. So I called the polizia.

We heard their arrival fifteen minutes later, the sound of sirens pulling into the village below and stopping down the slope where the cars could go no farther. After several minutes, five officers came into the door that I'd opened for them. They were all panting hard from their trot up through the steep village. The man in charge spoke excellent English.

"I am Ispettore Speranza. And you are?"

"I'm Owen McKenna and this is my companion Street Casey."

"From America," he said, recognizing Americans, as all Italians do, whether it be by speech or clothing or manner. He walked over and looked down at Valenti's body, touching the face, then touching the cornea on one of Valenti's eyeballs. With no reaction, it was an effective way of telling that there was no normal brain function. He drew his fingertips down over Valenti's eyes to shut his eyelids. They reopened half way. He did it again. They stayed mostly shut.

"Ispettore Speranza means...?" I said.

"Like a police inspector in America." He was proud.

I nodded. "I was with the San Francisco Police Department before I quit."

He looked at me, reassessing. "What was your rank?"

"I was a homicide inspector."

Speranza frowned.

"Like a sergeant who focuses on murder," I said. "Just as you're doing now."

"You said 'was.' Now you are retired? Or private?" Speranza said.

"Private."

"You are in Italy on business or pleasure?"

"Business."

He gestured at Bruno Valenti's body. "This is your business?"

"Right." I told him about the murders back home in Tahoe and the victims who had been interested in the Italian Renaissance and Professor Drago in Florence who told us about the Blue Fire of Florence rumor and how he said that if anyone could give us more information about the diamond, it would be Bruno Valenti. I explained how we'd spoken to Valenti for a bit and then, after we left, we were pursued and shot at by Valenti's assistant.

Inspector Speranza didn't react to anything I said, but he took careful notes.

"Was Valenti's man trying to scare you? Or was he aiming to kill?" Speranza asked.

"It seemed that he was shooting to kill. Several of the shots struck walls near my head. Stone chips flew. One stung me here." I reached up and touched my cheek.

Speranza nodded. "You have some dried blood. How was it that you escaped him?"

"We ran through multiple passages while he chased us on his motor scooter. When he followed us up to the church, I was able to tip one of the sculptures in front of him, which made him fall over the wall and slide down the slope. I climbed down to him. He was alive but unconscious."

The policeman turned to the other cops who'd come with him. He sent three of them out to find the man who rode the scooter. The fourth man stood near Valenti's body, his back to the window wall, waiting as if to guard Speranza should anyone else come into the room.

After the three men left, Speranza turned back to me. "You're pursuing the famous rumored diamond from the era of the Medicis. You came all the way from America to follow a rumor." He didn't sound scornful so much as disappointed that Americans could be so extravagant in chasing a fictional treasure.

"Yes," I answered.

"Did Mr. Valenti give you useful information?"

"He wasn't eager to be helpful. But I think he didn't want to seem too resistant because then we might think that he was hiding something significant. At first, he told us that he knew nothing about the diamond. So we left. Then his man chased us and shot at us. I took that as an indication that Valenti did, in fact, have information about the diamond. But after his man crashed on the scooter and we came back to talk, Valenti seemed quite stressed, and then he died." My statement was marginally correct. I worried that if I were more forthcoming, it would serve no purpose other than delaying us in Italy.

"Tell me again the series of events when Valenti's man chased you. How was it that you came back and let yourself into this house?"

I recounted what happened, step by step. Speranza consulted his notes from the first time I'd told the story. He was no doubt looking for any inconsistencies in my reporting. He was especially interested in our movements when we got back into the house.

Again, I told the truth albeit with a different emphasis than I might use in a future retelling.

"Bruno Valenti appeared to be bedridden," I said, "so when the young man who'd shot at us crashed and got knocked out, I took his keys so I could let us back into the house and inform Valenti. I assumed, of course, that Valenti had sent him on his mission to kill us."

"You might have gotten killed. Valenti could have had a gun under his leg. He may still." The ispettore turned and looked at Valenti's body.

"Yes, I was aware of that. I came up close to him before I woke him just so I could grab his arm if he reached for a weapon. But he didn't."

"Was he dead?"

"No. He was asleep. I said his name, and he woke up. He was startled to see me."

"Because he thought that you'd be dead." The policeman made it a statement.

"Probably."

"What happened then?"

"He clenched his hands and body, then took a pill and said that this was his fifth heart attack and that the doctor had told him that if he had another heart attack, it would kill him. Valenti said he wanted to die at his home. Which he then did. He made a long exhalation and went still."

Speranza made some more notes. He paused. "You are certain that the man who shot at you worked for Valenti?"

"Yes. He was the one who originally let us in to speak with Mr. Valenti. His key unlocked the back door."

"Did you have friction with the young man? Or do you think Valenti told him to kill you, and he was merely following orders?"

"I have no evidence either way. We had no friction. The man said nothing, and we overheard nothing."

Speranza nodded.

As a general principle, and also because of my background in law enforcement, I believe in telling the whole truth. But I'm willing to modify that principle under the condition that withholding information does not jeopardize justice and that it increases the safety of innocent victims.

In this case, the perpetrator was dead. So I decided not to mention Frank Sinatra. I knew that if Valenti's statement about stealing the diamond and delivering it to Sinatra's mother was made public, it would get back to the States and to Tahoe and create a huge media storm. The attention would likely cause the murderer in Tahoe to speed his plan and kill more people before we could catch him.

Speranza made some more notes. "Let me be sure I understand," he said slowly. "You came to Italy not knowing what BFF referred to. And even though Professor Drago told you the story about the Blue Fire, you've still found no actual evidence for this diamond."

"Correct," I said. I didn't feel bad saying it because, despite Valenti's story, I still had no evidence. Just a story from a convicted mobster who may have been enamored with the idea of a connection between him and Sinatra. And with the mobster aware of his impending death, what would keep him from spinning that story to grander levels?

Speranza looked up from his notebook. "Do you think you've come closer to understanding your killer's motive?"

"I don't know. Now that I know that BFF refers to a diamond, real or fictional, my best guess is that the killer believes the diamond exists and he thinks that other people he knows can find it. He may be killing those other people so that, if and when he finds the Blue Fire, he can keep it for himself."

Speranza nodded, his skepticism obvious.

The front door opened. One cop came in, stepped aside, and held the door for the other two. They carried the young man, one cop holding his shoulders, and the other cop holding his feet. From the posture and the skin coloring, it appeared that the young man was dead.

THIRTY-FIVE

They set the body on the floor.

"He was dead when you found him?" Speranza said to his colleagues in English.

They spoke back in Italian. I got the sense that the man had died as they carried him back to the house.

Speranza took more notes. One of the cops handed Speranza the young man's wallet. Speranza looked at the ID. They all spoke in Italian. They were animated. It was obvious that the young man's identity was significant. Eventually, Speranza spoke to us.

"This man is Mario Montana, someone we've been looking for. Informants associate him with Tony Scozzari. They are both reputed to be Cosa Nostra soldiers. They are subjects of interest in two murder cases in Palermo, Sicily. Now we have Montana, a very good thing. But we still need to find Scozzari. We heard from an informant that Scozzari had gone to the states and that Montana had come up here to Tuscany. But he was never spotted. Finding him here, working for Valenti, is an important event. It is unfortunate that he is dead. He could have given us useful information."

"If he broke his code of silence," I said.

Without pause, Speranza said, "We have techniques." He made a quick glance toward Street. Maybe he was embarrassed. Maybe not.

"I've never heard of the names Scozzari or Montana in Tahoe." I turned to Street. "Have you?"

She shook her head. "No."

Speranza said, "You've mentioned Tahoe. Remind me how it is that I've heard that name."

"Lake Tahoe is a large mountain lake on the border of California and Nevada," I said. "It's a very popular tourist area. The lake is surrounded by mountains with a dozen ski resorts.

There's lots of boating, hiking, skiing."

Speranza nodded.

"Scozzari is especially notable to us because the man we believe to be his grandfather was a boss in the Los Angeles crime family in the fifties. We don't know if Scozzari originally came from America. Or perhaps his father did and the young man was born here. Both Antonio Scozzari and Mario Montana are like apparitions, men made of smoke, of mirrors. More idea than substance."

"Similar to how you think of the Blue Fire of Florence," I said.

Speranza looked at me with hard eyes. "Exactly. And now that we've found Montana, it starts to make Scozzari seem more real as well."

"Do you have a photograph or description of Scozzari?"

"No photograph. Two descriptions from informants contradict each other so much, we thought maybe Scozzari was having people impersonate him. Tall, short, brown hair, blond hair, brown eyes, blue eyes, heavy, skinny, handsome, ugly, rough skin, smooth skin. Either that or he is very good at makeup."

One of the other policemen approached. He handed a piece of paper to Speranza and spoke to him in Italian.

After a moment, Speranza turned to us. "My men have searched Montana's room. The only thing they found that was somewhat unusual was this paper, tucked into a Bible." He handed it to me.

It had handwriting that said 'TahoeBlueFire@gmail.com.'

I handed it to Street. "I found this same email address written on Darla Ali's desk."

"Doesn't ring a bell," she said, handing it back to Speranza.

"Who is Darla Ali?" he asked.

"One of the murder victims in Tahoe."

He made a slow nod. "This certainly suggests that Montana was in contact with someone who is in Tahoe or knows Tahoe. Could the address belong to Darla Ali?"

"I couldn't find out. If so, she probably was in contact with Montana. If not, she was probably in contact with the same person who Montana communicated with. Either way, this is a connection between Darla and Montana."

Speranza said, "Normally, I would email an inquiry to this address and see if we get a response. But I'm thinking this is something you might want to pursue." He looked over at Montana's body. "I have a closed case. You don't. I'm assuming you would be kind enough to let me know if you learn anything."

"Of course," I said.

"This paper needs to go in the case file. Do you need me to write down the email address?"

"No, thanks. I can remember TahoeBlueFire at gmail.com."

Speranza said, "Is there any chance you can file a request with Google to learn the identity of the account holder?"

"From what I've heard, no," I said. "They may cooperate with requests from the U.S. National Security Agency, but not with private investigators."

Speranza looked over at Street. "I would like you both to come with me outside and show me where you ran and where Montana was when he shot at you."

We nodded. "Of course."

Speranza made a call, speaking in Italian. Then he spoke to two of his men. I gathered that he wanted them to stay at Valenti's house, maybe to wait for the medical examiner. He gestured for Street and me and the other two cops to come outside.

We spent the next two hours retracing our steps as best as we remembered. We showed him the locations where we thought we'd been shot at and where Mario Montana had been when he fired. Speranza took more notes.

At one point, a short, elderly woman came out of a small doorway. She spoke rapid words to Speranza and the other cops. Then she pointed at us. Speranza spoke back. After several exchanges, Speranza said, "Grazie," and the woman went back inside.

Speranza turned to us. "The woman says that she saw you two running up this passage, and a moment later she saw a young man come after you on a motorcycle. He had a gun and was firing at you. Just as you suggested, she said she was afraid to tell us until she saw my men carrying the man's body. So your story has been corroborated," he said.

I nodded.

We continued on our trek. When we got to the medieval church where the damaged scooter lay on its side near the bronze sculpture, I motioned for Speranza to come along, and I climbed down the embankment to show him where Montana had slid and where I'd found him. Speranza continued past me, angling sideways. Ten yards down, he broke a stick from a bush, bent down, and pulled a pistol out of the brush, using his stick to lift the gun by its trigger guard. He held it up. It was medium in size and had a three-inch-long silencer attached to the barrel.

"Looks like a Beretta PX-Four Storm," I said. "A reliable Italian semi-auto, but not especially accurate at a distance. Especially with a silencer."

"You know your weapons," Speranza said. "It is similar to our Ninety-two." He patted his own holstered sidearm. He walked up the slope toward me. Using a handkerchief, he pushed the magazine release button on the Storm and looked at the ammo. "Forty-five ACP."

"I'm glad he missed us," I said.

"What do you carry in the States? Something similar?"

"I don't carry."

"An ex-cop? I don't understand."

"Personal preference," I said.

He looked at me for a moment. "You had a bad experience."

"Yes."

Speranza let it drop, which I appreciated.

We climbed back up to the church where we all sat on the short stone wall and Speranza asked Street and me more questions about our movements and Montana's pursuit. He focused on Street's perspective of events. He also wrote down our passport numbers and our contact information.

One of the cops we'd left at Valenti's house approached with a man in dress clothes. We heard Italian and the word medico several times.

Speranza spoke to the medico at length, then nodded and said grazie. They left and Speranza turned to us. "The doctor said that his preliminary examination suggests that Valenti died of natural causes and Montana died of accidental causes, Valenti possibly by myocardial infarction and Montana probably by traumatic brain injury."

I nodded.

"I don't mind saying that I'm not sorry these men died," Speranza said. He closed his notebook. "I believe I have enough information. You may go."

"Will you want to see us again?" I said.

"I have what I need. If Montana and Valenti were still alive, we'd want you to provide testimony. But with them both dead, we have little need for your continued involvement. If something comes up, I know how to contact you. It is okay with me if you go home."

"Thank you. I think our business in Tuscany is done," I said.

As he shook my hand, he said, "I wish you luck catching your murderer." Then he turned to Street and took her hand in both of his. "It has been a pleasure to speak with you, and if you have any unattached sisters, please tell them I give free, personal tours of Tuscany."

Street smiled at him, the tight hard smile of someone who's trying to be polite despite their pain, and we left to walk back down the steep pathways to our little Fiat.

THIRTY-SIX

Later that afternoon, when we got back into our Florence hotel room, Street began trembling. I sat her down with me on the bed and held her.

"I'm sorry," she said, her voice wavering and tears building up and spilling over her lower eyelids. "I can pull maggots out of corpses, but having someone trying to kill us is different."

I rubbed her shoulders.

"I can't get those gunshots out of my mind. The flashes coming out of that gun barrel. Every little noise makes me flinch." She was crying now, tear tracks down to her chin.

"It's upsetting, sweetheart. When someone shoots at you, it shakes you deep." I leaned toward her and tucked her head under my chin and pulled her up against me.

"Do you think Bruno Valenti was telling the truth?" Street asked, her voice thick.

"About what?"

"That he didn't know what you meant when you said he'd made a mistake sending Montana after us." Street's nose was running.

"I don't know. I assumed he was just protesting. But I suppose it's possible he didn't know and that Montana acted by himself. Montana may have been working for Valenti so that he could find out about the Blue Fire Diamond. Maybe he's been feeding information about the Blue Fire Diamond to Scozzari back in Tahoe. Or maybe he was working with Darla. Montana may have already known I was working on the case in Tahoe. So when I showed up at his door, he decided to take me out of the way."

"I don't like it," Street said.

We sat in silence for 15 minutes, both of us probably thinking things we didn't want to put into words. The only sound was city traffic on the street below us and the occasional click of shoes in the hallway outside our door.

"Do you think you're up to eating some dinner?" I finally said.

Street wiped her face. "Yes. But I must look like a Halloween mask or something."

"You look upset is all. Everybody knows what upset is. And anyway, you're still beautiful."

"You lie," Street said, "but I love you for your kindness."

We headed out into the bustling medieval city and found an elegant but light dinner and with it, a bottle of Chianti Classico.

The next day, we caught the late-morning flight out of Florence, repeating our previous trip in reverse. The Alps were covered in clouds, so we couldn't see the spectacular peaks and glaciers. Frankfurt was socked in with rain and looked no more interesting than Newark. Our second flight followed the sun as we headed northwest up toward Greenland, but below us was only clouds. After another eleven hours nonstop, we landed at SFO in what appeared to be solid fog. Eager to get back to Tahoe sunshine, we boarded the shuttle flight to Reno only to find that the Sierra was having a spring snow storm intense enough to have pushed over the Carson Range on the east side of the Tahoe Basin and down into the Nevada valleys.

Our airport waits ate up the clock, and we'd been traveling for 21 hours. But because we followed the sun and went back through 9 time zones, our 21 hours had only moved us 12 hours forward on the clock. When we got into the Jeep at the Reno/Tahoe airport parking lot, the clock said 10 p.m. But our bodies were on Italian time, so it felt like seven the next morning. Because of our jet lag, combined with snow and high wind in the Washoe Valley, I drove the Jeep slowly, feeling the wheels struggle to grip on the wet, icy, compacted snow. The headlights were impotent in the face of waves of snow blocking all vision. I'd hoped that the snow would ease as we continued south and dropped down 400 feet into Carson City, but it seemed to intensify. Farther south, Carson Valley was enduring a blizzard. When we got to Diamond's house in Minden, Nevada, we pulled into his drive through eight inches of fresh powder.

Street had called Diamond en route, so he was waiting for us. He opened the front door as we got out of the Jeep. The light spilling out of his house lit up the giant flakes swirling down from the sky. Spot pushed out and raced around, possibly as eager to play in the fresh snow as he was eager to see us. We'd been gone only a few nights, so Spot was still on his Diamond-and-Danishes high. Having us come home might have been a disappointment. But he put on a good performance and wagged and bounced as we both hugged him.

"Snowing too hard to drive up to the lake, don't you think?" Diamond said.

We agreed.

"You want beer and chips or something?"

"It feels like tomorrow morning to us, so it would be best if we crashed."

Diamond understood. "You know where the guest room is. This way, Spot and I get one more party night together." Diamond turned to Spot. "Hey, dude, you want beer and chips?"

Spot wagged so hard his entire 170 pounds rocked side-to-side.

Street and I climbed up the narrow stairs to the attic of Diamond's bungalow. Spot followed and tried to play with me a bit, grabbing my hands as I play-boxed with him. I gave him a headlock, rubbed him, then sent him back down the stairs to Diamond.

Street and I climbed into the two narrow beds under Diamond's sloping attic roof and were asleep in minutes.

In the morning, we joined Diamond for coffee. Spot lay on the floor nearby. The snow had stopped falling, and the little desert town of Minden looked like something out of a Christmas movie. A foot of spring snow draped the trees and hung down from the eaves and stood up high on the mailbox. It was a strange perception shift. I kept thinking it looked like a great deal of snow, even as I knew that, were I out of the desert and up in Tahoe, I'd regard it as a modest little dusting of white, a thin blanket of no account.

Diamond looked at the time. "Civic duty calls in less than an hour. Gotta go give the taxpayers good value."

"Good to have a job," I said.

"Learn anything interesting in yonder Italia?"

I hadn't yet had enough coffee to cut my brain fog, so Street gave it to him in linear fashion, her recitation as precise as one would expect from a scientist. She turned to me. "Did I leave anything out?"

"Just the turquoise confetti," I said.

Street made a sly smile. "I'm thinking that Diamond wouldn't be interested in that."

I saw Diamond's eyebrows twitch. "Sounds like something that ain't my business," he said. After a long silence, he added, "So, where to now?"

"From what Bruno Valenti told us, I'm going to start with Sinatra. His whereabouts during the early sixties, for example."

"Tahoe, the Cal Neva Hotel, Palm Springs, and Vegas, of course," Diamond said.

"And his associates," I said.

"The Kennedy brothers, the Rat Pack, the boys at his little business he called Reprise Records," Diamond said.

"His association with the Mob," I said.

"Sam Giancana, Carlo Gambino, Lucky Luciano," Diamond said.

"His loves."

Diamond thought about it. "In the early sixties, he was between marriages. He'd recently divorced Ava Gardner, and Mia Farrow didn't appear for several years."

"Not much there," I said.

Diamond said, "Of course, he did have an affair with Marilyn Monroe."

"You may have just struck gold," I said.

"Or diamonds," Diamond said.

"At that time, she was the most famous and desirable woman in the world, right?" Street said. "Didn't Sinatra have a cabin at the Cal Neva that was set aside for her?"

Diamond drank coffee and nodded. "Yeah. And the secret tunnels made it so that he and she and all the others could come and go out of sight of the paparazzi."

"How do you know all this stuff?" I asked.

Diamond frowned. "If you moved south of the border and adopted it as your new country, I'd expect you to brush up on all things Mexican, which would include pop culture history."

Street looked at Diamond. "Let's say you had enough millions to buy the Blue Fire of Florence and you were in Sinatra's shoes. Would you make it a present to Marilyn Monroe?"

"Sure. Why not? She'd be a pretty good catch, huh? But I'd change the name. The Blue Fire of Florence would become… Let me think. The Tahoe Blue Fire." He glanced again at the time. "Gotta go. Lock up when you leave?"

"Thanks." I lifted my coffee cup toward him as a salute. "I appreciate you taking care of my hound even though I'll probably never be able to get him to eat dog food again."

Diamond nodded, gave Street a kiss, Spot a bear hug, and left out the kitchen door.

Spot stood at the closed door, his ears twitching as he listened to the inaudible sounds of Diamond as he shuffled down the snowy sidewalk, brushed the snow off his old, rust-experiment pickup, started up the noisy engine with bronchitis in the carburetor, and drove away.

"What about you?" Street asked me. "Would you have paid two million back then to buy a giant Medici diamond for Marilyn Monroe?"

I walked over behind Street and wrapped my arms around her, my hands exploring. "I don't know about Monroe," I whispered in her ear, "but I'd certainly buy it for you."

"Because I'm a classy broad?"

"Hmm," I said.

"Or because of my turquoise confetti?"

"Well, there is that," I said.

THIRTY-SEVEN

The hot spring sun popped out and quickly began melting what snow was left on the highways after the plows had done their nighttime work. By the time we climbed up from Carson Valley and crested Daggett Pass at the top of Kingsbury Grade, the roads were free of snow and ice, and, as the sun cooked their surfaces, they steamed billowing clouds in the air. But under the trees, away from the sun, the snowpack was even deeper than before.

Because we were still very tired, we skipped stopping at my office or Street's bug lab and drove up the East Shore toward home. The high sun was blinding on the snowfields of the West Shore mountains across the lake. I dropped Street off at her condo, and Spot and I drove up the mountain to my cabin.

There was another piece of paper stuck in my cabin door.

Like the first, it had the upside down pentagram symbol of evil Black Magic.

The message was once again written with a template, the block letters revealing nothing of the writer.

LAST CHANCE TO QUIT, MCKENNA. HOW MANY DEATHS CAN YOU TAKE?

I ushered Spot inside, away from any sightline from up on the mountain behind my cabin. The note may have been there for a few days, so it was unlikely a shooter was currently up on the mountain training his rifle's sights on me.

After considering the risk and danger, I had a little internal debate about the merits and demerits of a late-morning barbecued hotdog on the deck. I won the debate, so I lit the charcoal and shoveled two and a half feet of snow off the deck as the coals warmed up. I mostly stayed back near the cabin wall so a shooter couldn't hit me without running up on the deck, something I didn't think fit his style.

Because hotdogs burn easily, I put four of them on the side with the fewest coals and arranged half a bag of French fries crosswise to the grill wires on the side with the most coals. I set buns and ketchup out on the little deck table and sat down to wait and turn the hotdogs and fries. Spot came over, his nose held high. He inched closer and closer to the barbecue, wet nostrils flexing.

"Carbon monoxide, dude," I said, pushing him back. He swung his head and looked at me for a fraction of a second, his ear stud flashing, then turned back and stared at the hotdogs.

When the hotdogs and fries were done, I put half in Spot's bowl to cool, broke them into pieces, doused them with Ketchup, and let him dive in.

When I eat hotdogs and fries, I savor the taste as the upside of eating unhealthy food. When Spot eats hotdogs, he savors the speed at which he can ingest them. We think of dogs as salivating over taste and smell. But Spot proves over and over that the big concern dogs have about meals isn't how great they taste but how they can be a huge waste of time. Spot's speed suggested that his time was extremely valuable and he didn't have a second to spare. I'd almost finished chewing my first bite when he was done with his lunch. He licked the last drop of Ketchup out of his bowl, then lay down on the deck boards to enjoy the sunshine. The sun's heat was so intense that the boards that I'd shoveled just minutes before were now snowless and steaming. Spot flopped over onto his side on the warming boards, gave a big sigh, and began snoozing.

After I ate, I pulled my reclining deck chair back up against the cabin so that I was out of sight. It was only one in the afternoon, but that was ten in the evening in Italy. I tipped my broad-brimmed hat over my face and snoozed along with Spot.

When I woke, my transition to the non-dream world was predictably slow. I brewed some coffee and drank it as I thought about how, despite what I'd learned about the Blue Fire Diamond, I was still no closer to finding the killer.

I turned on the laptop and started composing an email to send to TahoeBlueFire@gmail.com. I didn't know for certain that the account holder was connected to the murders, so I wanted wording that would be suggestive but not accusatory.

I settled on, 'I know your identity, and I know you want the Blue Fire. Contact me, and we'll discuss terms. Owen McKenna.' I hit send.

Next, I did some research on Sinatra, his associates, his songs, and his Cal Neva Hotel.

I learned that while Sinatra had been wildly successful at singing for his supper, he also made real money as a businessman who started Reprise Records in 1960, and then sold it for big bucks a few years later to Warner Brothers Music. It was his ownership of Reprise Records that gave him the nickname Chairman of the Board.

Sinatra also bought the Cal Neva Hotel and Casino in 1960. It was a period of intense activity at the Cal Neva involving many famous people. They were able to escape the paparazzi and move about the Cal Neva grounds incognito by utilizing secret tunnels that connected the various buildings.

Rat Pack members Dean Martin and Sammy Davis Jr. performed there along with Sinatra. Will Rogers, Peter Lawford, Joe DiMaggio, and Marilyn Monroe vacationed there. Monroe came frequently enough that she had her own cabin near the lake.

In 1960, Monroe was filming in the nearby Nevada desert with Clark Gable and Montgomery Clift in what became the John Huston masterpiece, The Misfits. Sinatra invited the cast of The Misfits up to the Cal Neva, and he sang for them.

Monroe's marriage to playwright Arthur Miller was collapsing during the filming of The Misfits, a movie for which Miller had written the screenplay.

Sinatra had reportedly been seduced by Monroe back when he was married to Ava Gardner. So when Monroe divorced Arthur Miller, Sinatra began focusing on Monroe, possibly hoping for a more permanent relationship with her.

Unfortunately, Sinatra's misfortunes grew. He played too fast and loose with some Mob boys, especially Sam Giancana. And while the Nevada gaming bureaucrats had tried to give their most famous licensee a lot of wiggle room, Sinatra hadn't been appropriately respectful of them. So they yanked his permits, which forced him out of the casino business.

It was a tough period for Sinatra, and he had emotional altercations with a range of people. Maybe his celebrity was a magnet for people problems. But it could also be that he was predisposed to such issues, because he referred to himself as an 18-karat manic depressive.

I'd met several manic depressives over the years - a great colorful term now lost to the temperate, boring, and politically correct term bi-polar disorder, and I always thought that they were less crazy than our culture commonly presents them. Nevertheless, it seemed perfect that an 18-karat mania might help someone low on their meds justify purchasing a mega diamond to give to a girl.

Especially if that girl was Marilyn Monroe.

I called my friend Glennie Gorman, ace reporter for the Tahoe Herald.

"Owen, you bad boy," she exclaimed when I identified myself.

"Bad for what?"

"For not having called me in forever. What are you doing, where are you, and how is Street? Wait, never mind all that. Just tell me, how is His Largeness?"

I looked at him, sprawled on the rug in front of the wood stove. "He's sleeping off a barbecued hotdog/French fry lunch as we speak."

"This is how you augment the sawdust chunks? Where's the broccoli for vitamins? And what's this I hear about a quick trip to Italy?"

"The reason for my call. The Cal Neva Hotel on the North Shore," I said. "What do you know about it?"

"What's there to know? Nice place on the North Shore. Sits on the state line with half the lobby in California and half in Nevada. The swimming pool is split down the middle, too. Used to be owned by Sinatra. Currently closed for renovation."

"Zero in on the Sinatra part."

"Oooh, now my antenna is vibrating. What are you working on?"

"The truth is that I don't know," I said.

"But it has something to do with Ol' Blue Eyes," Glennie said. "Thus the Italian connection."

"Maybe."

"Okay. So this reporter could quote the book on his gaming license debacle and his fist fight with the Mob boss and his trysts with Monroe and his Rat Pack friends. But the most interesting thing about Sinatra wasn't about him."

"You lost me," I said.

"Sinatra is the guy who introduced Marilyn Monroe to his friends the Kennedy Brothers, who also frequented his Cal Neva. The evidence suggests that both John and Bobby had flings with her. Which was probably hard for Sinatra. He wanted to impress her with the mighty and powerful men he knew. But he didn't anticipate that she'd wander off into the presidential forest."

"But isn't that what sex goddesses do?"

"Like many women who hate to credit her with serious acting chops, I want to think that. But way, way back I remember doing a story on the famous acting coach Lee Strasberg. He said that of the hundreds of actors he worked with, it was Marlon Brando and Marilyn Monroe who stood above all the rest. And when I saw her last movie, The Misfits, I had to acknowledge that she was an amazing actor. Anyway, JFK was running for president at the time, and JFK's charisma trumped even Sinatra's. JFK and Marilyn Monroe embarked on a long affair that continued even after he moved into the White House."

Glennie's comment presented me with more reason for Sinatra to acquire the Blue Fire of Florence. With Marilyn Monroe succumbing to future President John Kennedy's allure, Sinatra might think that acquiring one of the most famous gems in the world would woo her back.

"You went silent on me," Glennie said.

"Sorry, you just got me thinking. Tell me, have you ever heard of the Blue Fire of Florence?"

"No. What's that?"

I gave her the basics of the BFF and how Sinatra acquired it.

For a cynical reporter who can't be surprised by anything, Glennie oohed and aahed at a pretty high amplitude. "What do you want from me?" she asked.

"I'm wondering if you can find out what the Blue Fire of Florence might be worth."

It was a moment before Glennie spoke. "This is a diamond that might not exist, and even if it does, we don't really have any information about it."

"Correct."

"Yet you want a value," she said.

I thought about it. "Tell you what. Let's just get a current value on the Hope Diamond, about which we know everything."

"Because you think the Blue Fire of Florence would have the same value?"

"No. Substantially less, because it has no provenance. But the Hope value would give us a ballpark indication."

"And how would I learn this?"

"You're the investigative reporter."

"Okay. I'll call you when I know something." She hung up.

THIRTY-EIGHT

The next morning, I decided to visit the safe house to check in on Adam Simms. On the way up Kingsbury Grade, I saw two rotary plows and a grader parked on a vacant lot. Maybe that's where the Douglas County snow removal contractor stored them. But they were probably too far from the South Lake Tahoe snow dump to be considered in connection to the murders.

When I got to the safe house, I left Spot in the Jeep. Adam remembered me, but he was slow and had about him a general air of confusion. Blondie seemed ecstatic to have me reappear into her life. She jumped on me, raced around, jumped again, her tail a blur.

Adam and I talked for some time. I told him about our trip to Italy. When I explained what the Blue Fire of Florence was, he didn't seem to have much interest.

After we talked, I asked, "May I look at the photos on your phone?"

Adam's face changed from resignation to worry. "Why?"

"Maybe I'll see something or someone that would give me useful information."

"So you suspect me of murder?"

"It's routine investigation procedure. It's my job to look for information."

"What if I don't show you?" Adam didn't look defiant. He looked confused.

"Then we'll get a search warrant."

"I could lose my phone before then. I could delete all my photos."

"True, but how would that look?"

"I could call a lawyer."

I wondered about the best response. "Yes, you could," I said. Adam thought about it. His eyes went back and forth like those of a guilty criminal.

Adam reached into his pocket and pulled out his phone. He leaned forward and handed it to me.

I turned it on and opened his camera roll.

There were 1814 photos. I couldn't give them all proper attention without a great deal of time. But I wanted to get a feel for them, so I started with the most recent one and scrolled back through them.

They were a strange collection. Faces up close, full figures at a distance. There were pictures of food, asparagus and onions in a refrigerator drawer, milk and orange juice, canned beans, a jar of spaghetti sauce, toothpaste, deodorant, a box of Kleenex. There was a picture of a road sign, a picture of car keys, a picture of a door with letters that spelled a doctor's name. There were pictures of all manner of prosaic objects. But there were no pretty pictures of scenery, no pictures similar to what other people had in their phones.

I clicked fast through all of the ones that were obvious memory helps or grocery lists and slowed for a close look at all of the ones of people's faces. Most of the people meant nothing to me. Eventually, I came to a picture of myself. Later, I came to a picture of Diamond and a closeup picture of his sheriff's name tag that he pins to his shirt.

Adam sat patiently while I continued to click through his photos.

Quite often, there was a picture of people that included a shot of Adam. I showed him one.

"This shot of you with these men, what was that about?"

He looked at it and frowned. "I don't know. I try to have people use my phone to take pictures of me with other people. It's supposed to help me remember what I did, where I went. Doctor's suggestion."

I kept scrolling through his photos. "Here's another one with you in a group of people." I held the phone out so he could see it. "Ring a bell?"

He shook his head. "I guess photos don't really help my memory."

After a couple of minutes, I came to a photo that stopped

me.

It was a picture of a rotary, the big kind with two engines. On the door was the South Lake Tahoe city logo. The rotary was chewing its way down a snow berm, shooting a giant arc of snow into the forest.

"Do you know when you took this photo?" I held out the phone.

Adam grinned. "That one I do remember. I saw that rotary when I was going to the doctor. I was walking into the office as it came down the street. It was blowing the berm. It was amazing and louder than a full-speed freight train engine."

"And you took the photo just because you liked it."

He nodded, his eyes crinkling with excitement. "I've seen them with engines running, but I've never seen them up close while they were blowing snow."

I'd never seen Adam look excited.

"I once worked at the yard where they store them," he said. "I got to look inside the auger and impeller and the discharge chute. And one time, one of the drivers let me climb up into the cab, and he showed me how it worked. But I never got to actually drive one."

That gave me pause. "Where was this yard where you worked?"

"The City of South Lake Tahoe. After I moved up to Tahoe to stay at Felicite's house, she thought I should try to get a job. She said it would be good for my brain. The doctor agreed. So I applied around town. I tried for a bagging job at the supermarket, a valet park at the hotels, a general grunt job at a construction company. It was the city that took me on. They put me out at one of their equipment yards in the industrial area. The place where they store and work on the rotaries. I liked it. Those machines are awesome."

"But you didn't keep the job?"

Adam's face lost its cheer. "I kept forgetting where I put stuff. Some of those tools are real expensive. After I lost a wrench set, I decided to quit."

"Do you remember the name of the guy in charge of the yard?"

Adam shook his head.

"Does Brann Crosen sound familiar?"

Adam frowned. "I don't remember."

"About five-eight. Bodybuilder."

"Oh, yeah. I didn't like him."

"Why not?"

Adam shrugged. "I didn't think he could be trusted."

"You might be right." I gestured with the phone. "Mind if I email some of these photos to myself?"

"Help yourself," he said.

When I was done, I handed Adam's phone back to him.

THIRTY-NINE

After I was done talking to Adam, I drove over to the industrial yard where the city stored the rotary blowers, let myself in the gate, and left it open.

Emilio came over to me. He held what looked like a sealed bearing assembly that had the seals removed. The bearings were caked in dirty grease as were his fingers.

I nodded at him.

"Te recuerdo. I remember you," he said. "You are to see Brann?"

"Please. He in?"

The man nodded, then tipped his head toward the little metal shed I'd previously visited. Then he walked back to his project.

I walked under the pole building, over to the shed, and pulled open the door without knocking.

Brann Crosen was sitting at a desk that faced the door. He was staring at a laptop screen that only he could see. He looked up at me, startled, his face instantly reddening. He quickly tapped several keys, then shut the laptop.

"Working hard?" I said, unable to combat my prejudice toward him. If a guy embezzles five thousand bucks, we put him in jail. If a guy uses a lawsuit to scam his employer for a hundred thousand, we happily pay out hoping he goes away. Then his lawyer uses the award for bragging rights to get more business. And if our conscience or fury causes us to make the mistake of saying anything bad about either of them, they can sue us for defamation. I knew that the legal system protects and helps many honest people, but I was confident that this guy wasn't one of them.

"Still pursuing your death-by-snowblower idea?" Crosen's grin had a touch of sneer. His face color was shifting back to normal. The light caught his face. His front teeth were capped.

In the light, his eyeliner and eyebrow edges looked more like tattoos than makeup. Probably used the lawsuit money for all three. Good to know he had his priorities in the right place.

"I heard you changed your name when you lived in Southern California," I said. "What was that about?"

Crosen's face began to redden again. "I don't know what you're talking about."

"You were given the name Brann Crosen at birth?"

"Who else would I be?"

I thought about Mario Montana, the man who tried to kill Street and me in Italy, and Montana's friend Scozzari, who Speranza had said was a Cosa Nostra soldier who grew up in L.A. "How about Scozzari?" I said.

Crosen paused as if wondering where I'd gotten that information.

"I don't know what you're talking about," he said. He opened his laptop. "I have work to do."

"You had an employee here named Adam Simms," I said.

"We sure did. That was an interesting experiment."

"How do you mean?"

"You try to train a big, dumb football player, and you'll see what I mean."

"He's not dumb," I said, feeling instant anger.

"Right. He walked around here like an old man who can't find his pants. He'd talk to himself, always looking for something but not remembering what he was looking for. Once in awhile he'd act like he had half a brain. But that was rare. About one to four, most of the time."

"What does that mean?"

"One good day for every four bad days. We could tell each morning when he showed up. Norman would usually see him first. Then he'd let us know. He'd say, 'up day,' if Simms had his half brain on. Or, 'down day' if Simms's brain was absent. Sometimes we'd place bets at night about whether the next day would be up or down."

"You bet on the state of his dementia?"

"Yeah. You got a problem with that?"

"Yes, I do." I was gritting my teeth.

"So that's, like, some politically incorrect thing? Guys can't joke around?"

"No, it's a decency thing. Joking about someone who's struggling with a severe disease is rude and obnoxious."

"Like I thought. You're politically correct. Like Emilio out there. He doesn't like to joke, either." Crosen picked his nose, watching me watch him. Then he flicked his finger so that whatever was on it flew onto the floor. "Simms could lift stuff, though, I'll give him that. I'm told he could play football twenty or thirty years ago." Crosen guffawed. "Imagine that. The guy's so big, no way could he move fast."

I tried to suppress my anger. "I'm here to ask if he ever drove one of the rotaries."

Crosen stared at me, frowning, then got a knowing smile. "Oh sure. I showed him, and he cruised it across the yard. He was like a little kid. He even crabbed it left and right. I let him eat one of the snow piles in that corner over there." He pointed. "The guy was a natural."

"Would you say he was good enough driving the rotary that he could have borrowed one?"

"Absolutely. In fact, if I had to guess who might have done your victims, I would have said him. All the other guys in the yard have ethics. But Simms, I don't think he knew the difference between right and wrong. 'Course, I wouldn't normally say that, but you asked. Anyway, it was too bad we couldn't keep him."

"Why not?"

"We had to let him go for incompetence. Big is good. Dumb is not. We have standards."

"What was your official reason for letting him go?"

"Like I said, incompetence."

I walked away without saying another word, my blood pressure pulsing in my temples. Crosen had irritated me in every way a person could. As I headed out of the yard, I walked by Emilio. "You ever see Adam Simms drive a rotary when he worked here?" I asked.

Emilio glanced over toward the shed where Crosen was. He turned a bit so he was facing the opposite direction. "Not that I have saw," he said.

"You think he maybe drove it when you weren't working?"

"I don't think. He love big machines, so powerful. If drove, he would be talking about all the time."

When I was back in the Jeep, I called Adam Simms.

When he answered, I said, "McKenna, here, at the city yard where you worked. Brann Crosen told me he fired you."

"I told you, I quit. He didn't fire me."

"Crosen said they let you go," I repeated.

"No. I quit. I realized that I was starting to lose it. It wouldn't be fair to keep working under those conditions."

"Crosen also said you drove the rotary," I said.

Simms said, "I never drove one. I looked inside the cab. I imagined driving one. They are amazing machines. I wanted to drive one, but I never did."

"Why would Crosen want to spread lies about you?"

"I don't know. He had it in for me from the beginning."

"Why?"

"One of the guys was trying to start the forklift so he could move the salt shaker."

"What's a salt shaker?"

"Oh, sorry, it's the salt and gravel spreader they put on the back of the dump trucks. So Leroy said, 'why not just have Simms move it?' And Crosen said, 'no way could Simms move a salt shaker.' And Leroy said, 'wanna bet?' So they started placing bets on whether I could move it, like they were betting on the horses or something. Crosen got dug in on his position, betting something like two hundred dollars that I couldn't move it. So I just walked over, picked it up, and put it where they wanted it. Crosen hated me after that."

"You're confident in saying that Crosen's a liar."

"He is," Simms said.

"How 'bout we talk to him about it. I could come and pick you up."

"What's the point?" Adam said. "Crosen's a jerk. So what?"

"He's spreading false information about you. He should know we're onto him."

The phone was silent a moment. "I have to go to the

supermarket. We could meet."

"Okay."

I told Adam where I'd be and then hung up.

We met, and Simms got in his pickup and followed me as I drove to the yard. We parked on the street and walked past Emilio who was outside of the gate looking under the hood of a pickup that was parked on the street. It had a city logo on the doors and a custom utility body.

Simms and I walked into the yard and over to a workbench where Crosen was leaning. His arms were crossed. He had a smug look on his face.

"You're a liar," Simms said to him.

Crosen unfolded his arms and moved his feet apart into a wide stance. "Nobody calls me a liar. I've got principles."

"You didn't fire me, I quit," Simms said.

"Sugar coat it all you want, but we fired you."

"No. I told you I was leaving before the end of my probation. And I told you why, because I thought my memory problems were making me ineffective."

"Ineffective," Crosen said. "Big word for not doing your job."

Simms took a deep breath as if to calm himself.

"And I never drove the rotary."

Crosen made a half smile. "Sure, you did. You don't remember? Must be like all that other stuff you could never remember."

Simms said, "I'm the first to admit when I can't remember stuff, but I can tell if an experience is familiar or not. I never drove a rotary. I looked inside. I asked about the controls. I remember being interested in the joystick for crabbing the rear wheels. But I never drove one." He leaned toward Crosen and said, "You lied."

"I told you, Simms. I don't lie. You'll pay for that." Crosen looked ready to throw a punch. He was a muscle-bound kid with hormones and attitude. Adam was a giant in his fifties. Whatever the result of an altercation, it wouldn't be pretty.

"C'mon, Adam," I said. "We've established that he's a liar. Time to go."

I reached my arm out, touched Adam's shoulder, and gently steered him away. We walked back across the yard. As we turned to go through the gate, I saw that Crosen was on his cell phone. He was gesturing with his free hand, stabbing his finger toward the ground, anger emanating like smoke. I could guess what he was saying, and it felt bad.

Emilio had the air filter off and was spraying WD-40 on a corroded metal component.

"Is Crosen always a hothead?" I said in a low voice as we approached. "Is he dangerous?"

Emilio looked out from under the hood, leaning so that he might glimpse Crosen back in the yard. His face showed fear, and I immediately felt bad for asking him. "I don't know to say hothead," he said in a low voice. "Señor Crosen is boss. I work hard, he gives me good schedule, gives me good lunch."

"Lunch matters," I said.

"Sí."

Adam and I walked down the street to his truck. When Adam was inside, Blondie tried to squeeze between Adam and the steering wheel, wagging vigorously. I leaned in the open driver's window.

"Don't look now, Adam, but I can see that Brann Crosen is mad. He's talking on the phone. Maybe it's nothing. But my cop warning lights are flashing. I could be wrong, but I think he might follow you. Worse, I think he might be calling some buddies."

"What, like he wants to rough me up?"

"Yeah." As I said it, I noticed the smell of cigar smoke in the pickup. Adam's ashtray was open. A half-smoked cigar protruded from it. I thought about the cigar butt that Spot had found on the mountain where Scarlett's shooter had targeted her. I felt confused.

"I could drive to the cops, right?" Adam said.

"You could," I said, thinking about the cigar.

Adam said, "But if I do that, Crosen and his buddies will go away and find me later, won't they?"

"Maybe," I said.

"What would you do?" he asked.

"I'd like to catch them. It would involve some risk. But I think it is less risk now when we sense they might come after you than it would be to wait and have them show up when you least expect it."

"I don't want them to come to the safe house, that's for sure. Felicite could be visiting. Where should I go?"

"I'd like you to drive out of here and go to the college. Drive slowly and take your time. Pull into one of the most distant parking lots and park in a space that is farthest from anywhere. That way they'll feel that they can come after you with little risk. I'll be following at a distance. I have my phone. And Commander Mallory at the police department is only a couple of blocks from the college."

"So the cops could come at the first sign of trouble."

"Yeah. But Adam, I want to be very clear about this. If Crosen really does come after you, now or later, the risk could be substantial. You don't have to do this now."

Adam stared at the dashboard. He put his hands on the steering wheel. "But like you said, if not now, then he might come some other time. I'm not a liar. He should have to recognize that. I'd rather get it over with. I'll see you whenever." He started his truck.

I reached in through the window and put my hand on his shoulder.

"I've got your back," I said, worrying that I'd set in motion something awful. But maybe some truth would shake out of it.

FORTY

I turned and walked to my Jeep, which was the other direction down the street.

Spot was excited to have me arrive, sniffing and wagging, no doubt smelling Blondie.

"What's the big deal, Largeness? A few minutes without me and you decide to love me once again?"

He stuck his nose on my ear, and made a single swipe at my neck with the other-worldly tongue. I would have been fine if I'd brought a bath towel to dry off. Instead, I wiped my sleeve over the slobber, reached behind my head, and rubbed him.

I pulled out, drove off opposite the direction that Adam was going, and turned at the corner. I went around the block and pulled over at a spot where I could see the city yard.

I waited, peering through branches back toward the yard.

A pickup, black and shiny, shot out of the yard and turned hard. It looked like Crosen was driving. He went down the road the way that Adam had driven. I pulled out and followed at a distance.

The black pickup went through town. In the far distance, I glimpsed Adam's pickup once. Crosen stayed back so that Adam wouldn't know he was being followed. I stayed back from Crosen for the same reason.

Before we got to Al Tahoe Boulevard, the turnoff to the college, I saw a red pickup come out onto the road in front of me. It slalomed around several cars, then drew even with Crosen's pickup. The drivers give each other the thumbs-up sign.

Crosen turned right on Al Tahoe, and his comrade followed. I remained at a distance. They turned into the college. A third pickup, this one white, came from the other direction. It too turned in behind the procession. In the distance ahead of them, I saw Adam's pickup. Four pickups, all late-model, all freshly washed and coddled, one the prey, three the predators. I was the distant fifth vehicle, a dirty, bullet-shot, used Jeep.

I saw Crosen turn into one of the parking lots. The two pickups behind him followed. As I approached, I saw Adam pull into a space at the far end of the lot and stop.

I passed the turn and continued on to the next lot. I sped up, and pulled into a space between two other vehicles so that I'd have a bit of cover. I jumped out and let Spot out. I took his collar so he couldn't run. We trotted to the end of the lot and stepped between some trees toward the lot where the three pickups had pulled in behind Adam's pickup, blocking him in.

A young kid of maybe twelve was leaning against one of the trees near me, playing some kind of game on his phone.

"Hey, you want to make a quick forty bucks?" I said to him.

He looked at Spot with fear and me with suspicion.

"Don't worry about the dog," I said. "He's friendly. I'm a detective. I could use help on official business," I said.

"You mean, like cop business?"

"Yeah."

"What do I have to do?"

I pulled out my phone. "I don't know how to use this very well. Can you tell me, does it shoot video?"

"Of course," the kid said.

"How many minutes does it go?"

"Depends on how much memory you've got left." He reached for my phone, tapped multiple times. "Looks like you don't even use this thing. You could take a couple hours of video."

"Perfect," I said. "I'm guessing I'll only need maybe five minutes." I pointed over to the next lot. "See those guys?"

He looked, nodded.

"The three smaller guys are chasing the bigger guy."

"The big black guy," the kid said.

"Yeah. I'm worried they're going to fight. If they do, I need you to record it all on video."

The kid looked worried.

"The most important part will be the very beginning. So if it looks like someone is about to throw a punch, start shooting. Or, if I make a sign to you with my finger, that means start."

"Got it," he said.

"Stay here near these trees."

"I can zoom from here," he said.

"Good."

I pulled on Spot's collar and trotted toward the men.

All four of them were out of their vehicles. Adam was standing alone, the other three made a shallow triangle with Crosen at the tip. His legs were slightly bent, his arms in a martial arts position. He was shouting at Adam.

"You called me a liar. No one calls me a liar."

"You lied," Adam said.

Crosen screamed, "No one calls me a liar!" Crosen shook with anger.

I raised my hand behind me so the kid with my phone could see. I held out my index finger and dropped it as if to say, 'go.'

Crosen shouted, "I don't care that you were a football player a million years ago. I'm gonna kick your ass."

He feinted a one-two punch, then spun, his upper body dropping, his leg rising as he rotated. His foot struck Adam a powerful blow on his shoulder. The kick drove Adam a foot to the side. Adam reached up and rubbed his shoulder. Crosen came in again, did a front snap kick to Adam's thigh. Adam pulled his leg back as the kick landed, reducing the blow a bit. Adam seemed surprised. He was big, but he obviously wasn't a fighter.

Crosen shouted at him. "Fight, you coward!"

I was approaching from behind and to the side of the three men, trying to decide how to intervene. The man closest to me was almost my height, much heavier, and fifteen years younger. I touched Spot's neck to prep him, then put a light foot tap at the back of the man's knee. He started to collapse to the ground, then caught his fall. He spun around, ready to dismember me.

"Growl, Spot," I said.

The man hesitated a moment as Crosen and his other pal looked over.

"Watch him!" I said to Spot as I pointed to the man I'd knee-tapped.

Spot growled. It wasn't much, but the man's eyes went wide.

"C'mon, Spot. Don't be shy. Show him your stuff." I tapped

Spot again on his throat.

Spot upped the growl. Deeper and louder.

"Show him," I said again.

Spot cranked the volume. The man started backing up.

I said to the man. "You try anything, you run away, you make a little bird peep, he rips your throat out."

I touched Spot's throat again. He lowered his head, lowered his stance, lifted his lips so that all of his fangs showed, and he started walking toward the man, his growl loud enough to rattle the man's chest. The man stepped backward, tripped, landed on his butt. Spot took another step, his bared teeth a foot from the man's face, which was pale with primal fear.

I turned to the other men.

Crosen shouted at me. "You think you're gonna save this guy? I'll show you what's coming to him."

Crosen punched Adam again. Adam had his hands up in defense. It was luck that Adam's hand took the blow, which slapped his hand back against his chest.

Crosen followed it up with another punch. Adam's hand was still up, blocking, and he caught Crosen's second punch. Adam grabbed Crosen's fist, reached out with his other hand, and grabbed Crosen's wrist.

Adam apparently squeezed down, for Crosen cried out, half yell, half scream.

Maybe Adam broke Crosen's hand, I couldn't tell. But Adam took Crosen's hand and arm and made a throwing motion as if hurtling a ball to the ground.

Crosen was jerked to the parking lot pavement as if pulled by his own hand and arm. He landed on elbows and knees, screaming with pain.

He shouted to his friend who was still standing, "Get him!"

The man advanced on Adam. I thought of leaping on him from behind when he exploded in a flurry of punches and kicks, mixed martial arts style.

Adam put his arms up, trying to block them. But many blows landed on him. His abdomen, his chest, his arms. He kept his arms up, forearms vertical, which prevented most blows from reaching his face. Like the man who was terrorized by Spot, the man doing the punching was bigger than Crosen.

The assault drove Adam back. He bent from the blows. With his head down, he took a punch to the face, another to his forehead. Then a kick grazed his ear.

Crosen, behind his man, was getting up from the ground, preparing to launch another attack.

Adam was lower now, taking more blows from Crosen's man. Maybe it was his lowered stance that triggered a kind of muscle memory. He lowered farther, elbows near his knees, then exploded forward.

It was as if he'd transported himself back thirty years to his time as a Nose Tackle. He hit Crosen's man low. His arms were out in a blocking position, and he was moving at sprinting speed. As he made contact, he lifted up, a classic move to get under the offensive guard. The man went into the air as Adam went through. As the man fell to the parking lot, Adam hit Crosen hard in the middle, his right arm around Crosen's body. He continued forward as if sacking the quarterback. Crosen and Adam went down, Adam pulling his arm out so it wouldn't get abraded as Crosen hit the asphalt. Adam landed on top of Crosen. Crosen's head bounced off the pavement, and he went still.

Adam scrambled up and turned around, still in his football position, bent down, ready to explode forward again.

The man Adam had blocked got up and ran once again at Adam, listing a bit with pain, making a sort of crazed war cry as he tried to launch some kind of leaping kick. It was an amazing strategic mistake.

Adam charged toward him. He hit the man with his shoulder. The impact barely slowed Adam down. But the blow took the other man in the middle of his abdomen. There was a whoosh of air as Adam lifted up. The man bounced off Adam on an upward arc. It was like a bull catching a lion with his horns and tossing it into the air. The man traveled eight or ten feet before he landed on the pavement. He struck the asphalt with an audible thump and lay there motionless.

Adam continued to run, arcing around in a semi-circle even though the two men who'd attacked him lay unconscious and the third man was lying under Spot's guard, frozen with terror.

I walked over.

Adam's eyes were wild. He looked around as if counting all three men on the ground. Adam pointed at Crosen. "He lied to me. He was the liar, but he attacked me."

"Yes, he did." I turned sideways next to him and put my arm around his massive shoulders. It was like hugging an elephant. "You defended yourself," I said. "You did what you had to, and you did it well."

"I never wanted to hurt anyone on the field," he said, his voice thick with sadness and distress. "I just did my job. But I wanted to hurt these guys."

"Me, too," I said.

The kid I'd given my phone to approached.

"Did you get it on video?"

He nodded. His eyes showed wariness but also amazement. He stared at Adam. "Are you Adam Simms?"

Adam nodded.

"That was the coolest thing I've ever seen."

I took the phone and dialed Mallory.

While it rang, I noticed that Adam was holding his arm.

"Hurt bad?" I said.

He shook his head. "It hurts. But nothing like being hit by Mike Munchak," he said.

"From the Houston Oilers," I said.

Adam nodded.

Mallory answered the phone.

I said, "I've got some dirtballs for your men to pick up, one of whom will give you some satisfaction to charge with assault."

"You got witnesses?"

"Yeah. Video, too."

Fifteen minutes later, they were hauling the three men away in handcuffs. Crosen had regained consciousness. As they carried him past me, he silently mouthed the words, "You're a dead man, McKenna."

FORTY-ONE

When Adam was back at the safe house and I was home, the phone rang. It was Glennie.

"That was easy," she said.

"What's the Hope Diamond's value?" I asked.

"It doesn't work like that. There is no standard for establishing value on a one-of-a-kind gemstone. It depends on a thousand variables. And some of the most important variables don't even have to do with the diamond itself."

"You're not making sense," I said.

"I spoke to representatives of the world's biggest diamond sellers. I found out that much of a diamond's value comes from factors such as the current investment climate and how other investment vehicles are doing. For example, when investors start to think that the stock market is overvalued, they will bid up the price of other investments such as art. And when the art market seems over-heated, they will put more money into stocks. When it comes to diamonds, there is an arcane…"

"Glennie," I interrupted.

"What?"

"I appreciate all of your hard-won information. But let's skip it for now. Just give me a figure. How much is the Hope Diamond worth?"

"You really know how to celebrate a girl's hard work."

"Sorry. I'm aware that you work hard and that your skills are top-notch. That's why I called you in the first place."

The phone line was silent for a long time. I was about to speak when she said, "Three hundred fifty million."

I was shocked. "The Hope Diamond is worth three hundred fifty million?" I couldn't even imagine that kind of money.

"That's what I just said."

"I know, but I can't believe it."

"I was trying to give you the background information that supports the number, but you cut me off."

"Sorry," I said. "You're right. Okay, I believe you. I'm still shocked. That's a lot of money."

"There's an understatement," Glennie said. "So you can assume that your Blue Fire of Florence is worth a lot. How much less than the Hope Diamond, I have no idea. If I had to just throw out a figure, I'd guess two hundred million."

I was trying to visualize $200 million. That kind of money would buy anything.

"Are you still there?" Glennie said.

"Yeah. Thanks, Glennie. That's a big help. A giant help."

We said goodbye and hung up as there was a simultaneous knock on the door.

Spot was wagging as I pulled it open. Street stood on my front step. She glanced at me, then turned and looked up at the mountain behind my cabin.

I kissed her and ushered her inside.

"I called your cell an hour ago, and the line was busy," she said. "I called your cabin a few minutes ago, and the line was busy. I was heading home from the lab and thought I might as well drive up the mountain and see what all the phone commotion is about."

"Sorry. I'd asked Glennie if she could learn how much the Hope Diamond is worth, and she called back to say three hundred fifty million dollars. She guessed that, without provenance, the Blue Fire might be worth two hundred million."

"You're kidding," Street said. "That raises the stakes an order of magnitude beyond what I was thinking."

"Does that kind of money make any sense to you," I said, "assuming that Bruno Valenti was telling the truth when he said that Sinatra paid two million for the diamond fifty-some years ago? Could something go up in value a hundred times in fifty-some years?"

Street sat on the edge of the rocker, her arm out and over Spot's back. "That's impressive appreciation, but many investments have done that. From the nineteen sixties, I'm sure that some Tahoe real estate has gone up a hundred times. Lots on the lake that once sold for twenty thousand probably sell for two million now. I remember reading that stock in Warren Buffet's company Berkshire Hathaway has gone up something like ten thousand times. So a hundred times is not hard to believe."

I thought about it.

"I suppose that no provenance is the major downside," Street added. "But the upside for a thief is that no provenance also means that it would be very difficult for someone to prove that they ever owned it and claim that it was stolen from them. Possession becomes the greatest claim to ownership."

"And if experts say it is real and it fluoresces red and such, whoever has it could be looking at an amazing payday," I said.

"Enough to make someone murder?" Street trailed off.

"Certainly. Let's say it sold at wholesale or on the black market for only a hundred million or a measly fifty million."

"Measly," Street repeated.

"In my career, I've met dirtballs who would kill for five thousand dollars. Bump the payout to many millions, and that would be enough to push any number of people over the edge."

"So where do you look now?"

"I've been reading about Sinatra, but there's no mention of any diamond. What I need is people who knew him or studied him, people who aren't historians. The historians write what they know, and that shows up in a Google search. I want to talk to people who might know something but never thought to write about it online."

"How would you find those people?" Street said.

"Fall back on the old gumshoe standby, pound the pavement and ask questions."

Street nodded, got up to leave, then noticed the pentagram note on my kitchen counter.

"You got another warning?!"

"Yeah. I'm being real careful," I said. "As should you."

"Because the killer might target me to get at you."

"I hate to think it, but yeah," I said.

Street moved in slow motion as she picked up the note and stared at it. "What can you do?" she finally said.

"Catch the killer," I said.

FORTY-TWO

"C'mon, Largeness," I said after Street left.

Spot jumped up, always eager for a ride.

I drove down the mountain on the private road, turned north on the highway, crawled up Spooner Summit, then turned north again to wind my way up the East Shore to Incline Village and around to Crystal Bay.

Once again, I saw a black pickup three or four vehicles back. With the sighting came the vague sense that it had been there some time. As I got to Crystal Bay, I turned off the highway, went around a block at speed, and pulled back out onto the highway. I was hoping to get behind the pickup, but as I sped forward, it was nowhere to be seen. Maybe it meant something. Maybe not.

I pulled into the Cal Neva and saw that it was still closed for renovation. I parked, reached under my seat, and pulled out my clipboard with the pad of pre-printed forms on it. The form had lots of illegible fine print and little boxes in a vertical row. I used a red pen and wrote "Cal Neva" at the top of the pad and put bold check marks in several of the boxes. From the glove box, I got the plastic clip-on sleeve with the photo ID and clipped it to my shirt pocket. The picture of me was fuzzy and the writing underneath even fuzzier. I told Spot to be good and got out of the Jeep.

There were trucks and construction equipment and chain link fencing setting off certain areas. I wandered over to where a group of men were unloading pieces of pipe from a pallet. They hauled it over and put it into a cargo box on a forklift.

"Looking for the foreman," I said to one of the men.

He made a single nod. "That's me."

I glanced at my clipboard, flashing the printed form toward the foreman, then looked up at him. "The county is working on a historical record of hotel renovations going all the way back. Nothing to worry about. This isn't about code violations or anything. We're just building a database of past remodels and using the cost-to-social benefit modality in order to expedite future projects and make our county more business friendly."

The look on the man's face showed frustration.

"I know you're busy, so I won't keep you," I said. "I just need to find whoever has worked construction around here the longest and ask him a few questions. Would that be you?"

He shook his head. "I just moved to Truckee from Kansas last year." He turned and called out to his men. "Hey, guys, any of you worked this area before this project?"

They all shook their heads.

"Sorry," the foreman said. "We're hired out of San Francisco. I guess you'll have to look elsewhere."

"Are there any other crews working here today?"

"Sure, inside the hotel. But you can't go inside without an appointment and someone from the main office accompanying you." He pointed to a long office trailer at the edge of the lot. "You could ask at the on-site office."

"Thanks," I said, and I walked off toward the trailer.

He called after me. "If the trailer's closed, check the Tahoe Biltmore across the street. Our Crew Chief went over there about twenty minutes ago looking for some..." he stopped.

"Looking for what? Did he get our mailer?"

"Looking for toilet paper. We ran out."

"Ah. Hate to run out of that, right?"

There was a portable three-step stairs at the trailer door. I walked up and knocked a couple of times, but no one answered.

The Tahoe Biltmore Hotel was a short walk across the highway. I waited for a break in traffic, then trotted over. Once inside the lobby, I walked over to the check-in desk and repeated my phony story to a young woman behind the counter. She glanced at my clipboard and frowned.

"Well, I'm kind of new, so I don't know everyone who works here. But no one comes to mind." She pulled out a business card from a cubby under the counter. "This is the manager. You could contact her in the morning and see if she can help."

I took the card. "Thanks much." I was about to head outside

when I about-faced and went back to the counter.

"Here's another thought." I gestured toward the casino area. "Is there any chance that you have any oldtimer customers? You know, someone who's been coming in for years?" I held up my clipboard and pointed to an unchecked box. "We actually have a space on the form for non-official information contributions."

She frowned again, maybe wondering why a supposed official like me would want to talk to anyone who wasn't part of the hotel staff. She must have decided the idea was benign for she said, "Well, I suppose you could talk to old man Joseph. He comes in every day and plays the slots. I hear he once won big dollars on the slots, and he's been trying for a repeat ever since."

"Old man Joseph?" I said.

"Yeah, that's what he calls himself. Like it's his actual name or something. He's here now if you want to talk to him."

"Sure. Where would I find him?"

"He still works the slots." She gestured toward the casino.

"What does Joseph look like?"

"You can't miss him. He's real old, and he has a crooked mustache and long straggly hair pulled back into a ponytail."

"Thanks."

I walked to the slot machines in the center of the casino. There were several customers scattered about, but only one fit the description.

"Joseph?" I said to him.

He had a plastic jug of quarters in front of him. He put a quarter into the slot and pushed the button. The electronic facsimile of wheels pretended to rotate. When they came to a stop, none of the symbols matched. The machine sang out its beeps, noise to some, no doubt music to others.

"Joseph?" I said again.

He turned and looked at me, his eyes seemingly dead from decades of staring at slot machines. He had earbuds in his ears.

I held out my hand and spoke louder. "My name's Owen McKenna." I flashed him my clipboard.

He didn't notice it. Nor did he notice my outstretched hand. I realized he was blind.

I changed my story.

"I'm a private investigator researching a case that may have connections to this area a long time ago. Fifty, sixty years, in fact. I'm wondering if you knew this area back then."

The man pulled his ear buds out. "What'd you say your name was?"

"Owen McKenna."

The man picked up his jug of quarters, hefting it as if to judge its weight. "Time for my lunch. We can talk in the bar."

He stood up, picked up his white cane, which had been leaning against the slot machine, carried his quarters in his other hand, and walked out of the casino. Joseph headed for the bar with the assurance of one who'd made the trip a thousand times, tapping the floor with his cane but not swinging it. He picked the barstool at the end, set his quarters on the bar top, hooked his cane over the bar rail, and pointed to the stool next to him.

"You can sit here."

I sat.

The bartender poured a draft beer and set it and a packet of peanuts in front of Joseph. "Your lunch, Old Man Joseph," he said as he winked at me.

Joseph took a sip, the head foaming over his mustache. He used his forearm to wipe the foam off his mustache. Then he reached out his hand. "I'm Old Man Joseph."

We shook. "Pleased to meet you," I said.

"You want some lunch? Will, bring this man some lunch."

The bartender pulled another beer and set it and another pack of peanuts in front of me.

"You want history from a long time ago, I'm the man," Joseph said. "The Biltmore's been here since nineteen forty-six, and I've been here longer than any three of their employees."

"I believe it."

"Why? Because I look so old?" he said.

"Well, that, but mostly because I'm good at reading people. You telegraph history."

"And I'm not senile, either. That's no small thing, you get to my age." He moved his arm over and bumped my elbow.

"Got it," I said.

"I'll be eighty-seven in two days."

"Wow. You don't look a day over ninety," I said.

Old Man Joseph threw his head back and laughed, his mouth open so wide I could see his gold crowns. "You're a funny guy," Joseph said. "Will, is this man a funny guy or what?"

"Yeah, Joseph. Wish I'd thought of that line myself."

"You come here often?" I said.

"Now he's trying a pick-up line on me." Joseph said, laughing even harder. Then he lowered his voice and leaned close to me. "I like you, but I'm more of a ladies man."

"Right."

"Anyway, yes, I come here every day. I live in a cabin just up the street. Sixty-two years. First, my wife and I rented it. I was twenty-five, and Stella was twenty-seven. I had a taste for older women, ha, ha. We saved our pennies and bought the cabin seven years later. Life was good. She worked bookkeeping, and I ran telephone lines, and we used to come to the Biltmore for dinner once a week. Thirty years ago, Stella caught the cancer. I couldn't stand to watch her as she died. That's what made me go blind. The doc said it was a neurological disorder, that the blindness was in my brain, not my eyeballs. So be it. Still can't see. After Stella passed, they told me not to make any major changes in my life for awhile. So I didn't. And I'm still doing the same thing all these years later. I've got my monthly check, which buys these." He rattled his quarters. "I've got Will to bring me my lunch." He turned and pointed toward the check-in desk. "And Mandra got me this." Joseph pulled open the front of his jacket and showed me an iPod. "Mandra put my favorite music on this pod. And every afternoon when I'm leaving, she plugs it into something that puts my favorite radio news show on this thing so I can listen to it at home with no regard to when it was actually broadcast. You can get interviews, too. Have you heard of that? It's called downloading."

"Yeah, it's pretty cool," I said. "What kind of music do you have on it?"

"Swing era. Big band stuff. Duke and the Count, anyone Riddle worked with. But mostly Sinatra. He's still the best. 'That Old Black Magic' was our song, Stella and me. I still get teary eyed when it comes on. That's what Stella had, and I was under her spell of magic until her last day. Strange that sightless eyes would still make tears, don't you think? But that's what happens when you really love a woman."

Joseph drank some beer, chewed more peanuts. "Our favorite joke was about the Norwegian who loved his wife so much that he almost told her. I can say that because I'm Norwegian. I told her I loved her every day."

Joseph drank more beer. "Tell me about your case," he said.

I decided to tell the whole thing starting at the beginning. I left out a few details to save time, but I explained the murders and how Sinatra had his mother buy the Blue Fire Diamond and my theory that it was a gift for Marilyn Monroe to woo her back from President Kennedy.

"So I'm looking for someone who might have known Sinatra or any information about the diamond."

Joseph nodded. "Stella and I saw Sinatra perform several times at the Cal Neva. He was amazing. But we never knew anything about his personal life. So we were surprised when that information about him and the Kennedys and Marilyn Monroe came out. I never heard anything about a diamond, though. I suppose the best thing would be to go where Sinatra hung out. Talk to people."

"That's why I'm talking to you. The Cal Neva is empty and undergoing renovation. None of the construction guys has been around for any length of time. Do you know other places where Sinatra spent time?"

"Well, you could search out the places where The Misfits was filmed. Marilyn's finest performance. I heard that Sinatra spent some time on the sets. He invited everyone in the cast up to the Cal Neva where he sang for them. There was The Mapes Hotel in Reno, too. He often stayed there and performed there along with many of the greats. But you can't go there because they tore it down in the year two thousand. There must be people in Reno who used to work there. You could run an ad or something."

"Do you know anyone who was a real Sinatra buff?"

"Well, I'm pretty much of a Sinatra buff."

"What about people who collect his stuff?"

"That would describe me."

"What kind of stuff do you collect?" I asked.

"You got some time? I started with an autographed napkin. It was so innocent in the beginning. Then I got an autographed drink coaster. From there, I started going to fan conventions, collecting various memorabilia. My first significant acquisition was one of his gold records. That really fired up my interest."

"How does someone get an artist's gold record? Isn't there only one? Why would Sinatra part with it?"

"I don't know anything about gold records. But a vender I'd worked with before - a guy I trusted - said he had one, and he sold it to me for only five hundred dollars. It wasn't one of those commemorative knockoffs. It was the real thing that Sinatra used to have on his wall. Every time I picked that record up, I felt like I could actually feel the gold."

"What record was it for?" I asked.

"'September Of My Years.' Nineteen sixty-five. A great piece of work."

"You collected more Sinatra stuff?"

"You can't imagine," Joseph said. "This wasn't like Roger Maris and Mickey Mantle baseball cards. This was a big time obsession. Of course, I never saw part of my collection, the stuff I got after Stella died and I lost my sight. But that stuff was like Sinatra Braille. I could hold and touch and admire."

"What, besides records, do you have?"

"I had notebooks, a fedora, a tie, more framed photos than you could count, lots of autographs, napkins, newspaper articles, statues and statuettes."

"Where did you get your Sinatra stuff?"

"Everywhere. There's a whole industry surrounding famous musicians. Lots of people make a living buying and selling memorabilia. But Sinatra is tops. There are shows just for Sinatra items. I used to go to those shows. I scoured flea markets and garage sales, always keeping my eye out for Sinatra stuff. But my biggest haul was the stuff from the Cal Neva."

"What was that?"

"They had a lot of stuff from the Sinatra years, and they stored some of it in a trailer. When I found out about it, I made the manager an offer, and he agreed to sell it, trailer and all. He just wanted it out of their hands. So I had a hitch installed on my car, they hooked it up, and I drove it home and parked it in my driveway. Of course, I went through it, and displayed some stuff in the house. But most of it I just left in the trailer."

"When was this?"

"Lemme think. It was just a few years before Stella died. So maybe twenty-five years ago."

"Did you ever know a woman named Scarlett Milo?"

Old Man Joseph made a huge grin. "Sure did. She was another huge Sinatra fan. Met her back during the heyday of the Cal Neva. She used to come there a lot. She was fresh out of college at Stanford. Living up here at the lake one summer. She had some kind of job nearby, I forget what. Real smart girl. But not all stuck up, you know, like some of those Stanford kids."

"Do you think she knew Sinatra?"

Old Man Joseph shrugged. "I don't know. I suppose it's possible."

"Could she have dated him?"

Joseph guffawed. "Now that's funny. Sinatra had an eye for women, that's true. But he was spending time with the likes of Marilyn Monroe. I don't think Scarlett Milo would have been very noticeable with that kind of distraction nearby."

"Have you talked to Scarlett Milo recently?"

"Nope. Not for years, best I recall."

"I'm sorry to tell you that she died recently."

Joseph's face seemed to lose its life. He frowned, deep and hard. "I'm sorry to hear it. She was one of the live ones. Big personality. Big opinions. I hate to ask, but did she get the cancer?"

"No. She was killed by a gunshot."

Joseph leaned his elbows on the bar and put his face in his hands. "Another one of those gun accidents?"

"It was intentional. She was murdered."

"Oh man, that's even worse. I don't know what to say. I don't have words for that. Did they catch her killer?"

"Not yet. I was the last person to talk to her. Scarlett wrote me a cryptic note in the last few moments before she died. I'd like to ask you about it."

"What did the note say?"

"It said, 'Medicis BFF'"

"What's that mean, Medicis?"

"They were a powerful family during the Italian Renaissance."

He nodded. "And BFF is like best friend forever, right?"

"You're sharp to know current lingo," I said.

"I heard it on one of those interviews that Mandra downloaded for my pod. So what does it mean, the Medicis BFF?"

"We believe the Medicis BFF refers to the Blue Fire of Florence."

"Ah. The diamond you asked about."

"Right."

Joseph was silent a moment. "It's obviously valuable if Scarlett Milo was killed because of it."

"Yeah." I saw no reason to name an amount. "That's why I'm asking about Sinatra memorabilia because I think the diamond may have once been in his possession, stuff which could have gotten into a collection such as yours. You said you went through all of the Sinatra stuff that was in the trailer?"

"Every single piece of paper, every photo, every letter. Every trophy, every award certificate, every knick knack, every bit of kitsch."

"I assume there was nothing that suggested a diamond."

"No. Nothing like that." Old Man Joseph shook his head. "When I lost my sight and later sold my collection, I had a friend help me go through all of the new stuff I'd gotten. No diamond there unless it was tiny and hidden well. Anyway, I decided that the collecting phase of my life was over, so I sold it all."

"Any chance you remember who bought it?"

"Sure. The radio guy. What was his name? He had the radio show about Sinatra back in the nineties. Vince something."

"Any memory of how much you paid for the trailer full of Sinatra stuff?"

"Three thousand."

"How much did Vince pay you for it?"

"Russo."

"What?"

"I just remembered Vince's last name. His show was called

Vince Russo's Sinatra Hour. Anyway, he paid me thirty-five thousand for my entire collection. The trailer stuff and all the other stuff, too. And he has lots of other stuff besides what he got from me."

"Did Scarlett ever find out that you sold your collection to Vince Russo?"

Joseph paused, thinking. "I don't know. Vince bought it several years ago. And it's certainly been several years since Scarlett and I have spoken. But I can't remember which came first or whether the subject of Vince ever came up with Scarlett and me."

"I'm hoping you can give me a little background about Scarlett."

"Like what?"

"Her friends, her acquaintances, any serious relationships."

"I would say that in the last years when we were in occasional contact, she had no real friends. Certainly none that would connect to being murdered. Scarlett was kind of a loner. Real private. From what I knew, being alone fit her personality."

"Why? Was she very shy?"

"Not to my experience. She just didn't need much input from other people. She was self-contained but in a good way. I don't think she was like one of those ornery, leave-me-alone types. More like independent. Like the stuff she liked to do was stuff you'd do alone."

"I'd like to leave you my card," I said, "in case you think of anything else. I'd really appreciate it if you'd call me."

"Card's no use unless it's Braille."

"Right. Sorry. How do you take phone numbers?"

"I remember them," Joseph said.

"Wow, I couldn't do that."

"You go blind, you develop lots of tricks. You get real good at observation that doesn't require vision."

So I told Joseph my cell phone number. He asked me to repeat it.

"Okay, got it," he said. "Can't imagine I'll think of anything else. But if I do, I'll call." He patted a buttoned cargo pocket on his shirt. "Got my phone right here."

"Do you know where Vince Russo lives?"

"Sure. Up at the lake in the Tahoe Keys."

"Thanks. You've been a big help."

Joseph grinned. "I'm happy to enlighten you with the world of Old Man Joseph. And you can call me, too, although I've learned that other people can't remember phone numbers like me. So just dial the Biltmore and ask for me. Mandra and the other receptionists take my messages."

"You're a regular VIP," I said.

"Two thousand a month in quarters gets me free answering service and lunch at the bar. Ain't that right, Will?"

"Right, Old Man Joseph."

"Let me pay for our lunch this time," I said.

"Nope," Joseph said. "That's the whole point of the VIP thing. My guests dine free. Right, Will?"

"Right, Joseph." Will's smile couldn't get any bigger.

"Okay," I said. "I'm grateful for all of your information. Thanks, Old Man Joseph." I clasped his shoulder, found his hand, and shook it.

"Welcome, Owen," he said, smiling like the sun.

FORTY-THREE

I was glad to see no more notes on my cabin door. I'd just walked inside when my phone rang. It was Sergeant Santiago from Placer County.

"Just wanted you to know that we still haven't gotten into Scarlett Milo's email account," he said. "We hired a consultant. Turns out that hacking email accounts is harder than it sounds. Most of the time, the hackers don't have an easy way to crack your password. So they trick you into giving it to them. Like a phony web page where you think you're logging onto your email. Can you believe that?"

"Yeah. Sorry to hear it. But thanks for the info."

"But the main reason I called is something else," he said. "Milo's house was broken into."

"Really? Any idea why?"

"It looks like a smash-and-trash. Kids who were looking for money or jewelry or prescription drugs they could turn into cash on the street."

"Or maybe something more exotic," I said. "Can't remember if I brought you up to speed on the Blue Fire of Florence."

"Sergeant Diamond Martinez did. So I wondered if Scarlett's burglar was looking for the Blue Fire Diamond and thought that Scarlett Milo had it. No way to tell at this point."

"Thanks for letting me know."

As soon as I hung up, I got a call from Commander Mallory.

"Thought you should know that Brann Crosen posted bail this afternoon."

"What a day brightener," I said. "But thanks for letting me know," I said.

"You might want to call the football player," he said.

"Right." We hung up.

I called Adam.

"Hello?" he said after several rings.

"This is Owen McKenna calling. I want you to know that Brann Crosen posted bail today. He probably doesn't know where you're staying, but be very careful."

"Who is this?"

"Owen McKenna. The detective. Remember me?"

"I don't take calls from strangers," Adam said. He hung up.

So I called Adam's stepsister Felicite and got her voicemail. I explained that I'd just called Adam and he didn't remember me and that I thought she'd want to know about it.

Later that evening, just after Spot and I had eaten, my cell phone rang.

"Hello?"

"I need help." The voice was weak, raspy, old. Maybe desperate.

My heart rate quickened. "Is that you, Old Man Joseph? Try to speak louder if you can."

"He beat me. Wanted to know where I put the diamond. I told him I didn't have it. I'm broke up pretty bad. But I couldn't exactly tell what I don't know."

My first impulse was to ask what the man looked like when I remembered that Joseph was blind.

"Where are you?" My breath was short.

"Don't know. Some house. They set it on fire. I can smell the smoke."

"Can you get out?"

"I'm tied to a rolling chair, so I figured it was a desk chair. I rolled around until I hit the desk. Then used the corner of the desk to get the tape off my mouth. I tried my teeth on the wrist tape, but I can't get it. Too many layers. I got my pocket button unhooked with my mouth and sort of leaned forward against my arm and mushed my phone out onto the desk. My phone's the old kind with buttons. I dialed it with my tongue."

"Did you call nine-one-one?"

"Yeah." He coughed, loudly. "They said I don't have the GPS in my phone, so they don't know where I am. So I hung up and called you."

"Did you yell for help?"

"I can tell no one's here."

"Okay, Joseph. We're going to do some fast detective work as I drive." I opened the cabin door as I spoke, and Spot followed me as I sprinted outside into the dark. "Walk me through what happened."

"I was walking home from the Biltmore. A vehicle pulled up. They grabbed me and put me in the back seat."

I let Spot into the back of the Jeep, then started it and headed down the mountain. "It was a four-door car?" I asked.

"Yes. I heard the driver's door close, then the back seat door."

"Did you have to step up high to get in? Or did you lower down into the seat?"

"Up high."

An SUV. "How many people?"

"Just two, I think. The driver and the guy who sat in back with me. The guy in back talked. The guy in front was quiet."

"Any sense of where they drove?"

"Well, let me think. It felt like they turned toward the east after they grabbed me. Then it felt like we went down a long gradual hill. There weren't a lot of tight curves, so I'd guess we went to Incline Village. I know we didn't go up the Mt. Rose Highway. That would have been noticeable."

"Then what? Think how it felt."

"We went at pretty good speed for quite awhile."

"So you were on the highway, not on neighborhood streets."

"Right. After a time, we went up."

"You think it was Spooner Summit?"

"Yeah, now that you mention it, 'cause they made a hard left turn. Then my ears popped on the long downhill."

I'd just gotten to the bottom of the private road, so I turned north toward Spooner Summit and floored the gas.

I said, "The road from Spooner comes down to the bottom

of the valley in Carson City. Even if the light is green, you have to slow a lot. Then there is a turn to the left or to the right. Do you remember which?"

"Left."

"So you were headed toward downtown Carson. What next?"

"Let me think. I'd say we went maybe four or five miles. We turned left for maybe a minute, right for a half minute, then left again. We drove for a bit, then turned into a driveway."

"Sounds like you went west of Carson City's main street. Toward the Governor's mansion." I was up to eighty as I raced up Spooner Summit. I had to slow for the curves.

Joseph said, "Yeah, I guess that makes sense."

"Then what?"

"They walked me into a house. Told me I'd die if I said anything or called out. I thought about trying to escape, but the guy holding me was very strong. I knew I had no chance." Joseph coughed again, sharp, difficult hacks.

"Is smoke coming into the room?"

"Yeah," Joseph said. "Better hurry."

"They say anything about the house? A comment that would help me find it?"

"No. But it's a big house. Maybe three stories. Probably an old Victorian. I could feel a cold draft coming out when they opened the door. Like there was a downdraft coming from an open window one or two floors up. Like the house was abandoned and had no heat on."

"Did they take you up the stairs?"

"Yes. Four flights with landings and turns between. So I think I'm on the third floor." He coughed again. His hacking was violent.

"If the smoke gets bad, try to tip the chair over so your face is near the floor. I'm on my way."

I heard more coughing. It sounded as deadly as any coughing I'd ever heard. "Tip your chair over!" I shouted.

There was no response. Then weak hacking. Then silence.

I pushed the accelerator down as I got to the straight section of highway that crests Spooner Summit. I raced down the mountain, tires squealing on every curve. Then I came to a section where the highway was moist from snow flurries, but it didn't feel frozen. I kept my speed as high as the turns would allow. Eighty on the straights, sixty-five on the sharp curves. If cops came after me, I could get them to help lead the way.

But there were no cops. I went down three thousand vertical feet, then raced north to downtown Carson City. I had no idea of where to turn left, so I picked one of the cross streets at random, rushing through the old neighborhood near the Governor's Mansion.

I did as Joseph said, turning right where he might have meant, then left again.

There were some newer small homes mixed in with a few older Victorians. I looked for any house that looked abandoned and dark, any sign of smoke, any old Victorian three stories tall, any flickering light that could come from a fire.

There was nothing.

I came to the end of the street, turned the wheel, and hit the gas. My tires spun on wet asphalt, and the Jeep skidded around. I floored it and sped back to the previous intersection. The Jeep slid again, and I slid sideways in the road, trying to find some balance between traction and speed. At the next turn, I skidded around the corner and raced down the street, once again thinking that the road possibly matched Joseph's description.

There were more houses, but none was tall, and none looked on fire or abandoned.

I repeated the process on the following street. There was a tall Victorian at the end. It had lights on. People were standing on the front porch talking to some people at a car in the street. I raced on by.

I was going to pull a U-turn at the next intersection, when I sensed a glow of light just beyond the next rise in the street. I pushed the accelerator to the floor once again and flew over the rise, feeling the Jeep nearly go airborne.

In the distance was a tall house, a Victorian design. Behind the first floor windows was a wavering yellow glow. I sped up even further, then hit the brakes, skidded to a stop, and was out the car door as the Jeep went still.

I let Spot out of the back. He couldn't help with a fire, but he could make a huge difference if there were still any bad guys around.

The windows on the lower floor of the house all had blinds of some kind. But they were translucent. The blinds glowed yellow in nearly every window.

The first floor of the house was engulfed in flames. I dialed 911.

When the dispatcher answered, I said, "Owen McKenna calling. I'm on the west side of Carson City, not far from the Governor's Mansion. There's a Victorian in flames." I gave the street name. "I believe a man is trapped on the third floor. I'll leave my phone on so you can get a GPS fix on the location." I set the phone on top of a fence post, then ran up onto the front porch. I was going to kick down the door, but I paused at the last moment.

Joseph had spoken of a cold downdraft when they took him into the house, a draft suggesting that an upper window was open. If that was still the case, and if I broke open a downstairs door or window, I'd create another draft, this time going up instead of down, this time much more powerful. A house afire with openings top and bottom will turn into an inferno just like a blast furnace and incinerate the entire house in a couple of minutes.

It would be much better if I could get in above and not create a draft.

I ran around the house in the dark, looking for a fire escape.

There was none.

I looked for roof gables or trellises or any other structure that I could climb.

Nothing.

There was no garage or other structure. Just an old fence separating the yard from the neighbor's yard.

I leaped over the fence and ran toward the neighbor's house. It was dark. Same for the house beyond that. Then came a dark open area. I saw no indication of people.

A third neighbor had a shed. I pulled open the door and shined my penlight into the dark. There was a ladder.

I lifted it off the wall hooks, backed out of the shed, then ran with it. When I got to the fence, I dropped the ladder over onto the other side, and vaulted the fence. Picked up the ladder. Ran to the Victorian. Leaned it up against the wall. Pulled the rope that extended the ladder.

When the ladder was fully extended, I saw that it only reached to just above the second floor windows. I could break into the second floor, but I would still create a draft that would be nearly as perilous as a draft from the first floor.

I needed to get the ladder higher.

I sprinted back to the Jeep, jumped in, and started it. There was a short fence at the front of the house. I shifted into drive, and drove toward the house, aiming between the fence posts. The Jeep blasted through the fence. Spot ran alongside the Jeep as I steered around to where the ladder leaned, pulled up next to it so the Jeep was ten feet out from the house and close to the ladder.

Leaving the front door open, I stepped on the driver's seat, then boosted myself up onto the roof. The metal dented in, but it held.

The ladder was within reach. I lifted it up and propped its feet on the Jeep's roof. It wasn't very stable, but it held as I climbed.

At the top of the ladder was a third-floor window just to the side. The window was shut and apparently latched. But this one I could break without creating a significant draft.

I used the back of my elbow to break the glass, then pulled the major shards out. Climbing through into the dark, I didn't realize how smoky the air was. My lungs filled with caustic, searing smoke as I dropped to the floor.

"Joseph!" I yelled, coughing, hacking, choking as Joseph had on the phone many long minutes before.

There was no answer.

I crawled through the dark. Forward to a wall, swatting at the air with my hands as I crawled so I wouldn't smash into the wall with my face. I turned about face, rushed back to the opposite wall, shifted sideways, went forward a second time, about faced again, went back again.

I kept my face low, trying to breathe the cleaner air next to the floor. I swept my arms as I moved, reaching left and right, trying to feel for Joseph.

Maybe there was a light switch somewhere, but I'd quickly succumb if I stood up to search the walls for it.

"Joseph!" I yelled again, knowing it was futile.

The smoke got worse as I crawled back and forth across the floor. I had to stop to put my lips right next to the floor to suck air, then hold my breath as I continued my attempt at a grid search in the dark.

I ran into a hard piece of furniture, striking it with my shoulder. Running my hands over it, it seemed to be a table, perhaps the desk Joseph had referred to. But I could find no desk chair.

Still sweeping my hands back and forth, I continued to crawl around the desk, counting the sides so that I could resume my grid search in the same place.

In the distance below me came the crash of breaking glass. Maybe someone else was coming to help. Or maybe the heat of the fire had broken a window. A steady noise began to grow, like a sudden wind. It grew to a roar. I felt vibration in the floor beneath my hands and knees. A sudden rush of hot air swirled around my head.

The draft I feared had started. The house was turning into a chimney of fire. If I wanted to survive, I had to get back out the window immediately.

But Joseph was here. Somewhere. Unseen. Unconscious. About to die if he wasn't already dead.

I crawled faster. Hit the far wall. Turned back. Raced on hands and knees to the opposite wall. Turned again. Sucked air off the floor. Crawled faster. My lungs burned. I put my lips directly on the floor to breathe air. But the smoke still made me choke. I didn't think I could make it. Even if I gave up on Joseph, I would still die from smoke inhalation.

Lips to the floor again, I sucked more air. Wheezed. Hacked. Felt a soft brush of fabric on my left fingertips.

I spun. Rushed toward the feeling.

A man. On his side. I felt his position. His arms were rigid, tied to the arms of a chair. My fingernails were claws as I found the duct tape, ripped it into pieces. I got Joseph free from the chair. Started to drag him. Got confused as to where the window I'd broken was.

I pulled Joseph to the wall. Went along the wall. Hit a corner. Lowered my lips to the floor as close to the corner as possible. Sucked multiple breaths. Turned and went down the next wall, pulling Joseph with me.

The roar of fire wind was an assault on my ears.

Yellow light appeared in what seemed like the middle of the room. A plume of sparks and embers shot up into black smoke from a hole in the floor.

I kept dragging Joseph.

The fire air and smoke blew across my back as I crawled. I stopped. That meant the smoke was exiting out an opening.

The window.

I backed up. I'd crawled right past the broken window.

I sucked more air off the floor. Three lungfuls. Four. Then held my breath.

Determined not to breathe, I stood up into a blast of smoke hot enough to singe my eyelashes. I lifted Joseph, got my arm around his waist. My movements were blind as I reached my leg out through the broken glass shards and felt for the ladder.

It wasn't there. I moved my leg sideways. Then down. I braced my free arm against the inside of the window frame and lowered my foot farther.

My foot touched the ladder. I found the rung, shifted my weight, held Joseph tight to my body as I got myself through the opening.

The fire blast blew hard into my face, searing my skin.

But I was on the ladder, and the moment I stepped down two rungs, we were back into clean cool air. I kept one arm around Joseph and used my other hand on the ladder as I carried him down to waiting firemen and paramedics.

FORTY-FOUR

The next morning, I was still hacking, but I could breathe better. The cold mountain air out on my deck was clear and clean, a gift for which I had new appreciation.

According to the doctor I got on the phone, Joseph was in rough shape with a broken arm and singed lungs. But the CPR had revived him, and they thought he'd eventually make a complete recovery. He was in Intensive Care, and he wouldn't be speaking for at least a couple of days or more. There was nothing anyone could do but wait.

I checked back in with the Carson City County sergeant I'd spoken to the night before. He had little to add to what we already knew. The Victorian was abandoned and had been tagged for demolition. The fire was so intense that they didn't think the fire marshal would find any clues.

We agreed to speak again if we learned anything more.

I realized that the killer must have followed me, saw me talking to Joseph, and decided that Joseph had information about the diamond. It was because of me that Joseph was attacked.

I thought again about Scarlett calling me for help. Then I remembered the terror on Felicite's face when the killer shot out the window at her neighbor's house, a shot that was no doubt intended for me. It seemed that I continued to make everything much worse instead of better.

Vince Russo was easy to find, but his voicemail said he'd be back in his office tomorrow. I hung up without leaving a message. Despite the voicemail message about being out of town, I found his house in the Keys and knocked on the door, but there was no answer.

I left and drove up to the safe house and spoke to Adam. He was having one of his bad days. He still didn't remember me. Then, gradually, he showed some recognition. His eyes went from unfocused to focused and back, as if he were fading in and out like a weak radio station. Adam gripped Blondie as she lay on his lap. Most yellow Labs are too big to curl up on their owner's lap, but Blondie was small against Adam's massive bulk. It was clear that her presence reassured him.

In time, I asked Adam to let me look through more photos on his phone. He looked puzzled, then handed it to me.

Before I clicked on his photo roll, I clicked the email icon to see if it was TahoeBlueFire, but it was password locked, so I couldn't tell his address. I didn't want to ask him because it could cause him to cut me off from his phone photos or any further information.

I started scrolling through his photos. After a few minutes during which Adam and Blondie didn't move, I came to a photo of a group of people. It was taken in dim light, as if indoors at night. The photo caught my attention because the person on the right side of the group was Scarlett Milo. And next to her was a young woman who looked like the photo of Darla Ali that her roommate Sanford Burroughs had printed out for me. To the left of them was a guy I didn't recognize, one in his late twenties. Sean Warner?

"Take a look at this photo." I showed it to Adam. "Do you recognize these people?"

He shook his head. "No. Photos d..."

"Don't?"

"Don't seem to help my memory," he continued.   .

"What about the woman on the far right? Recognize her?"

"No." He squinted at the phone, then shook his head. "I've never seen her before. I think."

"Does the photo remind you of any particular place?"

"No."

I looked at the photo details. "It was taken three weeks ago at eight p.m. Does that tell you where you might have been?"

"I can't remember what happened five minutes ago."

"Do you keep a calendar?"

"No."

"Then how do you remember to go to appointments?" I

asked.

"The only appointments I have are at the d..."

"Doctor?"

"Doctor's office. I give them my phone, and they set the time and date in the appointment app. My timer song goes off two different times before the appointment. Once in the morning as a reminder and a second time a half hour before I'm supposed to be there so I know it's time to get in my truck and drive down to South Lake Tahoe."

"Can you show me how it works?" I handed him the phone.

He pointed to an icon on the screen. "When it plays, I click on this app and then hit this button. That way they know I heard the message. This is the song that comes on." He tapped another button, and Jackson Browne sang 'Doctor My Eyes.'

Adam handed me his phone. I brought back the picture of the group. I pointed at Scarlett's picture. "The woman in the photo was the first person who died. She was shot and killed in Squaw Valley. Her name was Scarlett Milo. Does that information trigger any memories?"

"No. I'm no help to you. Something really bad is happening." Adam was gripping Blondie so hard, she squirmed.

I said, "Adam, have you ever met an older gentleman whose name is Old Man Joseph?"

Adam shook his head.

"He lives on the North Shore and hangs out at the Tahoe Biltmore."

"No. I never heard of him."

I resumed scrolling through Adam's photos. Adam sat patiently and waited. He seemed to fade away a bit as if unaware of my presence. There was nothing else that caught my attention. I turned off his phone and handed it to him.

"What are you doing with my phone?" he said, frowning.

"I was looking at your photos. You gave me your phone so I could look at your photos."

"No, I didn't. That's my phone. You have no right to look at my photos."

FORTY-FIVE

Adam began to get more tense and confused, so I said goodbye and left.

Back in the Jeep with Spot, I drove down Kingsbury Grade to my office. There were no phone messages and no email from the TahoeBlueFire email, so I sat at my desk and made some notes, trying to process what I'd learned. There were no clear indications for where I should look next. The picture in Adam's phone that showed Scarlett and Darla was possibly my biggest single clue yet, but Adam's failing memory made it a dead end.

I wondered if his step-sister Felicite might be helpful. She knew him better than anyone else.

I called Felicite, and she agreed to meet me at her house in San Francisco at nine o'clock in the evening. It was 4 p.m., which meant I'd miss the rush hour in both Sacramento and the Bay Area.

"Hey, Largeness, wanna go to the ocean?"

He jumped up from the rug in front of my desk, wagging.

Three hours later, we crested the coastal pass on I-80. I turned west on 37 and headed around the north end of the bay, figuring that it would be fastest to drop into The City over the Golden Gate and take 101 through the Presidio and Golden Gate Park to the Sunset District where Felicite had said she lived.

Because we'd made good time, I drove to the west side of Golden Gate park, found a parking place on Ocean Beach, and let Spot out for an evening run down the sand.

There was a thick-as-sea-foam fog pushing in off the Pacific. As Spot charged north up the beach along the breakers, his feet splashing in the advancing and retreating waters, he disappeared into the twilight fog. I continued to walk. After a time, he reappeared, an apparition in the mist that morphed into a Dane charging straight toward me. Spot raced past, close enough to threaten an injurious collision, then disappeared again.

When he slowed, I coaxed him back into the Jeep. He smelled of sea salt, and he tracked a half bucket of sand onto the back seat.

Felicite's house was a small bungalow in San Francisco's Inner Sunset. The Sunset District was mostly sand dunes in the 19th century, but it had been gridded off and paved with a regular network of north-south, east-west streets. The Sunset District was known for the fog pushing in off the Pacific, but the Inner Sunset was the least foggy part.

Except when I showed up.

The atmosphere was more liquid than gaseous and so opaque that I had to get out of the Jeep three different times and walk halfway up to a house and use my penlight to read house numbers.

I found Felicite's modest little terra cotta-painted bungalow two houses in from a corner. It faced west, so one would hope for occasional late afternoon sun. But on this night I might as well have been on the planet Venus so thick was the fog. It was 9 p.m. when I walked up to her door.

There was a small doorbell button that glowed a dim yellow in the late evening. I pressed it but heard no chime from within. I waited. Eventually, the door opened. Felicite smiled and ushered me in, standing aside as I walked into an entry bathed in soft light coming from a big spherical paper lantern with a single bulb at the center.

Felicite shut the door behind us, then walked past me and brought me into the small living room. She had a spare decor, a few simple pieces of furniture, two paper-shade lamps on little tables, and an old floor rug that looked Persian to my ignorant eyes. Felicite sat on a low-slung chair made of muslin fabric panels draped between the bars of an oak frame. She pointed me to a futon couch that was probably more comfortable for sleeping than sitting.

I got to the point.

"I think your brother Adam is somehow connected to the case I'm working on."

"You mean the murder of that woman?" Her voice was high-pitched and shrill. Her fear was obvious.

"Two women and one man."

Felicite looked horrified.

"You know that Scarlett Milo was shot. I don't know if you're aware that Sean Warner and Darla Ali were killed by a highway snow blower."

"I don't understand. What do you mean, a highway snow blower?"

"What Caltrans calls rotary plows. When the snow in Tahoe gets too deep for the graders to push it, they use the blowers. You should be familiar with them having owned a house in Tahoe for several years."

"Oh, yes. Of course. I've seen them a couple of times. I…" she hesitated. "I just didn't understand for a moment. I'm afraid to ask, but how would a person be killed by a blower?"

"Someone drove into them with the blower. It must have been a very scary way to die."

Felicite looked like she was going to get sick.

"You must also know that your brother Adam spent some time working at the South Lake Tahoe yard where they park and repair the rotaries."

The woman shut her eyes against a sudden flood of tears. She put her hands to her face, her palms covering her eyes like a child trying to block out the image of a boogeyman.

"You've worried about Adam," I said.

Felicite breathed short, gasping inhalations followed by staccato exhalations.

"Tell me what you've been thinking," I said.

I waited a minute, then another, while her breathing gradually slowed. She wiped her face with the backs of her hands. When she finally spoke, her voice was low and soft.

"I was eight years old when they brought Adam to our group home in New Orleans. He was younger than me by two years, but he weighed more than twice my forty pounds. I never knew why he was an orphan, nor did I know why I was. But I felt sorry for him. At the age of eight, I felt like the wise, older sister. I sort of adopted him. I showed him how to act, what to do, what to say. I helped him dress, taught him how to hold his fork, explained how to behave around the adults, everything. I guess I always had a desire to be in control, and with Adam, I was pretty much in control of his entire life. Like me, he had no one. But within a couple of weeks of him coming to the home, we had each other by mutual agreement. By the time Adam was eleven, he was the biggest kid in the home, two hundred pounds and strong as a man. It's not like I needed protecting, but all the other kids knew not to mess with me because Adam had my back. Like the other kids, we were misfits, and we had our problems, but we looked out for each other."

"What kind of problems?" I asked.

Felicite looked off toward one of the windows. Outside, the fog glowed yellow in the light from the door and the post light near the sidewalk.

"Adam had a temper. Normally, he was fine. But if he got frustrated trying to learn something difficult, something he didn't see the point of, things could boil over. Of course, many kids have a temper, but with Adam, he was so big that when he erupted, everyone kind of scattered. I think he learned that there was power in that, and it reinforced the behavior. Act out and the world cowers at your feet. It sort of gave him the wrong message."

"You think it encouraged bad behavior?"

Felicite nodded.

An ugly, unbidden thought came to me. "Let me guess," I said.

Felicite looked at me with alarm.

I said, "Adam set fires."

Felicite burst into tears for the second time, her hands back at her face, knuckles burrowing into her eyes and temples. She turned her head left and right as she cried. She turned sideways in her chair and drew her knees up to her chest, her sobs wrenching.

It took longer this time for her to calm. "I was there at my house in Tahoe, sleeping soundly, when Adam yelled up from the kitchen that the house was on fire. From the moment I woke up, it felt funny. He didn't come up to shake me awake. He called from downstairs. It wasn't like him. Adam wouldn't do that, calling from a distance."

"What would you have expected him to do?"

"The normal Adam would have run up the stairs and picked me up out of bed. I would have awakened in his arms as he carried me down the stairs. Instead, he was removed, awkward." Felicite looked at me with reddened eyes, swollen and tormented with sadness. "From the moment I awoke, I worried that he had set the fire."

We sat in silence for a minute.

"I'm so sorry," I finally said. "Tell me about the arson."

"I don't think Adam meant any harm. I really don't. He just lit a fire in the alley when he was a boy. He wasn't trying to destroy anything. It was more about experimentation. Unfortunately, the fire spread. They got it put out before any serious damage was done."

"Was anyone hurt?"

"No." Felicite shook her head vigorously. "It was just a case of a boy playing with fire. But the authorities treated it like it was a real serious crime. Like Adam was trying to burn down the building. It didn't help that he was so big. The authorities had a hard time visualizing a twelve-year-old kid in that big body."

"What happened?"

"He went through the juvenile court system. He spent some time in a lockup. Eventually, he was allowed to come back to the group home under court supervision."

"Does the idea that he could have burned down your house surprise you? Or does it merely disappoint you?"

Felicite shook her head again, repeatedly as she spoke, "I don't know. I don't know." Felicite looked at me with great worry, as if I were about to drop a bomb on her.

"Do you think Adam could have committed murder?"

"I don't know! He's not the type, I swear."

"But…" I said, prompting her to continue.

"There's something else."

I waited.

"I don't want to tell you, but you'll find it out if you start looking into his past."

"He got into more trouble?"

"No. In fact, it was something he did right." She paused, thinking, deciding how to tell me. "The summer after Adam was in the eleventh grade, he applied for a scholarship to attend a summer camp. He submitted a poem as his entry essay, and he won. So he went off to this rural camp for three weeks. They had lots of activities like learning to swim, which he'd never done before. But when he came home, it turns out that his favorite activity was shooting."

"Target shooting?" I said, a hollow feeling growing in my stomach.

"Yes. With rifles. Adam said they used air rifles, which were supposedly less powerful than regular rifles, whatever that means. A rifle is still a rifle, right? Anyway, Adam was very proud because he won the camp sharpshooter contest."

"I understand why it is an upsetting thought," I said.

We were silent a moment. "Let's say that Adam did commit murder," I said. "What would you imagine could drive Adam to do that?"

Felicite frowned. "You mean like, was it his temper and someone made him really mad? Or was he trying to cover up some crime? Or it was part of committing a crime? Like that?"

"Like that," I said.

"Then I would say it was his temper. Adam has never been able to express anger in a normal way. He always just acts calm."

"Unless someone pushes his buttons?" I said.

Felicite nodded. "Then he explodes. He once told me that was his secret to setting those sack records. He imagined that he was really, really angry at the guards blocking for the quarterback. So he would explode across the line and just blow through them."

I thanked Felicite and left.

It was ten-thirty as I drove away and two-thirty in the morning as I turned up the mountain to my cabin. Spot had snoozed the entire way.

FORTY-SIX

The next morning, I sent another email to TahoeBlueFire@
gmail.com, hoping to provoke some kind of reaction.

'I know what you did. I've found evidence. Your time is
almost up.'

Then I drove up Kingsbury Grade and knocked on the door
of the safe house.

"Last night, I drove into San Francisco and spoke to Felicite,"
I said to Adam when we were sitting in the living room.

He made another single nod, a move that I was beginning
to think was his signature, the mark of a taciturn man who was
polite enough to acknowledge that someone had spoken but not
loquacious enough to give every statement a verbal response.

"In my duties as an investigator, it's my job to look into every
person who is proximate to a crime."

Adam's face was impassive. I couldn't yet tell if this was a
good day or a bad day.

"She didn't want to say anything bad," I said. "She's naturally
protective of you. But when I pressed, she said you were once
charged with arson."

"I told you before that I've made mistakes. I was a kid. A
frustrated kid. Eleven or twelve years old. At a time when I should
have been playing softball or riding my bike, I played with fire."
He paused.

"You're having a better day," I said, hoping to make him feel
relaxed.

"Old experiences are still there. They're all muscle memories.
It's all the recent stuff that's disappeared."

"So you lit some fires."

Adam made another single nod. "Not a lot. But striking
matches, seeing how different things burned, being intrigued
with the flame and the heat. Just like every kid. If someone

had taken me camping, the campfire would have satisfied my curiosity. But in the French Quarter, it was sticks in the alley. An urban campfire. I'd seen old men huddling around a fire in a trash can, pouring whiskey into cups of coffee, warming their hands on a cold night. I wanted to try that."

"You're saying that you didn't try to burn anything down. Not with malice, anyway."

"No. But one of my fires lit a pile of leaves and sticks that were next to the back d…" He frowned.

"Back door?"

"The back door of a building. The fire in the leaves moved to the steps. I didn't realize how fast a fire could spread. Someone called it in, and a firetruck came. They put it out. They also arrested me. Was what I did wrong? Absolutely. Did I need to spend years in the Juvenile system to correct my ways? No. I learned my lesson when I first heard the siren coming."

I pondered what Adam said, thinking about how a well-told lie, especially a well-rehearsed lie, can sound like the truth. Even more, it can sound like complete innocence.

"Felicite also told me that you won a sharpshooting contest when you were in high school."

Adam smiled. "Yeah, it was great. We learned how to shoot, how rifles work, how to adjust a scope. Stuff like that. I wanted to learn about firearms and regular ammunition, but they only had us using air guns." He looked off, still smiling. "That summer camp was the most fun I ever had."

"Do you see that your background of arson and shooting and working in proximity to rotary plows makes you a person of interest in these recent murders?"

"Oh, man, my shooting was a good thing, not a bad thing! I won the contest. How many people in this country know how to shoot? A hundred million? Two hundred million? The arson was a bad thing, but I was a kid. And I already told you that I never drove a rotary plow. I was interested in them, sure. I asked questions about them. I looked inside of them. But I never drove them. You could see that two days ago. It was obvious that the yard man was lying when he said I drove them."

"And yesterday, the photo I saw on your phone was even

more suspicious than all the other coincidences."

"What photo?"

"The one with the two female murder victims."

"I don't remember that."

I reached my hand out. He handed me his phone.

I found the photo and showed Adam.

"I don't remember ever seeing that," he said.

"Nor taking it, I suppose."

"No," he said.

I handed him back his phone and stopped and thought about the case. After all of my inquiries and interviews and travel, I still had nothing solid to go on. I wanted to keep Adam talking, but maybe on a different subject where he might say something casual and unguarded, something that would give me a different window into his world.

I said, "Are you still writing your poems?"

Adam nodded. He reached into the side of his chair cushion, pulled out the sketchbook, and held it up. "But it's very hard to turn a good phrase anymore. I think I'm done writing anything decent."

"I'm curious about poems," I said. "What motivates you to write them?"

Adam said, "I suppose it's the standard poet stuff. My way of making sense of the world. The loss of wildness. The loss of innocence. The loss of my brain."

"All very frustrating," I said, wondering if those were the kind of issues that could make Adam mad, push him to explode as Felicite had described it when he lost his temper.

"Mostly, it really bothers me that all wildness is disappearing and most people don't seem to care. It's modern day manifest destiny. It's like people think that the forests and deserts and oceans and mountains and prairies are just there for us to cut and fish and mine and d…" Adam looked very frustrated.

It took me a moment. "Drill?"

"Drill. And if you don't believe in that inexorable progression, then you aren't a true American." Adam paused.

I was thinking, too, wondering yet again how a man coping with brain injury could sound so intellectual. I understood the concept of good days and bad days when it came to the brain, but his cycle seemed to be an extreme oscillation. Or a carefully-constructed lie.

"This is why you write poetry? Do you think your poetry is going to change the way people think about wildness?"

"No, because no one is ever going to read my poetry. And most of it already burned up in the fire. Who cares about poetry, anyway?"

"I do. It's like art," I said. "I like to listen to poetry the same way I like to look at art. I don't know much about it, but they both make me feel good."

Adam didn't respond.

"Maybe you should do a book," I said. "If your poems were available to the world, they might make a difference."

"I don't have any idea how to do that."

"I don't either, but I've read about it. It doesn't sound too hard. I think the basic principle is that you upload your poems to a company like Amazon, and they make the book and put it on their website. It doesn't cost anything. If someone buys your book, they print it and ship it, and they pay you a portion of the proceeds."

"I could never figure it out. My brain is too far gone."

"I'm sure there are lots of people who'd be willing to help you. Maybe I could help."

Adam frowned. "You're just saying that."

"No, I mean it. I think you have something valuable to say."

Adam shook his head. "People won't want to read about wildness. They would think my poems were a downer."

"It sounds to me like your poems are more celebrations of wildness. People might think your poems are inspirational. You could make it a kind of memoir. People would want to read the thoughts of their football hero. The presentation could be the writings of Adam Simms. And the subtle effect would be that your poems would sneak up on them, get them thinking about wildness."

Adam looked doubtful.

"I sacked everyone's heroes. Fans love the quarterbacks. They hate me."

"That makes you more interesting."

Adam was silent. I could tell I had him thinking. I waited and didn't speak.

"What would I call it?" Adam asked. "If I called it something like 'A Celebration of Wildness,' readers would fall asleep."

"Then call it something about you. 'Adam Simms, The Poetry of a Killer Sack Artist.'"

Adam looked serious.

After another minute, I said, "I understand the seriousness of your brain injury. And I've seen the effects. But I have to say that your brain works pretty well when you start talking about preserving wildness."

"That's because I think about it all the time."

I stood up, walked over and gave Blondie a pet. I said, "I have to go. Good luck with your poetry."

I let myself out and drove away, thinking about a man in the grips of approaching dementia yet who had ideas that could help the world. And, unlike nearly any other poet, millions of people knew who he was.

I also thought about his past history of arson and sharpshooting and working in the yard where they kept the rotary highway snowblowers.

Adam Simms might be a gentle poet, but he was also a murder suspect.

Which gave me a sudden, disturbing thought. Could Adam be faking the brain injury? If so, why would he have let me see the photo with Scarlett Milo and Darla Ali? Because anyone would assume that, if he were guilty, he would never let anyone see the photo. If he were guilty, he would have deleted the photo. But as I thought about it, the photo was no evidence of anything. So not deleting it and letting me and other people see it would add to the sense of his confusion, and it would make him seem innocent.

It could be a fantastic counter-intuitive cover and misdirection.

Maybe Adam was playing with me, bringing me into his web of deceit.

FORTY-SEVEN

The next morning, I had coffee with Street at her condo. Spot lay on the rug in her living room. He appeared to be asleep, but I could tell by his ears that he was listening.

"I'm making no progress," I said to Street. "I don't know who the killer is. I have no idea whether the killer is going to strike again, and if so, where or how. I'm not even sure why the killer is killing, although I assume it's because he wants the Blue Fire Diamond. Now if I could find that diamond, assuming it really exists, I'd have something."

"You would." Street was nodding. "What about putting the word out that you have it, and try to get the killer to come after you? Not that I'd want you to take such a risk, of course."

"I've already suggested that in my email to the TahoeBlueFire address. But putting the idea out to the public is a great idea. I could have Glennie write an article."

"Perfect! But would Glennie feel comfortable reporting a false story?"

"No. But she needn't report a false story. She could write the true report of Owen McKenna describing how he found the diamond. I would be the only one telling a falsehood. If Glennie reports it as something that I'm claiming and not as objective truth, then she won't compromise her journalistic integrity."

"The only question is whether or not she'll agree to your idea."

I got ahold of Glenda Gorman at The Herald, and I asked her if I could buy her lunch and tell her my story, and she said absolutely not because that would not be ethical.

"A reporter can never take as much as a cup of free coffee while getting a story, or she could be accused of bias."

"Just testing you," I said. "Hear me out, and you can decide if you think my story is news."

So we met, and I told her a story about the Blue Fire of Florence.

Glennie took lots of notes and went back to work.

She called when she'd filed the story. "If this story doesn't bring the killer after you, I don't think he's still alive."

The next day the headline was huge.

LOCAL DETECTIVE CLAIMS
SOLUTION TO TAHOE MURDERS

Private investigator Owen McKenna reported yesterday that he has solved the case of the recent killings in Tahoe, and he is on the verge of catching the killer.

According to McKenna, the case reaches back 500 years to the Italian Renaissance. If McKenna's reconstruction is correct, the famous Hope Diamond had an equally valuable sister diamond, mined from the same quarry in India, a huge blue gem that was hidden for centuries by the Medici family of Florence.

This diamond, called the Blue Fire of Florence, was purchased by Frank Sinatra back in the early nineteen sixties, the same period when he owned the Cal Neva Hotel in Crystal Bay on the North Shore. McKenna believes that Sinatra wanted the Blue Fire of Florence to help him win the affections of the most famous woman in the world, Marilyn Monroe.

McKenna says that the world will never know why Marilyn, who'd had a previous affair with Sinatra, was not swayed by this gem, which was upwards of 45 carats. Nevertheless, the diamond disappeared.

McKenna speculated that it may have been sold by Sinatra. Or, perhaps Sinatra, in a deep depression, threw it into Lake Tahoe. Whatever the history, the Blue Fire of Florence has remained hidden for all of these intervening years.

When asked how he knew if the gem in question is really the Blue Fire of Florence, McKenna stated that historical records show that it is a red fluorescing diamond, a rare characteristic that a few blue diamonds exhibit. McKenna explained that this characteristic is like fingerprinting, and it allows a positive identification.

The Blue Fire of Florence is estimated to have a value of 200 million dollars.

McKenna also stated that because the Blue Fire Diamond has never been authenticated and until now has existed only in the realm of rumor, there is no line of provenance establishing ownership. Thus, the diamond is like bearer bonds or treasure found at the bottom of the sea. It belongs to whomever possesses it.

According to McKenna, several people recently learned of the Blue Fire Diamond's existence, and the killer's motive is to eliminate the others so that he will not have to share ownership of the diamond when he finds it. McKenna said that the killer believes he knew where to find the gem, but, unfortunately for the killer, McKenna got to it first. In the absence of others who might claim to have discussed its location with McKenna, McKenna says that the diamond now belongs to him.

As to the question of what will happen to the diamond, McKenna said that its value requires him to keep it hidden until he's brought the murderer into custody.

FORTY-EIGHT

I stopped by the house where Darla Ali had lived before she was killed. Her roommate, Sanford Burroughs, had previously told me that his car was a silver Subaru Outback. I didn't see it in the street.

Nevertheless, I trotted up the stairs and knocked. There was no answer. I leaned off to the side of the stairway landing and tried to look in one of the windows. I couldn't see much through the narrow opening in the drapes, but I was looking into the kitchen area. The counters were clear and clean. It had been some time since my previous visit, but I thought there had been a collection of microbrew beer bottles along the back of the counters.

I went back down to my Jeep, where Spot stood in the back seat, watching. I realized that he wasn't looking at me but at a Post Office vehicle that was pulling away from a set of triple mailboxes.

Because it is so hard to maintain and clear snow from outdoor mailboxes in Tahoe, most people have P.O. boxes. But the Post Office has been trying outdoor boxes in some neighborhoods to see, presumably, if there is some advantage, cost or otherwise. Most people haven't signed up for them, but apparently, Sanford and Darla and the two apartments below them had given them a try.

Most of us detectives, whether private or employed by the police, don't have a big ethical problem with glancing at the front of someone's mail unless we think that it might produce critical evidence about a crime, in which case we like to get a warrant so that the evidence is admissible in court. But if we're just a little curious…

I flipped open Sanford and Darla's box and fanned through the mail. There was a gas bill, a credit card bill, and a clothing catalog addressed to Darla Ali. For Sanford, there was a letter from a credit union stamped 'third notice' in red letters, a notice from the DMV, and a magazine. I turned it over to see the front.

It was a magazine for rifle enthusiasts. This one had a cover story on a specialty sniper rifle made by Accuracy International. I flipped open the magazine and saw related articles on scopes and distance shooting with discussions of elevation and air density, wind velocity and direction, bullet drop, bullet trajectory, the Coriolis effect, many of the aspects of long distance shooting that military snipers grapple with.

It was obviously time for another talk with Sanford Burroughs.

I drove over to Pizza Pan International where he worked. There was no silver Outback nearby.

I walked in. A young woman was at the rear of the front room. She held a pencil and a pad of paper and was going through supplies in a tall cabinet, making marks on the pad.

"Hi, I'm here to see Sanford," I said.

"He quit."

"When was that?"

She made another mark on the clipboard, frowned, looked again at the shelf, erased what she'd just written, then rewrote it.

"Sorry. Yesterday. Talk about not giving us a two-week notice. He just called in and said something came up and he had to leave town. He'd only worked one day into the new pay period, so he said that we could just keep the money because he wasn't going to be reachable. Of course, we can't do that. So this will be a pain in the neck for us. We'll have to issue a check, then we'll have to hold it for him for who knows how long. I don't know the rule on that. We'll have this discrepancy on the books. It would be so much easier if he'd just give us a forwarding address."

"Did he say anything about why he had to leave town?"

She shook her head. "Nope."

"Had it seemed like anything was odd with him recently? Like he had any kind of trouble? Or did he talk about any big change that was coming for him?"

Another head shake. "The only thing different in the last few days was that he stopped talking about his never-ending microbrew plans. It used to be he couldn't be at work for more than a half hour without he'd bring up beer. He said he was going to call it Bold Brew. And he talked about the Bold concept incessantly. Then he suddenly stopped mentioning it. I even asked him if he was still going to do it, and he said he didn't know."

"What about his roommate Darla Ali? Did he talk about her?"

"Oh, you wouldn't believe. He talked about her so much it was like he was trying to convince us that he was worried about her. I mean, anyone would be worried if their roommate disappeared, right? It's not like we'd need convincing."

I thanked the woman and left.

FORTY-NINE

I called Vince Russo. This time he answered.

I explained who I was and that I'd talked to Old Man Joseph and learned that Vince had bought a bunch of his Sinatra stuff. I didn't volunteer over the phone that Joseph was in the hospital with serious injuries, nor that the persons who'd assaulted Joseph had likely been led to him by me.

It was one of the conundrums of my business. To pursue a murderer is to agitate and provoke and put innocent people at risk, a most unfortunate risk. But to let a murderer go free possibly puts more people at risk.

I decided I would talk to Vince first, then inform him of the hazards later.

Vince said he'd love to "talk Sinatra" with me.

I drove down the East Shore to South Lake Tahoe. During much of the drive I saw the same car in the rearview mirror, two or three cars back. It was a silver Subaru Outback, which, because it was all-wheel-drive, was possibly the most common car in Tahoe. It was also what Sanford Burroughs drove.

About four miles past the state line, I took a right on Tahoe Keys Boulevard and headed out to the Keys, an upscale neighborhood on miles of inland waterways that were dredged out in the 1960s. The roads can be confusing. When I couldn't find Vince's house, I realized I'd come down the wrong street. It seemed his house was just across the canal in front of me. But what was a short distance by water was a long way by road.

When I turned around, there was the silver Subaru Outback. Or maybe it was a different silver Outback.

I got back on Tahoe Keys Boulevard. The next intersection was a fair distance down and around a slight curve. I accelerated. When I got to the intersection, I'd come around the curve enough that I could no longer see the silver Outback. I jerked the wheel, pulled off, and stopped behind a group of fir trees.

It only took 30 seconds to realize that the Subaru had stopped or turned off.

I drove back to search. The Subaru was gone.

Maybe it was someone innocent. Or maybe it was Sanford Burroughs, and he realized that I was onto him.

I found Vince Russo's house and parked on the street.

The house was a large two story with a two-car garage tucked under the front portion. I left Spot in the Jeep and found the doorbell.

The door opened. A short grizzled man around 80 years old saw me and made a big grin. His teeth were numerous, perfectly lined up, and white as whipped cream. His thick, brown hair was styled like a heavy-nap, shag carpet. It sat crooked on his head.

He reached out his hand and gave me a strong shake.

"I'm Vince Russo. You must be Owen McKenna. Good to meet you. I was upstairs, and I saw your dog with his head out the window, and he drew a bead on me in the upstairs window. It was love at first sight. Will you bring him in, or do I have to go and cavort with him outside?" The man had a classic radio voice, deep and soothing, with crisp pronunciation.

"I'm happy to bring him in." I took a quick look inside Vince's house, trying to anticipate problems. Over by the big living room windows was an expensive-looking telescope. On a white pedestal near a black baby grand piano was a somewhat abstracted bronze of a singer at a mike, no doubt a loose representation of Sinatra. Many items that Spot could knock over.

"I see what you're looking for. Your dog's a wagger, huh? I have some delicate stuff that survived the recent earthquake. Hate to lose it to a Dane's tail. My sister, bless her soul, had three Danes years back. Two were waggers, one was not. I'll clear the tables and tail-proof the joint while you go get him."

So I went back to the Jeep and fetched Spot. Vince and Spot met like they were old friends who'd been apart for years. Vince rubbed Spot's neck, and Spot leaned against him, and then Vince got Spot to shake, catching his heavy paw with both hands and giving it a big up and down motion.

"He's a big fella, that's for sure." Vince led Spot indoors.

A large, reddish orange cat saw Spot and ran up the stairs into reassuring darkness. "Okay, Spot," Vince said. "You and me, we're gonna sit over here, away from the telescope and sculpture. I've got a rug in front of my chair and with the carpet, it's practically an American Kennel Club-certified doggie bed."

Amazingly, Spot did exactly as Vince wanted, lying down in front of Vince's chair.

"Okay, watch this." Vince winked at me as he sat down in the chair. He lifted up one of his legs and laid it across Spot's back. Spot didn't move. "Do I know Danes or what?"

"You know them," I said. "I hear you had a radio show devoted to Sinatra." I sat down across from Vince.

"Yep. Fifteen years. Those were fun days. Sinatra tunes brought out the camaraderie. Of course, everyone had a Sinatra story. Everyone had his records and watched his movies, and a large number had seen him perform at one time or another. My listeners were Sinatra's hard core fans. Sinatra's specialty was that he really connected with his audience. And I was the beneficiary of all that goodwill. Ol' Blue Eyes himself even called into my show one time. So I asked if I could get an autographed photo, and he sent me one." Vince turned and pointed to a wall of pictures. "There it is, second one down on the right. Signed to Vince. Is that a kick or what?"

I walked over and looked at the picture, then turned to the glass display case that was built into a corner. There were two shelves. Each one held a glass sculpture of Sinatra, about eighteen inches tall, and they were lit from below so they glowed. They showed two different sides of Sinatra, one the smiling charisma of the electrifying showman, and the other appearing to show Sinatra with a dramatic melancholy.

"Old Man Joseph, who sold you his collection of Sinatra memorabilia, said you also had other Sinatra memorabilia besides what you got from him."

Vince beamed. "I'm Sinatra's number one fan."

"I have a question for you. Have you ever heard of the Blue Fire of Florence? It refers to one of the world's greatest diamonds, possibly no more than a rumor, but possibly real. From my inquiries, I'm leaning toward real."

"Well, now, you sure know how to pique a man's curiosity. Of course, I already saw the newspaper article about you and the diamond. Maybe I know something. But you go first."

"You may have heard about the woman who was recently shot and killed at Squaw Valley."

He nodded.

I said, "Her name was Scarlett Milo. After she was shot, but before she died, she wrote a note about the Blue Fire of Florence. It wasn't clear what she was trying to communicate, but my sense was that she thought she'd been shot because of the Blue Fire of Florence. Another woman and man who possibly knew about the diamond were killed before Milo was killed. So I did some research on the Blue Fire of Florence and was told that Sinatra's mother Dolly bought it on his behalf."

Vince raised a single eyebrow. It seemed like he knew part or all of the story, but he wanted to see what I knew.

I continued. "Sinatra paid two million back in the early sixties. Dolly delivered the money in cash to an Italian mobster named Bruno Valenti, who stole the diamond on what he described as a custom purchase order. They made the transaction at a meeting in Genoa, Italy, where Dolly's sister lived."

Vince was still keeping silent.

I thought about what I'd recently learned about Sinatra. "I don't know what Sinatra did with the diamond," I said, "but if I were to make a guess, I'd throw out the very original notion that he maybe wanted it to woo a woman."

Vince grinned.

I continued, "Sinatra had been involved with Marilyn Monroe in the fifties during the time he was married to Ava Gardner. Around nineteen sixty, Monroe's marriage to Arthur Miller collapsed during or right after the filming of The Misfits. This was the time when Sinatra introduced Marilyn Monroe to John F. Kennedy. Shortly after that, Monroe had an affair with the president. I got to thinking that Sinatra hadn't wanted that result, and I wondered if he wasn't hoping to win Monroe back. He'd been with her once, and he knew what he'd been missing."

This time I paused.

Vince looked at me. "An interesting story, some of which I've heard before."

"From whom?" I asked.

"Back when I had the radio show, I would get letters from Sinatra fans. One day in the middle nineteen nineties, I got an unusual letter. Of course, that was before most of us had email. The letter was from Italy and it came to the radio station. It was written in English. The letter writer wanted to know if I had ever heard of the Blue Fire of Florence. She'd been going through old Italian newspapers at the library and had seen pictures of Sinatra in a gossip column. She said the column talked about a diamond that was rumored to have been originally acquired by the Medicis of Florence. The column also reported another rumor from the nineteen sixties speculating that the so-called Blue Fire of Florence had been stolen from a Florentine family and sold to an agent of Frank Sinatra. The column mentioned that this was during the time when Sinatra owned a hotel at Lake Tahoe. So the letter writer learned that I was in Tahoe and that I had a show based on Sinatra. Thus her question about whether or not I had any information about the diamond."

"And did you?" I asked.

Vince Russo grinned. "Give me a minute, and I'll show you something interesting."

He carefully lifted his foot off of Spot, stood up, and walked over to the display case with the Sinatra sculptures. He raised up on tiptoes, reached up to the top of the case, which was about my height, and removed a photograph.

"In the stuff I bought from Old Man Joseph, there were quite a few pictures of Sinatra. Most in frames. One day, I was pulling the backs off the frames to see if anything had been written on the backs of the photos. In one frame, I found this, a picture hiding in the back of the frame."

He handed a curved photo to me. "Careful not to straighten the photo or flex it, as the surface is brittle."

It was a five-by-seven, black and white photo, printed on glossy paper.

The picture showed Marilyn Monroe alone out on a pier on Lake Tahoe. She was wearing a filmy, white dress that appeared to glow in the setting sun.

"It was one of those mood shots," Vince said, "the beautiful girl who has everything anyone could ever want, right? But in that picture, she's looking very lonely, don't you think?"

Marilyn was standing at the end of the pier, her elbows resting on the railing. In the open palm of her left hand, she held a huge gemstone. It was the size of a chicken egg that had been sliced in half lengthwise. And even in this old black and white photo, I could see that it sparkled like it was lit from the inside.

Monroe was staring at the stone, a sad look on her face.

"Pretty obvious, don't you think?" Vince said. "That has to be the Blue Fire of Florence." Vince's resonant voice wavered as he said it. "You'd think that the moment Sinatra gave Monroe the Blue Fire of Florence, it would become famous, right? There would be pictures everywhere. Yet it didn't. And no one has ever seen pictures of it. So the question is why not?"

Vince sat back down. This time, he lifted his other leg to rest on Spot's back. "I think the only possible answer is that the diamond disappeared. Neither Frank nor Marilyn ever mentioned it. And there are no other photos of it. Otherwise, we'd have seen them a thousand times. So the only reason must be that Marilyn rejected it. And then Sinatra did something with it. Either intentionally or unintentionally, he hid it. Or maybe it's sitting on the bottom of the lake, sixteen hundred feet down."

"There's an idea to contemplate," I said. "Sinatra throwing a two million-dollar diamond into the lake. A diamond that might be worth two hundred million today."

"No kidding." Vince was shaking his head. "You said you heard that he paid the mob two million for it?"

"Yeah. Told to me in a little medieval town in Tuscany by the very mobster who stole it and then sold it. He was on his deathbed."

"Sinatra was extravagant," Vince said. "But I can't imagine him throwing away that kind of money. Plus, he had money issues now and then. Not your kind or my kind of money issues. But until he sold Reprise Records, he wasn't as flush as everyone thought. So there's another reason for him not to be too wasteful. Obviously, he was willing to spend the money, and, in his mind, Marilyn would have been worth the fuss. I've read several things here and there that suggest he was stuck on her. 'Course, who wouldn't be. But once the girl says no, any rational guy is going to do something else with the stone, sell it at the very least. Not throw it away, never to be seen again. Sinatra was rational."

Vince made a little lip-smacking noise. "There is, however, a possible extenuating circumstance. You've no doubt heard that Sinatra referred to himself as an eighteen-karat manic-depressive. Some people might think that he could toss the rock in a manic moment. But I doubt it. However, when I think of what I know about depression, I could see him tossing it when he was in the depths of despair." Vince reached out and pet Spot.

"Do you still have the letter you got from Italy?" I asked.

"Sure. It's upstairs. I'll go get it."

Vince got up and headed up the staircase.

After he'd disappeared into one of the upstairs bedrooms, the big red-orange cat appeared and sat on the top step. It looked down at Spot. Spot focused on the cat, but he stayed put.

I got up and looked out the big windows. Although the landscape was darkening with twilight, I could see down the canal that stretched out toward the big lake. There were two floating docks that had been left in all winter. One was Vince's and the other was some distance down. While the body of Lake Tahoe doesn't freeze in the winter, the canals in the keys do, so homeowners put their boats in storage during the winter. The water was now thawed in the spring sunshine, but most of the boats wouldn't return until summer.

The canal Vince lived on had a gentle curve. A hundred yards down, the canal joined the large open water area that was within the keys and near the channel out to the main lake. In that open area was a boat. As I looked into the gathering darkness, I thought I sensed a person standing up in the boat. The silhouette of the person went out to the sides as if the person had their hands up to their forehead, elbows pointing out.

My immediate thought was that the person had binoculars and was looking in our direction. Maybe even at Vince's house.

I walked over to Vince's telescope, bent down and looked through the eyepiece. All I saw was black. I tried turning a knob that may or may not have been a focus knob. Still black.

"You need to take the lens cap off," Vince said as he came down the stairs. "I often use it to look up at the stars. If I leave it pointed up, the main lens catches a lot of dust. The downside to having an actual wood-burning fireplace. So I've trained myself to put on the lens cap."

I looked at the large end and saw that there was a snap-on black cap. I pulled it off. Now I could see through the scope. I trained it back and forth.

The powerboat was no longer there.

"What are you looking for?" Vince asked.

"I saw a boat out there. Seemed like a person on the boat had binoculars and was looking this way."

"Oh, that happens all the time. Lakeshore people and boat people all have binoculars with them wherever they go." Vince pointed at his telescope. "My scope is the same thing, only more magnified. We're all looking at everything through a lens. Even at night. You get used to it."

The cat started walking down the stairs, looking away from Spot, nonchalant, uninterested.

Spot was still watching the cat. "Spot, stay," I said.

"That's Ruby," Vince said. "Probably the biggest she-cat in the county. But she'll run terrified from a terrier half her size."

"Smart cat," I said.

"She doesn't appear to be afraid of your hound. How's that? His head is bigger than she is."

"Spot isn't dangerous to cats."

"And somehow she can tell." Vince was shaking his head.

Vince handed me a piece of paper. It was a handwritten letter from the Italian teenager. After I was able to figure out the words, the message was as Vince had reported. There was nothing that suggested I could learn anything else.

"I've spent a lot of time on this," I said, "and I had to go to Tuscany to learn about the diamond. Yet, here you were all along with this information."

"Not all of it. From the photo, I figured the diamond probably existed. But I didn't know how Sinatra got it."

Ruby got to the bottom of the stairs, walked over to the baby grand piano, and sat down underneath. She appeared to not notice Spot.

"Why'd you stay so private about this photo?" I asked.

Vince made a half smile. "I own one of the largest collections of Sinatra stuff in the world, show announcements and movie posters, photos, award trophies and statuettes, Grammy Awards, Gold Record Awards, movie paraphernalia, clothes, even old shoes. I've been through it all many times, so I knew the diamond wasn't there, hiding in a watch pocket or something. But I wondered if somewhere in the notes and letters and songbooks and lead sheets might be an indication of where it might be, whether Monroe had in fact given it back to Sinatra, and where Sinatra might have stashed it."

"And if somebody knew about it, it could put you at risk."

"I already am. Someone broke into my house a couple of weeks ago. He went through my stuff, practically everything I have, and made quite a mess. But he didn't take anything."

"I thought I saw an alarm panel by your door."

Vince nodded. "I have an alarm. It is wired to the door and all of the downstairs windows."

"The burglar came in an upstairs window?"

"And went back out the same way. My alarm is quite old, so I don't have motion detectors."

I thought about how Diamond described the male victim, Sean Warner, as a burglar specializing as a "second-story man."

"Any idea what he was looking for?" I asked.

"Well, from the mess, he spent most of his time going through the Sinatra stuff, so it makes me think that he was looking for the Blue Fire Diamond."

"Any chance he found it? Someplace where you never looked?"

"There is no place where I've never looked. I've been very thorough."

"In your searches, did you ever find any reference to the Blue Fire of Florence? Any piece of paper with the letters BFF on it?"

"Other than the letter, no. But I found something very intriguing, if ambiguous."

"That's what we investigators look for. What was it?"

"A note that Frank Sinatra wrote to Marilyn Monroe."

FIFTY

Vince went over to a bookshelf and pulled out a biography of Sinatra. He opened the back cover, removed a piece of paper, and handed it to me. It was white paper, yellowed a bit with age and lined with light blue lines faded almost to the point of invisibility. There was a note written with a blue ballpoint pen. It said,

'M, I put it all on the line for you, but you rejected the whole concept. Yes, my reaction was too dramatic. But it's still there. That shows how I feel about you even if things will never be the same. - F'

I gestured with the note. "You kept this secret for some time, Vince. Why are you willing to tell someone about it now?"

Vince walked over to the photo wall and looked at two pictures of Frank with Marilyn.

"I think the Blue Fire is here in Tahoe," Vince said, "and I think that others have figured out that much. Three people are dead, and there have been attempts on you and others. I can no longer think it's right for me to sit on the info. Tell me what I can do to help."

"Let's start by having you show me your Sinatra collection."

"It's mostly just piles of boxes. This is a four-bedroom house, and I sleep in the smallest one. The others are stacked to the ceiling. Anyone who looked into those rooms would think I have a hoarding problem, which, I suppose, I do. I might sell the works. I looked up a bunch of items on eBay once. Whoa, was that an eye opener. It looks like I've got at least a quarter million dollars worth of stuff, if one were to carefully itemize it and sell it piece by piece. Maybe a lot more. But I'd prefer to find a good museum to take the collection. I'd be willing to donate the whole works, if it went to the right home. C'mon, I'll give you a peek."

Vince stood up and went upstairs. Spot jumped up and

looked at me. Ruby turned to stare at Spot, but she didn't move.

"My hound wants to come. That okay?"

"Sure."

So Spot and I followed Vince up the stairs.

"Here's the biggest part of it," Vince said, walking through an open door. "Fills the master suite."

Spot pushed ahead of me into a large room mostly filled with cardboard boxes piled in tall rows. There were two narrow aisles that one could squeeze through to get to the boxes near the wall.

The area near the corner windows was where Vince had put stuff that wouldn't fit in boxes. The largest item was a full-sized sculpture of Sinatra. It was made of metallic plastic that glittered in shades of red, magenta, pink, and orange. Nearby, standing up in a golden support was a golf driver, gold plated from handle to the club head. I picked it up. It was engraved. 'This club is filled with lead. Maybe now you'll be able to hit farther than 20 yards. Your fan, Dean Martin.'

"Got that from Caesars Palace in Vegas," Vince said.

We moved to the other rooms. I looked in many of the boxes, not for anything in particular, but to see if anything gave me a new idea. I saw autographed napkins, a set of shot glasses with Sinatra's picture on them, a jar of dirt with a label that said it was the first scoop that marked the beginning of the Cal Neva remodelling after Sinatra bought the hotel, bundles of letters, music award certificates too numerous to frame, copies of Nevada State files from the time when the gaming commission was investigating Sinatra's alleged ties to organized crime.

"How'd you get these?" I said holding up what looked like official Nevada government files.

"Everything you want in life gets down to who you know," Vince said. "I know a lot of people."

I spent 30 minutes looking but found nothing that might connect to the Blue Fire Diamond or Sinatra's mother Dolly or anything related. Of course, I didn't expect to find anything considering that Vince had been looking for the same thing for decades.

When I was done, I said, "Anything else that isn't in these

rooms?"

"Just the sculptures and the photo wall downstairs."

Back in the living room, Vince held his arms wide in a gesture to show the scope of the photo wall. There were several dozens of photos, most, but not all, of Sinatra. Many of the other people in the photos were famous, from presidents and foreign heads of state to royalty from around the world. There were photos of Sinatra receiving Grammy Awards and his Academy Award and Golden Globe Awards. There were photos of Sinatra performing all over the world from Caesars Palace in Vegas to Carnegie Hall in New York to London and Paris.

In its own area on the wall was a group of photos that were all taken at Tahoe, from the Cal Neva Hotel to boats out on the lake. There were pictures of Sinatra with his Rat Pack pals Joey Bishop, Sammy Davis Jr., Peter Lawford, and Dean Martin. There were photos of his friends and associates, including John and Robert Kennedy. There was a picture of Sinatra with mobster Sam Giancana. And there was Marilyn Monroe, sitting at a table at the Cal Neva, watching Sinatra perform.

"And these are Sinatra's records," Vince said, pointing at a substantial shelf on an adjacent wall. "I have them all, including the rare ones."

Ruby walked out from under the piano, strolled past Vince's feet, and sauntered over near Spot. Casual as could be, she lay down on the carpet near him, then stretched out her head until her nose nearly touched his. Spot shifted his head closer, but he didn't lift it off the carpet. His nostrils were flexing. It seemed as if Ruby was watching them move.

Vince stared. "I'll be damned. Look at that cat. It's like she's flirting with your dog."

Vince moved over near the fireplace. On a stand was a large aquarium with bright tropical fish, orange and yellow and blue, swimming elaborate patterns.

"This was at the Cal Neva. See the line on the bottom?" He pointed to a black line that went across the white gravel on the bottom of the tank.

I nodded.

"For years, this aquarium was inset at the end of the lobby

where the state line between Nevada and California ran across the lobby floor. So Sinatra had a line painted on the bottom of the aquarium, and then he put in a bunch of fish and asked visitors to guess which were the Nevada fish and which were the California fish."

"Are these the same kind that he had?"

Vince laughed. "I doubt it. I just picked what the pet store had. To my knowledge, there's no record of what Sinatra had. I saw one old photo with the aquarium in the background. The photo was in black and white, and the fish were nondescript, so it's anybody's guess what kind of fish he had."

"Anything else I should've asked about?"

Vince paused, then slowly shook his head. "But if I think of something, I'll give you a call. You're welcome to come back anytime and dig through boxes."

"Thanks." I turned to leave, then stopped. "Vince, I don't want to alarm you, but I'd like you to be very security conscious. Someone is killing people who knew about the diamond."

I told Vince about Old Man Joseph and how he'd been interrogated about the Blue Fire Diamond and then left to die.

"So I can't stress that enough. Be very careful. Lock your doors." I gestured at the windows. "Keep the drapes pulled."

"Will do. This place seals up tight. Ruby has her cat door, but it's tiny, and its frame is solid. No person could get through."

"You should also use your garage so that you're not visible when you get in and out of your car," I said. "Come and go at unpredictable hours. Don't let him know where you are at any time."

Vince shook his head. "That would be like living in prison. At my age, I won't spend the rest of my life, however little of it there is, hiding from the boogeyman."

I walked over to the front door. Spot followed. I turned and reached for the doorknob. "Thanks for letting me look at your Sinatra memorabilia. It is an amazing collection."

Vince came over and gave Spot a pet, then looked up at me. He seemed sad to see us go. And in his sadness, he looked his age. With his ever youthful false teeth and false hair and facelift, and, probably, nitro-freezing for age spots, and laser treatments for fading vision, he seemed like one of the awkward agers.

I appreciate older people who embrace their age, wrinkles, yellowed teeth, thick eyeglasses, and bald pates with the fringe of white fuzz. Yet, even as I thought that Vince's cosmetic applications looked obvious and goofy, I also realized that they did in fact make him look younger. Maybe the facades he put up to fend off aging were just a sign of youthful spirit. He still felt young, so he was going to try to look young. Screw the degradations of age. And if anyone had a problem with it, Vince didn't care.

Spot and I walked out the door into the night. I shut it and waited a few seconds to hear the reassuring sound of the deadbolt.

FIFTY-ONE

We got in the Jeep and drove away, turning onto Venice Drive and heading east.

The night was cold, and there was a mist coming off the canals. The Keys' houses were largely dark, empty vacation homes that would go unused by owners and renters alike until summer was upon us in July. The streets were empty as well, with none of the parked cars that spilled out of driveways and onto the streets on a normal summer night. The only one I drove by at the shoulder was a Fiat 500, just like the one Street and I had rented in Italy. I cruised on past, thinking about things Italian. Italian influence on America was pervasive. We ate Italian food, we wore Italian clothes, we drank Italian wine, we celebrated Italian movie stars, Italian art, Italian sports cars, Italian singers. Like Frank Sinatra.

It seemed that ever since Bruno Valenti told us about selling the Blue Fire Diamond to Sinatra, I kept bumping into people who celebrated Sinatra. People who'd seen Sinatra perform. People who'd watched his movies. People who collected Sinatra memorabilia. People who listened to his music. Like Vince Russo. Like the guy at the city yard who had Sinatra on his boombox. What was his name? Emilio. Wasn't Emilio also an Italian name? I'd thought he was Hispanic. But maybe he was Sicilian. Maybe the best way to disguise an Italian accent was to cover it with a manufactured Hispanic accent...

I slowed, turned around, drove back and stopped near the Fiat. It was parked near a canal. Like the canal near Vince's house, it would be crowded come summer. But now, this one had just a few floating docks and no boats.

But it could have held a boat an hour ago. And Brann Crosen had described Emilio as a guy who could make any engine run. Maybe even when he didn't have an ignition key.

I pulled out and sped back to Vince's street, slowed to a quiet stop some distance from Vince's house, got out with Spot, and we trotted through the dark.

The house was mostly dark. Vince had turned off his lights. But there seemed to be a glow of light on the side with the canal. I held Spot's collar as I went around the side of the house. The winter's blanket of snow had melted. The fresh snow of the last day was soft. We could walk quietly without crunching through crusted snow.

The glow of light was coming through the drapes on the windows that faced the canal. I heard voices. I couldn't make out the words, but I could hear the stress, the tension, the fear.

Nearby, was Vince's floating dock. Unlike earlier, there was a boat tied to one of the posts at the end of the dock, its bow facing the lake.

Spot's ears were focused, his eyes searching, nostrils flexing. I touched my finger across the top of Spot's nose, a signal to be silent. I wanted to rush in, break down a door, but I paused, considering my options.

I walked softly down the ramp to the dock.

The boat was a low profile speedboat with an outboard engine. The cockpit was small, protected from the wind by a tiny windshield.

"Spot, stay," I whispered, then stepped into the boat. It rocked and bumped noisily against the dock. I took out my penlight, shielded the rim of the light and turned it on. The boat contained the usual gear. Life jackets shoved under the bow deck. Dock bumpers in the side stowage just below the gunnel. A small anchor tucked into a stern bin.

The boat was moored by a single line at the stern. I saw another long line looped around a cleat on the bow. One of the ends ran back along the side of the boat and into the stowage at the stern. The other lay loose on the bow and was long enough to reach a dock post. I dropped it over the post with a running bowline knot. There was still some slack in the line, so I pushed it down onto the surface of the water so it would not be too obvious. If one of the men in Vince's house tried to make a fast escape and only unhitched the rear mooring line, he'd be in for a surprise as he tried to drive off and discovered that the boat was still lashed to the dock.

When I was back out of the boat, the line was noticeable even in the dim light from distant house lights across the canal. But perhaps the boat's operator wouldn't notice, because he would assume that the boat was as he had left it.

Spot and I tiptoed up the dock ramp and over to the windows. The voices were louder, angry. I thought I heard Vince say, "I told you, I don't know!"

I gently put my hand on the handle of the sliding glass door.

It was locked.

There was a small patio. At the outer two corners were large ceramic planters, empty now, waiting for summer flowers that were still two months off.

I did a test lift on one. It was nearly as heavy as the bronze statue I used to stop Mario Montana on his scooter at the church in Roccatederighi in Tuscany.

"Okay, Spot," I whispered in his ear in a tone that would prepare him for action.

I bent my knees, gripped the planter, and lifted it up. I gave it a backswing, then let it fly toward one of the floor-to-ceiling windows.

It was like an explosion as the planter crashed through window and blinds. The tempered glass collapsed all at once. I put my arm out to sweep the blinds aside, and I ran through into Vince's living room. Spot was at my side.

There were three men, all showing shock at what had just happened. All turned to stare.

Emilio from the city yard was on the left. His arm was up, pointing, telling the others what to do.

Brann Crosen was in the center of the room. His right hand and arm were in a splint, the result of Adam Simms crushing it with his hands. In Crosen's left hand was a large knife, a silent weapon that wouldn't alert neighbors to mayhem. Standing in front of him was Vince, trying to work a key into the lock of the glass display case that held the Sinatra sculptures.

"Spot!" I yelled as much to unnerve the men as to communicate to Spot. "Take the suspect! Take him down!" I dropped my lower arm in front of Spot's face and pointed toward Crosen.

Crosen was fast. He grabbed Vince and spun him around as a shield against Spot. Crosen held the knife against Vince's neck.

But dogs don't respond to threats. Spot jumped up, hitting Vince in the chest with his paws. Both Vince and Crosen toppled over backward.

Crosen rolled, got his left hand out, knife up toward Spot. But Spot was faster. His jaws closed on Crosen's hand, biting down. Crosen screamed as his hand was crushed against the knife handle enclosed in his grip. He tried to jerk away from Spot. But a dog's natural reaction to resistance is to bite harder. Crosen screamed louder.

I pulled Vince to his feet as I turned toward Emilio.

"I'm so sorry," Vince said, his voice shaking. "Ruby had gone outside, and this man appeared at my window, knife to Ruby's neck. I couldn't let him butcher her. I had to open the door."

Emilio picked up a chair and threw it at me. There was no time to duck, but I got my arm up. The chair knocked me back onto the couch. Emilio came at me. I rolled to the floor and reached out my leg to trip him. He fell. I leaped on top of him, pinning him to the floor. I tugged at his arm, trying to jerk it behind his back. But Emilio was very strong. He twisted sideways and swung back with an elbow punch that grazed my jaw. He got his knees up and kicked out, pushing off the couch, driving himself out from underneath me.

I jumped to my feet. But as I turned toward him, Emilio was already up, in the martial arts position used by Crosen and his men against Adam Simms. Emilio was bouncing on his toes.

"Good move, Emilio. Or is it Antonio Scozzari?" I said, as I circled, my fists up. "From the L.A. crime family. Friend of Mario Montana in Tuscany. Co-conspirator in chasing down the Blue Fire of Florence. Murderer of how many people? Two with a rotary plow? One with a rifle? More that we don't know about?" I danced left, then right.

"Each death was a pleasure," he said in perfect English. His lips were pulled back in a sneer.

"You're done now," I said. "And don't even think about abandoning Crosen. I've booby-trapped your boat."

Emilio/Scozzari blew air, trying to pump oxygen, sounding more like a hissing cat than a fighter. He feinted, snapped a punch that touched my shoulder, feinted again.

I'm not a boxer, and I don't know karate. What I do know is the fighting techniques that are taught to cops, a collection of blocks, holds, and punches mixed with some very effective dirty tricks.

Most fighters expect you to trade blows with them or move away. The pros know close fighting techniques, but they don't expect anyone but a pro to get close.

So I snapped a distracting kick toward his knee. As he danced back, I put my fists tight to my forehead, bent down, and charged forward, my head moving toward his chest. He punched twice in fast succession, but my arms blocked my face. He backed away as I pushed him, my head to his chest. I swept my hands out and up, my forearms pushing against his biceps. Then I hooked my hands over his triceps, trapping his arms in a clinch.

He struggled as I slipped around under his left arm, and locked onto him from behind.

He tried to stomp my foot but missed as I snaked my arm around his neck from behind and put a carotid lock on him.

The trick with any carotid restraint is to lift up and squeeze your opponent's neck from the sides, shutting off blood to his brain but without collapsing his trachea, which has the nasty habit of killing the suspect.

Maybe I didn't get enough pinch.

Emilio/Scozzari jerked up both arms as if to box my ears. Knuckles struck my temple, jarring my head. I still had my right arm around his neck, so I stabbed my left thumb toward his eye. It felt like I caught the edge of his orbit, my thumbnail gouging the bone as my thumb slid off into the flesh between eyeball and socket.

Scozzari made a guttural yell and charged backward, pushing against me. The middle of my back struck the fireplace mantle, hard stone contacting vertebrae with a brutal blow. Electric pain shot down my back, loosening my grip on his neck.

He twisted, pulled away, ran for the broken window, and leaped outside.

I staggered away from the fireplace, stumbled toward the door and looked outside.

Scozzari was already at the boat. As I ran after him, he unhooked the stern mooring line, leaped into the cockpit, started the engine, and threw the gear lever all the way to fast forward.

The outboard engine roared, and the boat raced ahead.

What occurred next happened so quickly that it was difficult to comprehend the details.

The line that was tied from the bow cleat to the dock post stretched out tight. The cleat ripped out of the boat. The other end of the line that went back along the boat was attached to the anchor in the stern. As the boat raced forward, the line that arced from the dock post to the anchor was pulled back. It caught Scozzari on the front of his neck. Unfortunately, his instinct was not to jerk the speed lever to neutral, but to simply raise his hands to the line at his neck.

The line pulled tighter. The anchor leaped up from the stern, swung wildly through the air behind Scozzari's back, and hooked itself over the line that stretched out to the dock post. It formed a loop around Scozzari's neck.

Scozzari was jerked out of the speedboat. It was as violent as the drop from a tall gallows.

I turned back to the living room.

Vince was standing in a corner, his eyes wide with fear. Crosen was still on the floor. Spot still held Crosen's hand and the enclosed knife handle in his mouth. The large, shiny blade of the knife stuck up in the air.

I put my hiking boot on Crosen's neck, pressing down hard enough to make him wonder if I would kill him at that very moment. I bent over and took hold of Crosen's wrist.

"Good boy, Spot. Let go. C'mon boy, let go."

Spot opened his jaws. Crosen's hand was mangled, misshapen, and bloody. It flopped to the floor. Crosen made a small scream. It looked like he was crying, tears pooling around the eyeliner tattoos. I removed the knife and tossed it some distance away.

I kept my foot on Crosen's neck as I called 911.

FIFTY-TWO

Three hours later, when I was done speaking to Mallory and his officers, I drove up to the safe house to tell Adam that we'd caught Crosen and his boss in crime, Antonio Scozzari.

Unlike the Keys, the high-elevation neighborhood north of Kingsbury Grade had gotten another foot of snow. The snow walls on the streets were still very tall.

Two blocks before I got to the safe house, I saw Adam Simms's pickup stuck in a snowbank. He'd slid in the turn where one narrow road split off from another. Under his tires, the ice was polished from ineffective spinning of his wheels. I pulled over and got out. Using my penlight, I could see that the pickup was empty. Shuffling boot prints led from the truck down the wrong road, away from the safe house. It must have been a bad day.

I let Spot out, and we followed the prints into the dark, thankful that the deep snow would prevent Adam from wandering into the forest. Spot instinctively sensed that the fresh boot prints in the snow were out of place and that he should follow them. He trotted ahead of me, into the dark.

The night air was cold and crisp, almost like back in mid-winter. To the east, the lights of Carson Valley spread out before me, 3400 feet below. It was a spectacular vista. To the west lay Lake Tahoe, a black plate almost 200 square miles large surrounded by mountains that were still cloaked in a heavy snowpack.

There was a mist of ice in the air, formed by a frozen precipitate of moisture as the night grew colder and water vapor condensed out of the air.

My concern for Adam ratcheted up as I went farther down the dark road. Spot had disappeared into the darkness in front of me. I wasn't sure where the road led, but my recollection was that the road was a dead end, kept clear of snow just to allow the plows a place to turn around.

The boot prints ambled in a confused way, at one point veering over to the snow wall, and at another, tracing a loop. I was shining my feeble penlight beam farther down the road when a distant engine revved. The sound rumbled like a big truck and then morphed into a giant roar behind me. As I turned to look, a rotary plow came into view around a distant corner. A surfeit of flashing strobes and flood lights and directional spotlights lit up the forest. With the accompanying roar, it felt like some kind of shock-and-awe invasion.

I'd fallen for the oldest trick in the book, following seemingly innocent footprints designed to lead the fool into a trap.

The realization that the rotary was coming after me hit hard, and it made my breath short. I thought of running back toward the rotary plow to try to slip by its side. But the road was narrow, and there was no promise I could escape past the wide auger housing.

In the other direction, where boot prints had been put to fool me, there was lots of room. I'd easily be able find a place to climb a snow wall and escape. I began running. After a dozen steps, I glanced behind to check if the machine was still coming down the plowed road.

It was already well into the narrow section of road. Definitely coming after me.

The machine dominated the landscape with an assault of light and roar. The sound shook my chest. I looked away. The floods and strobes created an ominous flashing in the cloud of icy mist that surrounded me.

The machine pursuing me had almost two thousand horsepower in its two engines, and both seemed throttled up all the way. Its auger was a wheel of giant spinning teeth, carbon tipped and sharpened, more powerful than a Great White shark or a killer whale.

The psychological component of defeat is stronger than the physical. I hadn't run far, so my legs had plenty of physical strength left. But with its flashing lights and crushing roar, the rotary plow seemed like a satanic spirit, a pervasive evil black magic that crippled my flight, slowing my steps, just like what happens to a rabbit when a coyote is about to grab it. I sensed that my death was inevitable, and that made my running footsteps weak.

I told myself it was still just a machine. The evil resided with the operator, a faceless, nameless entity behind black glass. Terror was like a punch in my gut. I looked back toward the dark black plate of the windshield and tried to see past flood lights. There was no movement or shape to perceive, no instrument lights reflected in eyeglasses, no glow of cigarette or cigar, no tooth shine revealing the hideous grin of sadistic torture. The flood lights blinded me. All I could see and hear was a giant snow blowing monster that was coming to chew me into pieces and spit them out into the forest.

I turned away and refocused on running. Pump the legs, pound the feet, swing the arms. Spot saw me run toward him, so he trotted ahead at a faster pace, not yet realizing that we were in danger.

The road curved around to the right. I followed the turn and saw that it was in fact a dead end. It was surrounded on all sides with snow walls. But they were not especially tall, so I knew that we could get up and over them to escape. I ran hard toward the enclosing snow walls, hoping that my pace was much faster than the rotary chasing me. Gaining some distance on the machine was a relief. I could escape into the forest and work my way back to my Jeep.

Without breaking stride, I jumped up onto the four-foot snow wall. Spot jumped up next to me. The snow was firm, and we sank in only a few inches. I took two running steps across the top of the snow wall, then broke through crust and fell into the snow up to my waist. I realized that the firm snow wall was the berm that had been pushed up by the road grader. Moving just a few feet back from the street meant I was off the berm and into the soft unbroken snow behind it.

The monster roared louder as I clawed at the snow with my hands. I pummeled the ground with my feet, trying to push down the snow and compress it enough to get purchase and climb back up onto the firm berm. Spot was also sinking into the snow, but he did some dramatic leaps, moved away toward the forest, then turned back to look at me, wondering what was taking me so long.

I didn't look up toward the rotary because I knew its floods would blind me again. But my periphery sense and the roar told me it was now only yards away.

My feet found purchase, and I got back up on the berm. I ran along the firm snow toward an area where the natural windflow had prevented much snow buildup off to the side of the street. There, the sculpted snow blanket was shaped like large waves. Between two high swells was a trough of thinner snow that would give me an escape path. If I could stay off the wave tops and run through the troughs, it would be easy. But when I ran away from the berm and toward the closest trough, I again sank in deeper than I expected, floundering in snow like quicksand.

I realized that my strategy was a mistake. I should have stayed in the wide, plowed part at the end of the street, taking my chances, hoping to feint and dodge my way to the side of the intake box and escape before the machine could turn around and come after me.

The rotary roar was louder still, like a jet on takeoff. Its floods were so bright they seemed like Klieg lights in the night. They showed every ripple of snow in the forest, illuminating my way. But as I clawed my way forward, toward the trees, away from the street and the monster blower, the areas that looked like they had the thinnest snow cover were still too deep for easy travel. But I dove forward, clambered back up onto my feet, then dove forward again.

For some stupid reason, I'd initially had a vague sense that as I went into the forest, I would leave the blower behind, stuck back on the smooth surface of the street. But in my peripheral vision, I saw the blower get to the end of the street then bump up over the curb. It kept on coming, not slowing at all as it churned away from the street, toward the trees, toward me, chewing up all the snow and branches and anything else between the machine and me.

Spot ran back to me.

I churned with my feet and pulled with my hands, swimming through snow that was thick enough to make it very difficult to move but light enough that it wouldn't support my weight.

The roar grew louder. Spot turned toward the rotary, growled and barked. The dim snow was transformed into a blinding white stage set as the rotary's lights shined on me and beyond. Now in the deep snow, the machine was moving three times as fast as I was. I knew I only had seconds before it was on me. I saw a fallen branch to my right, a skinny stick, two inches in diameter, leaning down from the tree where it had broken off. It leaned at a steep angle, still attached at its base to the tree that shed it. I jerked and scrambled and leaped toward it. I got a hand wrapped around it and a foot onto it where there was a bend in the wood. I pushed up, balancing on one leg, reaching out my other hand to other branches on the tree's trunk. I grabbed a smaller branch and pulled while I took sliding steps up the angled wood, desperate to gain some height above the snow. Spot looked up at me.

The lights blinded. The roar ripped at my eardrums. The noxious smell of diesel exhaust filled my lungs and choked me.

Spot looked at the rotary, then bounded away from it.

The sharp whirling teeth of the auger were about to grab my limbs and chunk-cut-pull me into the fast-spinning impeller to be dismembered and shot into the forest.

I pushed off the branch and leaped up and back toward the rotary. My right knee caught the top edge of the auger opening. My left leg hung down in front. I felt the auger grab at my jeans. I flailed my arms, grabbed a corner of blower chute with one hand. I pulled myself up and over the intake housing. I stood up on the top edge of the huge metal box inside which the auger churned. Out of the top of the box rose the big blower chute. It was like a metal chimney with a nozzle at the top out of which the snow shot at 60 miles per hour, arcing into the night.

The unseen operator immediately rotated the chute so that the nozzle swiveled toward me. He wanted to use the chute to blow me off the machine. I pulled myself up against the chute, which vibrated as thousands of pounds of snow per second coursed through the channel. Holding the back of the chute, I stepped up onto the cab, my body against the windshield behind which the phantom driver worked the controls.

The roaring teeth of the machine were now beneath me,

eating snow and branches and forest debris. I spread my arms and tried to span the cockpit cab, my body plastered against the glass as I floundered for a grip to keep from falling off in front of the auger. I saw Spot at the side of the machine. He was barking, but I only heard the roar of the rotary.

The machine made a sudden braking lurch. The deceleration threw me forward, off the cab and back down onto the auger housing. My arm flopped down and in front of the auger. I felt the spinning rotor grab at my jacket sleeve. I jerked my arm back, adrenaline making my breath short and my head throb.

I rolled back toward the windshield, flailing again for something to grab onto.

The rotary turned left, throwing me sideways. Then it turned right and braked again. I knew the driver wanted to toss me off into the snow so I'd be sucked into the auger intake.

My hand found a moving windshield wiper on the right side of the machine. I grabbed it and pulled the wiper out from the windshield, hoping to break it off. My arm went back and forth as the wiper made its sweep. I tensed my abdomen and pulled my legs up, scraping my shoes across the top of the rotor housing. The wiper broke off just as I scrambled onto my knees. The clouds of snow that billowed up from the auger entrance coated the windshield. If I could break off the other wiper, the driver wouldn't be able to see.

I got from my knees to my feet. The driver accelerated forward. I leaped toward the cab, planning to slide across the windshield and get the other wiper.

But the rotary lurched to a stop. I was thrown off the front into the snow. Spot ran to me.

"Go!" I shouted. "Run!" I pointed toward the forest.

The driver started up again, the auger roaring. Spot jumped away. I stared for a moment into the maw of the beast as it ground toward me. I turned and leaped, clawed and scrambled my way forward through the deep snow. There was a tree ahead, a misshapen pine. The trunk went up at an angle. The trunk was big enough to stop the rotary but small enough that I might be able to get my arms around it. About ten feet up was a dead branch, broken off a few feet out from the trunk. If I could get up to it…

I rushed forward, away from the rotary. I got foot purchase on a mound of heavier, firmer snow that had avalanched from branches far above. I grabbed the tree trunk as I stood up, balancing on the compressed snow. The roaring monster was almost on me. The cloud of snow it threw up surrounded me, and it glowed bright in the floodlight glare, making it difficult to see the tree. I felt the blast of swirling air from the auger. It was inches away. I had a second. Maybe less.

I leaped and pulled myself up at the same time. My momentum carried me up a few feet. At the top of my arc, I let go of the trunk and reached for the broken branch above, thrashing, catching air with my right hand.

But my left hand caught the branch.

I swung to the left, then back to the right. My right hand caught the branch. I did a pull-up, a stomach crunch, scraping at the tree trunk with my feet.

The edge of my right shoe caught on a small branch stub. My other foot swung in the air.

The beast was below, stopped just short of the tree trunk. My feet were a few feet above the roaring, spinning auger. I tried to pull up farther, but the dead branch seemed greased with wet ice. My hands started to slip. I stopped pulling and focused on just holding.

My phone was close by in my pocket, but I couldn't let go of the branch.

The rotary backed up, turned a bit, came back forward. It was now aimed so that when I fell from the tree, it could chew me up in a moment. But I was temporarily out of the auger's reach.

The engines on the rotary wound down to idle.

But the auger clutch must have remained engaged, because the auger kept spinning. The metallic grinding of the mechanism was more pronounced absent the engine noise. Despite the reduced power, the auger seemed to spin as fast as before. Even without 1300 horsepower on full throttle, just the inertia of the heavy auger would slice and dice me with impunity. If my hands slipped off the branch, I'd slide down into the auger even if the driver didn't come forward.

Spot was again at the side of the rotary, looking from the machine up to me, then back.

With the engines on idle, it was now possible to hear. Maybe I could delay the murderer by talking like a hostage negotiator, listening to his anger, telling him I wanted to help. I was about to call out when a thought pushed into my awareness. It was a memory that felt strange, an image I'd seen recently. As I clung to the tree, I remembered walking around the Zephyr Heights house that had burned down, the house where Adam had lived at the generosity of Felicite. I could visualize the wreckage, the broken truss, the cracked foundation. In the strange way that time slows down in moments of extreme stress, I thought about that cracked foundation. I realized that the burning, falling roof could not easily crack concrete. Then I remembered that the truss had burned and fallen and broken. But the broken ends had burned as much as the rest of the wood. Which meant that the break in the truss happened before the fire.

Cracked foundations and broken trusses come from more powerful stresses than a fire. Stresses like earthquakes.

My hands slipped farther on the icy branch. I jerked myself to get a better grip, seeing, as I grunted with effort, the time when I was talking to Felicite in the sun room and her tapping on her phone just as the shot blew out the window glass. Poor, stressed, fearful Felicite whose company makes actuators that can take a simple electronic input and create motion that can do anything from locking car doors to, presumably, triggering a rifle that had been previously set up on a sniper's bipod support.

I called out, shouting down toward the machine just below me.

"You don't have to do this, Felicite! We know that you and Antonio Scozzari killed Scarlett and Darla and Sean. We know that you terrorized Old Man Joseph. It was a great set up, I'll give you that. It was brilliant to frame Adam by using his past activity with fire and sharpshooting and working in the yard where they store the rotaries. You were the perfect, invisible culprit."

I was out of breath from hanging onto the branch, barely holding myself up above the reach of the auger. I paused to breathe.

"I now realize that you must have also participated in the summer program at that group home. It wasn't just Adam who went. Just like Adam, you learned all about rifles and sharpshooting. Once you had the rifle set up and carefully aimed at one side of your neighbor's window, you hooked up an actuator that was coordinated with your phone. That was also brilliant. How could I ever suspect you when you were with me as the supposed killer shot at us?"

I continued, "Between you and Scozzari, it was easy to coordinate borrowing the rotaries. He cut the wire to the oil gauge so that the driver would have a reason to abandon his machine in the street, allowing either of you to borrow it later. Then, when the earthquake damaged your house, you probably didn't have earthquake insurance. No surprise there. Most of us don't. Burn it down, however, and the insurance company might pay if they fall for your story. And you handled all the other details. One of Adam's cigar butts up above Scarlett's house. The photos in Adam's phone. But the Black Magic warning note was a mistake. I learned that your ancestors came from Saint-Domingue, which is now Haiti, a country where people still practice Black Magic, right?"

The rotary door opened. Felicite shouted up at me. I couldn't see her behind all the lights, but her shrill voice cut past the idling engine and spinning auger. "All my life, I watched as Adam was given every break! Even when he got in bad trouble, everyone, the foster parents, the cops, the teachers, they all felt sorry for the poor big kid who knew how to charm them. And then football made him rich, richer than you can imagine! But did he save any of that money? Did he give any of it to me? No, he just squandered it. And then when he was broke and starting to suffer from dementia, he came crawling to me. I never had a break in my life, and now I had to take him in, support him, buy his food. And what did he do to help? He wrote poetry!"

"That doesn't give you the right to frame him for murder," I shouted back.

"What difference does it make? He's going to die anyway. He won't even be aware of what's happening to him. He won't go to prison. They'll just stick him in a chair and let him stare into his stupid poetry book. I'm the one who found out about the Blue Fire Diamond from Mario Montana and Scozzari. I started the whole process. I found Darla, who worked at the Cal Neva. I showed her how to connect with people who could help, people like Scarlett who then traveled to Florence and found out more about the diamond. But they all double-crossed me. I paid them well. But Scarlett got them to shut me out so they could find and take the diamond themselves. When there's mutiny on the ship, the captain decides the punishment! And now the world will think that Adam arranged it all."

My hands began to slip again, and I lost my line of thought. I focused on intensifying my grip.

"The diamond's gone, Felicite," I shouted. "I talked to Vince, who got all the Sinatra effects from Old Man Joseph. There's nothing left to gain. Your financial windfall dream is never going to happen. If you back off now, I'll make the case to the DA that you were under extreme financial and emotional duress. We can plea you down and let the blame fall on Scozzari." I didn't want to tell her that he was already dead of a broken neck, floating in the Tahoe Keys.

My hands slipped an inch. My arm muscles were cramping. I wondered if I could swing out onto the top of the rotary cab. But she'd thought of that. She was just beyond my reach.

I shouted again. "You owe it to Adam! He needs you. He only has a short time left. If you abandon him now, he won't be able to face life." I was desperate for words that might distract her.

My right hamstring was knotting up as I gripped the tree.

Glancing under my arm, I could see the black rectangle of windshield. Nothing moved but the spinning auger. A high voice lofted above the machinery. No longer angry, but keening.

"He was always the babied one. The house mother doted on him and ignored me. She made him the helpless kid he is. I practically ran the household from the time I was a child because the house mom spent all her time helping Adam and the other kids. I was competent and didn't need babying. So what did I get for that accomplishment? I was ignored. Adam never did a day's work at a normal job in his life. He even failed when he tried working at the city yard. He was too busy living in a fantasy world. All my life I had to cope with harsh reality, while Adam coasted on his football career. And then, when he couldn't cut it anymore, he fussed about metaphors and meter and his ridiculous poetry."

"That was good of you, Felicite. You've made many sacrifices for Adam. The court will take that into consideration."

"No! I won't be subjected to any court. I've been a prisoner to Adam's needs all my life. Even when he became an adult, I practically had to feed and dress him. I'm done being a prisoner! He will be convicted. The evidence against him is overwhelming."

"But you've framed him for your crimes, Felicite. How can you live with that?"

"In another week or two, he'll be too far gone to even realize he's being prosecuted for these crimes. And he's dying anyway. It won't be long, and I'll finally be free of him. And when he dies, the killings will stop and they'll close the case."

"It won't happen, Felicite. They know about you. You're done killing, and you…"

The branch broke.

I fell, sliding down the trunk. My hand caught another branch, smaller than before. I grabbed with my other hand as I swung. Got both hands on the branch. Pulled myself up a few inches.

Just below me was the spinning auger, a few feet away.

The engines revved up to a roar. Chunks of snow and ice flew off the auger and stung my face.

The rotary started backward, then turned a bit, then came forward. The blower chute rotated.

I realized what she was doing. She aimed for more heavy snow. She was going to direct the shooting snow at me and knock me out of the tree. I was trapped with no exit.

The rotary started forward.

The spinning auger filled my field of vision. Spot was at the side of the rotary, leaping back and forth, barking, growling. The chute started blowing snow. The blast hit the tree trunk just above me. The moment she directed the chute down a few degrees, I'd be done, blasted out of the tree. I'd fall into the spinning blades, which were now a blur.

I saw another movement.

A vague figure appeared at the side of the auger, a shadow in the cloud of swirling snow. It was Adam. He ran up on the snow that had avalanched down from the tree. From there he jumped up onto the auger housing as the machine began to move forward. He gripped his hands on either side of the blower chute, locking himself in place like a boulder in front of artillery.

As the machine moved forward, the snow flew out of the chute directly into Adam's chest.

Adam shook as the blast of shooting snow threatened to cut him in two. The machine kept coming forward. Adam hung on like some kind of superhero.

Then the machine stopped, engines and auger winding down.

Felicite seemed to fall out of the rotary cab. She collapsed in the snow, curled up in the fetal position, sobbing.

I dropped onto the auger housing. Adam still stood there, a white sculpture of snow and ice. I helped get the caked, frozen mass off of him. As the snow came off, his jacket and shirt fell free, abraded to nothing by the shooting snow. His chest was already oozing blood across a wide expanse.

I helped him down to the ground, pulled out my phone, and dialed 911 for the second time that night.

EPILOGUE

Three days later, the hospital let Adam out of the ICU. When I went to visit, the doctor said that Adam would not succumb to his physical injuries. But he also warned me that Adam had not become self-aware.

So I went in and held Adam's hand and spoke to him, and told him that he needed to come around again to see Blondie, who was currently staying with Diamond.

I also told him that we were planning a poetry reading of his work, the poems that were in the one remaining sketchbook, and we would certainly appreciate it if he would at least grace us with a visit if not a reading.

After my visit, I called Vince and asked if I could come by. I explained that I wanted some people who worked on the case to join him and me at Vince's house. Vince was happy to accommodate.

When Vince came to the door, I said, "I believe you remember Old Man Joseph."

They hugged, Joseph using just his good arm as the other one was in a sling. Vince spoke, but Joseph wasn't talking yet.

I introduced Vince to Street as well. Vince put on his most charming manner. He was smooth and gracious, and he had Street laughing in no time. She probably didn't even notice the crooked hairpiece.

As we stood on the front step, Sergeants Diamond Martinez and Jack Santiago walked up. Behind them, Mallory was just pulling up in his unmarked. Glennie was next, and last was a young man named Abe Silverstein, a jeweler and reputed diamond expert. I brought them all inside and made introductions. Vince and Mallory knew each other because Mallory had come out the night Scozzari had broken in.

"You said you had something to show us," Mallory said to me, impatient as usual.

"Yeah." I opened my bag and pulled out a light. I looked at Vince, who was telling a story to Street. "Vince," I said.

He looked up, startled.

"Do you mind if I plug in my light?" I gestured with it.

He frowned. "Sure. What's the deal?"

"It's an ultraviolet light that can help authenticate the Blue Fire of Florence, which is a red fluorescing diamond."

"What's that mean?" Mallory said.

"You know how a glow-in-the-dark watch face is activated by shining a light on it? And after you turn off the light, the material glows? I don't understand the science, but apparently the electrons in some molecules get excited by light and they emit light afterward for some time. In the case of a red fluorescing diamond, the molecules are activated by ultraviolet light."

"A black light," Mallory said.

"Yeah. Just like what we had for lighting up black light posters in college. If you shine it on one of these special blue diamonds, it will glow red afterward."

"Sounds pretty trippy," Mallory said. "Is this conjecture, or is it something that's actually been observed before?"

"It's rare, but it's real. The famous Hope Diamond is a red fluorescing diamond. Right, Abe?"

"That's correct," Abe said.

"You still think the diamond might be here somewhere?" Vince asked as he looked over at the corner display case. "Like in those glass sculptures?"

"Worth checking," I said.

Vince walked over and lifted out the two large glass sculptures of Sinatra. They sparkled and shimmered and shot prismatic rays across the room and ceiling. He set the sculptures on the dining table.

Everyone leaned in to look at it up close. Spot walked over and stuck his head over the tabletop, wondering what all the fuss was about.

"A lot of stuff on this looks like diamonds," Mallory said. He pointed. "This, and this could be diamonds. And this blob

of glass here has what looks like diamond facets inside the glass."
He tapped it with his fingernail. "Could be someone dropped a
diamond into molten glass." He looked at me. "Would diamonds
melt if you dropped them into molten glass?"

"Got me," I said. I turned to Abe.

"Actually, most diamonds would not melt if dropped into
molten glass," he said, excitement in his voice. "The temperatures
of liquid glass aren't high enough. However, diamonds will melt
if heated to a very high temp. But at temperatures lower than
that of molten glass, diamonds will burn if the concentration
of oxygen is sufficient. I've even heard that diamonds will burn
explosively without any heat at all if they're dropped into liquid
oxygen. But then, most organic things will burn if dropped into
liquid oxygen."

Vince said, "Over the years, I've had both glass sculptors
and jewelers look at these sculptures. None of them thought this
could incorporate a large diamond."

Diamond pointed to the black light. "I've always understood
that ordinary glass blocks most UV rays. Hard to get tan through
a window, right?"

"True," I said. "But I was told that the red fluorescence of the
Blue Fire Diamond is very intense. So I'm hopeful that even a
little UV light will do the trick."

Abe nodded at my statement.

"What do we do?" Mallory said.

"We turn off the lights, shut the drapes, and shine the light
on the sculpture. After a minute, we turn the light off and see if
any part of the sculpture glows red."

"This is exciting," Vince said. He had an energetic step as he
trotted over to the windows and shut the blinds. Vince turned off
the room lights, and I turned on the ultraviolet light. It glowed
a strong purple, although I understood that the actual ultraviolet
rays were invisible to human eyes and the purple was merely the
closest visible wavelength.

I held the light in front of the sculptures. They looked dramatic
in the purple light, but there was no big reaction. Some portions
seemed more intense in the black light, but the biggest indication
of the presence of ultraviolet rays was not the sculpture, but the

few small white parts of our various clothing, Vince's white shirt, the top edge of Mallory's undershirt, some white marks on Street's sweater. Those areas fluoresced brilliant white.

After a minute, I said, "Ready? I'll turn the light off and we'll all look for any faint glow of red from within the sculpture."

"Ready," Vince said.

I turned the light off.

The sculpture was dark. Not even a hint of a glow.

"It didn't work," Vince said. "I didn't expect it to have the diamond, but I have to admit I was kind of hoping. Sorry about all your effort." He sounded sad. He flipped back on the lights.

"No problem at all," I said. "I didn't expect it to work, either."

"Really?" Vince was surprised. "You went to all the effort to get the light without expecting a result?"

I saw Mallory look around the room like I was wasting his time.

"I hoped for a result," I said. "Just not on this sculpture."

"What do you mean?"

"I keep thinking about the note you showed me. It was addressed to M and signed with the letter F."

"The note from Sinatra to Marilyn Monroe," Vince said.

"Yeah. Where he wrote something about putting it on the line for her."

"What do you think that meant?" Vince asked.

"I didn't know. Because of the picture you showed me of Marilyn out on the pier holding the diamond, I thought the note had to do with the Blue Fire Diamond. Putting it all on the line would be a metaphorical phrase, but I thought it might also be literal. And I kept thinking about the state line that runs through the Cal Neva Hotel. That state line was such a big deal, and it was even the source of the Cal Neva name."

Glennie jumped in, "So you think Sinatra put the Blue Fire Diamond on the state line?"

"Maybe."

"Where? Under the lobby flooring or something?" She sounded very excited.

I pointed at the aquarium. "Vince, you said your aquarium

was built into the lobby right over the state line?"

Vince nodded. "Yeah. It's even got a line painted across the bottom." As Vince said it, his eyes got wide. He walked over to the aquarium. "There's nothing here that could hold a diamond as big as what you are talking about."

"It doesn't have to be big."

"I don't get it. It was one of the biggest diamonds in the world."

"In its original form." I looked over at Abe Silverstein.

"A diamond can shatter," he said. "In fact, they are quite brittle." He walked over to the aquarium, his own eyes afire.

"What if Sinatra smashed the Blue Fire when Marilyn rejected him?" I said. "What if he threw it and it hit a hard surface? Or maybe it was an accident. If he scooped up the broken diamond pieces and dumped them in the aquarium, he might refer to it as having put it all on the line for Marilyn."

Vince said, "I've always noticed the gravel on the bottom of this tank. It's mostly yellow and white, but it's got a lot of what look like glass chunks in it. You think they could be pieces of the Blue Fire?"

"Let's find out."

I carried the black light over to the aquarium and plugged it in.

Vince lifted the top off the aquarium. "This way you can shine the light down through the water. Ultraviolet light maybe goes through water better than through glass, huh?"

"I don't know. We'll aim it so it goes through both the glass and water. Okay if you unplug the aquarium lights?"

"Sure." Vince unplugged the cord. With the aquarium lights off, the spectacular fish were now plain.

I turned on the black light and held it above the water. "Okay, let's turn off the room lights."

Street flipped the switch. The room went dark except for the fish, some of which now glowed in brilliant fluorescent colors.

"Oh, my God," Vince said. "Look at the bottom. The glass chips are beginning to turn a faint red."

Everyone came over. I held the light close to the water's surface. After a minute, the red of the chips was more pronounced. I said,

"Ready? Here goes."

I turned off the light.

The collective gasp of all assembled was like a fake soundtrack gasp in a movie.

The bottom of the fish tank was lit as if by a hundred little red Christmas tree lights. Each piece glowed a bright ruby red. The points of light were so intense, it was hard to imagine that they normally had a blue tint. The red light was so bright that we could see the fish silhouetted against the glow. They looked like they were hovering over a city of red lights.

Glennie giggled and bounced up and down.

Street was speaking into Joseph's ear, telling him what it looked like.

Diamond and Santiago looked at each other with amazed grins.

Gradually, the red glow diminished. After another minute, Street turned the room lights back on.

We were all quiet. Perhaps the others were, like me, considering the path the Blue Fire of Florence had taken from 500 years ago.

"Do you suppose these little diamond chips have any value?" Vince asked.

Abe said, "Each one can be cut into a new diamond. Some will end up very small. But there are a few that are pretty good size." He stared at the fish tank gravel. "Even without an extremely large single diamond, you have a serious fortune here. There appear to be several large chunks in the six or eight carat range and hundreds of tiny pieces a fraction of a carat. Of course, value is dependent on how they can be cut, but I'm guessing that just the large pieces, if cut well, will be worth a million dollars or more."

Vince said, "I can sell the big pieces to build a Sinatra museum. I'll leave the little pieces right there, in the tank, in the museum. I'll get one of those black lights so that people can see the Blue Fire glow red."

Two weeks later in the middle of May, at my urging, Glenda Gorman put a notice in The Herald saying that there would be a poetry reading for local poet Adam Simms, held at the Lake Tahoe Community College Library.

There was a full house of maybe 150 people, ranging from people who appreciated poetry to people who just wanted to get a glimpse of a football hero.

Glennie served as MC. At five minutes after the appointed time, she went to the front of the room, tapped on the mike, and asked everyone to take their seats.

When the room had quieted, she said, "Thank you all for coming. Tonight we are here to celebrate the written word and its power to captivate and enthrall. Not long ago, a man who writes poetry moved to our town. Years ago, he was known as a football player. But his words leave as big a wake as he used to leave on the field. Most people don't know that Mr. Adam Simms writes poetry. He's never published his poems. He writes them in sketchbooks, and he doesn't seek an audience."

Glennie looked around at the audience, her eyes searching. She grinned when she saw Adam sitting with me at the rear corner of the room. Adam's eyes showed worry and fear and confusion. His face was still puffy and purple from the snow abrasion that he'd taken saving my life. But at least his face still had normal skin unlike his chest which was severely abraded from the assault.

Glennie continued, "Adam Simms has never done a poetry reading. When I asked him why, he said he was too shy to read in public. When I asked him if others could read his poems, he thought about it and said that he didn't think that his poems were good enough to be read aloud." Glennie grinned. "But as some of you know, I can be persistent. Under my pressure, Adam finally relented."

Glennie lifted up a small sketchbook. There were Post-it notes marking various pages. She turned to the first one. "I will start by reading a poem called 'Wildness.'"

The poem was short and poignant and talked about the last bits of the untamed world. When she was done, everyone clapped loudly.

"The next poem will be read by Street Casey." Glennie handed the sketchbook to Street as she approached the podium.

Street said, "This poem is titled 'Dare I Sleep.'" Street read slowly and softly. The poem was a warning about species on the brink of extinction, yet it wasn't strident or shrill. Instead it spoke of the ephemeral nature of beauty in all plants and animals.

Street was followed by Diamond and then Sergeant Santiago. Even Commander Mallory, locally famous for being too much of a curmudgeon to participate in such events, got up to read a poem.

In all, twelve people read Adam's poems, all of which were about the forest and mountains and the untrammeled wild places and wild animals, haunting descriptions of hallowed ground.

During the reading, I leaned over toward Adam and whispered. "Looks to me like you have lots of friends." He didn't smile, yet he seemed amazed at what was happening. Blondie lay at his side. She wore her service dog bib.

At the end, the audience was quiet with contemplation and, perhaps, a bit of awe.

Glennie went back to the podium. "Let's give Mr. Simms a show of our appreciation."

The crowd clapped and stood and clapped some more.

I looked at Adam. He'd been silent, so I couldn't tell if he was having a good day or a bad day. But his cheeks were wet with tears.

The last week of May, I stopped by Street's lab on my way home from my office. She'd just opened the door and bent down to hug Spot when Diamond drove up in his Douglas County Ford Explorer.

He got out and walked over. Spot stared at him, wagging his tail.

"Sergeant," I said.

Diamond nodded.

"How's Adam Simms doing?"

"Going down fast," he said. "We moved him out of the safe house yesterday. I went in to check on him, and from the looks of things, he'd had another seizure, pulling the kitchen table and two chairs and the knife rack over onto the floor as he went down. Probably, he had a few seconds advance warning from Blondie. Fortunately, no knife stabbed him. He'd come back to consciousness before I got there, but only barely. His eyes were open, and he looked at me, but there was no recognition. He didn't know who he was, didn't seem to remember anything. He kept asking when Felicite was coming. I didn't have the heart to say that she was probably going to prison for the rest of her life. Adam had also left the stove top on with a pile of newspapers just inches away from the lit burner."

"That sounds terrifying," Street said. Her face was a network of worry lines.

"The worst thing was, Simms didn't recognize Blondie. He kept saying, 'who's that dog?' And he wouldn't pet her. Blondie was very traumatized. She stayed in a corner of the living room and wouldn't look at me or Adam. After we got Adam settled into the nursing home, I took Blondie with me, and she hasn't eaten a thing. She drank a little water, but not as much as I think a dog her size should. I'm worried. I called the vet, and they said to bring her in if she isn't drinking and eating normally in another day."

"What will you do about her?" I asked.

"That's a question I haven't answered." Diamond glanced down at Spot who was still wagging. Only now I realized that he hadn't been wagging at Diamond. He was looking at Diamond's SUV.

"I'm hoping we can find someone who's willing to adopt Blondie," Diamond said. "If we can't, I'll have to turn her over to animal control. I thought I'd ask if either of you has ideas."

"I can't fit another dog in my tiny cabin on a permanent basis," I said. "But let's not put her in the shelter just yet. Let's ask around. Maybe we know someone who would like a dog."

Diamond said, "I thought about taking her, but my job often has long days when I can't even get home for dinner."

Street said, "Is she in your car?"

"Yeah."

"We should let her out so she can run around."

"I don't think that's going to happen. She's had a pretty serious setback." Diamond walked over and opened the back door of his vehicle. There was no movement inside.

We followed him and took a look. Blondie was at the other

side of the back seat. She cowered from us. Her tail was between her legs, and her ears were back. She wouldn't look up.

"C'mon, Blondie," I said in my cheeriest voice.

She didn't move. Spot pushed his nose in next to me.

"Hey, Blondie, you can play with Spot."

No response.

I took Spot by the collar, brought him to the Jeep and had him climb into the back seat. "Stay," I said.

I walked back to Diamond's SUV and opened the other back door on the side where Blondie had pressed herself into the corner. She turned her head and looked at me but didn't move even as gravity started to slide her off the edge of the seat and out the open door. It was as if she were half comatose.

I cradled her in my arms and carefully carried her over to the Jeep, trying not to jar her. She still didn't move as I set her in on the edge of the seat next to Spot who seemed to understand not to be exuberant.

I shut the door.

"I'll take her home with Spot and see if that helps her forget what she's been through."

Diamond nodded. He pulled a large padded envelope out of his patrol unit and handed it to me. "A day or two after the poetry reading, Simms had a moment of lucidity, and he gave me this. He said, 'Can you give this to Owen McKenna when my mind is gone?' I agreed."

"Thanks," I said. I put the envelope in the Jeep. "Adam didn't have any money. How is the nursing home going to get paid? The state will cover some expenses, but not all."

"I talked to Vince. He said that if it hadn't been for Simms saving your life when you were chased by the rotary, you wouldn't have found the diamond pieces. So he's going to sell enough pieces of the Blue Fire to pay for Adam's care."

"Nice guy," I said.

"Yeah," Diamond said. "Nice is undervalued these days."

I drove the Jeep. Street said she'd follow along in a few minutes. When I got home, Blondie was still cowering.

A cloud front had come across the sky, shutting out the sun

as if someone had pulled a large sun shade across a huge skylight. A cool breeze had come up, and snow flurries whirled through the air. I let Spot out and brought him into my cabin. Then I fetched Blondie, trying once again to be gentle as I carried her inside. I pulled Blondie closer to me so that the cold weather didn't make her feel worse.

When I was inside the cabin, I kept holding Blondie. I said, "Spot, lie down on your bed."

I stepped onto the edge of his bed so that he couldn't take up all of the space. I tapped my foot where I wanted him to lie. "Spot," I said a bit louder. "Come lie down."

Spot ambled over, stepped onto his bed, sniffed Blondie in my arms, then lowered himself down onto his elbows.

I squatted down and set Blondie onto the other side of Spot's bed. She lay curled up, her snout turned sideways across her front paws. She was touching Spot with her side, but she didn't move.

I built a small fire in the wood stove, enough to warm Blondie but, I hoped, not enough to drive her away.

I heard the soft sound of a car door. In a moment, my front door opened and Street walked in. Spot lifted his head and looked at her for a moment. Blondie didn't move.

"How's she doing?" Street asked.

"Same," I said. "We'll just give her some space and time and calm and see if that helps."

Street nodded.

I opened a Sierra Nevada Pale Ale for each of us, and we sat in front of the wood stove. Street took the leather chair, I took the rocker.

I tore the end off the padded envelope and pulled out Adam's sketchbook. Tucked inside the pages was a hand-written letter. I read it aloud to Street.

Dear Owen,

This is a pretty good day as I write this. I can think. But I sense I'm near the end of that. I'm going to give this letter to Sergeant Martinez and ask him to give it to you when I'm no longer competent.

I'm writing this on the fifteenth day of May, my birthday,

and the day on which I found Blondie in the rescue shelter two years ago. I'd already been having seizures for six months when I got Blondie. Six months of feeling that life wasn't worth living.

I learned a lot from Blondie, starting with the first day. She was pretty much a wreck, just like me, but together we found that life once again became worth living.

Even on the worst days, when she got so stressed about my seizures, my brain eventually came back, and after a time, Blondie would calm down and go back to being as happy as a dog could be. Ever since I got that dog, when I've had dark times, I always reminded myself of that. I brought Blondie happiness. Imagine that. After all those years of football, the gift I gave the world that mattered most to me was bringing happiness to a rescue dog.

It must have been terrifying for Blondie to have me turn into the shaking robot, unresponsive to her, not noticing her licks or cries, not petting her, maybe even hurting her with my jerks.

But of course she also learned that I came out of the seizures, that the shaking robot left my body, and I always came back to her. She knew that no matter how often the seizures came and no matter how bad they were, I still came back.

This time I'm not coming back.

For me, that's the hardest thing about facing the end. It's not fair to an animal who thinks you're the most important thing in the universe. People understand, more or less. But Blondie - all dogs in this situation - Blondie will keep waiting for me.

So I have a favor to ask, Owen. I'm asking you because you know about dogs, you know their personalities and their needs.

Blondie would make someone a wonderful pet. She has more love in her than I've ever seen in anyone. I can't imagine her going back to the shelter. It would destroy her just being there again. Never mind that most dogs don't ever come out alive.

So would you please try to find a home for Blondie?

It would be a huge favor, but I don't know who else to ask.

Thanks very much for considering it.

There's one more thing.

I had the world in my hands when I played football. I knew a thousand people. Yet I never really had any close friends. But you showed interest in my poetry and talked to me about it. No one else ever came close to believing how important poetry was to me. You even organized the reading at the college. I've never had a friend who did that for me.

When you said you could help me do a book of my poems, I didn't know what to say. But I've never stopped thinking about that. I remembered that you said that more people would be interested if they thought my book had stuff about me and not just poems about wildness.

So I've written another poem for the book, even though I know the book may not ever happen. This poem is not about wildness. It's called Won't Need No Cane. In fact, I think that would be a good title for the book. I'm dedicating this poem to you, Owen.

Won't Need No Cane

A broke-wing hawk no longer flew
Looked up to see the trees and sky
Was grateful for the gift of view
He'd never seen from perch on high

Confined to ground, no longer free
He'd never grow too old to soar
With wisdom gained, he now could see
Though battles won, he'd lost the war

by Adam Simms for Owen McKenna

When I was done reading, there was movement over on the dog bed. Blondie began panting, clearly heated too much by the fire. She pushed herself up to her feet and, moving slowly, she walked off the dog bed, came partway across the living room and stopped. She looked at me, then at Street. Blondie's ears were back, her head hung low, and her eyes drooped with sadness. She looked very scared. Taking tiny steps, she gradually walked over to Street and looked up at her face. Then she lowered her head to rest it on Street's lap.

Street reached out with both hands and caressed her head. "I'll take Blondie," she said.

About The Author

Todd Borg and his wife live in Lake Tahoe, where they write and paint. To contact Todd or learn more about the Owen McKenna mysteries, please visit toddborg.com.

A message from the author:

Dear Reader,

If you enjoyed this novel, please consider posting a short review on Amazon. Reviews help authors a great deal, and that in turn allows us to write more stories for you.
Thank you very much for your interest and support!

Todd